Late Bl~~oomer~~

This book is a work of fiction. Names, characters, places and incidents are products of the author's imagination or are used fictitiously. Any resemblance to actual events or locales or persons, living or dead, is entirely coincidental.

Copyright © 2019 by Lisa K. Stephenson

All Rights Reserved, including the right to reproduce this book or portions thereof in any form whatsoever.

ISBN:

9781796290325

Printed in the U.S.A.

Join our Facebook Group: Lisa's Cabineers
Instagram: @lisak.stephenson
www.lisakstephenson.com

Hi Angeline

Lisa K. Stephenson
LATE BLOOMER

One taught me love,
one taught me patience,
one taught me pain....

CHAPTER ONE

Present Day

Noel pondered, listening keenly to the pugnacious woman outlining the play-by-play details of the affair she could figure was nothing short of karma.

He was successful, he was exhilarating, and he was married. Married to a woman who had made her way onto this excursion, tagging along with her a bitter and unpleasant revelation. With the truth stabbing like a thousand knives, Noel could do nothing but embrace the blessing she had growing inside of her.

Four weeks, six days, and eleven hours had her experiencing nausea, intense migraines, and insomnia to which Frances had yet to have taken notice. She was dozing off, misleading the woman who sat adjacent her into thinking she was listening.

Alicia was her name. Latina-American, five-foot-nine with long, flowing, straight brunette hair. Although she was beautiful and her tone soft, the words that left her mouth made her presence unflattering.

The story went on, but there was nothing she could do, no defense she could make. Everyone gathered around, confused on whether they were to console the wife, scold her, or rid themselves of her toxic company.

The room felt dark, and with little to no resolution, the ladies decided it was time, time to intervene the only way they knew how; turning to face Alicia, Frances said, "I think it best you leave."

Noel's best friend spoke as though she and Alicia had now become imminent strangers. The joy had been taken out of the room, the air now brisk as Alicia prepared to take her leave, the other women staring at her—their eyes glowing with malice. But it was not her they wished to have removed from their presence, despite her ongoing conversation; interrupting, Frances spoke with assertion,

"No, married lady! You need to leave."

It was at that moment Noel realized, despite this low point in her life, she could count on her friends to remain by her side. The thumping in her heart meant her anxiety was beginning to flare, and without so much of a second thought, as Alicia began to gather her belongings and roll her suitcase through the front door to await her driver, Noel said the words she knew was going to be enough to change both their lives forever.

Peacefully she said, "Alicia, please tell Nathan that I am pregnant."

Flashback

Seattle was cold in the winter, colder than she could have ever imagined. Walking around outdoors had become familiar whenever her parents quarreled. A perfunctory ritual, almost subconscious. Their voices would rise, and without realizing it, she would begin to dress in her day's ensemble to head outside and face the brutal winds that a city like Seattle could offer.

A young woman coming into her own, now twenty-six years of age, preparing to face the world, though her mother may not approve. Relieved by the fact that she had now escaped the den of parental disagreement, she found herself parked at a bench just five miles up from a creek across from the elementary school she attended. Mr. Kwon left to reason on her behalf, convincing his wife that the move would do her good, considering that one day the children would all have to leave the nest. Noel-Lee, Xavier, and their youngest, Daniel—who by now had learned the hard way that no one, absolutely no one, wins a verbal argument against Mom.

Noel was stumped, torn almost, as she watched the squirrels frolic around on the grass, playing, searching for food, looking as though they were having the time of their lives. Envious, she could not bring herself to admit that she had come to despise her mother. She loathed her for allowing her to grow up so sheltered all her life. She felt inexperienced, terrified to even consider going out on her own, to relocate and begin fending for herself.

But there was something telling her to do just that, something pulling her away from them, away from family, away from Seattle.

As the sun began to set, she continued to warm the park bench. Dear Noel, she thought to herself as she had many times, it is time to set yourself free.

Her eyes fell to the ground in devastation as she arose; she knew it was time to face the only person holding her back: her mother. Once home, she entered, shutting the door quietly behind her. It was half-past nine, and she wondered to herself how she had not yet gone mad. Half past nine on a Friday night and the house was so quiet you could hear a pin drop; everyone had gone to bed. Standing downstairs in the foyer of their Victorian home, surrounded by five thousand square feet, much of which she still could not account for, it dawned on her: this was her only chance.

Stepping lightly up the carpeted stairs, she realized she had to act quickly.

She entered her room. Closing the door behind her, she threw the closet door open and retrieved her suitcase, thrusting it onto her bed with the pink bedspreads. She began to throw clothes inside.

Ripping clothes from hangers, angry, her tears beginning to flow freely down her cheeks. She shoved her hair away from her face. As Noel looked at the clothes she found herself willing to travel with, she saw they were adolescent in nature. A tank top here, an oversized, homemade knitted sweater her grandmother had given her, jeans that were two sizes too small, and hats and gloves accompanied by overalls.

Noel halted. Taking a few steps back, she took a long look into her standing mirror, the one annexed to the back of her bedroom door. She felt trapped.

Placing her hands on her head, she felt bamboozled, tricked into a life she wished greatly she had avoided. Her eldest brother, Xavier, was thirty-three, living down the hall from her, and all she could think about was how one day she, too, would be just like him. No goals, no family, no ambition, just Mom and Dad and two brothers, the American family way as she had always been taught.

Sitting on the edge of her full-sized bed, she stared ferociously at the stuffed animals, throw pillows, and ornate pink comforter that her mother had purchased for her. She was ashamed to know she had gone through a portion of her adult life living like a child. Deciding to wallow no more, Noel changed her clothes. A tracksuit is fitting, she thought. Just then a faint knock came to her door.

Hesitant, she responded, "Who is it?"

"Daniel," the voice whispered. She loved her youngest brother; he was charming, intellectual, and welcoming—a heart of gold was what he had. Opening the door, she extended her arms hugging him tightly for she knew this was going to be it. The last time she would hold him for a long time.

Daniel remained clueless, and then it hit her: she needed his help. He was stealthy and could get her exactly what she needed to begin her new life.

She whispered in his ear, "Can you bring me the keys to the truck?"

Daniel was appalled. "Wherever you're going, take me with you!" he said. His eyes widened, "Take me with you, or I tell."

Daniel now peeked into the bedroom: He was no fool; he knew she was heading somewhere, anyplace but there.

Taking a long sigh, she said, "Daniel, no. Mom would kill me, and I have to do this alone." Gripping his shoulders, she knew he was not going to allow her to leave in peace.

"Fine," he snarled, removing her grip. "I am going to tell mother now."

She had never felt more afraid than she did now. His tone was calm yet frightening, but she felt he was bluffing until he was on the move. Making his way down the long corridor to the master's bedroom, he found himself face to face with the entrance to hell; at least that's what they had come to know it as.

"Please, please, please I am begging you! Do not tell Mom. Daniel, please," she whispered, her palms pinned together as she pleaded for what felt like her life. She knew if their mother became aware of her intentions, there would be no rest in their home ever again.

"Mom is a light sleeper; one knock and she will wake up!" he warned, balling his right fist as he prepared to thump.

"Stop! No, I will take you!" she lied. "I have no idea where I am going, but I will take you. You just have to pack, Danny," she said, feeling aggravated. She had hoped things would have gone smoother.

Daniel must have seen through her lies, as he began to bang on the bedroom door aggressively until their father came to greet them, erasing the sleep from his eyes.

Noel remained stationary, unafraid; despite what she'd thought she would have felt, she was relieved. Her mind was made up, and there was nothing anyone could do about it. Mr. Kwon, better known as Jin, faced his children, startled.

"What on earth are you two doing up?" he asked pushing his way between them, walking downstairs, begging for their silence.

"Please do not wake your mother. Noey, will you close the door? We can talk down here." Jin was a wise man; owner of three factories across the globe, he made a fortune from his candle corporation.

Slamming the refrigerator door, both Noel and Daniel sat at the kitchen island where they waited for their father to begin scolding them, which to their surprise he did not.

"Dad—" Noel decided it best to speak first. Jin lifted his left hand, palm open as he took a huge gulp of the Coca-Cola he had hidden to the rear of the refrigerator.

Sarcastically, Daniel said, "I guess everyone just wants to break the rules tonight, huh?" he scoffed.

"I haven't had one of these in seventeen years," Jin told his children as he took his first sip. "I know what this is about," he continued.

"Noel wants to leave, and if she goes, I go!" Daniel said.

Noel just listened, ashamed.

"You will go nowhere, and do not let me ever hear you speak like that again!" Jin scolded his son. "You are eleven years and will continue to stay under this roof until your mother and I see fit. Do you understand?" he asked.

Nodding his head in disappointment, Daniel reluctantly agreed. "But what about Noel? Why does she get to leave?" he asked. Turning to face her, Jin and Noel exchanged a look of understanding.

"My dearest daughter, you are my only daughter, but I know you have your need for space and companionship. There is a world bigger than our home that you wish to experience, and I for one cannot stop you." Jin could tell his daughter had been crying. Her sweet caramel complexion, dark brown eyes, and dark brown hair made him stare at her longer than usual. She had become a woman right before his eyes, and he could not bear to let her go. He understood this to be true of his wife as well, but knew it was simply selfish of them to deprive her of living her life on her own terms any longer.

"I will get your accounts set up first thing in the morning, and I will hand you the keys to the truck as well. Where exactly will you be driving to, my dear?" Jin asked.

Taking a long, deep breath, Noel could not believe her ears.

Envious now, Daniel said, "What! I hope when I reach my mid-mid-midlife crisis you and Mom are this generous with me!" he sneered.

"Oh, hush, young man," Jin playfully responded. "Your—your sister has not been happy for years! Have you Noey?" he asked, concerned.

"No," she said, tense now as she began to wonder if this was all some ploy. Hopelessly she said, "How will you get things going tomorrow? If Mom finds out she will not allow me to leave."

Jin took his Coca-Cola can and threw it into the garbage bin, where he then took out the bag, tying it tightly at the top.

"I am still the man of this house. Also, neither of you will speak a word of this to your mother! This includes my little drink," he demanded, and just like that, he began sliding his slippers across the elegant wooden floorboards back up to his master bedroom, where he closed the door ever-so-gently behind him. In a room where the lights were off and the street lights were beaming outside, Mrs. Kwon lay awake on her right side facing their nightstand, a tear falling from her eye.

Noel decided against sleeping in her bedroom that night; she awoke on the prime stone Ainsley sofa which faced closest to the den door. That piece of a three-sofa set was only a small piece of décor that made up their affluent living area. That morning, the malodorous scent of her clothing turned her face a blushing red. She needed a shower but decided against it as she could not stand the thought of stepping foot into her room ever again. The idea of Hello Kitty smiling on the back of her underwear repulsed her; what sickened her, even more, was that she had no other options.

"Breakfast is ready!" her mother bellowed.

The Seattle sun was now being generous, greeting them with natural light and bright-green, fresh cut grass. Making her way down the long corridor into the kitchen, she found what appeared to be a buffet-style, gourmet breakfast fit for any king or queen.

That morning, Jennifer had prepared waffles, oatmeal, sliced strawberries, strawberry pancakes, diced bananas, turkey bacon glazed with melted honey, freshly squeezed orange juice, and scrambled eggs. There was enough food to feed an army. Stepping into the kitchen and taking a seat at the kitchen island on the reupholstered stool, she realized what she would be missing.

As she reached in to grab a plate, her mother said, "Oh no, no, you are an adult and want your independence, remember? So, breakfast is not served for you until you cook it!" she said too politely. Noel was astonished as she listened to her brothers cackling from the dining room. Xavier had his mouth full, a complete disgrace in her mind.

"Where is Dad?" she inquired as she didn't give her mother's remarks a second thought; she was right after-all; Noel was moving out and therefore moving on to the real world.

Taken aback by Noel's lack of response, her mother was astounded, "You—you aren't hungry?" she asked, obviously disappointed to know her daughter was not seeking to grovel at her feet for the chance to indulge in the most important meal of the day.

Noel paced, frantically asking again,

"Mom, where is Da—" Just then, a horn began to honk outside. Immediately, the boys and their mother made their way outside onto the front porch. Their father was making his way up the winding stone driveway, the gates closing behind him as he pulled up to the front of the house driving a grey 2013 Land Rover.

Hopping out of the driver's seat, he shouted, "Surprise!" shaking his hands above his head in excitement, but Noel was not surprised. She once again felt coddled, deceived.

"What is this?" she questioned.

Her mother turned to face her. "This is your long overdue graduation gift. No more asking Dad for the car keys or bribing your brother into stealing them. This here is your very own car."

She was outraged.

"Dad?" she shouted as she turned to face him, no longer interested in what her mother had to say because, by now, she knew she was only hovering. "You promised me!" she said.

"Yes, I know, and then I spoke with your mother, darling, and you should have seen the look on her face—" Jin pleaded as he made his way up to the porch. But Noel was not happy.

"No, you both just want to keep me locked up here like some prisoner. Mom, you wouldn't even feed me this morning because you said I was independent now or whatever; I honestly thought you two had gotten it. But no, it seems neither of you do!" she argued.

"We get it! We get it!" her mother said.

Crying now, Noel turned to face her. "If you get it, then what is all of this?" she said, motioning to the car and her siblings.

"These things were wrong of your dad and I; we wanted to keep you here, and we thought that something materialistic would do the trick. But we were wrong, and we apologize," her mother said solemnly.

Xavier and Daniel both interrupted, "We all just want you to be happy, Noey," Daniel said.

"Yeah, we do," said Xavier.

"Xavier why are you still here?" she asked. "What—what makes you think being here is healthy or even somewhat attractive?" she continued.

"The truth is, I'm not as brave as you," he nonchalantly replied.

"That's just it though. I am not brave; I am scared as hell! But we must face our fears one day. You don't have to be brave, but goddammit, at least stop being such a coward," she scolded, making her way back inside.

Her parents asked to be alone. They were saddened by what they knew would have to come next. Wrapping her cardigan around her torso and throwing the front around her shoulders, Mrs. Kwon took a seat on the tiled porch step. Jin accompanied her. The cool breeze felt delightful; the weather perfect.

"We raised a smart girl," Jin said. His wife nodded in agreeance. Jennifer Jefferson-Kwon was born an African-American woman to her parents Mitch and Joanna Jefferson. A surge of nostalgia overcame her as she reminisced back to when she realized it was time to leave the nest. She was sitting adjacent to her mother, her father sitting to the right of her at their small wooden table one evening during dinner. Jennifer then politely told her parents that a cab would be arriving for her shortly, thereafter taking her to a hotel where she would be staying for a little while with her boyfriend until they found a place of their own. Of course, her parents were outraged, questioning whether or not she was pregnant. She was, but lied to avoid worrying them.

There she was, twenty-two years old, pregnant by a man she had barely known, Bryan Waters, who promised the world for both her and their unborn child.

Later that day, her father Mitch demanded to know where she was going and with whom, to which she later complied, telling them everything, from her pregnancy to her relationship to the possibility of her living with a man without having so much as a steady job. But she fought the urge to tell her parents the entire truth; Bryan was in his forties, a divorcee with two children from his previous marriage.

When Jennifer made the decision to leave, her parents did not quarrel. They simply expressed that she do whatever made her happy, and at the time, Bryan made her happy.

Once she and Bryan moved out on their own, things took a turn for the worse: infidelity, miscarriages, dishonesty, and domestic violence. It was single-handedly the worst time in her life; Jennifer swore from the day she left Bryan that should she ever have children, they would never suffer the same fate. They would be loved unconditionally and without question, never feel they were not welcomed home. She thought that was best.

"Honey, we have to let her go. She wants to experience the world," said Jin as he watched his wife's mind begin to wander, the expression leaving her face. He could tell she was afraid,

"What is wrong?" Jin asked as he consoled her.

"She can't go," Jennifer cried.

"Ah baby, she has to. We must let her go. Xavier too, he needs the boot! When they're gone, we can travel the world. Plus, Daniel is old enough to no longer need a sitter, and he'll be off to high school soon. We have to allow the children to grow up, sweetheart."

After a few hours, Jin managed to help his wife see things differently, Jennifer stopped sobbing now, thinking: a life without kids; at first, this seemed almost foreign, considering a child was beaten out of her, but now, she had no worries for she had a man who had been by her side for three decades and they too deserved a chance to experience their own freedom.

Stepping inside of her Victorian home, Jennifer had now turned a new leaf; having a new outlook, it was time she began living and learn to let go.

"Noel!" she shouted.

CHAPTER TWO

The car arrived, but Noel was not feeling optimistic. She was in love with the idea of a girl's trip, but who would have known that they would be completely isolated? Frances, who was responsible for this excursion, expressed her deep infatuation for the outdoors, but never did Noel believe this to mean that they would have to endure five long days of it.

"Hey, how is it going up there?" she bellowed from the back seat of the all-black Cadillac with tinted windows. A nervous wreck because she could not help but think during the entire ride how gullible she had been to have accepted this kind of generosity from a man who she sees no future with, she began to think. Maybe she is too lenient, too nice, too pleasant, too forgiving of the men in her life. Maybe, she needs to finally settle down. Her thoughts were all overwhelming, so much so that she did not realize the driver had not responded. Immediately she thought to herself, *what if he thinks I am the mistress? But then, why on earth would he possibly think that? What if he suspects something but just refuses to ask out of sheer politeness?*

Jesus Christ, she thought, *could I be going insane?* She turned to her one true source of comfort; onychophagia.

Only this time biting her nails didn't feel as good. A few long hours later they were coming face to face with what appeared to be a cabin lodge. They'd gone from the honking of the angry taxi drivers, the sirens of the obnoxious police officers, and the displeased pedestrians in the heart of Manhattan to the wooded areas of the Pocono Mountains.

This is home, well at least for the next few days or so. Not one for packing lightly, she could hear the luggage in the truck bouncing back and forth, a hard-shelled suitcase she purchased for a measly twenty-four dollars after convincing her lover that a Louis Vuitton would have seemed too affluent for a woman of her caliber to carry. Corey seemed to love that she was humble and grateful for all that she had, even though to him it was nothing compared to what he could give her.

To her, it was everything, because she worked for it.

Flashback

Noel was not a hoyden. She was, in fact, a simple Korean and Black girl who was now arriving in the big city at Penn Station—her mind blown: the tall buildings, the angry men and women screaming at their cellular phones, the taxi cabs honking their horns, the tall woman with the afro pushing Noel out of the way as she ran for the metro bus that read M54.

She threw her duffle bag across her shoulders; she was determined to start over, and that meant a new wardrobe. She packed nothing but her personals, some undergarments, hair products and her favorite bootie accompanied with her American Eagle sweatshirt and size 2 ripped denim jeans. Standing on the sidewalk by 34th street, her eyes wandered aimlessly. She was falling into a trance when a man bumped into her and shouted, "Pay attention!"

She was confused. After all, he had bumped into her, the second person to physically assault her in less than twenty minutes, and she couldn't be more thrilled.

Noel thought of her parents for a brief moment: her dad, this short Korean man, standing at only 5'4, she always wondered how the hell he managed to sweep her dear mother off her feet, literally. Jennifer stood at 5'7 on a bad day, and with heels...forget it, she loomed over him. Sometimes, Noel too.

Then she thought to herself, as she watched the afro-centric women saunter along the sidewalks in groups of five or more, confident, that she was just a Black girl mixed with Korean.

Jennifer had come to accept that she was indeed an African-American woman, however, she no longer found herself attracted to the African-American male. Noel despised this, though, as often times her mother would insist that Noel too, date outside of her race. However, with her caramel skin-tone, many African-American men and women had come to identify with her and she, them, but her dearest mother—all through Noel's childhood, Jennifer would not hear of such blasphemy. Jennifer only acknowledged her family on certain holidays: Martin Luther King, Jr. Day, Thanksgiving, and sometimes she would phone dear old grandma and grandpa wishing them a Happy New Year's, and that was it.

Living in the city, Noel just knew things were going to be different now.

Christmas time was always a happy time in the Kwon household. Her mother and her father always went above and beyond for their children. Thirty years of marriage, not one story of infidelity, and three beautiful children later, her parents were still inseparable and appeared to be as in love as two high school sweethearts.

As Noel reminisced on her past, she came face to face with the Hilton Hotel, where inside the lines were long and everyone appeared to be in a hurry. She continued to step lightly, everyone must have known she was a tourist; she was not moving with a purpose, but rather with admiration.

Noel took her place in line where she stood for what felt like twenty minutes. The yellow marble tiles and the high chandeliers were all indications that this hotel was out of her price range, but she decided since it was her first time in New York, she wanted to experience some form of luxury, plus she had no idea where she was going or even where she *was* for that matter.

Finally, she was next in line. An African-American woman stood behind the receptionist desk, her uniform slightly wrinkled. Noel stepping to the counter and requested a week's stay, removing both her credit card and identification card from her wallet. Noel noticed the receptionist taking glimpses of whoever stood behind her, causing her to become heavily distracted. Noel, intrigued, turned her head slightly to notice a man behind her engrossed in his phone. After a few minutes, the receptionist assisting Noel delivered some devasting news.

"Ma'am, I'm sorry, but this card is declined," the receptionist told Noel. Noel was both embarrassed and appalled because the woman had spoken loud enough for everyone to hear, but soft enough to sound polite. She was no fool, after all. Noel had managed to save enough money for her travels and had a secret credit card her parents knew nothing about; however, for the sake of saving money, she thought she would try her father's card first. Just then, she saw the hand of the gentleman standing behind her kindly express his interest in picking up the tab,

"Jade, honey, it is fine; you can just put her expenses right along with mine," the man said.

"It's great to have you back, Mr. Ramirez. Will it be you and your wife joining us this weekend?" She inquired.

Noel scoffed; turning to the stranger, she said, "Sir, while I do appreciate the gesture, you don't have to do that—"

"Please, it's most certainly my pleasure," he said, smiling as his eyes made their way up and down her body. "You aren't from here are you?" His eyes told a story of their own. Noel stood still even as the receptionist called to her.

"Ma'am! Ma'am! You're all set!" she said.

Noel remained fixated on the strange man as she stepped aside waiting for him to complete his transaction. Both Noel and the gentleman began making their way past the remainder of the guests waiting to check in. Noel felt grateful and compelled to repay him.

"I really appreciate you doing that for me," she said. "Maybe I can get you a drink?" she asked, pointing to the restaurant, but Nathan quickly declined.

"No, no, you go ahead and get settled in, maybe some other time," he said, licking his lips. He turned, placing his right hand into the pocket of his navy-blue suit pants and making his way towards the rotating doors and onto the city streets.

Looking over at the receptionist, Noel could not help but notice Jade's eyes piercing through her. As soon as she made eye contact, Jade looked to the floor, returning to her bidding with a look of shame across her face.

Noel was not concerned, she now had a free room and decided it was time to head out shopping.

That night, Jade enjoyed the jacuzzi located in the penthouse suite she had booked for her and her favorite person. A dark-skinned beauty with an afro that only came undone between hairstyle changes; her skin was smooth, her hair soft, and her body the shape of an hourglass. Jade was almost anything but shy; whatever she wanted was always going to be hers.

It was her edge that attracted him, her intellect, her ability to outsmart everyone in the room. A tiny nose ring pierced her left nostril in addition to the silver navel ring and the gold toe ring that accessorized the second toe on her right foot.

Nathan entered their penthouse, "Baby! I'm home!" he shouted, making his way into the dining area. Jade was never the type to become overzealous for any man, but with Nathan, she could never quite help herself. She stepped lightly from the jacuzzi wearing nothing but her gravity-defying curls and a string bikini.

The penthouse was nothing short of luxurious, and Jade found herself holding a glass of the city's finest wine; 2014 Chateau Lafite Rothschild Pauillac while overlooking the New York City skyline.

Two bottles of the wine had been delivered, compliments of the hotel manager for their gracious spending and frequent generosity. Jade felt like the luckiest woman in the world.

As the sun began to set, she noticed Nathan acting strangely. He had yet to compliment her since his arrival. Jade turned to face him as he was buried in his phone scrolling through what appeared to be social media. Jade did not like to be ignored; a woman of her exotic nature was never to be anyway. Seductively making her way over to him, removing his tie from his neck, she began to kiss him gently, moving his hands to palm her voluptuous buttocks. She kissed and kissed, taking his phone from his hand and placing it gently atop the black marble bar-top.

She felt a distance between them despite her being close enough to feel his heart beating against her chest.

"Jesus, what is wrong?" she said, growing jealous. "Is there someone else on your mind?" she whined, turning his face back to hers, for just then he had turned away, pursing his lips as he took a sip of the drink Jade prepared for him: bourbon, neat.

"No," he lied.

Jade took a few steps back, reaching for the beige silk robe she tossed across the feather grey plush sofa. Placing the robe across her shoulders, she pondered what it could be. Why he was acting so strange? Then it dawned on her and she became irate,

"You're seriously thinking about that girl, aren't you?" she questioned.

His head shot up and he scoffed. "No. Take off your clothes." Placing his phone down on the bar-top, he rose to his feet; Jade could do nothing more than to bask in his handsomeness.

Nathan Ramirez, Chief Financial Officer to Benner, Brown and Motley, PLLC, a known Fortune 500 company, stood at 6'4. He was sculpted and always very well-groomed. Hispanic-American, caramel complexioned with dark hair and a goatee, Nathan never missed a chance to show off his abdominals and toned thighs. Gripping Jade by her waist and seductively licking his lips, he used one hand to remove his garments, exposing his chiseled biceps and erection. Standing with his feet in the holes of his pants, his dress socks still on, he proceeded to lift Jade, spreading her legs to wrap around his torso as he kissed on her neck, simultaneously sucking and licking.

She moaned.

Nathan always aimed to please. He was a ladies' man, no matter the challenge he always found his way into the heart of the woman who was lucky enough to catch his eye. A voluptuous woman was what he craved, a woman with spice. Jade knew this as she began to tease him with her kisses before making her way down to his penis, where she took his shaft into her hand. Extending her body, she stood on her tiptoes. Bending forward, she began to take his penis in and out of her mouth.

The view for Nathan was marvelous, everything he could have imagined plus more. Jade was his trophy, she required little to no teaching and was always willing to do whatever it took to make him happy. Slowly, she began to pick up her pace, the saliva dripping from her lips creating a puddle before them.

Jade had the perfect posture to go with her perfect body. She continued to stand, both hands now thrusting around the base and the shaft of his penis, her long back extended as she poked out her booty, continuing to arch her back. Just then, a faint knock sounded on the door.

Both Nathan and Jade looked up, startled. Jade stopped, wiping the saliva from her lips she noticed a look on Nathan's face she had never seen before. It was a look of worry. Jade took a seat on the stool at the island where she sipped the bourbon Nathan left behind, crossing her legs with her toes pointed to the ceiling. She took a deep breath, admiring the ambiance around her.

Nathan refused to dress; he was pissed that someone had the audacity to interrupt him during his moment of glory. He began to turn the locks, one after the other, once he realized there was room service standing on the other side of the door.

"Oh, you nasty!" he said to Jade, smirking. "You done ordered us some freak shit." Jade continued to smile, sipping the last of the bourbon. As the door opened, Nathan froze. The room service concierge moved out of the way, and in his place stood Alicia.

"Ba-baby, what the—what are you doing here?" Nathan stuttered, his eyebrows knitted as he made his way to the bar where he shot Jade a look of anger, reaching for his boxers.

"Cheers, baby," Jade smirked.

Alicia made her way inside, her heels stomping ferociously. She removed the fifteen-thousand-dollar Hermes Box Birkin bag she wore to accessorize her look, hanging it on the door handle. Jade began to gather her things as Nathan now sat on the sofa wearing his poker face. Outside, he was calm; inside he was racked with fear. Jade had no desire to dress appropriately, she was living only a block away at the Phoenix. An extravagant four-bedroom, two-bathroom, one point five-million-dollar condo in a high-rise she convinced Nathan to purchase for her in her name only months after they began dating.

As Jade began to make her exit, she said, "Well, Alicia, he is all yours. You see, Nathan, I do not get booted. I make the grand exits. I saw the way you looked at that woman today; it was the same way you looked at me." Nathan remained silent.

"Oh, nothing to say for yourself?" Alicia teased. "Jade, goodbye. Oh, and for the record, you haven't won anything here. Tipping me off because you were afraid of being dumped was cowardly. But you aren't my problem and hoes, after all, will just be hoes," she said, slamming the door shut as Jade stepped into the hallway.

CHAPTER THREE

Shutting the door to the all-black Cadillac, Noel could hear the women inside cackling. She was filling with excitement, for she had not seen her cousins in months! The driver, Keith, began working to remove the luggage from the back seat, the luggage the concierge from Corey's apartment had been so kind as to assist with.

Nervously, Noel marched up to the ground floor entrance listening indistinctly to their conversations and began knocking on the door with force. Inside, Africa shouting with excitement, "Jesus, yes, about time, is that my cousin?"

Noel was growing so deeply ecstatic that she could not hide her smile any longer; as the doors clicked open, she simply began to envision hoping into her arms! Africa, her eldest cousin, was there in the flesh!

"Cousin!!!" Instantly, nothing but laughter filled the room as the ladies welcomed her with open arms, all except one. Noel took a quick glance, noticing one woman sitting on the sofa with her back to the door as the ladies all engaged; it was a moment for the books. Noel thanked Keith and he hastily took his leave. Stepping into the cabin, Noel making her way around the ground floor, noticing the commodious lodge!

"Girl, we have the margaritas!" shouted Abigail as she handed Noel a glass. Abigail, Africa, Frances, and an unknown face were all there to greet her. Noel then decided it best to extend her hand to the unfamiliar face, smiling, joyful to make her acquaintance.

"Pleasure to meet you, my name is Noel," she said harmoniously.

Smiling at first, her eyebrows then knitted, Alicia was staring at her as though she had known Noel from somewhere. Initially, she had stretched her hand to meet Noel's, only to then retract it slowly. Frances could sense the tension and made her way over to them both as Africa and Abigail looked on.

The stranger then said, "Noel? As in Noel-Lee?" She continued a smirk along her face as she looked Noel up and down.

Noel continued smiling, too, careful not to spill the drink she was now holding, confused. She made eye contact with Frances, then looked back to the stranger, "Yes, my name is Noel-Lee, but most of my friends just call me Noel." She continued to smile despite the now insidious look on this woman's face.

Tranquilly, Alicia crossing her legs, staring into her eyes as Frances now felt the need to interrupt. "Alicia, girl, what's going on? I told you about Noel."

"Yes, Frances dear, you did tell me about Noel, the woman who is fucking my husband." The room grew silent. She continued, relaxed, "Oh, and was that Keith?" She pointed to the door with her eyes fixed on Noel and her posture unchanged, as if to indicate the anticipation of her arrival.

Flashback
The clock read 12:04 a.m. and Noel could not sleep. The plush king mattress was far too comfortable, unlike anything she ever felt in her life, and yet she had insomnia. Tossing and turning was doing her no good. She started to feel things. A tingling feeling between her legs. She turned to lie on her back, staring at the ceiling above her when a knock came to the door.

Noel frightened, it was late and she was not expecting anyone. Not to mention, she was forced to sleep in the nude considering she had not brought any clothes along with her and was having too much trouble locating any familiar stores in the area. She rose, wrapping the silk sheets around her body and stepping onto the freshly cleaned beige carpet.

She scurried over to the door where she checked the peephole and noticed a familiar face. Nathan. Unlocking the door, she did not unhook the security door chain. Peeping through the door now, she made eye contact. "Hey?"

"Hey, yourself," Nathan said. "So, I couldn't sleep and decided to go for a walk," he said nonchalantly, but Noel was not impressed.

"How did you know what room I was in?" she inquired.

However, Nathan politely responded, "Believe it or not, despite the fact that I paid for this room, they wouldn't tell me the room number, so I had to resort to other shameful tactics." He smirked. But again, Noel was not moved, rather she found his behavior to be officious.

"Look, I don't know what kind of woman you think I am, but I don't sleep with men for nice things, and I am not some woman you can bed just because you took it upon yourself to stretch your black card across the counter. In fact, it was kind of rude of you to have done that. I think you should go," she demanded. Noel proceeded to close the door, but Nathan was not taking no for answer.

"Please, I promise you, there is no funny business here. I just want someone to talk to. I have been drinking, and I promise you that if you let me in and you begin to feel even the slightest bit uncomfortable, I will leave. I will, in fact, leave," he assured her. His face innocent. His wardrobe seemed trustworthy. Draped in navy blue silk pajamas, bedroom slippers, and the matching button-up pajama top, he looked like a rich fool. Noel couldn't help but chuckle. Closing the door to unhook the security lock, she stepped aside as she opened the door, granting him access.

Nathan moseyed inside, swinging his arms from side-to-side like a classic schoolboy. "Do you mind if I have a personal from the refrigerator?" he asked. Noel struggled to keep her sheet wrapped around her as she motioned for him to help himself. After all, he was the one footing the bill.

"So, Miss...? I do not believe I caught your name," he said as he took a seat on the sofa closest the window. Noel sat on the edge of her king-sized bed.

"My name is Noel," she said.

Nathan was intrigued. She was shy, perhaps, a woman of mystery. "Noel is a beautiful name. Aren't you going to have a drink with me?" he said, motioning for her to take a sip of the Jack Daniels.

"No, actually, I don't drink. I grew up in church and my parents were both pretty strict. Never had a drop of that poison a day in my life," she said drawing a long sigh.

Nathan stopped drinking. Shocked, he asked, "Noel, how old are you?"

"I am grown, and I have never had a drink. I believe that is all you need to know," Noel snapped. She was holding her sheet so tight the back of her hands turned white.

Leaning back in the sofa, Nathan crossed his legs. For a moment, he stared into her eyes.

"Why—why are you staring at me like that?" Noel questioned.

"Because you're beautiful," he said. Rolling her eyes, Noel could not help but notice how handsome he was. Nervously, she put her hair behind her ears. She still gripped her sheet as she pulled her legs closer together.

"So, tell me about yourself," she said.

Nathan took a deep breath and downed the remainder of his Jack Daniels. He stood, making his way back to the refrigerator for another, and now wobbled back to the sofa. He was no doubt inebriated—reeking of alcohol when he strolled inside. But now he was ready to speak his truth. "Are you sure you want to hear my sob story?" he asked. Noel nodded her head yes. "Well, can you take a drink with me?" He asked, his soft eyes asking her as well.

Noel wanted to say no, and so she did. "No. I told you I don't drink."

Throwing his hands up as if to indicate giving up, he said, "Of course—of course, and I respect that. Sorry to have asked. Now, where would you like me to start?" he asked, slurring his words now as he took another sip of his Jack Daniels.

"Why don't you start by telling me about your wife," Noel said.

Nathan was stunned,

"Wife? Who told you I was married?"

"The receptionist from this morning." Noel reminded him.

"Oh!" His eyes widened. "Okay, here is the backstory. I married my high school sweetheart when she told me she was seven weeks pregnant with our child. She was seventeen and I was nineteen, and even though I was on my way to college and she was beginning her senior year of high school, I felt that marrying her was the right thing to do, so against everyone's better judgment I did it," he said.

"Well, that was noble of you. Especially considering you were both so young," Noel said.

"Noble, ha! More like fucked up. I was selfish; her family told her to get an abortion and I begged her not to, and it wasn't because I was ready to be a father and a husband, it was because I didn't want her resenting me. I didn't want to feel like I had disappointed her by simply giving up and letting her go at that alone. So, I convinced her to keep our baby boy and, um," he took a long breath before continuing,

"We uh, took a flight to California, then drove out to Vegas, and the rest is history."

"What did her parents say?" Noel asked.

"They became volatile. They would hit her. My family, on the other hand, didn't mind it. They accepted it, I was man enough to get a woman pregnant, so I had to raise that baby and take care of my woman, and that's exactly what I did. When I learned that her step-father had put his hands on her, man, I wanted to kill him, he—he touched my wife, the woman carrying my baby. She begged me not to, she begged me to keep calm, and so I did. Instead of allowing myself to catch a felony, I took extra classes while she was pregnant and worked a day job, had her staying with me at my parents' house, and once I graduated and got my CPA license, I went on to work for a law firm, and before I knew it, I was working my way up."

"Why do you look so sad? Sounds like the perfect love story to me," Noel said, crossing her legs.

"She died," said Nathan. Noel's eyes widened. "When she was giving birth to Junior, she had a seizure. Blood pressure got too high and, um, she didn't make it. But Junior is safe, alive and flourishing, thanks to my queen," he said, his eyes now looking down. Nathan was beginning to cry. Noel let a tear fall before wiping it away. She was not going to console him. After all, he was still a stranger.

"What was her name?" she asked.

"Charlotte." A moment of silence fell upon them. Just then, Noel asked, "So, did you ever re-marry?" She had two reasons for asking, she needed to know if he was indeed a widow or an adulterer.

"I did, and her name is Alicia. But I can't bring myself to tell her the truth," he said, now taking another sip of his Jack Daniels.

"What truth is that?" Noel asked, now slightly intrigued.

"She was a rebound. She wasn't meant to be my wife. I married her because I did not want to be alone, I've been horrible to this woman and for no reason, no good reason at all. I don't deserve her," he said. The room felt cold, Noel was slowly beginning to let her guard down as she watched Nathan bathing in tears. She knew that he was only showing this level of vulnerability to get her to trust him; to give him exactly what he wanted.

"So, tell me about yourself. What brings you to New York?" After all the tears had dried and another bottle bit the dust, Nathan made his way back into the refrigerator, this time grabbing two bottles of Jack Daniels.

Noticing this, Noel said, "Hey, I said I don't drink!"

He turned to face her, the lamp from the desk hurting his eyes. "I know, who said any of these were for you?" Noel quickly decided it was time to change the subject, and so she went on to describe her life in very short detail,

"I am a square from a box neighborhood, and my parents were and still are very strict and overprotective. I came to New York to find myself, to have some type of a life, to experience something outside of the nothing that I've grown so accustomed to," she said.

Nathan could not help but chuckle. "Square from a box, huh, I can't imagine how that would work. But if that's what you're calling it... You know, you are truly beautiful," he said before seeming to doze off a tad bit.

"Hey! You can't sleep here!" she shouted, tossing a throw pillow at his head. But Nathan was not moved. Instead, he positioned himself in the fetal position. Noel's eyes widened and she knew she would not get a good night's rest with him in her room.

"Please, I am asking you to leave, otherwise I won't sleep well. Please," she begged.

Nathan heard her cries and decided it best that he be on his way out of respect for her, and so he stumbled over to the exit. Feeling relieved, Noel assisted him in opening the door. As he stepped into the hallway, she shut the door behind him. Noel took a long, deep breath behind the door as she made her way back into her king-size bed. She thought of Nathan the entire night as she pleasured herself before finally falling asleep.

The next morning, she woke to find breakfast and a present by the foot of her bed. Frightened, she called, "Is anyone in here? Nathan!" Nothing. Still, with nothing to wear, she stretched down to the foot of the bed to retrieve her gift. The long box was orange and ornate with white ribbons. As she tugged on the ribbons and revealed the contents inside, she hollered. It was a Versace bomber with ripped jeans and a silk purple blouse. Noel wondered what she had gotten herself into.

Just then, a note slipped out that read:

Meet me in the lobby at noon

Looking over to the nightstand, the clock read, 10:34 a.m. She knew she had time, however, she had no undergarments, but for the first time in a long time, she felt alive, she felt excited, she felt intrigued. Noel dialed down to the front desk where she inquired whether or not the hotel provided such personals, as in undergarments, and surprisingly enough they did. Noel then requested panties and toiletries. The underwear arrived, all black Hanes, six in a pack, but what did she care? At least they were underwear.

Noel ran to the bathroom where she showered, shaved and shoved food down her throat. Then came the hardest task of her life: hair.

Noel toyed with whether to leave her hair down or pin it up. She felt a ponytail made her look like an adolescent and she wanted a grown woman look, and so she decided to apply heat and let her shoulder-length hair flow freely. By 11:35 a.m., Noel was adding the finishing touches to her makeup. She went for a neutral look and by the time she was finished preparing and slipping into her gift, she felt a surge of confidence. It was the first time in a long time she was happy and pleased with her attire, not to mention the Jimmy Choo heels she'd found on the floor once she had climbed out of bed. She could not wait to see Nathan, because for once she had a good feeling.

Once the elevator dinged, she began making her way down to the lobby. Exiting, she paced—looking at her watch, the time now read 12:04 p.m. which meant Nathan had to have been somewhere, and so she searched, but she could not find him.

Just then she felt a soft hand grab hers. Alarmed, she turned, coming face to face with a familiar face,

"Hello beautiful, it's me, Kenneth."

CHAPTER FOUR

Noel stood still—the world stopped spinning. It was a twilight zone. Growing anxious, she could do nothing but make eye contact with the one person in the room she knew was going to be the most disappointed: Frances. And she was. Her face said it all.

A nefarious plot by a demonized wife seeking revenge, she was eerily calm, so much so that a look of satisfaction made its way across her face. Alicia knew she had won, she came into the domain of a woman she had loathed for months and finally, finally, she was getting her revenge the only way she knew how, or so she thought.

Just then, Frances bellowed from across the hall as Noel prayed for impunity.

A hamartia this was, for nothing good could possibly happen now, Frances thought.

Alicia was busy now downing the remainder of her margarita. Doing as she was told, Noel took long strides to join Frances down in the basement where she decided it best to retreat, and just like that, as the door shut behind them, Frances went on the attack.

"What in the flying fuck!" Frances screamed. Meticulously, Noel placed her margarita down on the mantle alongside the sectional. The basement was spacious, there was even a pool table and a complete bar. The ladies were no doubt getting the royal treatment, and Noel could not help but feel guilty for causing the first disturbance of the day.

"I can explain, I promise!" she said nervously, for she was terrified and no match for Frances.

An irritated Frances began pacing back and forth. Her mouth opened, but she made no sound. Instead, she raised her index finger and began to race up the basement stairs after having what looked like an epiphany, which worried Noel.

Noel decided to follow, but as she began to follow her friend, Frances turned to face her, shouting, "Stay your ass right here!"

Upstairs, Frances did what any best friend would do, she began to demand answers from the party who opposed them. "Please wipe that smug look off of your face. I mean, who do you think you are? Why here and why now? My friend is wrong, but so is your husband, if in fact any of these allegations are true. I mean, what is his deal? Have you spoken to him? Are you divorcing him?"

Africa decided to intervene as she noticed Alicia did not have much to say. "Franny, she isn't worth it." A beautiful woman with a tender heart, Africa spent her adolescence raised in a suburban home in Long Island with her mother Aubrey, her father Michael, and her younger sister Abigail.

As Abigail looked on, she knew nothing good could possibly come next but remained hesitant to check on Noel. If the accusations were true, she knew she would never look at Noel the same. Africa knew this too.

Frances was beginning to feel confused; she could not bring herself to face her best friend, nor could she imagine losing her over something like infidelity and her being the other woman.

Alicia continued looking on, confused on why the ladies were acting distraught, she realized then that her reaction was not what it should have been; then came the confirmation of her realization.

"How are you so calm?" Africa asked. "I mean, not only did you come in here accusing my cousin of sleeping with your husband, but you don't seem the least bit upset that he is having an affair." Abigail began to cringe and after a few seconds, a discouraged look came across her face. By now, the entire room was filled with discomfort.

"We need to find out what's really going on here." Frances' words were muffled.

Africa turned to face her, "What?" she asked. Alicia remained seated, taking in the view as she witnessed the slow transformation of a previously amiable gathering.

"We need to speak to Noel and find out what really happened," Frances concluded as she let out a disappointing sigh. This debacle was one no one could have predicted,

"We're all so confused and worried and here is this woman so calm! How on earth are you so calm? I am by no means condoning violence, but you just confronted the woman who you claim was sleeping with your husband and yet, you just seem okay with the events playing out here today. Can you explain that?" Africa pleaded. Africa knew her behavior was off, she was never typically out of order, always the most level-headed in the room as she always believed in leading with logic. But today was different. Today, she felt nothing but a surge of emotion because if any of this information proved true, her relationship with Noel could change forever.

"I had time to deal with my emotions, and that is all I am going to say until Noel-Lee comes back out here to look me in my face and deal with this head-on, the same way that I am," Alicia responded.

"If any of this is untrue, you will be handled accordingly," Africa assured her

"Well, who is going to go down and speak to Noel?" Abigail asked. Everyone exchanging looks.

Flashback

"Kenneth, oh my goodness, it's so good to see you!" Noel shouted with glee, smiling. But she couldn't help but wonder how he came to know of her whereabouts. "Wait, how did you find me?" she asked as she retracted from the wide hug she had given him.

"Well, your dad contacted me when you told him you'd arrived," Kenneth said. Noel's eyes widened, she'd had no idea her father knew anyone in the city.

"You speak to my dad?" she inquired as she prepared to take her seat at the table out on the patio by the bistro located inside. By now she could only assume Kenneth had sent her the clothes and the note. Kenneth was slender but fit, tall with a medium to dark skin tone and light brown eyes. He was draped in a three-piece Charcoal Gray Armani suit, which looked uncomfortable given the weather. Small sweat puddles began to build on his forehead. The weather demanded something a little lighter.

"Well, no, not personally, but my father speaks with him," Kenneth said. "You see, after graduation I came out here to live because I got accepted to NYU. I studied public relations with a minor in social media marketing, and now I manage a PR firm here in the city. I saw you yesterday checking in, but I couldn't say anything then because I was checking in one of my clients and didn't want to look unprofessional. But, of course, my girlfriend wanted to meet my client and so, a favor for a favor, huh?" He said, chuckling. "By the way, your dad was the happiest I've ever heard him, once I told him I located you."

As his lips moved Noel followed like a dog following a steak on a stick. Kenneth looked delectable and spoke with such eloquence.

"So, do you live here in the city?" Noel asked. As the words left her mouth, a young woman made her way to them. She stood, hovering by Noel and Kenneth as she extended her right arm around his shoulder, bending down to give him a kiss on the lips. She looked familiar.

"Noel, this is my girlfriend, Jade. She works here at the hotel," Kenneth said amicably.

"Nice to meet you," Noel said as she shook her hand. Jade was wearing a red maxi-dress with beige Gucci flip flops and her hair slicked to the back with a puffy ponytail to the rear of her head. Her facial features were soft and her skin as smooth as silk. She looked perfect.

Noel admired her until their eyes locked, and Jade, beginning to feel uncomfortable, announced her sudden urge to leave.

"Well, Noel was it? It was a pleasure meeting you, and Kenneth, baby, I will see you tonight for dinner. I love you," she said as she protracted her lips to meet his. Kenneth was no doubt smitten by Jade; as she walked away, he continued to stare despite Noel seeking to make conversation. Before she knew it, her complaints about the garden salad had become a soliloquy.

"Well, it seems like you've hit the jackpot with that one," she said sarcastically, raising her right eyebrow. Noel wondered if Nathan had, in fact, sent her the clothes and the card. If so, then where the hell had he gone?

"Hey, I have a crazy idea. If you're not busy, why don't you and Jade hit the town? She can show you some nice places to shop and maybe take you down on Fifth Avenue; you look like you have expensive taste." Noel blushed as her eyes broadened—looking down at the misleading clothes draping her body.

"Sure—"

Before she could retract her confirmation, Kenneth replied, overjoyed, "Great! I think she just went over by the greeting desk, I'll go fetch her," he spoke as he made his way out of his seat.

Noel wondered if he was truly anxious to get them going out or whether he simply could not wait to lay his eyes on Jade again. She decided to give him the benefit of the doubt by thinking the former of the two. Jade then made her entrance, motioning from the doorway for Noel to join her. Placing a twenty on the table, Noel arose and began making her way towards Jade.

Stepping out in the spring sun, Jade took out her posh Chanel glasses to frame her face and protect her eyes.

"That bomber is making *me* hot," she teased. Noel was burning up, so she removed her bomber and began throwing her hair into a high messy bun where she twisted the top despite knowing it was destined to fall. Jade extended her arm in the middle of the street to hail a taxi, and a yellow cab pulled over. The ride was short, about ten minutes of silence between them with Jade checking her pocket mirror and the taxi driver yelling at the sports broadcaster over the radio. The noise of the New York City traffic gave her a headache.

Finally, they had arrived at what appeared to be a boutique. Jade stepped out after punching some numbers on her phone, which had the cab driver thanking her profusely.

"What's that on your phone?" Noel asked. Jade raised her eyebrows,

"It's an app for paying the cab drivers. Wait, what kind of phone do you have?" she inquired, standing with her handbag falling slightly from her wrist, her manicured nails noticeable.

"I left my cellular phone back home. But I had one of those touch key-pad phones. Nothing too fancy." Jade let out a huge sigh of disappointment.

"Well, perhaps this is fate's way of telling me you need Nathan more than I do. I mean, it's obvious you're sleeping with him," she sniped as she began making her way into the boutique.

"No, no I am not sleeping with him. He and I literally had one conversation."

Jade turned in disbelief. "One conversation and he has you wearing a seven-thousand-dollar Versace bomber? Girl, save it. What other incentives would he have to spend that kind of cash?" she asked.

"Hope," Noel snapped.

"Uh-uh, that was a rhetorical question. He wants something from you and he's just buttering you up. But just you wait, you'll be throat first on that dick when the time is right."

"Speaking of which, if you're sleeping around—"

"No, you don't get to do that! I am not sleeping around. I made a mistake, as do many other people. I know what you're going to say, you think I don't love Kenneth or that I am doing something horribly wrong here. But Kenneth and I have not always been in a good place. He's made mistakes, too. We both did."

"You can't cheat on someone you love," Noel said.

"What do you know about love?" Jade snapped.

"Anyways, Kenneth asked me to treat you well, so we have his black card and, um..." Before she could finish her sentence, Jade took a few steps back to see if she had recognized the cashier. She did.

"Frances!" she called. Jade scurried over to the fragrance counter where she greeted a young woman who appeared to have suddenly smelled something putrid.

"Listen, please do not act like you don't miss me, roomie." Jade smiled.

"Noel, this is my abhorrent ex-roommate, Frances Cooper," Jade said sarcastically. Frances was clearly growing annoyed,

"I am not unpleasant, I just do not like you," she snapped. Frances turned to face Noel. "Pleased to meet you, girl." She swiftly moved to walk away.

"Noel."

"What?" Frances turned.

"Oh, my name is Noel; you called me girl," Noel said assertively.

"Oh, I don't see why you're hanging out with this gold-digger," Frances said.

"Gold-digger? Frances, why on earth are you being so rude? And, why are you working here? What happened to your teaching job?"

"Really, Jade, why did you even come over to speak to me? Must we pretend like we're buddies, chums? Well, we aren't. I absolutely despise you," Frances said. Jade decided it best to end their conversation as she motioned for another associate,

"Hello, may we have some help over here? I would like to purchase the Dior 1.7oz." Jade decided to continue examining the counter as Noel and Frances stood witnessing her desperate attempt to behave with indifference.

Noel decided to break the ice once Jade was out of view.

"So, why do you hate her so much?" she asked Frances, who was now pricing items behind the glass window.

"Jade and I were roommates throughout college, and she managed to sink her teeth into my younger brother. He slept with her, their relationship turned ugly, and she moved out overnight. No one in my family ever heard from her again and she left me to struggle with rent, and now here I am, working two damn jobs, and my brother is engaged, but I can tell he sometimes blames me for bringing her into our lives. She destroyed him. Take it from me, okay, Noel? She's like a hellion, I don't know what she's planning, but keep your eyes open and don't fall for her tricks. I have to go. It was nice meeting you." Just like that, Frances disappeared.

Moments later, as Noel stood alone in the center of the large store, Jade appeared holding three bags with the name *Crystals* written across them. "I wonder what lies she told you about me." Jade looked as though she wanted to cry, so Noel decided it best to change the subject.

"Are we going to another store?" Jade nodded. She took one sadder look at Frances, who was now busy with a customer. Returning her Chanel shades to her face, she stomped past Noel with an extra show of confidence, making her way out of the glass doors and stepping onto the sidewalk to hail another cab. Noel prepared herself for what was going to be a day filled with redundancy and mindless shopping.

When Noel arrived back at the hotel that night, she fell onto the bed, dropping her shopping bags at her feet. Eight hours and thirty-seven minutes later, she was feeling completely exhausted. But thanks to Kenneth and Jade's fashion sense, to which she had slowly grown accustomed, she now had outfits to complement the woman she was becoming. Noel thought of Nathan all day. So much so that she'd prayed to hear from him when she returned to the hotel. A message, a note, something; at this point, she would have even taken another gift.

The phone rang. Unsure of whether or not she should answer, she did.

"Hello?" She said.

"A black cocktail dress will be arriving. Put it on. The limo will be out front in two hours." The dial tone sounded before she had a chance to say anything. Before Noel could place the phone back on the receiver, someone knocked at the door.

The dress was spectacular, a Dolce and Gabbana Lace-Trimmed Cady dress that fit her body like a glove. Noel was not the curvaceous type, but in that dress her body looked voluptuous. She wore her heeled sandals with the red straps and carried a red clutch she purchased earlier that day with Jade. Noel having no idea the clothes she purchased would come in handy so soon, but they did.

She wore her hair parted in the center and slicked down at the sides to create a massive bun at the rear of her head. She looked sophisticated.

Making her way down to the lobby where she would await the stretch limo made her heart beat with excitement. Nathan was different from the men she knew, and this was unlike anything she had ever experienced. Jade and Noel made eye contact as Jade stood behind the receptionist desk wrapping up what appeared to be her last customer for the evening. She was wearing her trench coat and had her knapsack on.

A few minutes later Noel observed the stretch limo appearing outside. Jade knew who it was but decided to keep her composure. She told herself that Nathan was her past and she was determined to move on, no matter how many lies she had to tell herself. Noel stepped lightly through the glass doors, the humidity causing her to sweat and her makeup to run. She raced into the cool limo where she turned the vents to face her as the air conditioning pumped from them. The ride was uneventful at 8:45 p.m. on a Sunday night.

The limo stopped. The tinted windows made it impossible for her to see where she was. The driver instructed her, "Ma'am, please remain seated," in a modulated tone. A few minutes later the door opened and Noel was greeted by what appeared to be a valet. She extended her hand to feel the soft hands of a man, looking up she watched as Nathan admired her with his eyes. Their hands intertwined. She wanted to kiss him, she wanted to mount him, she felt herself falling in love with his chivalry.

Stepping into the French-inspired restaurant *Adour*, Noel felt like a queen. The restaurant was empty, and as they made their way further inside to take their seat, red and beige rose petals were thrown at her feet by the waiters—the hostess stood by with a chilled bottle of champagne. They were seated in the center of the restaurant, and the ambiance was exceedingly romantic. Noel speechless, she was far too busy taking in the experience.

A violinist began to play his rendition of "Song Without Words, Op. 2 No. 3" by Tchaikovsky, at that moment Noel felt compelled to say, "Nathan, I am a virgin," just as the waiter began pouring their first round of Cristal Brut.

Nathan, although shocked, remained calm. He was draped in an expensive black and beige suit. Choosing to ignore her statement, Nathan raised his glass for a toast.

"To Noel, tonight is your night. I am happy to have met you and I hope that I can continue to sweep you off your feet and perhaps one day make you the happiest woman alive." Nathan then took his glass and tapped hers. Noel and Nathan both took a sip of their champagne.

Their conversation lasted for hours. Topics ranging from college experience to high school pranks and bullies were discussed. Nathan and Noel were bonding over exquisite food, tasteful champagne, and having been the root of many pranks during their adolescence. Noel did not know what it felt like to fall in love, or even to fall in like, and for the first time in her life she had a sip of alcohol, which made her view of Nathan far more appealing.

Noel felt like she could conquer the world, feeding one another tartines and sharing their main courses, three hours felt like three years, and Noel was ready. She was ready to make this man her life. Nathan was perfection from his decorum to his career to his romantic nature to his physique. Noel knew she could have asked for nothing more, and so she didn't. She simply enjoyed what was and imagined what could be, which at that moment was enough for her.

Once their course ended, Nathan requested a photo from the waiter, who was happy to oblige. Noel felt self-conscious, claiming that her makeup by now perhaps had faded away and she would resemble a goat rather than a human. Nathan found this to be quite humorous and he let out an undelightful cackle. But she decided to put on a brave face and a smile, and before she knew it the flash came and went.

That is what her night felt like. The night felt like the brief flash of a camera; it was ending too quickly.

Noel and Nathan exited the restaurant, and the only thing Noel could think of was sex. She was ready, she was willing, she was going to give Nathan her innocence.

Once they arrived back at the Hilton, Nathan walked Noel to her room, where he removed her dress and her shoes as she continued to speak mindlessly on politics and the injustices within America. He kissed her on the forehead and then proceeded to tuck her into bed. She was inebriated, and despite her many attempts to seduce him, he would not indulge her.

That night Nathan allowed Noel to hold onto her self-respect, for he was not the type of man to take advantage of a drunken woman. On his way out of the hotel, he politely asked that someone check on Noel and contact him with an update every two hours, this request came at a fee in the amount of six hundred dollars to a Dillion Matthews, who was more than happy to accommodate Mr. Ramirez after thanking him abundantly for his generosity.

CHAPTER FIVE

As night came it was the howling winds that worried Noel more than the possibility of her face being bludgeoned by not only one woman, but several. She knew no one would condone this behavior, not now, not ever, especially if anyone were to catch wind of the unbearable results. Just a few more minutes, she thought to herself as she continued to wait patiently for one of her executioners to make their way down the stairs. Yet no one came. As the night began to fall and the wind speeds continued to pick up, she figured it best to take matters into her own hands and go and face the woman who she was trying so hard to elude.

Who was she kidding, trying to hide? There she was, in a cottage with the wife of the man she was sleeping with. Escaping now was merely wishful thinking as she paced downstairs, thinking now it may be a good idea to face her problems head on—deciding to do so, Noel began marching up the stairs.

Meanwhile, upstairs after a slight pause, an irritated Frances concluded that it was perhaps best if she confronted Noel. Both Africa and Abigail reluctantly agreed. Just as Noel was beginning to make strides up to the main floor, Frances opened the door, looking down at Noel like a lion to a gazelle.

Noel backed down, calling to her.

"Franny? Franny?" she repeated, hands now placed together in the position of prayer, "Look, I can explain. So here is the thing. I had no clue that man was married when he and I first met." Noel pacing as Frances continued to stand by the staircase with an infuriated look on her face. Noel continued to speak, her voice breaking as her eyes began to well. However, she fought through it. Taking long, deep breaths, she continued to provide an explanation that only Frances had earned.

"You know Nathan, I had no idea he was still married until the other day when he mentioned it to me," she lied. "But, I just, um... I just...I figured it wouldn't be a big deal...since...I don't... see myself with him..." Noel stuttered.

"Cut the shit! I could lose my fucking job over this, Noel! That woman is married to one of the richest men on the island. They have connections, and you don't know how far she will go to enact revenge. I mean, and who the fuck is Noel-Lee? Huh? I thought I knew everything about you!" she said, disappointingly. Noel could no longer resist, she allowed the tears she had been working so hard to hold flow freely from her eyes.

Gasping, she said, "You do, Franny, I swear you know everything."

Shaking her head in disbelief, Frances said, "Listen, those tears can't save you! Do you know who this woman is? She can destroy us both! I teach her fucking daughter."

"She can have us destroyed with the snap of her fingers. I had no clue you were screwing her husband!" she shouted. Noel thought for a moment, realizing Frances was right, they could both lose everything they had worked so hard to build. However, she felt it was only fair they were both exposed for their skeletons. Noel despised the idea of being labeled a home-wrecker, especially when she was not alone in her treachery.

Everyone upstairs was growing impatient. Abigail toyed with the idea of leaving, "I think I just want to go home," she confessed.

"We can't just leave them here," Africa said. Both of the ladies took a long look at Alicia, who was now taking a tour around the cabin, her feet carelessly gliding across the wooden floors

Suddenly she asked, "Did you ladies all put together for this cabin?" Africa and Abigail exchanged a look of worry, unsure of whether or not they should respond. For a moment Africa argued with her inner-self, trying to convince the hellion in her to simply not entertain such a question, for she knew the question came with intent. But the hellion won.

"No, it was a surprise excursion courtesy of Frances. Figured you would know that considering an invitation was extended your way, which I am still not exactly sure why."

"I see. Well, if I am not mistaken, Frances is a school teacher; she teaches my daughters' third-grade class. So how is it that she can afford such an amenity?" Knitting their brows, Africa and Abigail exchanged a confused look.

"What exactly are you trying to say?" Abigail interrupted. Africa folding her arms now as she slouched in the Sierra lodge sofa.

"My husband is quite wealthy, and we've taken trips with the Brimson's for business purposes, of course, and so I know their family engraving from anywhere. This is definitely a Brimson estate," she said as she continued to wander, Alicia now made her way into the kitchen where she slowly ran her manicured nails across the cabinet knobs and the marbleized countertops.

"So, my friend hit the jackpot, she knows a wealthy man who was kind enough to offer his estate for our trip. I mean, it's 2018, anything is possible." Abigail shrugged, trying hard to keep her composure when they all heard shouting come from the basement, startling them.

"Wait, okay, just wait a damn minute!" Noel shouted.

"You don't get to simply point the finger at me. I know whose cabin this is, and who is funding all of this. It damn sure isn't no Maxwell."

Frances was growing violent, her tone increasing. "Bitch, what the fuck did you just say? Are you seriously trying to turn this around?"

"I said what the fuck I said!"

"You could get us fired! Fuck a cabin and an all-expense paid excursion. You are fucking a married man!" Frances shouted.

Noel continued, refusing to lower her voice, "Okay, alright, well what about you? Huh, Mrs. Pro-black. I saw the engraving on the door handle; this is a Brimson estate. Shit, Maxwell, he can't even afford a motorbike—he lives with us. This is from Michael Crawford, alright, and his family are one hundred percent Caucasian Republicans, along with him. They are avid Trump Supporters, they even sponsored his campaign. You want to talk about not knowing one another," Noel snapped.

The howling winds increased, blowing against the wooden door frames.

Frances scoffed, "Oh, listen to me, you ungrateful bitch, we have a roof over our head right now, an all-expense paid trip and much more to come because of the man I spread my legs for. But because of who you decided to fuck, we could be unemployed and homeless! So think about that before you decide to go checking somebody!"

Noel went blank. All she could wonder is *how did we reach here?*

Flashback

The next day, Noel awoke once again to the fresh smell of strawberries, pancakes, eggs sunny-side up, and coffee freshly brewed on a wood veneer room service cart. Noel was thrilled. She had never been catered to and she knew this was only the beginning.

As she wolfed down her food hoping to nurse her hangover, she noticed a tiny box hanging off one of the stainless-steel bars, a blue box with white ribbons. Meticulous, she removed the box, shaking it as she opened it with excitement. Inside she found a small jewelry bag with the words *Tiffany & Co* written across it. She proceeded to open the bag, shaking out the contents onto her bed. What fell out were two 18-karat gold circle pendants hanging from a 20" gold chain.

Noel was ecstatic; she stood on her bed and danced to the sounds of her own inner tune. She was being swept off her feet—something she had only seen in movies—and she could not have been happier. Noel wanted to thank Nathan for his kindness but realized she had no way of doing so other than waiting for him to call her. But Noel had other plans.

After she had taken a long hot bath and rubbed her skin with an Orchard Mile intense day cream, another form of luxury hand-picked by Jade, she smelled of expensive cotton. Noel dressed in her khaki pantsuit, a mocha colored cashmere blouse accompanied by the black-strapped Tom Ford sandals she purchased the day before during her shopping trip with Jade. Then, to complete her look, she added her new gift. Placing her hair into a tight, sophisticated bun, she proceeded out the door. Walking past the other guests, she felt right at home. She blended in as she struts with confidence looking like money she did not have.

Noel made her way past reception, where she and Jade briefly made eye contact, but Jade was not stopping there. "Hey! Loser, where do you think you're going?" she shouted as she reached her on the sidewalk, waving down a taxi.

"Am I under surveillance?" Noel snapped. Jade was annoyed, but she was also impressed. She scoffed before making her way back inside, jealous that she had to succumb to wearing a crimson midi-skirt that came slightly past her knees, a white button-up long-sleeved shirt, bowtie, and crimson vest with a pair of thirty-dollar heels that hurt her feet when she walked, but she was a working girl. Noel climbed into the back seat of a taxi and asked to be taken to *Crystals.*

Once outside, Noel sauntered her way into a Starbucks where she purchased two venti-sized iced coffees with cream. Heading next door, she stood by the entrance searching for Frances. When she caught her eye, Noel began making her way towards her, but Frances did not react nor respond.

Noel placed the coffees on the glass countertops and re-introduced herself. "Hopefully you remember me from yesterday," Noel said amicably.

"Of course, I remember," said Frances as she snatched one of the coffee cups and began to take a sip. She was draped in a yellow sundress with flip-flops, her toes undone and her hair in a tight ponytail, un-straightened. Frances was a spontaneous, amicable, free-spirited woman with questionable priorities. She reminded Noel of a Barbie doll.

Standing at 5'8, enriched with melanin, Frances had an afro-puff with the most beautiful, exotic facial features one had ever seen. Noel caught herself daydreaming as she stared into Frances's soft hazel eyes, longing to see her beautiful smile.

"Why are you staring at me like that?" Frances questioned. The boutique empty, not a customer in view. "And, my oh my, don't you clean up well. Did you and Jade swindle a millionaire after you both left here yesterday?" she asked, chuckling.

Noel let out an uncomfortable sigh. "We're not all users, and to be honest, Jade is a working woman,"

"I didn't call her a *user* per se. For the record, you said that. Anyways, what brings you here? Can I interest you in something?" Frances asked.

"No—but I figured maybe we could hang out today. You know, see the sights," Noel said taking a sip of her iced coffee.

Frances let out a loud exaggerated laugh, almost as though she was mocking her. "Hang out? I take it you don't have a job. A pretty woman like you will just get all the men and their money, huh?" Frances teased.

"Actually, no, I do have my own money. I just really liked your vibe yesterday and I want to learn more about you." Noel felt kind of strange. She felt like she was hitting on Frances, but Frances knew better, and so against her better judgment, she agreed.

"Okay," Frances said, much to Noel's surprise.

Frances grabbed her bag, and throwing it over her shoulders, she made her way out of the front door where Noel now stood. Turning the sign from **OPEN** to **CLOSED**, she then turned the lock and she and Noel headed down the street until they came to a crosswalk. The sun was shining and Noel could not have been happier. She found herself in a trance every time she looked at Frances. She was truly one of a kind—gracious and despite her Tom-boy demeanor, she was playful and open to adventure. This excited Noel.

"Have you ever been to the New Museum?" asked Frances as they continued to stroll. After walking one block, Frances took a look at Noel and decided she had to change.

"You're not going on a city outing with me in those heels. First of all, you look like a Park Ave stuck-up bitch, and second, you need flats."

Noel chuckled because she felt like a Park Ave stuck-up bitch and knew the occasion had not called for it. The ladies turned around, returning to Frances's boutique where an unhappy woman was seen waiting outside. Frances and Noel exchanged a look, and Frances decided it best not to return.

"Why aren't you going back?" asked Noel.

"Because that's Amber, and I know if I go back, she'll try to convince me why I should stay at work and not take breaks and not close the store when it's supposed to be open," Frances mocked.

"You mean to remind you of your morals?" Noel teased.

"Precisely," Frances laughed.

Noel was in no mood to negotiate, especially considering her feet were beginning to hurt.

"Okay, the pinky toe is suffering," she cried, but Frances did not console her.

"Heels are meant for taxi rides and exquisite dates with CEO's and CFO's and those investors on Wall Street. Not places like the Village. Just some food for thought. Now, the quicker we walk, the sooner we will find you a store for some shoes," she said. So they walked. Noel continued to struggle in her heels for what felt like an hour before they finally came face to face with a small shoe store located on the corner of W 24th Street. Noel felt relieved. Once inside, she removed her right shoe, noticing the red imprints the straps left on her foot. Groaning as she struggled to remove the shoe on her left foot, Frances stood in amazement.

"Why must women torture themselves like this?" she laughed as she walked away to explore their collection.

Noel continued to sit, taking long, deep breaths as her feet were finally free from burning when a pleasant voice said,

"Looks like you're having a rough day, even though the day's pretty much just getting started." Noel turning to face the source saw a Caucasian man standing behind her holding the hand of a little girl with curly brown hair and a light-skinned complexion. Noel smiled as she remained eye-level with the young lady, who by now was tugging on the strange man's hand, begging to leave.

"We're going darling; can you give daddy one minute to talk to the beautiful lady?" he pleaded. Noel continued to smile as Frances tried on boat shoes in the adjacent aisle.

"Sorry about that, I wasn't trying to intrude. It's just that I saw you and your friend come in and couldn't help but notice how beautiful you were." He smiled. His daughter looked away in disgust.

"Eww daddy." She laughed, Noel joining her.

"My name is Noel, and who you are?" she said to the little girl.

"My name is Ana," she said, shying away behind her father's leg.

"Nice to meet you, Ana, and who is this handsome man you call dad?" Noel asked as she looked up to face him.

"My name is Abram, and it is very nice to make your acquaintance, Ms. Noel. Do you mind if I take you out for dinner sometime?" he asked. Ana stood behind him making funny faces,

"Daddy, this is embarrassing," she cried. Noel continued to chuckle.

"How old are you, Ana?" she asked.

"Seven," her soft voice responded.

"I think I'm going to let your daddy take me to dinner, is that alright with you?" Noel asked, smiling.

"Sure, can you bring me back a burger?" Ana asked.

"Sure, if dad says it's okay." Noel smirked. She stood now, her bare feet on the carpet. Extending her hand to Abram's, she said, "It is definitely a pleasure to meet you both, too. I, um, don't have a cellular phone at the moment. I just moved here from Seattle, long story. But, um, I am staying at the Hilton Hotel over on the Avenue of the Americas." Noel said Abram raised an eyebrow; he was impressed.

"Well, Ms. Noel, I can give you my card here and hope you give me a call sometime, and it was a pleasure meeting you," he said.

"Sure—dinner tomorrow at 8?" she asked as Abram and Ana prepared to take their leave.

Smiling, he said, "Of course! Should I pick you up at the Hilton?" he asked, confirming.

"Perfect." Noel smiled with her eyes and just like that, they were gone.

Frances made her way over, holding in her hand a box with a pair of blue and white Keds. Noel quickly took a glimpse of the shoes—her smile turned into a frown, wondering why Frances would even consider purchasing those.

"Those are ugly, Frances," she said.

"Great, they're not for me, they're for you. Just a whopping twenty-two dollars for comfort. Go on now, Ms. Unemployed. Get your sneakers so we can go!" Frances said, handing Noel the box. "And please wipe that repugnant look from your face," she continued as she made her way to the entrance. Eyes wide, Noel took the sneakers and put them on, along with a pair of thick stockings. She took one look in the mirror and scoffed; her entire look had been thrown off.

Once Noel purchased her sneakers, she placed her sandals in the bag and off they went.

"So, tell me about daddy guy," Frances said.

"Oh, my goodness, wasn't he like super handsome?" asked Noel.

"He definitely was some nice vanilla, and I was totally impressed with that save!" She chuckled.

"Yea, I knew once I said I had no phone he didn't believe me, probably thought I was blowing him off or something. But dinner tomorrow night, secured. If I knew it was this easy to meet good-looking men, I would have come to New York a long time ago and probably wouldn't still be a virgin." Noel spoke with excitement, not realizing Frances had stopped walking.

Turning, she asked, "Hey, why'd you stop walking?"

"Did you just say you're a virgin?" Frances asked. Noel, feeling embarrassed, began to massage the back of her neck as she looked up at the high-rises before responding.   "Can you at least get back up here so we can discuss my private parts discreetly?" she asked.

Frances skipped to her. "Yes, please explain yourself. Aren't you like—grown?"

"Well, yes, but the conversation of sex never really came up in my life and I didn't really meet anyone I liked, so I just never had it, and then at one point I decided I wanted to wait until marriage, but then decided against that. So, here I am, a virgin," Noel explained.

"Do you mean re-virginized, as in, you didn't like the dicks you had, and—"

"No, I mean virgin, virgin, as in, never had sex," Noel clarified. "Yes, I know, I am twenty-six and never had sex. Shame on me, and I'm turning twenty-seven this October, I might add." She smiled.

Frances and Noel continued walking as Frances made fun of Noel, "We have to get you laid before your twenty-seventh birthday. For sure. What kind of flavor are you leaning towards making this happen?" Frances asked.

"Flavors?" Noel questioned as she opened the door to a small restaurant serving brunch.

"Black dick, white, dick, caramel dick, do you have a preference is what I'm asking." Frances smiled.

As they made their way inside Noel pondered her answer. When they were greeted by the hostess, Noel politely advised her they were dining for two. Making their way inside the cozy restaurant, Noel placed her clutch beside her. The restaurant was small but ornate. The table cloths decorating the tables resembled that of a picnic blanket, blue and white squares with knitted ends. Atop each of them was a personal bottle of wine, two wine glasses, plates with napkins neatly folded, and a centerpiece of green plants. Noel quickly opened the bottle of wine—a screw top, helping herself as the waiter made his way over to them.

"Hello ladies, my name is Maxwell and I will be your waiter today. Can I get you both started with some water? Well, maybe water to accompany the wine, I should have said." He blushed as he smiled. Noel swished her wine around and Frances was careful not to make eye contact as she buried her head into the menus he placed before them. Maxwell, was average height for a guy, standing at what appeared to be 5'9 with dark black waist-length dreadlocks that he pulled into a ponytail. He was wearing a fitted black shirt that hugged his muscles perfectly and had a beautiful white smile that was driving Frances crazy. Noel shot her a sinister look.

"Can you come back in maybe ten minutes, after we take a look at the menu?" Noel asked, her eyes gleaming. As he walked away, Noel turned to Frances, "If you bury your head any further into that menu, you're going to start eating the pages," she whispered.

Frances looked up, ensuring that the coast was clear of Maxwell, she said, "I don't know what it is, but I haven't had sex in almost a year and it's like every good-looking man I see, I just want to sit on his private parts. You'll know what that's like, once you dust those cobwebs off your Mary and start getting with the grinding and whining. Speaking of which, you didn't answer my question," Frances said as she extended the napkin across her lap, preparing to look into the menu once again.

"Nor do I intend to, because I truly do not know. I feel like whoever takes my virginity now should at least be deserving of it," Noel said.

"Deserving? Well, maybe Mr. Necklace might be. I didn't notice that around your neck yesterday. Where did that necklace come from?" Frances asked, extending her hand to Noel, gently lifting her pendant to get a better look.

"Well, he might be a good candidate. I'm still weighing things," Noel spoke with uncertainty.

"Don't wait too long. Gifts like that usually come after there's some serious time invested; it seems like maybe you guys have a few years in. So why not him? Is he in Seattle?" she asked. Noel raised her eyebrow, she did not want to lie but felt the truth would be overbearing; this was their first time hanging out.

"Yea, he is. He'll be in town tomorrow actually." Noel felt ashamed.

"Tomorrow, don't you have a date with the daughter-guy?" Frances chuckled. "Well, hey, if Seattle guy isn't your boyfriend, have him check into a different room and live your life, girl," she said, raising her glass for a toast. Just then, their waiter approached,

"Are you beautiful ladies ready to order?"
Scurrying to review the menu, they both simply said yes.

As the afternoon continue to pass them by, the ladies ate, laughed and talked for hours as they enjoyed their wine and dessert. The neighboring tables began to fill one by one as more people came piling inside. The wooden floors creaked as patrons filled the room. Noel looking around, enjoying the aesthetic. The bar where the wine was kept hung high, at least fifty bottles loaded into the overhead. Just beneath it a table

50

filled with fresh fruit, bread, butter, spices, and carrots. There were plants everywhere; the room resembled a greenhouse.

As Frances took her last sip of wine, she was feeling rather tipsy. "I want him so bad!" she murmured.

Noel took a look at their waiter, who was standing behind her waiting on another table. "So go get him," Noel said as she purposefully dropped her utensils. Frances's eyes widened, the loud clatter embarrassing her as everyone turned to stare.

An innocent Noel said, "Oh, my goodness, clumsy me!" Maxwell hurried over, as he bent down to clean up the mess she had made, the look in Frances's eyes was telling.

"Maxwell?" Noel whispered as she bent down to speak to him.

"Oh, sorry, not to worry ma'am, I'll get this all cleaned up for you," he said while wiping the floor and picking up the knives and forks.

"No, Maxwell, my friend here is very interested in getting to know you," Noel whispered.

Standing now, as Frances turned away, Maxwell blushed. "I mean, I was intending on taking a less messy approach by just leaving my number on your receipt, but I guess this works, too," he said, smiling at Frances.

Noel chuckled loudly. "I am so sorry about the mess!" She laughed.

Frances was relieved. "I would like that very much," she said smiling from ear to ear. Once the bill was settled, Frances walked out feeling like she had just met the man of her dreams.

"New Museum here we come!" she screamed.

Noel gave her a benevolent stare as she proceeded to the middle of the road to hail a taxi. Once the driver pulled over, both of the ladies hopped in. Noel and Frances arrived at the New Museum in Soho where they explored, and Noel felt like a kid again. The attractions had an enigmatic feel. She and Frances stayed for hours walking, meeting new people, and engaging with natives and tourists alike. It was like something out of a dream.

Noel began to realize she had a friend in Frances. Frances was genuinely a happy person who at all times seemed to have Noel's best interest at heart. When they arrived at the museum, Noel insisted that they take photos: funny photos, vogue-inspired photos, and photos of the art. Frances had over one hundred pictures of them by the time they had readied to leave.

It was 6:14 p.m. when the ladies contemplated parting ways. Noel insisted on dinner, but Frances was not hungry. Instead, she insisted they go for a walk down the Hudson Pier, taking in the beauty of the riverbank.

Arriving by way of taxi, the ladies walked for a few minutes before Frances took a seat on a bench—she now appeared to be deep in thought.

"Is everything okay?" Noel asked, taking a seat next to her.

"Yea, right now things are perfect. Interestingly enough, when I was a kid my mom and I used to ride our bikes here. But we don't seem to be that close anymore," she said as she continued looking on.

"Is your mom here in New York?" Noel asked.

"No, she remarried and moved to California," Frances responded. There they sat, watching now as the sun began to set just over the Hudson Bridge, Frances resting her head on Noel's shoulder.

CHAPTER SIX

Africa felt she needed to intervene realizing she did not hear a sound come from the basement in more than twenty minutes. Both Alicia and Abigail remained upstairs, their girls' trip had become a nightmare. Peeking her head down the stairs, Africa stood watching as Noel and Frances sat on the floor, both upset with one another.

"Should we just all go?" Africa called down to them.

"No!" shouted Frances. "We may as well make the best of this trip."

Africa went down the stairs. "There is nothing to make the best of, Franny. Noel, I love you and we're family, but you know we can't condone this. Frances, we're not condoning this, right?" she begged.

"What are you trying to say, Africa?" Noel snapped.

"What I'm trying to say is we're family and that's never going to change, but I don't think we can be friends. Noel, Jesus, you don't sleep with married men! There are a plethora of single men out there for you to have sex with, why have sex with someone else's? How would you feel if it were you, huh? What if a woman was sleeping with your husband and her friends and family made her feel it was okay, or that it was the right thing to do because a man filled her head with lies?" Africa scolded her.

"I don't need this right now," Noel barked, placing her hand on her head.

"Neither did we. Our trip is ruined because of you," Africa continued.

"She didn't ruin the trip, Alicia did. First of all, she tricked me into even inviting her, all along her motive was to ambush you," Frances said, pointing at Noel.

"This wasn't an ambush, this was a confrontation. The only way she knew how to get one. You teach her daughter, Franny. I mean, how else was she supposed to get close enough to Noel for a conversation? As women, we shouldn't be blaming one another. It's that bastard everyone should be mad at! He gets to sleep with two women, lie and use two women. Meanwhile, one of them had a choice in the matter, and now we're all stuck up here on what was supposed to be a rekindling of our friendships, arguing because of that degenerate," Africa said.

"You don't have to talk about him like that," Noel interrupted.

"Don't you dare defend him," Africa shot her a loathsome look. "You may be my cousin, but just because we're family doesn't mean you can't thoroughly disgust me, and so far, you've done a pretty good job at that. Please, let's not add defending his character to the list of stupid things you've managed to get yourself involved with during your time here," she snapped.

The room grew dismal. "You're being way too harsh," Frances said.

"What? Are you kidding me? Am I the only person in this room who realizes this is a married man! He isn't separated or pending a divorce! He is a married man!" Africa screamed.

"We do get it! Saying it one hundred times doesn't make him unmarried, Africa! Jesus, just give us some time to think," Frances said.

"There's nothing to think about!" she replied.

"Oh, so what's your solution for me, huh?" Noel asked. "Give me the electric chair? What exactly would you like everyone to do, Africa, go home and cut me off? Never speak to me again because that would make you so happy." Noel was always soft-spoken and never raised her voice, even when she truly wanted to. Today was one of those days. The room stood still.

"What are you trying to say?" Africa, turned to face her, folding her arms.

"Be honest, you were always jealous of the relationship between Frances and I. Cousin or no cousin, here I come, befriending one of your best friends, and you didn't like it too much. But Africa, get over it. I didn't know you two knew each other, and even if I did, I wouldn't have changed a thing between Franny and I," Noel said.

"Everyone just needs to calm down," Frances said as she struggled to stand. She was growing tired of looking up at Africa and feeling like a child. She placed her hand on her head, annoyed by the bickering. "Maybe we should all just go to bed and re-convene in the morning. Africa, she made a mistake. As her friends and as her family, we have to try and forgive her," Frances said softly.

"These are my morals, Franny, and Alicia is trouble. I mean, she's up there inquiring on how we could even afford a place like this. Says she knows you're a school teacher and can't afford this cabin on a teacher's salary," Africa said.

"Well, that's none of her business. Why didn't you tell her we all paid for it?" Frances asked as Noel looked on.

"Why would I lie?" Africa said.

"Right, because you're just so perfect! So, what did you tell the stranger about how this cabin was afforded?" Frances snapped, growing impatient.

"Look, if you're sleeping with some rich, racist republican asshole, I want to know about it!" Africa said.

"What?! Oh, that's what she said, huh?" Frances asked. "I've had enough of this." Pushing Africa out of the way, she made her way upstairs.

"Don't you see she's just trying to turn us all against each other," Noel pleaded. Frances slammed the door behind her as Africa prepared to make her way out of the basement.

"You don't get to speak," Africa scoffed.

Standing now, Noel replied, "Excuse me, who the hell are you talking to? Just because you're my older cousin doesn't give you the right to speak to me like I'm a kid."

"Well, considering the fact that you've damn near been breastfed all the way up until your twenty-sixth birthday, I'd say you probably still are one," Africa responded.

Frances made her way to her bedroom, but not before instructing Abigail, "You might want to get down there before they kill each other. Good night, everyone." And just like that, she disappeared for the evening.

Meanwhile, the quarreling sustained downstairs.

"You're just being so disgusting right now!" Noel said as she prepared to leave.

"No, disgusting is when you lay with another woman's husband; and don't pretend like you're some cherub by insinuating that I am jealous of the relationship you have with Franny. All you've managed to do since arriving here is ruin a marriage and steal my best friend," Africa said.

Abigail shouted from the top of the stairs, "Both of you stop it right now! Africa, what the hell is wrong with you? She's family!"

"Yea, and from now on that's all she's ever going to be. Just because we're family doesn't mean we have to speak or be friends," she said, stomping past her sister and up to the living room. Gathering her duffle bags, Africa made her way up to the second floor.

Flashback

Arriving back to her hotel around eight, Noel completely lost track of the time as she made her way to the restaurant where she placed an order for baked salmon, rice, and vegetables. The hotel now filled with tourists—some of which were checking in, but Jade was nowhere in sight. As she waited for her food, Noel caught glimpses of the television where she watched as the news broadcast aired the presidential debate. Noel, gratified to see an African-American by the name of Irving Houston, waving his right hand in admiration to members of the overcrowded room. He steps confidently across the stage taking his place behind the podium.

As the cashier handed her a bag and advised her that the condiments were inside, a pleased Noel prying her eyes from the television moseyed her way onto the elevator where she took a few deep breaths before reaching the seventh floor.

Entering into the room, a sweet pea aroma hit her that she was not accustomed to. Stepping lightly, she saw Nathan sitting on the edge of the freshly-made king-sized bed in her suite. Placing her food on the desk, she quickly demanded answers,

"What are you doing here?" she asked, dropping her shoes to the ground. Nathan turned to face her, his hands pressed together,

"Where on earth were you? I called here several times."

Noel was in shock, she could not imagine why he would be speaking to her this way. "I was with a friend," she said.

"A man?" he interrupted.

"No, a female friend. Are you okay? Why on earth do you look so upset?" she asked. Noel was growing fearful now. She had no idea what he was planning. Next to him was a bag, she prayed it was not another gift, because by now she felt he was being far too paranoid.

"Baby, I just need to know where you are. That's all. I was worried sick," he said, stepping closer to her. Noel took a few steps back. Nathan chuckled.

"I hope I'm not scaring you. I was just honestly worried, and if you don't want me showing up like this, I promise you it will never happen again," he said. "But this is for you." While he walked back to the bed to retrieve the gift he bought her, Noel became hesitant. Handing her the bag, Nathan took a seat back on the bed. "Open it," he instructed as Noel continued to stand unmoved, forgetting the food on the desktop.

Once she began unraveling its contents, she found it was a cell phone, an iPhone to be exact. "You bought me a phone?" she said, alarmed.

"Well, yes, the phone number is on a receipt in the bag, and the phone is brand new, hasn't been set up yet, so you can do whatever you need to do with it. Personalize it," he said, smiling. Nathan was ecstatic, but a bit disappointed that she was not happier. "Did I do something wrong?" he asked.

Noel placed the phone and the bag on the desk next to her food. "I think this is a bit much for me. I mean, I barely know you and already you've bought me this chain, wonderful food is delivered here every morning, this room, and now a phone. I don't want to feel like you're buying my affection. I find you very striking, I do. But you're married, Nathan and this isn't ideal for me—"

Nathan stood, placing his index finger along her lips, shushing her. "You know I don't love my wife. I am there for the kids. I have a moral obligation to them, and right now things between you and I are new. But Noel, I promise you, I am attracted to you; I like that you're spicy and I just want you to give me a chance. I promise you, once I can get a handle on things with my wife, I will leave."

Nathan continued to look into her eyes as he spoke. He wanted to ensure that she was hearing him and that she believed him. Surprisingly enough, she did. Nathan leaned in to kiss her on the forehead, but Noel wanted more. Raising her head, she kissed his lips. She felt like a criminal, like the acts she was thinking to commit were an absolute crime and in the eyes of God, it was something worse. A sin.

Rubbing her head against his chest, she muttered, "I can't take the phone. I can't take any more gifts from you. I can return the necklace too and be out of here by morning—"

"No, no, I won't hear of it. I want you to keep everything, and please stay here. I really just need you to stay," he begged. "I know I probably make you uncomfortable, so I'll go, and of course before showing up I will give you a call first or shoot you a text. But please don't go," he continued.

Noel knew she was going to regret her decision, but she simply could not help herself. She wanted him by her side, and with her, so she asked, "Can you spend the night with me?"

By now, Nathan was already preparing to take his leave but stopped before exiting. Turning, he asked, "Are you sure you're ready for that?"

Noel snickered, "I was ready last night."

Nathan heard enough, turning down the lights, he turned, taking three long steps over to her and began to kiss her lightly. Nathan was going to make love to Noel for the first time. He stopped for a moment to admire her, staring into her eyes, he looked her up and down, palming her breasts as he kissed her gently on the lips.

"I promise I will go slow," he said, kissing her.

Noel was inexperienced, but she knew how to tongue kiss, and so she did. She went with his pace; he was indeed taking things slow. A lick here, a bit of tongue there and before she knew it, he was lying on top of her in the dark room, both of them wearing nothing but the white sheets. Nathan licked Noel from her neck to her torso to the playground between her legs. Her body was ready to receive him, but he was not ready. Nathan teased her, licking her and pinching her nipples as he caressed between her legs. Noel moaned.

Just then a loud bang sounded on the door. Nathan tossed his head in the air as he nervously began to rummage around for his clothes. Noel sat upright with the sheets covering her body, wondering why he was in such a hurry.

"Who is that? Are you okay?" she asked.

"Yes, I'm fine. I will see you tomorrow, I promise, and I am very sorry," he said as he ran out of the room.

Noel wanted to see where he was heading off to and with whom, so she quickly gathered herself off of the bed and ran to open the door, looking nervously down both ends of the hall, but there was no one there. She could not have imagined he'd have gone so fast, but she knew of no other options.

A few hours later she was still up, playing on her phone and trying to figure out what games Nathan was playing. He seemed to have known who was knocking, otherwise, he would not have left as quickly as he did. This did not sit well with Noel. She felt like a fool but was now longing for someone to touch her as Nathan did. Feeling hungry now—her appetite returning, she decided to get dressed making her way down to the lobby area where she found a microwave.

Her hair thrown into a messy bun, Noel waited patiently for her food to heat up.

As she turned to see the empty lobby, she noticed Jade strolling past the receptionist area wearing a silk robe with bed slippers, her hair pulled back into a tight ponytail. Noel hid, she did not want to be seen by Jade. She found it odd that Jade would be at the hotel, instead of being home with Kenneth. Just then, her phone pinged. It was a text from Nathan asking, "Where are you?"

Noel was in no mood to play games. As she stuck her head back out to see Jade, she realized she had gone. Noel took a few moments before replying, "Lobby. Food warming."

Just then her phone pinged again, "I am back, will wait in the hall."

Noel felt a mix of emotions. She wanted to confront him. Grabbing her food from the microwave after checking if the coast was clear, she made her way back to the elevators where she returned to the seventh floor. She watched as Nathan stood outside her door playing on his cellular phone. Once she approached him, his eyes fell to the ground as though he were ashamed. Inside the room, Noel opened her food and proceeded to eat. Nathan looked on from the sofa after grabbing a personal of Bacardi from the refrigerator. Watching Noel devour her food despite her petite frame turned Nathan on.

While chewing on her salmon, she said, "So, explain." Nathan took a sip of his Bacardi before answering.

"That was no one," he said. Noel grew angry.

"What? Is there someone I should be worried about? Was that your wife? What if she tries to come back when you're not here and tries to hurt me?" Noel shouted as she knitted her eyebrows placing the food on the desk; losing her appetite once more.

"I very much would just love to lie next to you and wake up next to you. Please, can we not fight?" Nathan pleaded.

"Finish eating your food, my love, so I can finish eating mine." He shot her a seductive look.

Noel wanted answers from him, yet she couldn't bring herself to inquire further. She stood, removing her robe, she took a few steps towards him. Parting her legs, she climbed on top of him.

Tossing the Bacardi aside, Nathan lifted Noel. Turning her over as he mounts her atop the bed. Nathan made love to her soul that night.

Nathan was gentle, but by the third round, Noel became aggressive. Five orgasms later she realized it was time for bed once Nathan ejaculated and there were no more condoms. Snuggling her head onto his chest she rubbed along his nipples before falling fast asleep in his arms.

CHAPTER SEVEN

The ladies all retired to their respected bedrooms. Africa and Abigail shared the conjoining rooms to the rear of the hall while Frances had the room closest to the staircase. Noel in the center, and Alicia on the first floor in the room nearest the patio.

That night, Alicia pondered her approach. She was not trying to be unpleasant, however, she was trying to get her point across. Alicia was known for her benevolent nature. It was what made her husband fall in love with her in the first place.

Alicia took pleasure in knowing that her husband was a hopeless romantic; what made her sick was knowing that he romanticized other women the way he did her. How unfair, she thought. *I am the mother of his kid, the woman who helped him raise his son, and now I must compete with strangers for a heart and a love he vowed was only to be mine.* It was not the cheating, it was not the other women, it was the blatant disrespect which kept her up at night. It was knowing that Nathan went to her father, begging for permission to marry her, only to hurt her after all of the years she had given him. Noel was not to blame, but how could she ever confront him, the one man her heart will never let go of?

As Alicia sat upright in her bed, listening as the howling of the wind increased, she played with the curls in her hair, twirling them strand-by-strand. With nothing left to do, she finally decided to go to sleep. *Tomorrow is a new day*, she thought.

Meanwhile upstairs, both Africa and Abigail decided to engage in some late-night unpacking and alcohol consumption once Abigail made her way back into her quarters.

"Where did you go?" asked Africa as she removed her clothing from her purple-shelled suitcase.

"I went to make a call," responded Abigail as she took a seat on her sister's bed. In her hand she held a glass of bourbon, swishing it around as if to take in the sweet smell. The girls laughed and laughed, reminding themselves of why the trip was necessary. Now a senior in college on winter break, Abigail knew for sure an excursion like this was just what she needed. Africa, as well. Abigail told stories of her experiences in school as Africa multi-tasked: unpacking, listening and sharing her own experiences in comparison.

"Why did you choose to go to Spelman again? I mean, you could have simply stayed in New York, Abby," Africa said after unpacking for almost forty-five minutes, distracted constantly by conversation and booze. The rooms they occupied all had the same décor. The twelve by sixteen square foot rooms were large enough to fit the queen-sized beds that occupied them, the sofas, nightstands and wardrobes. The sliding door in Abigail's room overlooking the rearmost part of the lodge, the forest covered in a blanket of white was what she was missing all those months while she was away.

"I needed to get away from mom and dad, and to be honest, sometimes you, too. You're all so occasionally overwhelming," she confessed.

Africa had a look of sympathy. "Sis, I get it, I was honestly only teasing because I miss you. I mean, things just haven't been the same. I feel alone now. I feel like we aren't as close as we used to be and things are just changing," she said, tossing her arm around Abigail's shoulder.

"I know, but I graduate in a few months, so you'll have me all to yourself again very soon!" said Abigail. They both exchanged a warm smile.

"Have you finished unpacking?" Before Abigail could respond, Noel and Frances came rushing in.

"You are a crazy person! You called my mother!" Noel tried to shout. But, as always, her low-pitched voice made it hard to decipher when she was truly irate, though by now she was ready to get physical.

Alicia listened to the commotion, as it had awakened her, but she thought it best to remain discreet as she tiptoed to the foot of the stairs, eavesdropping.

Noel continued her rampage. "Africa you are just a jealous, vile woman. Funny, no, how one minute you're saying my mother breastfed me up until twenty-six, but the second you hear something about me and my shortcomings, here you go gossiping about me like a damn adolescent! I understand how upset each of you are about the situation, but get over it! I did what I did, but everyone in here has or is currently making mistakes. No one is innocent, and to have involved my overly zealous—" Africa remained standing, a sardonic smile on her lips. "Oh, you think this is funny?"

"Noel, back off," warned Frances as she and Abigail both continued to look on. The ladies had endured enough drama for one night.

"You want to smile because you think you're better than me?" Noel continued as she took steps toward Africa. They were now face to face. Africa, however, decided Noel's theatrical episode was mere blather as she now prepared herself for a shower. But Noel was in no mood to be ignored, smacking the toiletries from Africa's hands. Both Abigail and Frances rushing to restrain her—Africa turning quickly to face her,

"Noel, I said back off!" Frances shouted as she held onto her best friend, finding her decorum to be unbecoming. The room had become an uproar, everyone shouting simultaneous words of confrontation.

"I am not going to waste my energy on you. Can't you see that you're a mess? Just look at you, you've become a fool for a man who does not want you!" shouted Africa. "You were just a good fuck, and now his wife, oh, let me tell you what she wants. The reality is she wants to let you know your position and what role you actually played in her husband's life. She isn't here to be your friend, she is here to let you know that you need to back off because at the end of the day, he goes home to her. He lives and breathes her. Not you, not the easy lay," Africa over-enunciated her words to drive home the point.

Standing downstairs, Alicia sighed before returning to her quarters where she slept peacefully for the remainder of the night.

Upstairs, the room grew quiet. Noel fought back tears; she knew Africa was telling the truth. As she exited their room, she wondered to herself, how did this happen?

Once the room emptied, Abigail closed the door behind them. She stood with the knob in her hand, looking down as her sister continued unpacking

"It was me, and you didn't tell," she said, her voice breaking up as she fought back the tears.

"You called her damn mother, Abby?" Africa asked.

"No, I called mommy and told her. I think she called Auntie Jenn," Abagail whispered.

Africa shook her head in disbelief. "It's alright. Go get some sleep," she instructed as she took a sip of her sister's bourbon before falling onto her mattress. Feeling regretful, Abigail exited.

Flashback
The next morning, Noel awoke to the fresh smell of pancakes, eggs sunny-side up, strawberries, and strips of turkey bacon. She was ecstatic despite the fact that she was alone. She wondered what time Nathan had gone.

As she devoured the strips of bacon, she searched frantically for her cellular phone but could not locate it. She looked under the bed, on top of the desk where her salmon was now beginning to smell. Tossing it into the garbage along with the rice and vegetables, she felt sick.

Noel removed her long, curly hair from her face. Slipping into her robe, she paced all throughout her suite searching anxiously for her phone, as she wanted desperately to continue setting it up. Feeling thrilled she could now communicate with Frances. But, no luck.

Just as she made her way to the nightstand to turn off the light now that the sun was shining in, she noticed a small piece of paper with the words,

Took the phone, has a glitch,

will return tonight.

XO Nathan.

Noel was not sure how to react—disappointed. However, she had more food to finish. A few moments later came a knock at the door similar to the one she heard the night before. She was midway through her breakfast, and as she poured on the maple syrup for her pancakes, she contemplated answering. She thought if she remained very still, whoever was on the other side would, well, go away; but no. The banging continued, this time longer and louder.

Just then, a voice said, "I know you're in there!"

Noel threw her fork down and sauntered to the door, looking through the peep-hole she saw no one, but was now curious about who it could possibly be. She unlocked the door, and standing on the threshold was a fair-skinned woman who jumped out to surprise her.

"Surprise Noey!" she screamed. It was Abigail, Noel's youngest cousin. Noel was surprised to see how much Abigail had grown. She extended her arms to hug her, and they held onto one another for quite some time, tottering in the hallway, smiling and laughing in excitement.

"Oh, my goodness, I have to get a look at you!" said Noel as she pulled away to examine her baby cousin, who was by far no longer a baby.

"Wait, how on earth did you know I was here? On my goodness, come inside, Abby, oh my God, you're so big." Abigail continued smiling. She was so overjoyed to see her cousin she could do nothing but continue to hug her. Noel was always so gentle.

Abigail's features were strong. She was short, exactly 5'0, with kinky dark hair and a light-skinned complexion, still wearing braces.

"What-what—are you hungry?" asked Noel, as she continued to look her cousin up and down. "My goodness, you've grown so much, I think the last time I saw you, you were like nine and we were all playing on the jungle gym and you fell and your dad got mad at mine," Noel reminisced, both of them laughing. Noel reached in once again to hug her. She was ecstatic.

Just then, Frances and Africa began making their way down the long corridor conversing. Noel overhearing her; ran into the hallway screaming and galloping towards Africa, throwing herself into her arms, both women were falling to the floor. Frances decided it best she move out of the way.

"Africa!" Noel screamed. Noel kissed her cousin all over her face; she was surprised to see her and by far delighted. As they both stood, Noel could not help but smile. She felt her life was slowly beginning to come together. Turning to face Frances as she kept her arms wrapped around her cousin, Noel was in a world to herself.

Africa, returning the gesture, could not stop smiling either, both of the ladies filled with excitement and overwhelming joy, Noel began to fight back tears.

"How did you guys find me?" she whimpered.

"You know my best bitch—it's a small world after all. Which room is yours, cuz?" Africa said. Noel scurried towards her room as she dried her eyes, the ladies piling inside taking in the ambiance. The suite Noel occupied was surprisingly large.

"Seattle bae?" asked Frances as she knitted her eyebrows and used her hand to motion the space. She smiled a sinister smile, impressed by his exquisite taste in the lap of luxury.

"Seattle bae," Noel confirmed, chuckling.

"What is there to drink, I am parched!" said Africa.

"Well, you all are just in time, I was starting to work on breakfast. There's enough for everyone. Eat up!" Noel said as she maneuvered around the suite, taking everyone's bags and accessories and placing them neatly into the front closet. Noel felt like a new woman, she could not point a finger to it, but she suddenly felt the urge to be responsible and welcoming. And she couldn't wipe the smile from her face.

"So, details, how does everyone know each other?" asked Noel. She was intrigued, no longer having an appetite as she begged her family and friends to devour the food she was given, and they did. Frances helped herself to the bacon and eggs. Africa went for the strawberries, pancakes and orange juice, while Abigail stuck with the pancakes, and eggs as well. Noel was happy to see everyone enjoying themselves, and with the room large enough to accommodate them all comfortably, she was finding herself even more smitten by Nathan for all he had done for her.

With everyone now settled, the conversation commenced.

"I can't even believe how small this world is," said Frances as she made her way towards the mini-bar. "Wow, Noel, you've really been working on this bar huh?" The scarcity of its contents made her question her friend's drinking habits.

"Says the woman looking for alcohol at ten in the morning," Noel snapped. Everyone let out a warm laugh.

"I need to know how you all know each other, this is like so surreal," said Noel. She was jubilant as she sit amongst them.

"Crazy story," began Africa, but Abigail interrupted.

"No, no, no, let Franny tell it because you're always too serious."

"Okay, braces!" teased Africa.

Laughing as she poured the 1.7 ounces of Jack Daniels, Frances took a seat on the sofa. This reminded Noel of Nathan, and despite the presence of her friends bringing her complete joy, she simply could not take her mind off of him. But she decided to remain focused, despite her taking glimpses of the phone every ten to twenty seconds.

"Okay, well now that I am settled with my drink, I will tell the tale of how Africa became my favorite continent," Frances teased.

"Oh, you are so corny for that!" said Africa as she tossed a throw pillow towards her. The room was filled with happiness as the ladies talked,

"Well, Africa here tried to steal my boyfriend while we were undergrads at Columbia. I was studying journalism and she was studying psychology with a minor in art design, which my boyfriend at the time was also studying. Well, they met, they kissed, well she kissed him—"

"I did kiss him, but in my defense, I didn't know he had a girlfriend, plus he and I were both drunk at a party," said Africa. "But please, carry on."

"Yes, anyway, this is how we met and bonded. We both wanted to join Delta so bad that we wrote the president at the time, begging her to bring a chapter to our campus. She responded to Africa's letter and not mine, but when the sisters arrived on campus, they asked Africa for me by name,"

"And I was super pissed," Africa interrupted.

"Yes, because after I found out about the boyfriend thing, I had her labeled a whore all over campus by my interest group," Frances confirmed.

Africa smiled.

Noel continued to listed as she watched for the phone to ring, Frances continued, "So, when I arrived at the rush I was aggravated and annoyed and tried my best to get everyone I knew, including the Delta sisters, to dislike Africa. I thought she was shady and, of course, a girl who stole boyfriends," said Frances.

"Wait, so I have to ask. Did you even get with Frances's boyfriend?" Noel interrupted.

"Nope, once I found out he had a girlfriend I wouldn't even give him the time of day. There are too many single men out there for me to be sharing any with another woman!" Africa said. Noel took a deep breath.

"Yep, so long story short, we pledged together, I learned of her morals, and we've been inseparable ever since. Africa, you're seriously my line sister and real sister. Like, I freaking love you," Frances said. Noel still could not believe her eyes or ears.

"So, last night, Noel, after we left the restaurant and I went home, this chick calls and she goes, where were you? I went by the boutique and you weren't there!" Frances laughed.

"So, I said I was out with a friend and she's like, what friend? How many other women are you friends with in New York?" Frances continued to chuckle. "So, I go, one other, her name is Noel and she's really dope. You know, calm, I like calm women." Frances confirmed. "So, Africa is like, I know a Noel, she's my cousin, but we haven't spoken in months. By now, I'm on the phone half-drunk, struggling to even keep my eyes open and I say, she's this Korean and Black queen and then out of nowhere Africa screams, that has to be my cousin!" Frances let out a loud chuckle, Africa joining her.

Their laugh in sync; they were adorable to watch as they played off of one another. Finishing sentences, smiling profusely and making one another happy.

"Then this morning, of course, I gave Jade a ring and she was acting all stingy with your information, but then to my surprise, Kenneth took the phone and after he and I spoke she was more than happy to relinquish your information." Frances continued.

"Kenneth? You know him?" asked Noel.

"Yes, creepy Kenneth. I've known that clown since the third grade," confirmed Frances. Noel's eyes widened.

"Kenneth and I went to school together, in Seattle," Noel said.

"Yea, when his parents divorced, his dad got custody and took him to Seattle, but then he came back a few years ago and now he's some hot shot at a PR firm," Frances said tranquilly.

Noel couldn't help but chuckle at the coincidence. "Perhaps, we were destined to meet," she said.

"We should all head out. Noel, by the way, your cousins know far more attractions than I do. So, get dressed, doll, you're coming with us." Frances smiled.

By now both Africa and Abigail were buried in their phones answering text messages, emails, and scrolling through social media. Smiling, Noel said, "You guys go ahead, I, um, think I'm going to pass."

"What? No way, why do you want to stay cooped up in this room?" Abigail asked.

"I went to bed pretty late you guys and I think I want to just rest today," Noel lied. She was fully aware, that she wanted to be there in case Nathan called.

"Are you sure?" Africa confirmed.

"Yea, cuz, I'm sure. Can you come by tomorrow or later on to check on me?" she asked Africa.

"Yea, of course. How is Auntie Jenn, by the way?" Africa asked.

"She is very well. Didn't want to let me leave, but here I am, I managed to get away somehow," she said nervously.

"Yea, and it seems you're doing pretty well for yourself, keep up the good work. I am very proud of you and you look absolutely breathtaking as always," said Africa. Noel smiled, she had not realized how much she missed her cousin, but at that moment, she knew she needed her.

"Please just come later," she begged. Africa felt it had been a cry for help, and after the laughter faded and Abigail and Frances concluded their selfies, she gathered the ladies and they took their leave.

That day, Noel remained stationed in her quarters, ordering room service and adjusting the pipe levels during her shower so they were low enough she would hear the phone ring, but nothing. That day she started her diary,

May 26, 2016

Dear Noel...

CHAPTER EIGHT

Noel was timid, but she didn't allow her fear to get the best of her. She knew she had to speak to the only person who could understand her. The faint knock initially went unheard as Frances had her headphones in playing the latest from musician Trey Songz while unpacking her suitcase. Then the knock came again, louder this time. Demanding. Removing one of her earphones, Frances sauntered over to the door where she cracked it open slightly to see who had decided to disturb her; seeing Noel, she quickly opened the door with her lips pursed.

"What is it?" she said, removing the other earphone. Frances had come to see Noel as the little sister she never had, so no matter their differences she was always going to be there for her, even if it meant her needing some space to clear her mind.

Noel stuttered, for she and Frances had not quarreled often in the past two years of knowing one another, and so, she fidgeted.

"I want to tell you the truth," said Noel.

"Oh, about you sleeping with a married man? I think the lady downstairs beat you to it. Close the door behind you." Frances said as she walked in towards her bed where she had her clothes laid out to be placed away.

"No, not that." A timid Noel walked into the room, shutting the door behind her. "You have to promise me that after I say this you and I will still be the sisters we are. I can't lose you, Frances," Noel cried.

Frances shot her a questionable look, "If you have to ask me that, then that means whatever you're going to say to me will make me look at you differently and so, I can't promise that, Noel." Frances said as Noel continued to sob.

Sniffling, she remained by the door with her hands together and her head held down in shame, "There was never a Seattle bae, Seattle bae's just always been Nathan," she whimpered.

Frances placed her hands over her mouth, her eyes widened.

"Oh, my God, that makes so much more sense!" she shouted. Just then, Noels' phone rang, startling them both. It was her mother. Hesitant at first to answer, she decided to take the call-in hopes that Frances would have processed and calmed by the time she returned. Answering the phone, she said, "Hello."

"Noel-Lee Kwon the whore! That doesn't seem to have a nice ring to it! How could you sleep with a married man? How on earth could you travel miles away from home only to embarrass us like this?" she screamed.

Noel was speechless, but knew she needed to respond, and fast. "Mommy, no, mom, no, whatever you heard is not true. I promise."

"Noel! You cannot possibly be sleeping with a married man! There is no way! We did not raise you to wreck homes! Please, you are young and beautiful. Married men do not want anything with you but to use you and waste your time because they themselves are unhappy and filled with lust and regret. Do not involve yourself. Noel? Noel? Can you hear me?"

Noel was listening, but she was too busy sobbing to provide a response, but for the sake of not appearing rude, she mustered up the courage to say, "Yes, I am here." She spoke through her tears as Frances watched in horror. Frances ceased her bidding as she decided to cradle Noel. She did not know the words that were being told to her, but she had never seen Noel this sad and it pained her to watch. Once the call concluded, Noel grabbed Frances, squeezing her as tight as she could muster before letting out a loud scream as she continued to sob. Finally, she dried her eyes and began making her way down the hall to confront the woman she knew was responsible, Frances trailing behind her...

Flashback
It had been three days, eleven hours and twenty-one minutes since Noel had last seen or heard from Nathan. She stayed in her suite, writing in her diary and listing all the wonderful things she hoped to do whilst in New York. She planned to get a job, but one of those fancy office jobs in a high-rise building making at least six figures, and she wanted to live in a penthouse where she did not have to worry over bad weather and maintenance. She would soon then send for her brothers and help them get jobs where they, too, could earn a substantial living. Oh yes, Noel had big plans as her eyes darted back and forth between the notebook and the telephone.

As she completed her fourth entry, the phone dinged. Her heart skipped a beat as she thought it had finally been Nathan, but once she scurried over to answer it, the phone stopped ringing. Noel decided to answer anyway, figured it may have been a minor glitch, but that was not the case for all she heard was the dial tone on the opposite end. That evening, Noel flipped through the television channels searching for something good to watch. Again, the phone rang. By now she had not left its side and picked up on the first ring.

She cleared her throat. "Hello," she said.

"Hey there!" The voice on the other end did not sound too familiar. But she decided to play along anyway.

"Hey, how are you?" she said.

"Good, good, was just calling to see if you'd mind if I came on up. I just got back from work and Jade and I just finished dinner," the stranger said. Immediately, Noel realized who she was speaking to. It was Kenneth. Noel grew anxious; she hadn't showered in nearly forty-eight hours and was in no condition to have any visitors, but considering that Kenneth had been nothing but kind to her she decided to agree.

"Sure, can you give me about thirty minutes?" she asked. As Noel prepared for her first visitor in three days, she dreaded the thought of Nathan showing up. And she decided against going a date with Abram a few nights before out of fear that she would miss Nathan once he called. Thirty minutes came and went and Noel was nowhere closer to looking rejuvenated. She had taken a quick shower, thrown her hair into a high-top messy bun, and put on her robe and carried the ice bucket to the vendor so she could get ice and water for her tea. Upon her return, Kenneth was waiting outside preparing his fist to knock on the door. Noel slid towards him, using her free hand she leaned in to give him a hug.

"Hey there, beautiful little lady," He said as he greeted her with a warm smile. Noel returned the gesture. Smiling with ease upon realizing some company was exactly what she needed. Entering her suite, a malodorous scent attacked them. Noel didn't realize how putrid her room smelled because she had been sitting in it for days wallowing in her own self-pity. Embarrassed, she quickly opened the windows and turned up the air conditioning, apologizing profusely, but Kenneth had not noticed a thing.

As he unbuttoned his blazer, removing it and laying it nicely across the crème sectional closest the window, he realized just how beautiful Noel truly was. He stared at her as she continued to apologize for the mess and the stench, straitening up the linen and picking her clothes up from the floor.

"So," she said as she took a seat in the president's chair in front of the desk. "How have things been going?" She sighed multiple times, and Kenneth grew uncomfortable as he began to wonder if he were boring her.

"Hey, is everything alright with you, you seem a little out of it?" he questioned, leaning forward to get a better look into her eyes.

"Yea, I'm completely fine. Just waiting for the ice to melt so I can make some tea. I think I'm just feeling a little lightheaded is all," she said. "Nothing to worry about." She chuckled nervously. Noel could not put her finger on it, but shortly after they began to converse, she came to the realization that Kenneth was no longer the boy she had known in high school, he was a man, a handsome man whom she was beginning to grow shy around.

Kenneth continued speaking as Noel tuned him out, she watched the sweat build up around his groomed goatee and the muscles on his chest move each time he laughed or smiled. The shirt he wore quite fitted—a forest green to complement his complexion. Noel was beginning to find herself attracted to a man she once referred to as her brother.

There was no way.

As he continued to speak, and she pretended to listen, Kenneth leaned back into the sofa, placing his right leg across his thigh, his auburn dress shoes pointing horizontally. Noel now kept her head down as she decided to stop basking over his looks and finally give him her undivided attention.

"So, you were saying, you like the firm?" Noel confirmed as he concluded his last sentence.

"No, no, I love the firm. Hey, so, are you thinking about working at all? We need a receptionist. I don't know if you'd be interested." Kenneth had this invested look on his face; meanwhile, Noel was lusting after a man she had known for years, who then, as a simple boy, she easily ignored. But now he was breathtakingly handsome, making it difficult to overlook him.

"I think that would be great," she said, her tone dismal.

"Wow, I thought you'd be more excited. It is a real job that pays real money—yay!" he shouted, raising his hands in the air. But Noel could not remain focused, she continued to notice the print on his pants. Then, without warning, he began making his way towards her.

"Aw, Noel, you seem so out of it. I think someone can use a hug." He spoke in a child-like manner, extending his arms as he leaned forward to wrap his arms around her torso. Noel tilted back to give him a kiss on the lips. Much to her surprise, Kenneth did not reciprocate. Quickly, he pulled away, stepping back to the couch, his brows knitted and his eyes widened in shock.

His cowardly reaction after the kiss became concerning as he questioned whether or not he should have reacted differently or defended himself.

"Noel, Jesus, you know I have a girlfriend. What—what were you thinking? Why'd you do that?" he questioned.

"I have no idea. I—I wasn't thinking. I've been dealing with a lot these past few days and I just, um, thought that's what you wanted," she said. As the words left her mouth, she knew she was doomed.

Kenneth scoffed. "You thought I wanted you to throw your morals out of the window to kiss me, despite knowing that I had a girlfriend? I have never thought that low of you—ever," he said, unsure of how to proceed.

"Please, look, I am really sorry. I wasn't thinking," she begged. Noel felt weak, like her mind was playing tricks on her, because despite the commotion going on in front of her, she couldn't help but take glimpses of the phone. Three days, no breakfast, no Nathan, no calls. She was devastated.

"Look, I'm going to go, so Monday morning just meet me at my loft. Here's the address. My driver will take us to my work." Kenneth took a piece of paper from the nightstand, scribbling his address and work phone as he spoke. Blazer in hand, he proceeded to take his leave.

That night, Noel wrote in her diary, where she began to question her sanity. Why was she allowing the absence of a man to bring her such grief? One hour later, Noel decided to go to bed. Turning off the lamp and the television—the room pitch black. Outside, she could hear the footsteps and laughter of the guests in the hallway.

As Noel drifted to sleep, a faint knock was heard coming from the door. She opened her eyes gently, listening for it again—nothing. Going back to sleep, there it went, this time a little louder. She switched on the lamp by the nightstand, checking the time on the clock. It read 4:14 a.m. Noel stood, wrapping herself in her sheets, she scurried over to the door where she looked through the peephole but saw no one.

Noel was growing frustrated now. She hated being awakened in the middle of the night, just as she turned to walk away a loud thud startled her. She ran back to the door and unclicked the locks and in came Nathan, rushing in wearing an Adidas track-suit, a hat, and a pair of Nike sneakers, laughing hysterically.

Noel watched him. She did not know whether to be angry or relieved.

She continued standing by the door, her arms folded, her soft-pitched voice asked, "What the hell? What are you doing here?" Inside she was leaping for joy, outside she was ready to behave aggressively out of bravado. Nathan ignored her as he reached into the refrigerator, kicking off his sneakers, removing his pants, socks, and zippered hoodie to expose his glistening abdominals.

"I said, what are you doing here?" she attempted to shout as she made her way to the foot of the bed, her arms still folded. Nathan was now lying down with one hand bent under his head, the other hidden under the sheet as he watched her.

"You're so beautiful." He smiled.

Noel knew he was mocking her. She reached over to grab the bucket of ice that was now filled with water thrusting it upon him. The splash of water created what looked like a tsunami. Water drenched the sheets, carpets, nightstands and some parts of the sectional. Nathan immediately stood; his boxers soaked.

"Noel, what the fuck?" he shouted.

Noel was not moved. She was angry, and she wanted answers. "I am the wrong woman for this bull crap. Do you hear me?" she said.

Nathan continuing to wipe his face with his hands. Surprisingly, he was turned on. The pair continued to stand, Noel had not moved an inch, she was ready to confront him, for she knew if she allowed this behavior to continue, that is exactly what would happen.

"Noel, Goddamn it, you know I have a wi—"

Noel interrupted, "Don't give me that excuse. I didn't ask you to come into my life and disrupt it, you took it upon yourself to do that. Now, if we're going to be in a serious relation—"

"Wait, whoa, relationship? Is that what you were going to say?" he asked as he dried his face with the linens. Noel was now shocked. She was quickly learning her place. "I thought this was just a casual situation, nothing too crazy. I wasn't thinking about a relationship. I mean, Jesus, I have a whole wife and two kids, I can't just leave them and be in a relationship," he explained.

Noel could not believe her ears. "Where is my phone?" she questioned.

"My son needed a phone, and so I thought it was best he had it," Nathan replied. "Any more questions?"

"Just one," Noel said as she continued to stand with her arms folded. "Can you leave?"

She was failing at keeping her composure. She was hurt, devastated, the tears were coming and she couldn't stand the idea of Nathan seeing her cry. Foolish, thinking she had not known this man long enough to have felt such strong feelings.

Scratching his head in confusion, Nathan said, "We both need to leave; the place is soaking wet. There's no way we can stay here. Grab your things," he instructed.

Noel did not oblige. "No, I want you to leave."

"Noel, you're being very sensitive right now. Please stop with the theatrics. I will get us a new damn room to sleep in." Nathan was growing agitated as he stepped past Noel, grabbing his sweater and pants—also damp—and sliding them over his legs and torso, rolling his eyes and sucking his teeth as he made his way out the door,

"Have your things packed by the time I get back so the transition can be easy, please," he begged.

Unbeknownst to her, Nathan had now developed a great deal of respect for Noel. He wanted to do right by her.

Noel could not face him. As the door slammed, she raced over to the nightstand where she searched frantically for the paper Kenneth left her, dressing quickly. She grabbed the paper, shoving it into the back pocket of her jeans. Noel was rummaging around, throwing her things into a duffle bag and the shopping bags she had kept. She decided to leave behind the dress Nathan had bought her. Now in her jeans, a distressed crop top and the Keds she'd purchased, Noel was packed. As she sneaked out of the suite, she overheard Nathan and the concierge walking towards her.

Noel began to panic, a loose thread from her shirt now caught in the door, she continued to rummage with the bags and her duffle as she struggled to break free, their voices drawing nearer. Just then, she ripped her shirt free, leaving a small piece of it in the door as she ran down the hall into the vending room to hide. Noel knew he had arrived and entered the room when she heard him racing up and down the halls screaming her name.

"Noel! Noel!" he shouted. The concierge politely asked him to quiet down as the other guests were sleeping.

"Sir please, you cannot scream in the hallway."

Noel continued to sit tight between the Coca-Cola machine and the snack machine cached in the corner. She could feel his presence near the vending room, but he never entered. Noel held her breath for as long as she could, then let out a deep sigh, listening on as she heard Nathan banging on another door. Noel stood, peeking her head through the vending room door. Nathan was seen standing in front of the door adjacent hers. He knocked again, this time louder as the concierge continued watching him. Housekeeping, with a large cart was preparing to enter Noel's suite in an effort to clean it. Noel squinted her eyes as she waited for the door Nathan had been banging on to open. A few moments later, a woman appeared.

The woman stood on the threshold tying a loose knot on the front of her silk fuchsia robe. Noel could not believe her eyes, unsure of why Jade would betray Kenneth, and so she trusted her ears instead as the woman now said, "What on earth do you want? It's five in the damn morning."

Nathan leaned in to kiss her on the cheek, "Are you still mad at me?" he asked in a loving way. The woman then asked.

"What happened over there? Did your prized possession bring you some trouble? And why the hell are you wet?" she inquired playfully.

Nathan, now smiling, began to kiss the woman passionately on her lips. The housekeeper and concierge incognizant to their affairs.

"Jade, you know I will always love you," Nathan said in between kisses.

"Oh, I know," she said, wrapping her arms around him and pulling him inside. Noel felt crushed, not only for herself but for Kenneth as well.

That night, Noel took a taxi to 89758 Lafayette Avenue, the meatpacking district where she watched the sun begin to rise as the driver dropped her off in the center of the bricked road.

She wandered aimlessly, looking for a loft, any loft. At first, she thought she had read the address incorrectly considering it was so heavily smudged due to the water, but then she looked up and noticed a tall building with a fire escape annexed. She stepped frantically inside, closing the elevator door to the lift and making her way to the third floor.

As Noel reached the third floor, she lifted the gates and grabbed her bags. She stood in front of the steel door with the numbers eighty-five written across it. Underneath were the words *Anderson Residence* engraved in script.

She knocked. Nothing. She knocked again, nothing. Noel then knocked once more, until an elderly lady from the fourth floor hung over the staircase railing, she bellowed,

"What on earth are you doing here, woman?"

Noel stuttered, "I-I am trying to reach my brother!" she attempted to shout, embarrassed by her timing. Just then, the doors began to unlock and Noel saw before her a faultless shadow. Kenneth stood wearing nothing but a pair of Versace Paisley silk pajama pants. Noel clutched her duffle bags, her jaw dropped as she remained stationed.

Kenneth could not help but feel flattered as he pulled her inside, watching as she tripped over herself, picking up her bags and wishing the elderly Mrs. Hammerstone a good night.

Shutting the door behind them, Noel continued to clutch her duffle bag as she took a few steps into his lavish, high-ceilinged loft. She couldn't believe the home he was living in. It was exquisite. The sixteen-foot ceilings, exposed brick walls, cast iron columns, open kitchen equipped with nothing but stainless-steel appliances, hardwood floors, central air, and a laundry room. Kenneth had two brown leather ottomans that decorated the downstairs living room in the open space, a beige barrel chair, and a sectional with red throw pillows and modernized recessed ceiling lights.

Kenneth cleared his throat. "So, can you turn to look at me?" he asked.

Noel slowly turned to face him. "Sure," she said, duffle and bags in hand.

Kenneth took a long look at her face and could tell she had been crying. "Noey, what's the matter?" he asked, concerned as he placed her cheeks between the palms of his hands. Kenneth looked down at her and, noticing her beauty, he kissed her. The kiss was passionate and far better than any kiss she had ever received from a man.

Noel dropped her bags as she pulled Kenneth closer to her. Suddenly, Kenneth stopped. Pulling himself back, he wiped his lips as he turned to make his way into the kitchen.

"I'm so sorry, Noel." His hands were trembling.

Tumbling over her belongings, Noel chased him. She was like a dog to a bone; she wanted every inch of him. She wanted to touch him—caress him even. Noel then grabbed him, kissing again, aggressively. Kenneth, again pulled himself away,

"I can't do this, alright? Jesus! Why did you even come here?" he asked, slamming his fist against the marble countertop. Noel was confused,

"What, what did I do?" she asked. Touching his hand, she knew he was hurting as his fist turned a dark red. Noel slowly raised his hand and began to kiss his knuckles. Kenneth was resisting the urge now to push her away as he pulled away once more,

"What the fuck is wrong with you? I said we have to stop," he scolded.

Noel was frustrated now.

"Why?" she said, walking up to him. Removing her ponytail, she let her hair flow freely. Aggressively, she pulled him towards her, shoving her hand down his pajamas as she stroked his penis, staring him in the eyes. His heart beat fast, as did hers. She knew what she wanted and she wasn't going to stop until it was hers. Kissing him passionately on the neck—standing on her tiptoes now. Kenneth was growing impatient, but he reciprocated her act as he lifted her shirt and began to palm her breasts.

Attempting to pull himself free once again, Noel refused to let him go anywhere. She whispered,

"Let her go! She's sleeping with a man named Nathan."

Kenneth pushed her away, staring long and hard into her eyes. Fueled by anger, he kissed her hard, grabbing her buttocks and lifting her atop the counter as he pushed away its contents, everything hitting the floor from the cookie jar to the kitchen utensils, but none of that mattered. That night, Kenneth and Noel made love, their heavy breathing, hair pulling, teeth clenching escapade lead them to every inch of the loft now christened by their growing infatuation.

CHAPTER NINE

It was a new morning and all the ladies slept in. Noel could not bring herself to sleep alone, and so she and Frances shared a bed, sleeping toe to head, no bags unpacked as she found herself feeling less like completing the trip as the hours pressed on. Alicia was up early, as she was awakened by the sound of a beating door. Closest the entrance, she tiptoed out of bed, screeching as she forgot her bedroom slippers and felt the cold chill shoot up from her feet.

That morning, she'd heard from her husband who begged her profusely to simply come home for he had come to learn the reason for her abrupt leave of absence. But she had decided against that. Although she was not amused with any of the females, she knew had she simply gone home there would have been no resolution, and that was simply not something she could live with.

As she opened the front door, she noticed a gentleman standing outside wearing a large red Canada Goose down jacket, a hat, a scarf, mittens, and black pants. He was carrying a large suitcase,

"Good morning, ma'am," he slowly introduced himself, distracted by her beauty.

Alicia was not going to allow him to stand in the cold any longer. "Wow, where are my manners, can I invite you in? It's freezing," she said. Alicia wore a silk nightgown and was in no mood to catch a cold as the wind began to pick up.

"Sure, thank you," he said, making his way inside, dragging his suitcase behind him. At the door, he began to remove layers of clothing, exposing what appeared to be a black chef's coat.

As he stood by the door holding his garments, Alicia asked, "May I take those for you? We have a closet just around the corner there."

"Yes, thank you," he said enthralled by her endearing hospitality, handing her his garments. As Alicia paced to the rear for a place to hang his belongings, she listened as he spoke.

"My name is Angelo. I was hired by the owner of the house to cook for you ladies today and tomorrow. I was wondering— is it just you? Or are the other ladies still asleep?" He was nervous, but Angelo had nothing to fear, Alicia knew once the ladies took a look at him they would be flipping a coin to see who would get dibs.

"No, no, they're all upstairs. I slept down here, that's how I was able to hear you. I believe I just heard some pipes turning on so they must be getting ready to come on down. My name is Alicia, by the way," she said, extending her hand.

"Pleasure to meet you," he said. "So, if you don't mind, I'll just head over to the kitchen and get started."

Angelo looked to be in his late forties, grey and black hair with a dark fade and a full beard. He didn't look like he made it to the gym often, but was surely someone great to look at.

"Not a problem at all, I am going to head to the back and take a shower," she said, exiting the kitchen. Angelo washed his hands and decided it was time to get to work. Pinning his name-tag to his coat, he removed ingredients from the refrigerator he had placed there a few days prior and began to prep.

Thirty minutes later the island was growing populated with bacon, hash brown, sausages, ham and eggs, pancakes, freshly cut strawberries with grapes and blueberries in a basket. Angelo had also made omelets, three to be exact. Learning earlier on of the ladies preferences, he prepared their meals accordingly.

Noel had not showered or gotten out of bed. Instead, she looked on as Frances stepped out of the tub, wrapping herself in a clean towel and applying her facial products and lotion.

"Are you going to just lay there staring at me, or are you going to get out of bed sometime soon?" Frances inquired.

Lying on her back now, watching the ceiling, Noel said, "Why should I? Everyone hates me, including you. So, this seems like the most fitting place for me to be right now."

"You know I hate it when you start to feel sorry for yourself. I think you should stop being so selfish and see the situation for what it really is. I can't continue to speak on this topic, it's like beating a dead horse. But, we have to find a way to get past this. I know we can," Frances assured her, but Noel was still not feeling optimistic.

"Franny, my cousin hates me and my mom thinks I'm a freaking home-wrecker. All I could think about last night was how disappointed she must feel. I mean, what if a woman had done to her and my dad what I was doing to Nathan and Alicia." Noel now sat upright,

"And Corey—" Frances replied.

"Yes, and Corey," Noel said with her head down. "He's been so damn good to me and I just—I just had to get myself involved with this crap!" she said, tears now falling from her eyes.

Frances, now dressed in a pair of jeans and an American Eagle button down shirt, went over to console her.

"Listen, I can't say that he will forgive you, but you have to just be strong enough to tell him exactly how you feel and why you did the things you did. He may not understand right away, but with time he may be in a more forgiving mood," she said, though in her heart of hearts she knew she would never take back a cheater. Truly, she would be disappointed in Corey if he decided to forgive Noel given that her actions were intentional, but she could not dare bring herself to say that.

Noel continued to lie in bed. Frances opened the bedroom door and watched as both Africa and Abigail were making their way downstairs without so much as a word.

"Hey! You two weren't going to say anything? I mean, come on, it's a whole new damn day," she cried.

Angelo overhearing the women from the kitchen.

"Look, I just want to have fun. When we leave, it'll all be a different story," Abigail said.

"No, no one is going to fake for the sake of it. Let me know how you both really feel so we can make some decisions as to who needs to simply leave and who wants to stay," Frances now interrupted.

"Please, can you guys just stop? I will leave if I need to, I mean really—" Noel was now gathering her things as she climbed out of bed.

"What? No, you're not leaving!" shouted Frances. "Ladies, I love you all, but we can't continue like this, so, what's it going to be?" she said, facing Africa and Abigail. Frances secretly wanted everyone to simply put the past behind them and move on like adults so they could enjoy their trip like the amazing best friends they all are, but she was beginning to realize that with her group of friends a wish like that might be impossible.

As the morning pressed on, Angelo was growing worried. He was now alone with a seven-course breakfast waiting on someone, anyone, to join him. Listening on as the women grew louder; he became uncomfortable but could not allow that to deter him from doing his job. He now stood with his arms behind his back, patiently waiting. He had spices all meticulously placed by the meals, whipped cream, biscuits, and two containers filled with orange juice. By now, Alicia was completely dressed and decided to Facetime with her children if her cellular phone service would permit. It did.

Once the phone lines opened up, Nathan appeared holding their youngest. Despite the bad signal, Alicia was able to get a glimpse of her daughter.

"Hi my pumpkin!" she said, smiling.

"Hello Mommy!" her daughter said, her voice angelic. Nathan continued to hold the phone.

"Lauren," he said, turning his face to see her.

"Yes, Daddy?" she said,

"Please go play, Daddy and Mommy need to have a grown-up conversation."

"Okay Daddy, I love you Mommy," Lauren said, turning out of view. The phone was now lagging,

"What is it, Nathan?" Alicia sounded anything but pleasant.

"I know what you're trying to do. I just want you to come home so we can talk about this and figure out what's next for us," he pleaded.

"I know what's next for us. I am going to get this woman to leave us alone for good and we are going to counseling and we are going to fix our marriage. Now I just need some time to clear my head," Alicia said. She hated herself for saying this but feared more than anything the thought of being alone, and she and Nathan had come so far and were excellent parents.

"No, Alicia, you're not listening to me. We have to have a serious talk. There will be no counseling," Nathan said. Just then, Alicia decided it was time for her to go, she took a long breath before responding,

"Listen, kiss Lauren for me, enjoy these next few days before I return home and we figure things out. Goodbye." She said before turning the phone down. Alicia made a promise to herself; she would never end up alone, especially raising a child.

Standing now, she brushed her curly hair before braiding the ends, creating a loose braid, which she then used a hair bow to keep in place.

Alicia made her way to the kitchen; the view was absolutely stunning. Angelo now stood by the refrigerator, his hands behind his back. Militant.

"Good morning once again, ma'am. Please help yourself," he said, and Alicia did just that.

The ladies could be heard bickering upstairs until Abigail began making her way down, motioning with her hands to be left alone. Looking over into the kitchen, she noticed Angelo and stopped in her tracks. Both Africa and Frances followed suit, all standing atop the staircase, the ladies admired the view.

"Hello," she said. Alicia had now taken a seat on one of the island stools as she filled her plate with fruits, pancakes, sausages, and grits. Looking up, Angelo replied,

"Yes, good morning, ladies. My name is Angelo," he said, removing one of his hands from behind him, gently placing it on his chest.

Her eyes wide, her right eyebrow raised, Abigail responded, "No D?" She was now tiptoeing down the stairs,

Alicia quickly thought; *we have a winner* as she bit into her sausage link.

Angelo blushed, "No D." Abigail had now come face to face with him impressed that he was able to comprehend her sexual innuendo.

Extending her hand, blushing, she said, "My name is Abigail, but my friends call me Abby." She smiled. Both Africa and Frances could not help but laugh as they too began making their way down to the kitchen. Noel decided to enter a few minutes later once everyone had filled their plates and made their acquaintances and were beginning to devour their first meal of the day.

Noel took a bite of the strawberries and pancakes from Frances's plate after she too made her acquaintance with Angelo. The ladies thanked him profusely for all the hard work he had done.

"This taste brings back memories," said Noel as she smiled.

Overhearing, Angelo responded as he took a seat and began to converse with the women, mainly Abigail, who asked him a different question between each bit.

"Ahh, yes, from the Hilton. Oh man, those were the best pancakes I had ever eaten!" said Frances.

Noel chuckled. "Yup, the very same." It pained her to speak about that, but she did not want the moment to be awkward.

"I couldn't help but overhear, you said the Hilton, the one downtown right?" asked Angelo.

"Yes, do you know of it?" asked Noel as she continued to stand and eat from Frances's plate. With every piece she ate, Frances replenished her dish.

"Of course, I am the head chef for the Hilton on Americas. Have been for the past five years." He smiled.

Abigail gasped, "Oh my, you're a head chef?" She quickly asked. Angelo turning to face her,

"Yep. Those pancakes are my signature. I have a secret ingredient I add to the batter." He chuckled. "If you've had those, you must have stayed with us before as a special guest or some sort. I don't usually make that unless it's requested, and I don't think we've met," he continued.

Noel grew silent. "Right. I was there a few years ago." Noel said slowly. She was dying inside.

"Oh, okay." He looked disappointed, as though he had hoped he knew who she was. Angelo was big on finding new clients and maintaining relationships.

"Well, I mean, now you know Angelo's Signature Pancakes, just ask for it by name if and when you do ever come by again and I'll be sure to whip you up a batch," he confirmed.

Noel smiled. "Will do."

Abigail continued her interrogation. "So, like, who typically orders your signature?" Abigail was secretly hoping she would learn of the mystery man Frances was sleeping with.

Angelo took a deep breath, "Wow, I mean, I have so many clients. Um, there's Nathan, Ricardo, Marian, Jeannette, some tourists who after networking with some of my previous clients ended up learning about the signature—"

"Wait, did you say Nathan?" Alicia interrupted.

Innocently Angelo responded, "Yes, he is actually one of my best clients."

"How did you meet him?" she inquired. The ladies took long sighs as they grew annoyed. Noel's face flushed.

Angelo sensed everyone's frustration. "Through another one of my clients, actually. But he rarely has me cooking for him; it's mainly for the people he brings by. He'd let me know someone's checked in and ask me to take care of them. Typically, though, by the time their stay is over he'd almost always introduce me and that is usually that. Nathan is a stand-up guy, you know," Angelo said, grinning nervously.

Alicia now stopped eating. "Is his name Nathan Ramirez by chance?" She asked. Angelo quickly turned,

"Yes, that's him. Do you know him? Tall kind of, stocky build and wears a suit almost always?" Angelo said, politely. The ladies remained quiet as they realized Alicia began turning red—embarrassed.

"Latino? Yes, I know him. He's my husband, has been for the past seven years," she confirmed with a disappointed look on her face as she removed the napkin from her lap slamming it onto the kitchen cutlery.

Angelo, turning to face her, said, "Oh." Shortly after, followed up with another, "Oh!" This time he was feeling empathetic as he realized just who Nathan truly was.

"If you will all please excuse me," Alicia said, standing.

"Noel, so, I guess you were a special guest." She scoffed. "What are the odds, huh? You didn't get to meet the great chef once your stay was over. I wonder why that is," she said as she walked away. The room remained quiet.

"I'm sorry," said Angelo.

"You have nothing to apologize for. That guy is a pig," said Africa.

Flashback

Noel awakened to the sweet smell of fried eggs and bacon. She turned to find she was in bed alone. The king-sized mattress with all white bedding made her feel like a queen. Kenneth's bedroom was affluent in nature and especially large. It held an exercise bike, a sofa, two nightstands, and a large walk-in closet just in front of the winding stairs.

Noel took a shirt of his she found at the foot of the bed and began making her way down the iron-plated stairs. The loft was very warm, her hair messy from the activities performed the night before. As she made her way into the kitchen, she noticed Kenneth standing by the stove whipping up pancake batter and sizzling bacon.

"Good morning," he said, his back still turned. Noel could not help but notice how well sculpted he was, his back had muscles in all the right places. Kenneth was gorgeous.

"Good morning," she said softly. Kenneth then turned to face her as he placed cutlery before her; plate, knife, forks and a spoon along with a cup of coffee.

"You like cream or sugar? I have brown if that's okay," he continued.

Noel was shy, she watched as he maneuvered from one end to the next, grabbing her coffee, placing her sugar gracefully inside. Noel was enamored. He was so gentle, except where he needed to be.

Just as he began turning the stove down and handing Noel about five slices of bacon, he placed his hands on the counter behind him turning to face her,

"We should talk," he said. His pajama pants falling just below his V-shaped cut by his lower abdominal region; Noel, now taking small bites of her bacon, nodded her head in amazement.

"So, um, last night probably shouldn't have happened," he continued. Noel almost choked. She took a quick sip of her coffee.

"Are you alright?" he asked; he had not moved an inch. Noel's eyes widened.

"What do you mean, exactly? I thought we both had a good time," she inquired with a concerned look on her face.

"We did, but I have a girlfriend and you know that. I mean, yes, last night took two of us to make it happen, but I'm not a cheater, Noel. I feel like I at least owe it to myself and to Jade to get an explanation or something," he said.

Noel was confused, "So, are you saying, we're like, not going to be a thing?" she asked.

"If what you said is indeed true, to be honest, I won't be looking to get into anything serious with anyone for a while," he confirmed. Noel felt upset. She had no idea how to respond and no intention of finishing her food. Her appetite gone.

"I mean, you aren't surprised, right? I mean, we don't really know one another anymore and last night was a spur of the moment thing," he continued, but with each word he was hurting her far more than she could stand.

"No, please stop," Noel said as she ran upstairs to gather her things, tears filling her eyes. Kenneth quickly followed behind her.

"Hey, you don't have to leave! I can stay on the couch downstairs. Noel, Jesus, will you stop packing and listen to me?" he screamed.

"No! No, I won't. You say you aren't a cheater and, well, you cheated. But you cheated on a terrible woman who doesn't deserve you. She doesn't deserve this luxury, the life you're trying to provide for her. Maybe I'm not exotic enough, you know," she sobbed. Kenneth grabbed her by the face,

"Noel, you are astonishingly beautiful and I promise I never meant to hurt you. I just want to close one door before I open another one. I believe that's fair." He kissed her gently on the lips.

"Kenneth, I've known you almost my whole life. I just thought..." Noel could not bring herself to say the words, and so she begged him to let her go and he did. As she made her way down to the ground floor in the lift elevator she sobbed placing her hands atop her head in confusion.

Where does she go from here?

The morning sun was brutal. She walked for what felt like hours until she reached the main road calling for a taxi. Once one arrived, she began stuffing her things in the back seat, "Can we go to *Crystals*, please?" she asked.

Outside of the boutique, she noticed a blonde woman opening its doors. Stepping out to face her, struggling to carry her plethora of bags, she asked,

"Hi, does Frances come into work today?"

The blonde woman continued her bidding, taking a deep sigh she said, "Yes, but later on. How can I help you?"

"Well, you see, I'm her best friend and I need her address because as you can see, I just got kicked out of somewhere and I need to speak to her." Noel knew her request was outlandish, but surprisingly the blonde woman did not turn her away,

"Tell you what, why don't you stay here until she gets comes in? She usually arrives around two, but please do something about those God-awful clothes," she sniped.

Noel was thrilled, "Yes, of course, and thank you." As the doors opened, Noel rushed inside, her arms burning from carrying around her duffle bag and shopping bags filled with the clothes she purchased.

"My name is Amber, by the way," the blonde woman said, extending her hand. Noel reciprocated,

"Noel. Very nice to meet you," she said, dropping bags, her shoes falling to the ground, exposed from their boxes—a clumsy Noel merely chuckling, looking up to face Amber who decided against assisting her.

Noel could not bring herself to not aid Amber throughout the day. She helped with the steaming, folding of merchandise, and even purchased new clothes to wear as she worked. Noel headed into the bathroom where she combed her hair, swished a pocket-sized Listerine around in her mouth, and applied a brush of foundation to her face. Amber was happy to have her. The customers came in and although Noel could not personally assist them, she found herself growing more comfortable by the minute. Amber was kind; she offered her breakfast and complimented her customer service skills and work ethic.

"For someone not on the payroll, you sure work hard," she advised as she cleaned the glass countertops with Windex.

"My father taught us the importance of working hard. Plus, he owns many businesses, so I think I got it from him," she replied.

"That sounds plausible," Amber said.

The ladies enjoyed their lunch, but now customers were piling in and Amber was finding herself to be a little flustered.

"Noel, do you mind monitoring the fitting rooms?" she asked as she tended to a customer with a big bill.

"Absolutely," Noel replied with glee. She was happy to finally be engaged in something that kept her mind occupied from both Kenneth and Nathan. By the time 2 p.m. came around, Noel watched as the door opened and closed, each time praying she would see Frances make her way inside.

"She's late," cried Amber. Just then, Frances made her appearance, looking rejuvenated. Her hair neatly cornrowed, her ends extending past her shoulders well into the depths of her back. She sported a black blouse with khaki dress pants and flip-flops with her handbag thrown over her shoulder; she was heavily accessorized as each piece spoke to her personality, the bohemian feather pendant necklace, the zodiac charm bracelet, and the classic black stacked bracelets.

Stepping inside, Frances immediately noticed Noel who had now been draped in garments from the boutique; a purple maxi dress which hugged her perfectly and a pair of white sandals.

Noel noticed that Frances was staring and decided to spin, her dress flowing freely from the ground.

"So, what do you think?" asked Noel, smiling. Much to her surprise, Frances did not have a reaction,

"Amber, can I speak to you in the back for a minute?" she asked.

Stepping past Noel, Frances and Amber made their way to the rear of the store once Amber concluded her transaction,

"Um, what is she doing here?" Frances asked.

Noel waited patiently in the front, minding the counters as more customers began making their way inside.

"What do you mean? She said she was your friend." Amber replied, "Also, please tell me you're going to comb out your hair."

Frances shot her a gruesome look. "Please don't speak on my hair," Frances snapped reaching into her handbag to grab her wide-toothed comb as she began to unwind her hair strands, resulting in a beautiful crimpled finish.

"Well, I rescind my last statement, your hair is beautiful and I wasn't trying to offend you..." Amber imploded into a nervous babble.

"Please, just let me know what is she doing here?" Frances repeated for she was far more interested in that piece of information.

"Well, when I came this morning to open the store, she saw me and initially she asked for your address, but I told her she can wait here for you instead," Amber replied. "Did I do something wrong? I mean, are you and her not friends?" she continued.

"I mean, I've only known her a few days and, I don't know, she seems cool, a bit unstable for me, but cool nonetheless. I just thought maybe you'd have called or texted me to let me know she was here," Frances replied as she oiled her ends and styled her hair.

"You are absolutely right, I am so sorry. Today was actually so busy and I honestly wasn't thinking," she cried.

"Hey, it's alright. I'll go and speak with her," Frances said.

Both Frances and Amber made their way out of the storage room and onto the main floor where Noel was gathering her things once more.

"Hey, where are you going?" Frances said.

"I'm leaving. I just didn't want to leave the floor empty, but now that you two are back from your little chat, I guess I'll be off," Noel snapped.

"Wait, seriously, you can't be upset," cried Frances.

"Of course, I am. You walk in and don't even say so much as hi or hello like I'm a complete stranger. You weren't solicitous at all," said Noel.

"Well excuse me for not hearing from you in over three days and then coming to work to find you working at my job, *Single White Female* ring a bell?" Frances joked. Amber chuckled.

"This isn't funny. I don't have a phone and I'm not some crazy psycho trying to take over your life or find myself infused in it, I just—I had nowhere else to go," she said, taking a deep breath as she fought back tears.

"That's understandable, and I am sorry for making you feel like I don't want you here. But, Noel, we have to get you a phone. Here in New York, popping up without notice on anyone is simply a no-no unless you're a lover trying to make things right again," Frances explained. "And we are not that."

Annoyed. "Look, I know we're not some lesbian couple. Can you please stop acting like I am some stranger stalking you?" she asked.

"Relax, what are you doing here anyway?" Frances said as she motioned for Noel to put her bags behind the counter, with Amber now on the register, both Frances and Noel made their way to the rear of the store.

Multitasking as she folded clothes and began her interrogation, Frances prompted, "Noel?"

"Well, Seattle bae and I didn't work out. Then I went to stay with a friend of mine and things took a turn for the worst, now here I am," she said.

"Okay, you've only been in New York for all of a week and so far Seattle bae was a fail and another friend bit the dust? Perhaps you're the issue," she teased.

"No, Seattle bae was trash and the other friend was a guy who is sleeping with trash and just doesn't know it yet," she confirmed.

"Wait, so these are both men? Are you still a virgin?" asked Frances.

Noel took a deep breath before answering, "Far from it at this point."

Frances let out a shrieking cry, elated by the news. She wanted to give Noel a long hard hug but decided against it, her friend did not look too receptive of the gesture. "So, was it Seattle bae or the other bae?" asked Frances now completely invested.

"Well, it was both," said Noel.

Just then Amber called, "Frances!"

Frances could not believe her ears, two men in one week, she knew Noel was not as innocent as she looked.

"This has been the longest, shortest week of my life," Noel complained. Frances was now making her way to the front of the store to assist Amber but took notice when the store was empty.

"Hey Amber, what's going on?" she asked politely.

"This lady wants to see you," she said. Frances quickly turned to find herself face to face with Jade, who had been standing with her arms folded, a baleful look on her face.

"Jade, what on earth do you want?" asked Frances mildly exasperated. Jade was glowing, her complexion refulgent as she stared relentlessly into her eyes.

"That whore you call a friend slept with my man, and I know you and I haven't spoken in months, nor are we on good terms, but please keep your friend away from my boyfriend! I may have left the hood, but the hood is still in me, Frances." Just like that, she began making her way out the door, "Oh, and another thing—you know what? Never mind. Just keep her away from Kenneth." And just like that, she disappeared, her long weave flowing freely behind her.

Amber and Frances exchanged a worrisome look as Frances beckoned,

"Noel," she shouted. "Storage room, now!"

Noel dropped the clothes she held and followed behind her like a lap dog, "What is it?"

"You slept with Jade's boyfriend?" she questioned. Immediately, without answering, Noel ran to the entrance of the store where she scurried out the door, searching frantically for the messenger.

The weather was cool and after only a short minute, Noel spotted Jade clacking her heels down to the block past the Starbucks and the deli.

"Hey!" Noel shouted. "Jade!" Pedestrians pretending not to notice were now intrigued.

"You little bitch!" Jade said, marching towards her. Frances, now in view, ran towards them.

"Wait!" She cried. But Jade was stomping fast and Noel had not moved a muscle, coming face to face they had now become the center of attention right on the corner of Lexington Avenue in the East Village.

Completely out of breath, Frances now stood in between them, huffing. "Ladies, please, let's talk about this inside," she pleaded.

"There's nothing to discuss. Noel, Kenneth does not want you, or else he wouldn't have told me about you. How dare you have sex with my boyfriend?" She screamed. Spectators continued to look on,

"Ladies, this is embarrassing, we need to get inside, now," Frances said.

"You have some nerve asking me about Kenneth. He may love you, but you don't love him, and what's even worse is that you're trying to confront me about something you, yourself, are doing—sleeping with a married man!" shouted Noel. Jade was speechless.

"How the hell do you know about that?" she inquired.

"Wait, who is married?" asked Frances.

"It doesn't matter; all that matters now is that you keep a close eye on Kenneth because I am coming for him," Noel warned.

"Is that right, just you try, bitch." Jade smiled as she took her leave.

Frances continued watching them, shocked. "Thank goodness I talk to one dick and he's poor," she joked.

Noel and Frances made their way back to the boutique. The spring was becoming quite festive; Frances wondered how her life had been before Noel, far more peaceful, she would gather. Noel had no idea the fuss she was causing, nor did she care.

As they strolled back to the boutique, Frances could not help but ask, "So, who is married?"

"No one, these guys are nothing but clowns in a circus," said Noel passively as she opened the boutique doors.

The next few hours went by quickly, and just as the ladies were beginning to lock up, a stretch limo appeared. The windows tinted, Frances, Amber, and Noel all looked on as Frances assisted Noel with her bags, offering a spot on her couch for the night.

The limo stopped, a tall man stepping out of the backseat with a bouquet of flowers and a Louis Vuitton bag in his right hand.

"Um, who does he belong to?" Amber asked playfully, as Nathan approached,

"Good evening, ladies," he said. Turning to face Noel who was now standing still. "I just wanted to say how sorry I am for everything. Will you forgive me?" he asked handing her roses. She quivered, and besides, she could not take them, her hands were full.

Nathan chuckled. "Looks like you may have some trouble holding onto these. I will help." He smiled as he removed the bags from her hand, instructing his driver to assist. Frances handed over her items, shrugging her shoulders, unsure of how else to proceed. Nathan smelled of Hugo Boss cologne and was wearing a three-piece all-black Tom Ford suit with diamond cufflinks.

Noel was mesmerized, she felt her point was made and although her mind was elsewhere, her feet were no doubt going to accompany Nathan. "What—what are you doing here?" she stuttered.

"I made a mistake; I want to start over and I am very sorry about the way I behaved. I know you want better from me, especially considering the short time we've known one another. I think I can definitely make an effort to be a better person towards you," he said, licking his lips after every word.

Noel forgave him, instantly. "Where are we going?" she asked.

Amber began taking her leave as she clicked the padlock closed. "Good night, ladies," she shouted from down the street.

"Well, how about dinner?" interrupted Frances.

Noel chuckled. "Sure, dinner," she reluctantly agreed. Nathan nodded his head in compliance, if that's what Noel wanted, then of course, that's what Noel would have.

"Is that a gift?" she asked, looking down at the Louis Vuitton bag Nathan was still carrying.

"Oh, yes, of course it is." Accepting the bag, Noel opened it. The contents were a small black box with the initials *LV* engraved. As she continued to remove the ribbons, she came to find a Tambour black faced 34mm pink alligator strapped watch. She almost fainted. It was exquisite. Noel leaped into his arms. She felt like she was living a fairy tale.

Gathering their things, Frances, Nathan, and Noel all piled into the backseat of the stretch limo and off to dinner they went.

CHAPTER TEN

As the cold air blew a draft into the cabin, Frances remained silent as she continued unpacking her clothes. She could hardly bring herself to face Noel, but she did.

"So Nathan, huh? Nathan is this woman's husband? I would have preferred to not have never met him, especially now that I'm meeting her. Ramirez, the name now sounds familiar. I have never seen him pick up his daughter, it was always some nanny. For three years, that girl's been a student at my school and not once did our paths cross. Had I known, Noel, if I knew it was that little girl's father you were screwing, I don't know, but things would be different. It shouldn't matter either way, but just when I find myself at a place where I can somewhat sympathize with you, something new comes along. So, this was it, Alicia knew I was your friend, and knew you were fucking her husband and lied her way onto the trip so she could meet you I guess." Frances scoffed. "What a bunch of bullshit," she said, rolling her eyes.

"I haven't slept with Nathan in over a year, ever since Corey and I—" Noel said.

"I'm going to stop you right there! What is it with you and the lies? This woman would not be here if she didn't have the slightest inclination that you are still sleeping with her husband, and poor Corey, why do this to him?" she yelled.

"Frances, you're not listening to me, this is bigger than just you, me, and this woman with low self-esteem. Why won't she just leave him, huh? You'll be shocked to learn this is not the first time she's had an *inclination* or some gut feeling about his infidelity," Noel pleaded.

"So, what are you saying exactly, Noel; out of all the women screwing her husband in New York, why plot to meet you?" Frances asked.

"I can't tell you yet," Noel said.

"Wait, what? So you know why she's here and you've been acting aloof this whole time?" Frances asked.

"No, just give me time, please," Noel asked. "I swear I will explain everything.

Flashback

After dinner, Nathan had Frances dropped off her at Brownstown in Harlem. Noel was surprised to see that she, too, lived so lavishly. Frances bid her farewell. Once alone, Nathan and Noel exchanged a seductive look. Noel could not help herself; she began kissing Nathan passionately before dividing her legs to climb on top of him. She wondered, was she simply missing Nathan and using Kenneth as a crutch? Or did she truly like Kenneth and felt crushed by his rejection? Despite her wondering if either were true, she focused her attention on her own satisfaction. Nathan made the perfect lover. Despite her many attempts to overpower him and perform a blow-job, he would turn her over to please her first, always teasing her body from soft, wet kisses along her neck to the long, hard kisses on her torso causing her body to quiver.

The limo driver continued at a pace he knew was adequate enough, as though he had done this far too many times. Noel moaned, afraid she would disturb him.

"Keith, turn on the radio!" Nathan shouted from the backseat. Keith obliged, and the loud, sensual sounds of the Isley Brothers came blaring through the speakers. Noel continued to moan as Nathan blessed her with his tongue. She kept wondering who was better. Kenneth or Nathan? Nathan was far more patient and Kenneth was rough, not anywhere near as attentive to her body and the sounds it made as Nathan was—a professional at lovemaking. Nathan and Noel made passionate love in the backseat of the stretch limo for what spanned well over two hours, the music continued to play and Keith continued to drive. Noel felt loved. She felt overjoyed, and with two back-to-back orgasms, what woman wouldn't?

Their lovemaking coming to an end, Nathan reclined, his back to Keith, staring into Noel's soft brown eyes. She asked, "What is it?" Smiling as she dressed.

"Nothing," he said. Noel blushed as the limo came to a halt. She looked around, confused as to why they had stopped and watched as Nathan pulled up his pants, stretching past her he opened the door and stepped outside. They had arrived at a building on Park Ave. Noel wondered where Keith had taken them for two hours because from the looks of it they had never left the city. But she was in no mood to question him. As the night fell upon them, Noel watched as Nathan removed her shopping bags and duffle bag from the back seat.

Meanwhile, on the opposite side of town, Frances was home, undressing, tossing bills and sending provocative text messages to her new beau, Maxwell. Frances worried that it had been a couple of days since the two began conversing and yet he had not asked her on a date. She wondered if perhaps she was expecting too much too soon, but then she realized maybe not and so she gave him a call. Sitting on the edge of her bed massaging her toes—after three rings he answered.

"Good night, beautiful." His husky voice sent chills down her spine as she no doubt found this appealing.

"Good night yourself. How was your day?" she asked, now lying in a supine position staring blankly at the ceiling.

"It was good; thinking of joining the Air Force so I went to see a recruiter today. I'd have to cut my dreads." He laughed, but Frances heard nothing funny. She was naturally possessive over people she found herself caring for, and he was one of those people.

"Air Force as in the military?" she confirmed.
Maxwell chuckled again. "Well, yes."

"When are you thinking of leaving," she said, her tone different. Max could tell she was not happy.

"Not anytime soon, I still have to take the exam. Please don't be sad," he said.

"I mean, I'm not too sad, I just wonder if you're even really into me. We speak every night and you still haven't asked me on a date," Frances said.

"Well, to be quite honest I am trying to save for a car so I haven't had the funds to really take a girl out. I mean, I understand if that's not what you're looking for right now, I know all women want to be catered to and things like that, but right now just isn't a good time for me. I mean, I was saving to take you out, just wouldn't have been this week or next," he confessed.

Frances smiled, she liked that he was honest and his tone maudlin as they continued to speak. She knew Maxwell was a humble man. "What are you doing?" she asked.

"Lying down about to get up and feed my cat," he said.

"Can I come over?" she asked.

Maxwell was surprised, but he agreed. "Um sure, have you eaten, we can order some take out?" he asked.

"Oh, that's okay; I had dinner with some friends earlier. Text me your address and I'll let you know when I'm on my way," she confirmed.

"Oh okay, no problem," he chuckled.

"Okay," she laughed before getting off the phone. Frances sat upright, pondering her next move as she scurried into the bathroom to prepare for a shower. One hour, a long hot shower, Shea Butter and a head full of Bantu knots later, with light makeup and her nose piercing in, Frances was ready to go. She threw on a pair of distressed jeans, a crop top sweater, and slid into a pair of flip-flops right before dialing her Uber. As she stepped out of her brownstone she went out to stand on the stoop waiting for her driver, who according to their mobile application was only four minutes away. Maxwell's address was unfamiliar territory; before her shower she found herself on Google whilst waiting for the hot water to come up.

As she approached the high-rise building about five blocks away from Canal Street in SoHo, she wondered how he was able to afford such living, then she realized it was public assistance housing. Frances had two choices, either be a shallow woman and turn her cab around, or follow through and spend time with a man who otherwise seemed perfect in every way. She chose option number two.

Standing outside she texted him to let him know she had arrived. Maxwell advised he was on his way down. Frances stood outside waiting patiently until she heard her name. "Frances," he shouted trying to get her attention amidst the New York traffic. Frances turned to face him, gripping her shoulder bag as she stepped religiously towards him and the open door. Once inside there were elevators and a laundry room to their left where women were seen folding clothes.

Arriving to the ninth floor, Maxwell let them inside of his apartment, Frances was taken aback. The décor in his apartment was untoward; he was a man, a bachelor at that, she thought.

The apartment was not big, nor was it small; it was home for a single man and his pet. Inside, Maxwell had a bicycle leaned against the wall and beside it a line of shoes, sneakers and loafers. As Frances stepped further inside she noticed the red leather sectional, a small coffee table and a flat screen television in the living room sitting atop a glass television stand. Frances had not noticed that she passed the kitchen until she placed her bags down and Maxwell was standing behind her holding two bottles of Poland Spring water.

Frances took a few steps over to the large window in the living room area where she watched the city lights gleam. His view from the high-rise astonishing. Maxwell, standing beside her, turned, their eyes interlocking,

"I know this isn't what a woman like you would expect from a man. Maybe into the mansions and the penthouse suites," he chuckled nervously.

But Frances remained quiet as she watched him make his way back to the sofa. "Do you smoke?" she asked, noticing the ashtray on the coffee table as she placed her water on a coaster.

"Yea, I do. I just didn't want to ask you that, because I figured that would be too forward." He smiled.

"No, no, it is fine. Can we smoke in here?" she asked, removing her purse.

"Yea we can, I can get some now," he said.

"Yes, that sounds really good," Frances watched as he made his way into his bedroom, which wasn't too far away. She sat on the sofa flipping through the channels and then he appeared holding three pre-rolled joints.

"Wow, you're prepared," Frances said.

"No, I mean, please don't judge me." He chuckled nervously. Maxwell having a boyish charm to him Frances could not help but adore. "I try to make my life as easy as possible since most of the time I'm working long hours and mostly come home to sleep or ride my bike for exercise to the gym and back. Life is pretty boring, but I was telling you this," he continued. "You're quite foppish by the way, I like it and love the hair," he said as he sat down, striking a match. Maxwell took two long puffs before handing it over to Frances, who took two of her own, inhaling and exhaling deeply. She was starting to like him even more as she checked off every box in her head: handsome? Check. Taller than me? Check. Not an idiot? Check. Kind? Check. Has goals? Check. And smokes? Check. Frances felt she had found her soul mate.

As the night pressed on, so did the joints. Hitting them one by one, both Maxwell and Frances lowered their eyes, reclining as they stared at one another, and for the first time, Frances made the first move. She removed her crop top as she arched her leg, placing it firmly across his lap, kissing him gently as he prepared himself for a night filled with satisfaction.

Removing his black crew neck t-shirt, Maxwell lifted Frances thrusting her legs around his torso. He stood, turned around, placing her gently on her back using one arm, driving Frances crazy as they continued kissing passionately.

Maxwell completely removed his shirt and fell to his knees as he slid his tongue up and down her chest, back to her neck, and then down to her thighs. Gripping the sides of her legs, he placed his head gently between them as he began to lick her clitoris. Frances let out a loud moan as he motioned his tongue like a man on a mission. Forcefully he took control like a real man, a whole lot of man. His hands were firm as her thighs began to shake. Biting her lips, Frances felt herself have an orgasm as Maxwell used his tongue to vibrate on her clitoris for at least five minutes, never once letting up.

Frances was no stranger to good sex, and she reciprocated the act, her Bantu knots now falling as her natural curls hung lightly past her shoulders. She moaned in ecstasy. Maxwell turning to position himself upright on the floor as Frances slid her way onto the ground. A second later taking his penis into her mouth, Frances stroked and sucked using her hands to rotate around the shaft. Maxwell, tilting his head back in satisfaction—Frances playing with his balls, stuffing them into her mouth as her saliva dripped along the floors. Maxwell moaned in ecstasy, holding onto her hair and twisting her curls into a fist, he finally allowed himself to release into her mouth and Frances gladly welcomed his gift as she took a huge gulp.

The two kissed passionately as he lifted her, removing the remainder of her jeans and carrying her into the bedroom where he plunge her onto the bed. Frances moaned as he prepared to enter her. Looking up, she saw his silhouette, the black stallion, teasing her clitoris now as he reached for a condom and placed it firmly on his penis. He entered her.

That night the two made love until the sun began to rise. Once they were done, Frances sat upright, caressing Maxwell from his shoulders to his chest, twirling his chest hairs around her fingertips, her hair now completely bouncing around as her Bantu knots had all come undone. Smiling from ear to ear, Frances could not get enough of him. She kissed his chest and began making her way back down to his penis where she gave him another blow job before calling it a night.

Maxwell was pleased.

The next morning, Maxwell and Frances had awoken to the sunlight beaming in on their faces.

"Good morning, beautiful," he said.

"Good morning." She turned to face him, grabbing his baby face to give him a kiss. Frances was happy.

"I'll make us some breakfast. What do you normally take?" he asked, getting out of bed.

Frances now staring off into his eyes, "Why are so perfect?" she asked.

"I am far from perfect, but I feel like we're going to be great." He smiled as he leaned in to kiss her.

"Just an omelet, baby, and thank you," Frances replied as she buried her head into the pillow—Maxwell taking his leave.

Moments later her phone rang; it was Africa.

"I'm here with bagels, where are you?" she asked. Africa was standing in front of the Brownstone, waiting patiently for Frances to rear her head. But this time it was different.

"I am actually not home," whispered Frances.

"Um, are you whispering?" questioned Africa.

"Yes, I am with a guy," Frances said quietly. Africa immediately let out a loud shriek.

"Oh my goodness, did you have sex?" she screamed. "See, I was almost mad at you to have me standing out here with bagels and hot coffee, but get you that dick, girl, I am not even mad, I am proud. Who is he, Franny? Why am I just now hearing about this guy?" Africa inquired. She was ecstatic, Frances was content, she knew her halcyon days were here.

"He's this guy I met at a coffee shop a few days ago. Noel and I went there," she said.

"Beautiful. You sound happy, aw but you're the Joan Clayton of the group, whose house are we going to pop up to now?" she joked.

"There's only three of us, how am I Joan?" Frances joked.

"We found Lynn the other day, Noel, my dear," Africa said laughing.

"Listen, my favorite continent, I will call you later when I get home," Frances said. As she was wrapping up her call, she felt Maxwell slide into bed with her, kissing her butt cheeks and causing her legs to tremor. "Africa, I have to go," she said as she ended the call.

Noel had awoken to an empty house. She was excited to be staying in the Park Ave apartment but missed Nathan; she also missed breakfast. After taking a few deep breaths she decided to wander the apartment. Inside was huge, three-bedrooms, three bathrooms, a balcony, long ceilings with a kitchen large enough to fit another apartment. But Noel was not the cooking type, more like the eating type. She searched the refrigerator for something to eat, she saw food, but it was all uncooked.

She was bored. Here she was in a million-dollar estate, no phone, no access to her friends, simply waiting for a man to notice her. Just then the doorbell buzzed. She pondered for a moment if she should answer and decided against it. Tiptoeing to the peephole she saw that it was Jade. Noel felt her heart sink to the bottom of her chest, just then she heard Jade jingle keys. She was flustered and with no time to plan, she hid in the coat closet behind the entrance, holding her breath and placing her hand over her mouth as Jade entered the estate.

Jade was stark raving mad. She stomped all throughout the apartment, searching for something. Just then her phone began to dial out; placing the call on speaker she placed her handbag on the center mantle.

"Hello," the voice over the phone said.

"Where is it?" asked Jade.

"Where is what?" said the person on the other line.

"My damn watch," she screamed. Just then Noel squinted. She was embarrassed by the fact that was hiding in the closet, but even more embarrassed that she was hiding from Jade. She loathed Jade, pitied her, and yet, she was the one hiding.

"Look, you said you wanted to end things and so I obliged. When I tried speaking to you, you called my wife and then pulled another ass stunt the other night," the voice said.

"Listen, just because I want to work on my relationship doesn't mean I don't still care about you. But you can't keep giving handouts to every mini-skirt you see, that's unfair to me. You're jealous of Kenneth and I get that, but for Christ's sake, Nathan, you are married! If anyone should be jealous here it is me. If anyone should be securing a back-up plan, it should be me. You keep trying to make me jealous with every woman you encounter and frankly, I am sick of it," Jade scolded.

"I have to get back to work," said Nathan as he hung up the phone. Jade's iPhone beeped twice indicating the end of the call. Noel couldn't help but feel bad—she continued to hide.

At work, Nathan began to panic. He knew Noel was in the apartment and wondered what was going on.

Jade stomped and sobbed as she pulled up a seat in the dining room. She had paced all throughout that apartment and knew Nathan had brought another woman there. But knowing she could do nothing was the worst feeling of them all, she could not get upset because he was a grown-boy who would never take accountability for his own actions. An hour later, Jade had arisen from her seat of self-pity, brushed her weave and begun making her way to the front door. As she turned the lock, she felt the need to open the closet door next to her, in there she found Noel had fallen asleep on the ground curled into the fetal position. She kicked her.

Noel twitched for a moment trying to figure out what had happened. She groaned as Jade continued to look down on her in disgust.

Noel noticing the foot before her eyes, immediately sat upright, looking up at Jade, trembling, she felt ashamed.

"Well, well, well, look what we have here. Just as I suspected," Jade said as she began to remove the key from her keychain. Noel yawned, she was truly feeling exhausted.

"You can keep him and this life, because look at what you've been reduced to," Jade said as she dropped the apartment key. Shutting the closet door, she made her exit. Noel felt relieved, she took a deep breath before realizing she now had a copy of the apartment key and could leave, and so she did just that.

Noel showered, she noticed in the master bedroom there was a walk-in closet completely filled with clothes and shoes, she only prayed they were her size. Not all, but some, and that was enough for her. After her shower, she turned on the record player where she sang along to the smooth sounds of Otis Redding, using her brush as a microphone to lip-sync the words to "Try a Little Tenderness," her curls bouncing back and forth. Noel felt free.

She reached into the walk-in closet where the carpets were beige and the shoes all lined shelves in rows of twenty. Each garment sorted by color, and she was feeling very pastel. Noel reached for a crème, ivory and light grey outfit. As she dressed and looked into the mirror, she saw a whole new woman, a chic woman. Noel then tamed her curls. She first straightened her hair and then proceeded to place it into a tight bun. She then reached into her duffle, where she located some makeup, applying minimal foundation, she found herself ready to face the world, and by the world, she meant Frances.

As she prepared herself to take her leave, now stepping into a thirteen-hundred-dollar pair of stilettos, she made sure to have the apartment key tucked away in her clutch. Opening the door, she was startled by a young gentleman wearing an all-black suit with a hat.

"Who are you?" she quickly asked.

"My name is Stewart ma'am, and I will be your driver for the day," he said.

Noel was confused. "Driver?" she asked.

"Well, yes, Mr. Ramirez specifically said that I am to take you wherever you please, oh, and to give you this." He reached into his suit jacket, pulling out a white envelope which held an Amex gold card, a key, and a note.

Will be home around 8, please order food.
Stewart will take you wherever you need to go.
Manicure and pedicure baby.
XO

Noel looked at Stewart.

"How long have you been standing here?" she asked as she crumbled the note, tossing it to the floor.

"Since 4 a.m., ma'am," said Stewart. Noel was disgusted. She was on the move.

"What time do you get relieved from your duties, Stewart?" she asked as they rode the elevator down to the lobby.

"Whenever Mr. Ramirez says I can leave, ma'am," he said apprehensively.

"Okay, well, tell you what. How about you tell Mr. Ramirez that you spent the entire day with me and I had a hell of a time. Okay, so, between you and I, you are now relieved of your duties," Noel said. Stewart gazed at her with a puzzled look. Noel stepped out into the scorching sun where she walked about a block to the main street as she hailed for a taxi.

"*Crystals,*" she said.

Arriving at the boutique, Noel watched as the black Audi pulled up across the street. As she stepped out of her taxi, she stepped lightly, hoping that she would see who was coming out from the car, but she did not. Opening the doors to the boutique, Amber noticed her but was with a client and could not engage at the moment, however, her face said all that her lips intended to.

Minutes later, Kenneth appeared as Amber made her way to the rear of the shop to fetch a client's personalized order. Standing behind Noel, he removed his sunglasses. He did not notice her but was intrigued by the scent of her perfume.

"Smells wonderful," he said. Noel turning to face him, as they made eye contact, the world as she knew it stopped spinning.

CHAPTER ELEVEN

By noon the ladies noticed a parked car in the front of the cabin, intrigued by its presence Noel asked, "Frances, who is that?"

Frances turning to face her. "They're here to take us to the Sky Top lodge," she said as she zipped her Obermeyer jacket, preparing for the brutal cold. Africa made her appearance, standing by the threshold completely dressed from head to toe in her ski gear. Posing now, she was trying to get the woman to let her know if her curves were still palpable. No one confirmed,

"Where is Abby?" asked Frances.

"Downstairs, talking up the chef. I have a strong feeling they'll end up in a relationship by the time he prepares to leave," Africa teased.

"That is sickening. She must return to school anyway, so I hope she doesn't play with that man's emotions. Can someone go check on Alicia, the car is here we need to get a move on. Noel, how much longer until you're dressed?" Frances asked as she stuffed her feet into her boots. Immediately she felt nauseous, stepping into her bedroom Noel catching a glimpse of her facial expression,

"Hey, are you alright?" she asked.

Standing swiftly to avoid an uncomfortable conversation, Frances arose.

"Yes, I'm fine, grab your shoes and let's go," she instructed. Noel did not like feeling rushed, but because it was Frances, she allowed it. Shoving her feet into her snow boots, she ran down the stairs, zipping her jacket and brushing her hair into a ponytail. Just as the girls were all preparing to leave, Frances took notice that Alicia was nowhere in sight. She made her way to the back of her room where she called to her. Alicia was standing outside on the patio sipping a glass of Hennessy,

"Hey, I thought you were coming to the lodge with us? They have skiing and stuff," said Frances, but she knew the reason Alicia was in no mood to parlay.

"You girls go ahead, I have some thinking to do, and to be honest, I'd just rather be alone right now," she said tranquilly. Frances hesitantly agreed as she knew the reproof was not needed.

"Okay sure, well, Angelo is going to be here preparing supper. If you need anything just let him know," Frances said, and just like that, they were gone. Alicia sobbed with each sip of her glass. It was 12:04 in the afternoon and she was facing a bottle of Hennessy in her room, alone, in the Pocono Mountains. She felt defeated.

After a few sips, Alicia mustered up the courage to contact her cheating husband via FaceTime. Holding the phone outside by the patio for better service, the phone continued to ring. He did not answer.

As she pouted and tossed the phone onto her bed, she heard a faint voice ask, "Hey if you're hungry I can make you some Coquilles Saint-Jacques," he said in his impeccable accent with hand gestures as well, and for a brief moment, Alicia was impressed.

"That sounds quite fancy for my taste," she teased.

"Your husband is an affluent man, a dish such as this should be familiar, especially to such a beautiful woman and considering the fact that it was him who recommended it to me after returning from his trip to France in 2014," he said. Angelo was slowly beginning to wonder why he had spewed such words, immediately he wished he could have taken it back. But Alicia was flattered and bewildered, it had been quite some time since someone, anyone, complimented her, hiding her disappointment, she forced a smiled,

"Thank you," she said.

"This is the first time I've seen that glow on your face. Why are you drinking so much?" Angelo asked as he motioned her to follow him to the kitchen where he was growing excited to begin making his favorite appetizer. Alicia took a seat on one of the swinging island stools. Having brought along her bottle of Hennessy, she poured herself another glass. She was growing weary.

"What glow?" she mumbled sadly. Leaning forward, Angelo placed his index finger under her chin, lifting her head slightly, their eyes met and a soft blissful kiss was exchanged.

Alicia grew angry, stumbling off of the stool she stood upright, grabbing the bottle of Hennessy, she raced back to her room, Angelo following,

"Please, I am very sorry!" he pleaded, pacing to the rear of the corridor. But Alicia was in no mood for apologies, she wanted only to think. Slamming the door in his face, she threw herself onto the mattress, her hair now coming undone as she sobbed herself into a deep slumber.

Flashback

Kenneth could not bring himself to carry on a conversation, although Noel wanted answers. She was livid,

"You told Jade about us?" she screeched.

Kenneth continued paying her no never mind as he glanced around the ladies' boutique, looking over Noel's head, waiting patiently for the owner to greet him. Minutes passed, and while Noel was growing anxious, her tone now importune, she decided it best to cease her plea and carry on to the rear of the store where Amber was there to greet her.

"You have a degenerate waiting for you by the front door, Amber," Noel advised in an undermining tone.

Amber quickly noticed as she arose from her desk and made her way to the front of the store, her eyes fixated on Noel, puzzled by her aggressive demeanor as her client scurried outside.

"Oh, hello!" Amber said as she extended her hand to formally introduce herself,

"My name is Amber, you must be Kenneth?" she confirmed. As they made their way into the office, Noel quickly made her exit. Noticing Frances walk out of the lady's room, she stood just on the outside of the glass counter, frowning.

"Another day of Bohemian Chic," Noel said.

"Sure, it beats another day of rich man's trophy," Frances replied. Noel laughed hysterically.

"So, you have to tell me, who the hell was that guy?" she asked as she spritzed the Windex atop the counter. Noel backing up swiftly.

After a slight pause, she replied, "That was Seattle bae," she reluctantly said. She wanted to choke on her lies.

Frances was not easily convinced. "Seattle bae? Really?" she questioned as she knit her eyebrows. "So, does he have you staying back at the hotel?" she inquired. Noel now had to think fast,

"No, actually, he rented a penthouse over on Park," she hated herself. With every word leaving her mouth she became absolutely repulsed by her own actions.

Frances was shocked. "What! How long is he here for? By the way, you look amazing!" she said, snapping her fingers for extra emphasis as she pulled the sleeves up on her Bohemian print dress.

"Thank you and, honestly, I'm not too sure. I think maybe a few weeks. He may be thinking of buying some property out here," she said nervously. Frances had a look on her face that told a story of its own: skeptical.

"But, enough about me. How was your night after we dropped you off?" Noel said. Frances was now folding clothes in the plus-sized department where she began grinning from ear to ear.

"Oh, my goodness, Noel," she said as she continued to smile, wondering if she would ever stop long enough to tell the tale.

"Oh man, you can't stop smiling, was it that good?" Noel teased. Frances slapped her gently before composing herself.

"It was, um, it was the best time of my life," she said.

Noel let a loud shriek slip just as a customer had made her way inside. "How big is he and just to make sure, we are talking about coffee boy right?" she whispered.

"He is a great size for me," she chuckled as she squeezed her way past the mannequins to greet the guests who were now piling in,

"Hello and welcome to *Crystals*. My name is Frances, if you have any questions please let me know and I will be happy to assist," she said. Noel was impressed, just as the soliloquy ended, she turned to face Noel, mouthing the words, *best sex ever*. Both Kenneth and Amber appeared, continuing their conversation,

"I am so happy you decided to go with our firm for your pop-up event. I promise you, you won't regret it," Kenneth remained professional as he stood hovering over the ladies in his three-piece Giorgio Armani forest green suit and chestnut colored dress shoes. He was well groomed and smelled of YSL, nails freshly manicured and his teeth a snow white. Noel hated herself for caring so much about a man who showed no respect for her.

Frances interrupted, "Hi there Kenneth—so, you're the expensive guy who's going to make our pop-up sensational?" she teased. Amber laughed, she loved Frances for her outspoken personality. Kenneth and Frances, despite their familiarity, were cordial but not friends.

"Well," placing his right hand over his heart, "I will most certainly try my best." Briefcase in hand, he began to make his way towards the door with Noel, pacing behind him as he turned to once again bid his farewell. Kenneth was annoyed, he knew Noel was up to no good and despite his many attempts to avoid her, he decided to finally give in.

Standing outside the two conversed. "Kenneth!" shouted Noel.

"You don't have to shout, I am standing right here," he said, growing impatient.

"Why are you treating me like this?" she begged.

"Like what?" He shrugged. "I told you I apologized for the other night, but it can't happen again and Jade and I are trying to repair things. She and I are even now, so it's a little easier," he advised, gripping his suitcase.

Noel could not believe her ears. "What, so you're just going to stay with a cheater? Revenge cheating, it's that like...some...toxic relationship shit?" she inquired.

"Her and I both made mistakes, neither of us are perfect, but we're willing to work through it. Noel, again, I am very sorry," Kenneth said, pulling that staged move again, placing his left hand across his heart, bending slightly to reach her eyes.

However, Noel began to fight tears as she heard nothing but the word mistake. "So you think I was a mistake?" she asked.

Kenneth gazing into her eyes began to pity her. "To be quite honest Noel, I shouldn't be speaking to you. So, I'm going to go. Once again, I apologize." Just like that, he began to walk away. Frances now stood outside, her hands formed above her head to block out the beating of the sun.

"We need to talk," she said.

Noel could not face her now, as she watched Kenneth confidently walk away. She felt heartbroken. Moments later, Noel turned to Frances,

"Can I come to your place after work?" she asked, sniffling.

"Of course, you can," said Frances, wrapping her arm around Noel and bringing her close to her shoulder. Frances did not like to see her friends sad, especially over a man. Inside, Frances clocked out for her one-hour break. Both she and Noel strolled down to a pizza shop on the corner of Madison where, after placing an order for their 12" sliced pepperoni pizza, they each took a seat at a table where they began their conversation.

"So, who is that guy to you, and please don't say Seattle bae," inquired Frances as she removed a napkin and began to shake both the salt and pepper onto it creating a mound she would twirl her index finger in. "Habit, since I was a kid," she explained when Noel shot her a questionable look.

Noel took a long sigh. She had no desire to take a trip down memory lane, but she had come to trust Frances.

"I probably don't even deserve him," she said. "Well, that's Jade's boyfriend, the one she tried to kill me over. Kenneth and I grew up together. Our fathers were friends, and although he and I went to different high schools we would sometimes be with our dads at work. I remember when we were kids and he would constantly ask me out and I wasn't interested, you know? He was the square. I mean, skinny, shorter than he is now. I mean, he ran track in high school which probably explains the slenderness, but he just wasn't my type and who was I, you know, to even tell someone they're not my type?" Noel now joined Frances as she stuck her finger on the napkin, twirling the salt and pepper tracing infinity lines.

"Do you think maybe he fell in love with you?" Frances asked.

"He did, and then for prom, he asked me to go with him— I told him no. We made out a few times but I still didn't see much in him. He was just not like the football players. He slouched, he had greasy hair, he never clipped his fingernails or his toes, he would wait almost three months to get a haircut. I mean, he was a mess." Noel chuckled as she struggled to find humor in her sadness.

"So, it was a physical thing for you back then?" Frances asked.

"Yea, I mean, I was young, Frances, goodness, don't tell me you've slept with every boy in high school who ever liked you," Noel questioned. "I mean, how am I still being punished all these years later? I had no clue he was going to come here and begin looking like that or acting like this or make something of himself," Noel complained.

Frances chuckled as she rose to fetch their food after hearing their order called by the cashier. Disbursing nineteen dollars for two slices of pizza, she made her way back to the table. Placing Noel's slice in front of her, she took a bite of her own before saying,

"Well, he's a man. Now, tell me, how did you know he was in love with you?" Frances sunk her teeth into another bite, wiping her mouth profusely as the oil dripped.

"He asked me to prom and at first I said no, so then he started working for his dad and earning some money. He went and bought me a necklace with a heart pendant from Pandora. I was in love with that necklace, but I wasn't in love with him. I mean, we continued to hang out—" Noel continued, her mouth full.

Interrupting, Frances said, "Why on earth would you accept the necklace?"

"He worked every day with his dad for two months to save and buy me that necklace, why on earth wouldn't I take it?" Noel responded. The pizza shop now getting crowded.

"Well, for starters, because that gives him the wrong idea. You're pretty much telling him that you're somewhat interested. You pretty much led him on," said Frances.

Noel chuckled. "Jesus, I was like seventeen years old, I knew nothing about men, or even my emotions, let alone my own damn body. Who could I have led on? I mean, I do think I could have handled things differently, but I think what sent him over the edge was when I went to prom with someone else. Someone the complete opposite of who he was," Noel said.

"Yep. That'll do it. You take his chain and then wear it to prom with another man. Congratulations on being a cold-hearted bitch. Let's just thank God he still believes in monogamy and he isn't out here punishing every other woman for your mistake, he's simply punishing you and I am now, all the way here for it!" exclaimed Frances.

"Seriously, because I was seventeen and hardly knew any better? Plus, he looked like a twig with arms and wasn't confident at all. He made me feel like I scared him," she said, rolling her eyes.

"Well fool, that's because he loved you. Are you going to finish the rest of that pizza? I get it you're all Manhattan now and want to stay slim, perhaps, but don't go wasting my money," Frances said playfully.

After three bites of her pizza, Noel wasn't hungry, she was confused and now Frances made her realize why. "So, after you're done stuffing your face can you tell me what I'm supposed to do?" Noel pleaded.

"Sure, you leave that man alone," advised Frances.

Noel knitted her brows. "Um, no, I want to be with him now, especially after the sex. He's perfect. Hell, maybe I need to marry him. Frances, I need better advice than that." Noel panicked.

Just then, Frances stopped chewing as she took a napkin to her lips, wiping meticulously.

"If you and Kenneth grew up together, wouldn't that make him Seattle bae?" she asked, a perturbed look on her face, she feared that she had been lied to and was impatient for a response.

"Um, no, he is not Seattle bae."

"So, when do I get to meet Seattle bae?" asked Frances.

"When the time is right, I mean you've met Nathan and—" Noel stuttered.

"Noel, breathe, is there something you're not telling me?" Frances asked, just then her watch buzzed, signaling lunch was over.

"Look, I have to get back to work. I don't mind you coming by later, just let me know, or if you're staying at the store until I get off, that's fine too," Frances said. She stood, stretching her dress and stepping outside to make her way back to the boutique. Noel remained seated as she took notice of everyone around her, how content they were, happy. She felt a part of her was missing. Deep in thought, she heard a voice call out to her,

"Ms. Shoe-lady," an angelic voice said. "Look, Daddy, it's the shoe lady." Noel turned to find Abram and his daughter Ana standing by the counter placing an order. Quickly, Noel stood. She was speechless and embarrassed; she stood him up and now here they were, face to face.

Noel greeted Ana with a smile, to which she reciprocated. Abram could not bring himself to be angry for he was far too mesmerized by her beauty.

"You look beautiful, as usual," he said nervously.

Noel continued to fidget, her hands developing a mind of their own as she could not bring herself to stay still.

"Thank you, you look good as well. Um, about the, um, the day, well, evening, we were supposed to have dinner..." she stuttered as she continued to fidget. "I am so sorry," she continued, dropping her hands.

"It's really okay. I mean, I'm a pretty understanding guy, and I know things happen and so, it's fine, really. Don't worry about it," Abram said, smiling.

Noel fought herself before saying, "Would you like to go on a date with me this weekend?" she felt uneasy, as though she was only suggesting another date out of sheer pity. Awaiting an answer, everything came to a halt, including her ability to breathe.

Abram smiled. "I think that would be great," he smiled.

"Great, um, I can meet you here at six on Saturday?" she asked. A tad bit skeptic, Abram half-heartedly agreed.

"Why here?" he asked. Almost impatient, he continued. "How about I give you my number again, and if anything changes you give me a call and let me know?" he said. Noel agreed. Again, Abram decided to write his number on the back of his receipt, which he handed Noel and she was pleased.

Backing out of the pizza shop slowly, Noel felt herself smiling from ear to ear. Abram was truly a great guy.

That night, Noel decided against going to Frances's apartment, returning to the Park Avenue penthouse after Frances's shift ended. She was exhausted, but on the cab ride home, she began to wonder to herself if the life she was living was a life worth living for. As she exited the taxi, handing the driver twenty-seven dollars, she sauntered onto the elevator where she passed the concierge, greeting him. Arriving at the front door, she turned her key stepping inside, she attempted to navigate the stygian home. Closing the door behind her, she was welcomed with a smack across the face.

CHAPTER TWELVE

Just as the sun began to overlook the mountain and the white blanket of snow gave an alluring view, the limo driver stopped in front of the beautiful ornate Ski Lodge where tourists were gathered. Frances placed her ski mask on; she was ready as they stepped inside to register. The large building resembling a cathedral church from the outside, the high ceilings, bright lights, expanded balconies, and the benches outdoors. Frances could not help but feel grateful—having never been skiing before. The ladies all conversed amongst themselves. Noel, feeling slightly hungry, was growing irritated.

"Food?" she complained, turning to face Frances who now held onto her stomach frantically in search of a latrine. No one else taking notice as she ran inside, her right hand over her stomach and her left hand covering her mouth, her snow boots weighing her down and making it hard for her to move as quickly as she needed. She felt the lumps of vomit begin to erupt. Noel quickly followed as Africa and Abigail stood in line, pending registration.

Inside the lodge, Frances went straight towards the restroom, where she entered one of the white stalls and began to hurl. Noel waited patiently for her as the other patrons made their exit and entrance. Noel smiled to avoid any suspicion.

Just then, Frances emerged, her eyes red and filled with water, her kinky curls dangling in front of her, her ski mask in hand. Placing it on the sink to rinse her hands, Frances was beginning to feel tired.

Looking on, Noel said, "Franny, are you pregnant?" Noel placed her hand on Frances's shoulder. Frances let out a long sigh.

"I have no idea," she said as she stared at herself and Noel through the mirror.

"Well, you probably shouldn't get on the slopes, at least until we find out," Noel advised. Frances agreed as they both made their way out of the latrine. Amidst the large crowd, Noel spotted Africa, who had her hair in large braids that she styled into a high-top bun. She was hard to miss. Both of the ladies were excited to begin, Abigail especially,

"Black girls on the ski-slopes!" she teased. Everyone chuckled, as she was known to be the jester of the group.

"So, I think we have to go out back, and it is freezing you guys, but we have our wrist bands, so let's head on out," Africa said. Noel and Frances both exchanged a look before Frances said,

"Girls I'm not feeling too good. I think I ate too much at breakfast and my stomach is doing backflips," she said as she placed her hand atop her stomach. She saw the look of disappointment in their eyes but knew she was making the right decision.

"Ah man, do you want to go back home?" Abigail asked, secretly hoping her friend would say no,

"No, no, of course not. I'm going to hang out here and drink some hot cocoa, find some magazines to read. You guys have fun." She smiled. Frances was always kind-hearted in nature and it hurt her that she was letting her friends down. As Noel continued looking on, a part of her felt she should stay back as well, but she knew the other ladies would no doubt become wary, so instead, she gave Frances a hug whispering,

"Love you."

Knitting her brows. Africa overheard her. "Jeez, it's just skiing, we aren't going on a suicide mission. Why must you two look so down?" she snapped. Abigail chuckled as she took a long look at Frances.

"Well, we're told we're skiing on the green circle, which apparently means that's the easiest slope to go down, so we have to head on the ski lift now you guys," Abigail said. Moments later the girls were headed on the ski lift and making their way up the mountain accompanied by two women who were vacationing from Australia.

Frances stepped outside. Removing her phone from the inside pocket of her winter jacket she started snapping pictures; once everyone realized, they began to pose, shaking the lift slightly. The tourists decided to join in the fun.

"Have fun, you guys!" Frances screamed.

The ladies skied for hours, Africa and Abigail began making their way from one circle to the next; Africa now on the black circle and Abigail on blue. Noel decided after two hours of trying to simply give up as she remained stationed on the green circle just inches away from the bunny slope. Back inside the lodge, Frances decided to enjoy a hot cup of chocolate and Ski Magazine and an Archie comic book she was lucky to locate by the gift shop. As she sat on the couch enjoying the hot chocolate and her good read, she couldn't help but wonder if there truly was something growing inside of her.

Frances placed her hand atop her stomach as she began to think of all the wonderful joys parenthood could bring to both her and Maxwell, and then a dreadful thought crossed her mind, one she wished she would never have to consider.

Flashback

The apartment pitch black, Noel now faced down on the hallway floor, what appeared to be armed men began to pat her down, sliding her clutch away from her and shouting to one another.

"Get the watch!" one man said.

Another shouted, "Fuck, get everything man! The watch and the chains. Hell, check the closet." Noel turned her head to see the man standing above her wearing a pair of black and silver New Balance sneakers. She continued to lie still until she heard a muffled sound coming from the living room. Immediately, she turned her head to see a dark shadow had been seated against the wall, their hands bound. She hated that she couldn't see anything and wondered how many of them were there. They were moving swiftly, shouting, ransacking and cursing all throughout the home.

The stranger then grabbed Noel by the wrist, lifting her. As she tripped over her feet, she felt a slight pinch in her wrist, a pinch that became a bruise soon after. She was thrust against the hallway wall where the man began to frisk her, parting her legs with the tip of his gun, he removed an ankle bracelet, her watch, and the earrings she wore. Noel knew better than to struggle. As she was pushed into the living room the base of her pants ripped. The muffling grew louder now, she wondered if it had been Nathan. The masked man pushed her inside the living room where she was instructed to stay seated next to who appeared to be Nathan, his forehead gashed, his eye bruised and his hands and feet bound, duct tape across his mouth. Noel was now scared, more than before as she listened as the men continued to shout.

"Grab the shoes," another one yelled, their guns now waving back and forth. She felt her shoes snatched from her feet, a thirteen hundred pair of stilettos.

"Hey, Donald Duck, bind the bitch," one man shouted to another who was standing adjacent Noel and Nathan. Noel was too afraid to scream and too numb to want to. Her mind had not yet grasped that they were, in fact, being robbed. The sound of glass shattering began to resonate throughout the apartment. Donald Duck now proceeding to bind Noel, tying her wrists so tight she let out a shrieking cry, Nathan now staring deeply into her eyes as he continued to try speaking past the duct tape and fight to free himself.

Noel let a tear fall from her eyes.

Donald Duck now holding the barrel of the gun to Noel's forehead,

"Stop moving or I shoot your bitch," he said. Noel's eyes widened. Nathan placed his head back in silence. Deciding to comply. Noel continued to take deep breaths as a piece of duct tape was now stretched across her lips. Her long hair covered her eyes. Donald knelt, looking up at her. She stared into his eyes, the only part of him visible.

"You are way too beautiful for him," he said as he used the gun to remove the hair from her face. Noel closed her eyes tightly, remembering home, remembering her father, her mother and brothers. She did not want to leave them but felt she may not have a choice. She wept.

"Awe, don't cry beautiful, there's no way we're going to hurt you," Donald Duck said as he arose. The rest of the men, four, Noel counted, continued their wreckage and determining what was of value. Forty-five minutes later, the five thousand square foot apartment with high ceilings and wooden beams had become a complete catastrophe. The beige couches now stained with red blood from Nathan's dripping wounds Noel wanted so bad to nurse.

As the men stood by the door, Noel and Nathan's backs turned, the light from the hall shined in.
Noel wondered if they were not going to untie them.

"Dude, do we untie them?" one man asked, reading her mind almost. She muffled as her level of discomfort rose.

Another responded, "No, press their panic button and let's go." The stranger did just that; after a few buttons were pressed a loud noise blared through the apartment. Noel could not hold it in any longer. Once the door had shut, she broke down into tears as Nathan moved closer to her in a sad attempt to provide comfort.

Fifteen minutes later, the police were at the door, banging loudly as the door squeaked open.

"Hello, is anyone home?" a voice called. Noel and Nathan screamed, their sounds muffled. Immediately the officers entered, scattering, they searched the large apartment from the front to the back with their guns facing forward. A man named Bellinger, the name written across his badge, removed a pair of razors as he began to whittle down the restraints binding both Noel and Nathan. Once freed, Noel grabbed Nathan by the hand, squeezing him tightly, his dress shirt now drenched in sweat and soiled in blood.

"This man needs a hospital," an officer said.

"It's okay, ma'am, we're going to get him to the hospital to get him the medical attention he needs," Bellinger said, placing his hand atop her shoulder to comfort her. But Noel did not feel comforted, she felt afraid. She was now trembling as she came to realize her adrenaline had worn off.

By the time the EMT arrived, Nathan passed out on the Ushak Rug his wife won at an auction years ago. Noel cradled him as she sat on her knees whilst the police officers collected evidence, placing caution ropes in and around the Park Avenue apartment. An EMT positioned Nathan on a stretcher where they wheeled him down using the elevator, Noel following, ignoring the witnesses who heard the commotion and wanted to know what caused it.

As the ambulance drove, Noel could think of no one but Kenneth. She wondered how he would handle this situation, she wondered if he would have stood to be robbed at all. She pictured his muscles flexing as he fought aggressively all the men who would oppose him. She fantasized as the EMT called to her. Nathan, now hooked up to an oxygen tank, was waking up, his eyes fluttering open.

"Ma'am, it looks like he's trying to wake up, can you call to him? If he hears your voice, he may awake faster," the EMT said. The middle-aged Asian-American woman was growing impatient as Noel remained unresponsive.

"Ma'am? Ma'am? Ma'am!" her tone increasing as she now flashed a light into Noel's eyes.

Noel twitched. She was present.

"Yes," Noel responded, waving her talons as she began to knit her eyebrows.

"Please call to him," the middle-aged woman requested again. Noel was growing nauseous as the truck moved side to side and the sirens wailed. But she did as she was told,

"Kenneth! Kenneth!" she began to shake him, just as the EMT interrupted her,

"His name is Nathan," she said, gritting her teeth as she whispered. Noel felt embarrassed, slapping her head she began to sob. The EMT grew sympathetic, her nitrile gloves now gripping Noel's hands, she said, "Listen, I know this is traumatic, but I really need you to focus so we can keep him awake," she begged.

Noel nodded in compliance as she took Nathan by the hand, squeezing his palm into hers, she called to him, "Nathan, Nathan sweetheart, you have to wake up. I hope you can hear me, please wake up." The longer she spoke, the more afraid she became. She had no idea what to do or even say. Sensing this, the EMT asked her gently to take a break.

"I think you should rest. We can try again once we've arrived at the hospital," she said.

Noel continued to fight back tears, but she was no longer strong enough. She broke down as the ambulance docked at the Davidson Memorial Medical Center. Once the back doors opened, the driver proceeded to assist Noel with stepping down from the back of the ambulance. She continued to tremble despite the temperature being well into the nineties. Noel had a scratch on her cheek from where she was slapped, and after being nursed once inside, she watched as Nathan slept peacefully from just outside of the room where he would now occupy. Her arms folded, the doctors and nurses all wondered if she was a mate or a hooker, her detachment raising doubt. A doctor soon approached, clipboard in hand, as he extended his right hand to greet her, but Noel was in no mood for pleasantries.

As the doctor retracted his hand, he said, "My name is Dr. Walker. I take it you must be Noel-Lee Kwon?" he said.

Noel nodded.

"Right, so he took quite a beating, had some internal bruises and required some stitches, but he should be fine to return home within a few days, maximum three-to-five," he concluded. Noel continued to stare lifelessly into the room.

"Do you need anything else from me?" she asked as she began to feel that the role she was expected to play was quite cumbersome.

The doctor, turning to face the nurses, looked back at Noel and said, "No, but we do not recommend he be alone. Are there any friends or family members we may call?" he asked. Noel could not understand why the doctor was advising that Nathan not be alone; he was after all in their care. Annoyed by his arrogance she was ready to go home, and that is what she did.

Stepping outside, she waved for a taxi from the corner. She had no idea where she was, but knew she had to be far from home, wherever home was now.

She feared the idea of returning back to the apartment but knew she had no choice. She had no phone and could no longer remember the address for her friend's. Noel wanted a drink, she needed one badly, and so she requested an address mindlessly. Arriving at the Hilton, she walked inside as the angry cab driver shouted obscenities. After making it past the double doors, he was now behind her demanding payment.

Jade looked on witnessing the tussle between them, and against her better judgment decided to intervene. "Hey," she shouted as she walked over to them. She was annoyed, Noel was the last person she ever hoped to see again, but Noel had no idea where else to go. Her pantsuit now ripped, her hair a mess, a bandage across her cheek and her blouse stained with blood, Jade knew she could not ignore her.

The cab driver spoke quickly once Jade appeared,

"This woman, this woman owes me thirty-four dollars!" he exclaimed. Reaching into the pocket of her uniform vest, Jade handed the unprepossessing man two twenties and a ten-dollar bill.

"Here you go, sorry for the inconvenience," she said as she turned to face Noel, who now had her hands wrapped tightly around her torso as her eyes darted back and forth. Wrapping her arms around her, Jade walked her over to the counter where she gathered her things and advised her co-worker that she would soon return. Jade knew something was wrong.

Noel noticed that the room Jade was letting her into was directly across from the one she occupied, room 714. Inside the resemblance exact.

"Why did you help me?" Noel asked breathing shakily.

"Well, because you look like shit and I don't know, I still have a soft spot for you. Just don't ever forget I did this, just in case I want to cash in a favor," she said as she took her leave.

"Wait," Noel called. "Do you have Frances's number?" as the words left her mouth, the tears began to flow once again. Jade turned to face her.

"I will have someone bring it up and some food, okay? Just take a shower and relax," Jade said.

An hour later, Jade had made good on her promise. Food was delivered, a burger and fries, a salad, and Frances's number written on the back of a napkin. One hour later and Noel had not showered. She paced back and forth, replaying the events in her head over and again like that of a broken tape recorder.

She sipped on two Bacardi personals she removed from the refrigerator. Noel jumped over to the telephone where she began to dial Frances. Excited she answered on the second ring; Noel began to sob.

"Wait, who is this?" Frances asked.

"It's Noel," she said crying.

"What's the matter?" Frances asked, concerned.

"Franny, someone robbed us!" Noel allowed the words to leave her mouth, but she was shaken.

"Oh my God, where are you? I am coming right now. Where are you!" Frances demanded.

"The hotel, Franny, room 714, please, I just, I don't know, I'm such a mess," she continued.

Unbeknownst to her, Frances was beginning to cry, she hated that Noel was going through this,

"I am on my way!" Frances confirmed, immediately following came the dial-tone. Noel continued to sit on the edge of the bed where she now examined her injured wrist, playing with the purple bruise, she waited until the clock read 12:09 p.m. before deciding it was time to head into the shower, and so she began to undress when a faint knock came at the door, startling her. Pushing the food cart aside, she tiptoed to the door where she looked through the peephole to see both Frances and Africa standing on the opposite side in jogger suits and sneakers. Unlocking the door, Noel threw herself onto them, gripping them tightly as she sniveled. Both Africa and Frances returned the gesture.

"What happened?" asked Africa once Noel allowed them to breathe and they stepped inside.

"I was at the Park Avenue apartment and when I walked inside it was really dark; I took a few more steps and was hit in the face and then thrown to the floor," as Noel explained she continued to sob, loudly and uncontrollably. She was terrified.

Frances and Africa exchanged a worrisome look, Africa kneeling down to console her cousin, she felt guilty. "Listen, forget these men, you've been bouncing around all over the city like some hooker. Just come and stay with me. I know I don't live in the city, but I'm here every day for work. I can make some space, maybe get a futon," Africa rambled.

Noel nodding in compliance.

"This is ridiculous, I have a two bedroom and we can get you a job at the boutique. Africa, let's make things easy on all of us," Frances said with her arms folded.

Africa was grateful. "Thank you so much, Franny. So much, you have no idea how much this means to me." Africa continued hugging her cousin, a part of her feeling responsible. As she wiped her tears she said, "I'm your older cousin and I should have done more to protect you, Noey, I am so sorry," she whimpered.

Frances continued to look on resisting the urge to cry.

"Why don't we go now?" she said. The women gathered, preparing to take their leave as Jade stood in the hallway overhearing them. The food untouched and the beds left unturned, Noel felt it was time she did some re-evaluating. Opening the door, Jade stepped aside as Africa thanked her and she and Noel began making their way down the long corridor.

Frances said nothing, with her back turned, Jade said, "Hey, I got your homegirl together, a little gratitude would be nice," she sniped.

"Gratitude for? Just a few days ago you wanted to kill her and now you're her hero? C'mon Jade, there's a catch somewhere, we just don't know it yet." Frances turned and said, placing her hands in her pockets.

"There's no catch, okay, she needed help. She couldn't even pay her damn taxi fare. I helped, okay, I helped and you know? I know you don't like me, but you have no idea how hard it was for me to leave Freddie," Jade cried.

"Oh, my moronic brother who thought he could turn a hoe into a housewife, yes, hard for you, I bet," Frances snapped.

"Yes, because I loved him. You and I are two beautiful melanin-dripped goddesses and we fight like cats and dogs instead of embracing one another all because you never got the story straight. Freddie and I were in love, but we weren't good together, Franny. I mean we fought all the time, and I know it seems as though I just abandoned him, and you're his sister so of course you're always going to be biased, but Freddie was controlling. He hated for me to have a life outside of him, and I wasn't sure if it was because he loved me so much that the mere thought of losing me would kill him or if he simply enjoyed the idea of me being dependent on him. Well, it was the latter. You know my family was destitute, nothing was given to us, and Freddie knew that too, but what he didn't know was that I wanted my own life, my own individuality. I loved him, but it was for the wrong reasons Franny."

"I still don't understand, why didn't you say any of this? You always came around us and you smiled and you made everything seem like it was okay. You made us fall in love with you, and then one day after he announces to the entire family that he was going to marry you, you disappear! Not only from him but from me. You moved out while I was at work, changed your phone number and made us feel like the culprits. You turned his world upside down," Frances scolded.

"I admit the way I did it was so wrong, Franny it was so wrong and you meant so much to me, we were best friends and I am so sorry that I left you high and dry like that, but he was just so controlling and manipulative and I couldn't stay, I just needed to get away. It was toxic Franny, but I don't know, I thought time and time again that he and I would be able to move past it, that I could look past his imperfections, but then I couldn't see myself dealing with that for the rest of my life. I am sorry, I've missed you terribly," she sobbed.

"You broke my brother's heart and mine. Um, I have to just think for a while, Jade," said France. Noel and Africa remained in the lobby.

Frances began to step backward. Staring into Jade's eyes, she sensed her genuineness but felt she would betray her brother if she ever thought to allow Jade back into her life, and just like that she disappeared. Jade continued to stand by her hotel room door. Minutes later she went inside. Pondering as she showered, she stepped outside, draped herself in a pair of distressed jeans to enunciate her curves, and put on a sweater as the spring night winds blew cold. Jade dialed a taxi,

"Yes, I am at the Hilton," she said to the operator.

"Where are you going?" the groggy voice on the other end said.

"Davidson Memorial Medical Center," Jade replied.

CHAPTER THIRTEEN

Awakening from her nap, Alicia felt strange—sluggish. She knew there was a reason she stopped drinking hard liquor in the middle of the afternoon. As she turns around squinting her eyes, the time now, 3:44 p.m. The lodge remained peaceful, which meant the ladies had not yet returned home. She was regretting the decision to remain back at the cabin. Feeling as though she was allowing a man who had broken her heart several times to win, even if he weren't around to do it.

Alicia arose from her bed. She hated that bed; it was nothing like her mattress at home—already she felt her back beginning to ache. As she stood, she sorted her outfit for the evening, showered, and headed out to face the world. And by the world, she meant the painstakingly attractive chef. She stepped lightly in her ocean blue strapless maxi dress, her waist-length hair straightened, her makeup light and her skin glowing. She smelled of Dior J'adore, a scent which over the years had become her signature.

Angelo having yet to take notice; remains seated on the sofa on the other side of the wall with the fireplace, nibbling on snacks and reading through a magazine he seemed quite immersed in. Alicia, standing behind him, cleared her throat, starling him.

"Sorry, didn't mean to scare you," she lied. She found this to be quite hilarious as he had clearly been comfortable. He removed his shirts, exposing his toned biceps. Alicia was fascinated. Lifting her dress just above her ankles, she stepped with caution, joining him on the couch as she set aside his chips and magazines.

"Maybe we should talk," she suggested. Angelo blushed as her beauty continued to blind him.

He simply could not focus, and without thinking, he said,

"You are the most beautiful woman I've ever seen." Again, he wished he could retract this statement, as he feared her leaving, but this time was different. Alicia yearned for some affection; she had not made love to her husband in over two years. She was in need of it, and Angelo seemed perfect. As her silence began to worry him, he added, "I know that I am being completely inappropriate, but I know Nathan, and if what you're telling me is true, a man like that doesn't deserve a woman as beautiful and as charming as you," Angelo said. It was the passion in his eyes, the meaning behind every word, and his soft approach that made her lean in and give him a kiss. Every single bone in her body desired him, but she could not bring herself to explore his manhood, and so, she arose,

"Can you show me to those French delicacies?" she asked politely. Angelo happily obliged as he stood, bowing and making a pathway for her to pass while motioning for her to head into the kitchen. Once on the other side, Angelo did not bother to put his shirt on, he was in the mood to show Alicia just what she'd been missing. Angelo, turning on the oven, began by taking her hand, escorting her towards the counter where he grabbed her waist seating her on top. A few minutes later the Coquilles Saint-Jacques were now heated to perfection, he reached into the oven after applying his oven mittens, removing them and the pan, Angelo standing between her legs, parting them with his torso, slicing into the Coquilles Saint-Jacques creating bite-sized pieces. Alicia was enjoying every moment.

Angelo's lips kissing her delicately, he then said,

"Close your eyes and open your mouth." Alicia did as she was told, feeling the warm delicacy grace her tongue. Closing her mouth, she felt Angelo's finger—sucking the taste from his fingertips—removing his finger Angelo took pleasure in watching as she began to chew slowly.

"This—is—amazing," she said, reaching for his hand, as she placed the tip of his index finger back into her mouth licking and sucking it gently after opening her eyes. Alicia waited for the next serving and seconds later she received it. Alicia felt confident, a feeling she thought she had lost, as she reached in to kiss Angelo passionately on the lips. He reciprocated and their moment was blissful, filled with peace and admiration.

"I respect you," he said. Alicia continuing to pull him closer.

"I am a Christian woman and my vows are everything to me, but Lord knows I just want to ask for forgiveness," she stressed.

Their moment soon interrupted by the ladies as Abigail stepped inside,

"Well, well, well," she teased, standing by the front door.

Angelo and Alicia panicked. Quickly the two looked to scatter as Angelo searched frantically for his chef's coat and Alicia hopping from the counter, standing in an awkward position for she had no idea what else to do.

"Welcome back," she said nervously. But Abigail was not pleasant; instead, she stood aside as the remaining ladies now piled in. Angelo after retrieving his coat, now looking like the professional he was hired to be. Abigail struggled to remove her garments as she couldn't help but feel disappointed.

"Welp, another Black woman loses to the Spanish," she mumbled. Noel knitted her brows as she overheard.

"What?" she questioned.

"Oh, those two, they're fucking now," Abigail said making her way up the stairs. Noel was not accustomed to Abigail showing signs of frustration, and so decided to brush it off as pure sarcasm. Alicia greeted everyone as she trembled, hoping no one would have taken notice of her brief moment of weakness. But once Abigail brushed past her, shoving her slightly, this confirmed she was doomed. Angelo taking notice arose to object, but Alicia begged him not to as she mouthed the words,

"Please don't," continuing to assist the women with the removal of their gear.

Flashback
It had been two months since the robbery, and as Noel turned the key to Frances's first-floor apartment, the sweet scent of her aromatherapy hit Noel's nostrils like a cool breeze on a summer day! Lavender, to be exact. The spacious twelve hundred square foot apartment had twelve-foot ceilings, two bedrooms, a washer and dryer, and was two blocks from the mall house in central Harlem. The apartment came equipped with slate matte appliances, granite counter tops, ceiling fans, glass tile backsplash in the kitchen, and best of all an 11x9 square foot bedroom Noel could call her own. As she entered the front door, she placed her keys on the kitchen counter to her right. Her bedroom was to the left, and the walk-in closet, now empty, was all that she could have imaged plus more. Frances and Noel shared a conjoining bathroom, with Frances's room closest to the patio area found to the rear of the building. The dining room was large, 12x15 square feet with a flat screen television, cable, and a three-piece dark blue leather sectional. As Noel watched movies, she would see Frances just in the kitchen in front of her whipping together her famous sweet potato pie.

Noel was home.

Four short steps and she was standing in the middle of the kitchen, raiding the refrigerator for something, anything, to eat or drink aside from Cognac, lemon, or Poland Spring. No success. They were the worst bachelorettes, neither of them knowing how to cook, clean properly, or even shop for adequate furniture. Noel was reminded each time she plopped onto the navy-blue bean bag located closest to the kitchen island. The same island where stools are supposed to go. But she dared not complain, she felt happy for the first time in a long time, and with fall now approaching, Frances was preparing to head back to school to teach the children of the third grade. Noel, on the other hand spent another unsuccessful day searching for a job. Her money was beginning to run low after contributing monthly to rent, furnishings, and replenishing her clothing.

Immediately it dawned on her: this is what struggling felt like. With each passing day, Noel thought of Nathan and worried that he had no idea where she was or even how to find her. Kenneth never left her mind either, and although she and Abram never had a chance for that date, she missed him, too. She had sequestered herself from the outside world, socially, as she focused on strengthening her mental health, getting a job, and finding her inner peace again.

Noel now had a cellular phone she absolutely despised, the thought of paying over a hundred dollars a month to communicate with her friends, to her, was an absolute waste of money. Money she could have been using to buy clothes or repay Frances the loan she had borrowed. She was feeling defeated. Noel began to do the one thing she always did when she was feeling down on her luck, bite her nails and fondle her shoulder-length ponytail as the sound of keys began to rattle in the door. It was Frances returning home.

The night was coming down quickly and there she was, the woman of the hour Noel thought as she continued to sit by the kitchen island.

"Well, don't you look...pitiful," Frances said as she made her way inside, tilting her head as she found herself standing in the middle of the kitchen. Her goal—same as Noel's had been—food.

"What the fuck? Why are we so broke?" she cried as she opened the refrigerator, holding it open as if keeping it open and staring inside would make food appear. Noel sauntered into her bedroom as Frances closed the refrigerator door and began to prepare herself for bed. Standing now by her bedroom threshold and fiddling with a piece of thread she'd removed from her clothing, she could not help but stare at Frances. She is gorgeous, she thought.

"Maybe we can order UberEATS or Door Dash?" Noel finally said. Frances was now in the bathroom taking a shower.

"Sounds good to me. Chinese?" she screamed.

"Yes, on me! What do you want?" Noel bellowed, now scrolling through her phone after opening the UberEATS application browsing their selection for Best Chinese Harlem.

"Chicken and broccoli with fried rice, Noel!" she said.

"Gotcha," Noel confirmed as she noticed a brochure on the bathroom countertop for a place in the *Poconos.*

Once the pipes shut off, Noel began her interrogation. "So, tell me more about this getaway!" she said, pointing to the brochure once the curtains shifted and Frances was now reaching for a towel to dry her naked body.

"Do you mind if I dry off first? Nosy!" she joked.

"Um, no, can we talk about this trip please?" she said, fanning the brochure her way. Frances couldn't help but chuckle.

"I'm going to give you a pass for being the ultimate creep right now because I know you still can't find a job," she teased. Noel smiled from ear to ear, for she had come to appreciate and love the nature of their relationship.

"Okay so, to answer your question, Spruce Camp is in the Pocono Mountain and it is so beautiful," she said as she slid into her negligee—turning to face Noel with a sly look on her face. Frances then reached for her iPhone where she scrolled through her photos before handing the phone off to Noel. She then sat on her bed to lotion her skin, her moisturizer of choice raw, pure Shea Butter. Her talons clacking as she rubbed the lotion between her hand, distracting Noel slightly.

"How many bedrooms?" she asked as she continued to scroll.

"I am told there are five in total," she said. Frances was now seated meticulously in front of her vanity, preparing to cornrow her hair and grease her scalp. Hair as healthy, thick, and long as hers took quality maintenance, which she always provided.

"So, I mean, this looks really expensive," Noel said as she continued to twirl her thread.

"It is very expensive, but, I mean, this isn't a trip I'll be taking any time soon. Maxwell simply asked where I would like to go for our anniversary one day and I told him about this place, so we're both saving,"

Amidst their conversation the doorbell rang. It was their food. Noel made her way to the front door where the delivery man was standing with two bags in each of his hands, evidence they were busy tonight. Noel politely mentioned her name, to which he searched for the bag with the corresponding receipt annexed. Handing the bag over to her, she exchanged with him a seven-dollar tip, nodding his head in acceptance, Noel wished him a safe night.

"The food is here!" she screamed in excitement. As Frances prepared herself to head into the kitchen, her cellular phone rang. Clearing her throat, she answered as she wiped the grease from her hands. Noel, now in the kitchen, continued to do her bidding as she reached for a plate from the cupboards. Seconds later, Frances began making her way towards her,

"Hey, do you mind if Max comes by tonight?" she asked politely.

Noel laughed. "Have I ever minded, plus that's good, I get to ask him if his job is hiring and tell him we have food!" she shouted loud enough for him to hear her over the phone. Frances turned giddily,

"She says it's fine," she said. "Okay, see you soon baby." Frances hung up the phone as she skipped her way into the kitchen after finishing her hair.

"Why are you always so painfully happy when that man comes around?" Noel asked as she took a large bite into her broccoli tree.

Standing now by the counter, Frances began to prepare her meal, "Well, he makes me very happy and we don't get to see one another that much anymore since he started studying for his CPA license," said Frances.

"Oh, wow, that's impressive," Noel said.

"Yes, so which television series are you going to have us suffer through tonight?" Frances teased.

Noel felt slightly offended. "What? You love the shows I recommend to you," Noel cried. The blithe Frances smiled as she stepped with a leisurely gait into the living room where the television was located.

"Whoa, you don't get to ignore me, you do like the shows I recommend, right? Otherwise, why suffer through them?" asked Noel.

Sitting now, Frances hated that she had to come clean. She knew Noel was very sensitive,

"Well, the shows you like are very romantic or lackluster," she admitted. Noel was shocked,

"What? Excuse me, well okay, let's see what you'd recommend," she said, handing her the remote control as she took large gulps of her rice.

"See, that's the thing, I don't watch television all that much. I'm a school teacher, my evenings are spent grading papers and creating new assignments for the next day," Frances said.

"Oh, that's bull. What about the summers when you're off from teaching?" Noel questioned. The ladies both now sat on the leather sofa, a black television screen in front of them,

"Still, no television. I am working to supplement my income, and when I'm not working, I'm sleeping or visiting my brother and my parents. This summer those visits didn't happen as frequently as I would have liked, though," Frances said frowning.

"Why is that?" Noel inquired as she continued to eat her food.

"Well despite the fact that Freddie is engaged to be married, he still blames me for Jade leaving," Frances said just as the doorbell sounded. She arose quickly as the conversation was beginning to make her uncomfortable.

Placing her food on the kitchen countertop, Frances tiptoed to see who had rung her doorbell, stepping into her slippers and her robe, she slithered into the hallway where she opened the front door to find Maxwell standing; his face hidden behind a large bouquet of red roses. Frances, smiling, leaned in to kiss him as she continued standing on her toes.

"These are beautiful baby, thank you so much!" Frances said as she walked him inside.

"Noey, how did the delivery man get inside?" pondered Frances as she came to realize Noel had not gone outside to retrieve their order.

"I have no clue, maybe Shawn was heading out when he was coming in," she responded. Frances hated this; she was surely going to be making a complaint in the morning. Their landlord never liked it when strangers were allowed to tailgate, yet he remained oblivious to this? Maxwell stepped inside wearing an Adidas solid black hoodie and denim blue jeans with a pair of black Airmax sneakers. Frances and Maxwell conversed in the kitchen as Noel now began making her way into her bedroom,

"Oh my, those flowers are beautiful!" she screeched as Frances searched for a vase to place them in.

"Thanks, how have you been, Noel?" Maxwell asked.

"I've been okay," Noel responded.

"Where are you going? You don't have to leave, we can all just hang for a while. I'm not staying the night or anything, just wanted to stop by and check on Fran," Maxwell said. Before she had a chance to respond, Frances turned to face him,

"Why aren't you staying the night?" she asked.

"I have to be at work early tomorrow, I changed my shift," Maxwell said.

"Why'd you change your shift?" Frances asked.

"Because I need more time to study, babe," Maxwell said, his brows now knitted. Noel felt uncomfortable for him, she had never heard Frances this inquisitive.

Whispering now as she was beginning to feel a growing tension, Noel said, "You know, I can always just go in my room, leave you two lovebirds alone, plus my food is getting cold, you know Chinese food is nasty when it is cold," she said nervously.

"No—stay—please—join us," Frances said as she stood staring into Max's eyes. She did not believe him.

Maxwell decided to change the subject. "Noel, do you smoke by chance?" he asked.

"No, I don't think I ever have. Like cigarettes?" she replied, her hands now hurting, she decided to place her food atop the counter next to Frances.

"No, like a joint. Weed?" Maxwell said to clarify. He remained standing next to Frances who was now engrossed in the conversation as she stood by the sink finishing her meal.

"Oh no," Noel said laughing.

"Would you like to?" Maxwell said. Frances interrupted,

"She would love to," she said. Noel looked bewildered.

"Plus, if we don't smoke, she's simply going to find some boring television show for us to watch where I'm going to end up falling asleep anyway," Frances teased.

Noel chuckled as she placed the remainder of her food in the disposal. Both Noel and Maxwell made their way to the sofa, where Maxwell removed four joints from his back pocket before taking a seat. Reclining, he took four puffs of the one he lit first and handed it to Noel,

"Okay so, you want to take a long hard pull, feel it in your lungs, let your lungs fill up and then exhale," he instructed. While Frances poured him and herself a glass of Cognac over ice.

Frances made her way to the sofa where she sat across from them, taking a pull and then following up with a sip of her alcohol, she proceeded to turn on the television.

"Max, can I ask you for some guy advice?" Noel said. Maxwell turning to face her as he replied,

"Of course, what's going on?" he said.

"If I didn't like a guy when he liked me, but like him now that he looks different and has a good job, how do I convince him that I like him now and want to be with him?" Noel asked, her eyes beginning to lower.

Maxwell chuckled and Frances continued flipping through the channels on the television.

"Well, I mean that depends. Um, men aren't stupid, so surely when you initially denied him you probably bruised his ego a bit. So, he knows that now that he's successful and he has a good job, he can have any woman he wants. Um, it's very rare that men like this find themselves going back to entertain the woman who bruised their ego," he said.

"So, you're saying there's absolutely nothing I can do?" Noel was growing sad.

"I mean, you can let him know how you feel about him and acknowledge the fact that you know you hurt him. Then, make up some nonsense about you not knowing any better back then and just hope that he buys it," he said nonchalantly.

"But what if that was the truth?" Noel said, yawning now as she took a sip of Frances's cognac. Frances turned to look at her,

"I hope you can handle all of that," she laughed. Turning to face her, Maxwell said,

"She can't, there's no way. But this should be interesting," he said, feeling the effects of his high. Maxwell pondered lighting a second joint after the first had finished and the ladies were reclining, enjoying their blissful state.

Maxwell took a few sips of his cognac, Noel stepped up and ran into the bathroom to shower. Frances and Maxwell exchanged a confused look,

"Want to go check on her?" he asked Frances, but Frances was in no mood. However, she checked. Noel was in the shower, the water steaming hot.

Shouting over the water pressure, Frances said, "Noey be careful, if you need me just let me know!" she said.

"I will," Noel slurred.

Twenty-five minutes later, Frances and Maxwell were cuddled together in the dark, both working on their second joint now watching a movie called *Doubles* on TNT. Noel emerged, gathering her things and making her way outside. Immediately, Frances sat upright.

"Where on earth are you going?" she asked.

"To heal an ego," she replied, shutting the door behind her. Frances and Maxwell exchanged a look after shrugging their shoulders before leaning in to kiss one another. Maxwell lifted her, diving her legs, placing her on top of his lap, minutes later the pair began to make love.

Noel was dressed in her most fitting ensemble; with fall approaching she felt the need to express her feelings one last time. She felt she had spent enough time running away from her problems. Her hair in a bun, her jeans a dark blue and her blouse a cashmere top she borrowed from Frances, she smelled of a sweet perfume. As she skipped along the sidewalk to the main road, she stretched her hand to signal a taxi. Once one arrived, she hopped inside,

"Can you bring me to a flower shop, please?" she asked. Later she'd arrived at a shop just a few minutes from the brownstone where she purchased two lilies. Heading back into the taxi, she was feeling foolish.

"Can we head down to the meatpacking district?" she asked as the driver drove slowly along the highway, allowing the smooth music of jazz to resonate through his speakers. Noel looked through the window, taking in the nightlife view of New York City.

The taxi arrived and although Noel had forgotten Kenneth's address, she remembered the look of his building. Making her way inside the lift after stumbling all over the rocks outside, she had forgotten her phone was in her back pocket as she struggled to lower the elevator door, causing it to fall. An older gentleman stepping towards her picked it up.

As she arose slowly holding the lilies, she extended her hand to retrieve what was hers from the polite stranger,

"Thank you," she said as she continued to admire him as he walked out of the building. A few minutes later, she was there, and she knew he was, too; she could hear the sensual music playing on the other side and wondered if he was with Jade, but she did not care. Noel banged on the steel door.

She banged again before finding herself face-to-face with Kenneth, who she was sure was going to shout obscenities before sending her on her way. Kenneth scoffed as her eyes widened with surprise.

"Um, so, yea, I have this big speech that I had all prepared in my head and, um, I'm really sorry to be here like this, I, um, I was robbed at gunpoint and that changed me," Noel stuttered. As the words left her mouth his expression changed from nonplussed to empathetic,

"Come in," he said, stepping aside. Kenneth smelled wonderful, this time he was wearing a black silk Versace top and bottom pajamas. Noel hesitated at first until he motioned with his hands for her to come inside.

"Do you want some hot cocoa?" he asked, sauntering into the kitchen as the door slammed behind her.

"The flowers I have are for you," Noel shouted as she turned to follow him, placing the flowers on the marble kitchen countertops.

"Wow, you bought a man flowers?" he asked.

Noel was nervous, her palms sweating now,

"Well, not just any man. I wanted to have a conversation with you. I am honestly amazed you even let me inside. I know how much you hate me," Noel said.

"I most definitely do not hate you, I think you're a beautiful woman, a bit too persistent for my taste, but considering our history I felt it only to right to be civil," he said as he stirred the hot cocoa, he was now going to serve Noel. She felt disrespected.

"I don't want you to pity me, Kenneth. I know that when we were younger, I hurt you and so I just wanted to apologize. I felt like, maybe because of that, you didn't want to truly have anything to do with me. So, I just wanted to say sorry for that," Noel explained.

"You traveled to my house in the dead of night to apologize to me for not liking me when we were seventeen; something that happened fourteen years ago, Noel? Come now, that's just silly," he said.

"No, it's not, you're still hurting obviously and I wanted to just make amends," Noel cried.

"Make amends, so because I won't cheat with you or leave my cheating girlfriend for you, you believe that it's because you broke my heart all those years ago?" Kenneth mocked. "I just want to make sure I am hearing you correctly." He grinned with one eyebrow raised.

"Okay, so when you put it like that, it sounds ridiculous, but I just thought..." she said, her eyes hanging low. Kenneth adored how innocent and awkward she was behaving.

"Noel, may I kiss you?" Kenneth asked. Noel lifted her head in excitement,

"Yea," she whispered. Kenneth made his way over to her, tilting her head back and running his fingers through her soft hair. Kenneth kissed her passionately on the lips. As he stared deep into her eyes, he asked, sensually massaging her temples.

"Tell me about the robbery. Did anyone touch you?" he said. Noel loved the way he asked her that, it was just as she thought. He would fight to protect her.

"Yes, they only took some of my shoes and jewelry and this guy hit me and I had to get stitches, but nothing too crazy," she said as she fell into a hypnotic state as he continued to caress her hair.

"You'll be safe from now on," he said kissing her once again. Stretching his arm under her thighs, he lifted her. Noel felt safe and warm as she wrapped her arms around his neck, burying her head into his chest whilst he carried her up the stairs to make love to her for the rest of the night. The next morning the sun came to greet her as she laid comfortably between the plush white blankets outstretched across the king-sized mattress, the sound of a woman clearing her throat startled her.

A woman stood above Noel, a maid, who looked unkind. Her face read disgust.

"The master has a car waiting for you downstairs to take you wherever you please," said the woman, her accent British.

Noel was appalled, she demanded to speak to Kenneth.

144

"Where is Kenneth?" she said as she scurried to get dressed. Struggling to find her bra, she continued to pace along the room, dragging the sheets over her body. The maid clearing her throat once again as she focused her eyes to the foot of the bed where her bra had been located.

Vehemently, Noel asked again, "Where is Kenneth?"

"Never does the master see the women off in the morning, that is my job. Please have your belongings ready to go within the next five minutes, our driver is quite impatient. Thank you," she said as she began making her way downstairs. Noel ran her fingers through her hair. She had no idea why Kenneth was treating her this way and she demanded answers.

Stomping down to the kitchen she wandered aimlessly searching for that maid, but she was nowhere to be seen, until suddenly she said,

"Ahem, ma'am, please, the driver is waiting" She was standing by the front door. Stepping outside, Noel thought it was best she did not embarrass herself further. She decided to walk a few blocks, passing the black town car with its tinted windows, she looked over to see the man from the night before jogging in a tracksuit by the railroad, and despite making eye contact, Noel decided it best to continue walking alongside the brick road.

CHAPTER FOURTEEN

As the night came the ladies bid their farewell to Angelo, all except Abigail. She was in no mood to converse as she now looked forward to basking in the enjoyment of his absence, choosing to enjoy the meal Angelo prepared after hours. Feeling like a pariah, Alicia retired to her quarters at seven, winding down; Frances enjoying a nice hot cup of tea, Alicia remained in her room reading through a novel she purchased from the book store near her condo.

The view from her back room frightening her as she watched what appeared to be shadows lingering just outside, darting back and forth. A deer, she thought, but no, it was the shadow of a man. He appeared suddenly. Standing on the outside of the sliding doors stood Angelo. Alicia could not help but chuckle, inspired by his pearly whites as she slid the door open, cringing from the sudden thrust of the cold air and the snowflakes that managed to seep inside. Stomping his feet to clean his boots, Angelo began removing his jacket, gloves, and hat.

"I couldn't stop thinking about you," he said. Alicia did not know how to react. She was no doubt smitten by him, but loathed the thought of infidelity, let alone engaging in the act itself. She took a few steps back, her pajamas, a bright red, slid across the floor. But Angelo was not persistent; the look in her eyes told him all that he needed to know.

"I am not here looking for us to do anything, I'd just like to spend some time with you," he continued. The lamenting look on her face was caused by thoughts swelling her mind about the choices she had made, replaying the signs she ignored, the man she once loved, and the reasons now she wished she had simply listened to her parents. Alicia was filled with regret but was determined to not allow her devastation to ruin a potential friendship.

"I think I would like that very much." She smiled.

Angelo was elated but careful not to let it show as he removed his pants—never one to wear his outside garments on the bed—climbing next to her as he examined the book she was studying.

"So you're into fantasy, huh?" he asked.

Alicia now staring into his eyes, nodded. Their conversation lasting all night, the room filled with nothing but laughter and genuine happiness, Alicia felt she had a friend in a house where she had made nothing but enemies.

Africa, overhearing the cackling, tiptoed to the bedroom door where she placed her right ear firmly on the wall to listen as both Alicia and Angelo chatted. It was a brief moment before Frances spotted her,

"What are you doing?" she said, holding a bottle of water to take to her bedroom. Africa was startled, preparing to lie as she searched her mind for the quickest possible answer.

"I think Alicia may be into the cook," she whispered.

"Well, that's none of our business," snapped Frances. Knitting her eyebrows, Africa sauntered over to her friend. Tugging her slowly, she gave her a hug.

"I just felt like you needed this," she said, laughing, and it was true. Frances needed it. Stepping back, Africa analyzed her friend. She was not herself, and so Africa demanded answers. She motioned for them to make their way over to the electric fireplace where they sat and talked for hours on end.

"The baby will just change our lives, I guess, and I don't think I'm ready to be a mommy," Frances cried. Africa leaned over to console her once again.

"Franny, I am your best friend, you can tell me anything, and something like this is nothing to fear. I will be there too, every step of the way," Africa emphasized. The expression Frances now had on her face was one Africa had never seen before,

"Franny, what is it?" she said firmly. "There's something you're not telling me, isn't there?" she said.

Frances, crying, was not in the right state of mind to continue the conversation and decided to end things abruptly,

"I'm going to go to bed. I feel tired," she said, standing and making her way to the top of the stairs where she went into her bedroom, closing the door behind her. Africa knew better than to berate her, so she sat quietly as Frances took her leave. Africa let out a long sigh.

The next morning the cabin felt perfect, the temperature was just right as the ladies stretched and Abigail made her way down to the living room where she extended her yoga mat and began her exercises. Noel, waking in her room, found herself feeling quite some confusion as she checked her phone to see there were no missed calls or texts from anyone. She thought it was poor reception, causing her to step into the hallway where she moved swiftly to the back window closest the rooms both Africa and Abigail occupied.

"No luck," she thought as she went back into her room to snuggle under the throw blankets and pillow. Just then, Africa appeared draped in her beige long johns and a cashmere blanket she packed from home. Noel now sat upright as she invited her into the bed. Africa ran, thrusting herself onto the mattress. Both Noel and Africa laughed.

"How much weight did you gain, woman?" Noel joked.

"Just a few pounds in the right places," replied Africa as she made herself comfortable. Noel had grown to be a stoic individual, learning the hard way that wearing your emotions on your sleeve is not always rewarding.

"Do you hate me?" Africa said, turning to face her. This question took Noel by complete surprise.

"Of course I don't hate you!" Noel said. But her tone was less than convincing. Africa proceeded with a follow-up question.

"Then why have you been so distant, Noey?" she asked.

Noel did not have an answer; rather she had a moment of nostalgia. "Do you remember when we were kids and Auntie Nora would leave us in the house while she went to the supermarket? We would take Jackson's water guns and make a huge mess inside spraying each other?" She laughed.

"Oh my goodness, yes, but you never got the whooping, only me. Mommy never hit you," Africa laughed.

"Your mom. My mother used to tear my butt up when I got home. Or the time we went to play in the treehouse and Jackson pushed you down the slide?" Noel laughed. Africa now sat upright.

"Why do you seem to only remember me getting abused?" she teased.

"Because no matter how hard anyone hit you, you always stood right back up and faced them, always. I've admired that about you my whole life. I am not like you at all. I find myself coerced into making decisions that I know go against everything I believe in, and yet I take on the challenge and fold when it is time to face the consequences. You don't fold," said Noel. Noel and Africa were now falling into a state of sadness; Africa could not put her finger on what was plaguing her cousin. She pondered how she could have made things better, and as she laid back a thought quickly came to mind.

"Let's go for a hike!" she said.

Noel rolling her eyes. "You see this melanin, I do not hike," she said as she slid back under the covers.

"Well, I am not trying to coerce you into anything, but I feel like we all need to do something that requires teamwork, sort of like a teambuilding exercise," she said. Noel quickly reverted back to her place of comfort under her blankets, head stuffed between two throw pillows, her ponytail now coming undone.

Africa caressed her. "Come on, Noey. I know if you agree, Frances will too. Abigail will come as long as I go, and Alicia, well..." Africa did not realize her facial expression had changed, an enigmatic look now causing Noel to seek answers.

"What is it? Why did you make that face?" Noel asked as she removed one of the throw pillows to expose both of her eyes.

"Nothing. We need to talk about hiking." Africa tried her best to deflect, but it was not working. Noel now sat upright once again.

"Africa, you have to tell me," Noel begged.

"I think she's sleeping with the cook," blurted Africa.

"No way!" Noel screeched as she turned to stare off into space. "Well, isn't that interesting," she said.

"Listen, I didn't tell you that for you to gloat, I am still disappointed in you," Africa said as she placed her hand on Noel's cheek, turning her face to meet hers. "We are so much better than second place, doesn't matter how good we think it feels in the moment," she continued.

Noel sympathized, her head now hung in shame. "I know I have to fix some things when we leave here, okay?" she said.

"Good! And now, teambuilding!" Africa shouted with glee. Noel buried her head back in between her throw pillows.

"Why are you bringing all that non-profit babble up here in the wilderness?" she said, her voice muffled.

"I didn't learn that from my job, I learned from therapy," Africa admitted.

Exposing her head again, Noel shot her an astonished look.

"Therapy?" she questioned.

"Yes, therapy. I go now twice a week, I told her I was coming up here and she recommended that we do teambuilding exercises to keep my mind as occupied as possible," Africa said.

"Wait, therapy? For what? Are you okay?" Noel was now worried.

"I was not okay for a while after Morris left. I had a nervous breakdown and then Franny and I started looking for therapists in the neighborhood and we found a good one for me," Africa said calmly. She was now gathering her blanket to take her departure.

"Morris left you?" Noel asked as she stood.

"Yep, for his trainer, um, about five months ago actually," Africa said, biting her bottom lip, her eyes beginning to well. She was now ready to go.

"So, he—he—cheated and left? I just—I don't understand," Noel said.

"Yes, the gym we frequented, he slept with his trainer, who knew he was in a relationship. She saw me with him almost every week and then, boom, he left. One night I got in late from a luncheon and saw his duffle bag packed sitting on the stairs. We had a brief conversation where he let me know that he was leaving, who he was leaving me for and told me he apologizes. You know, the key stuff," she said sarcastically.

It all made sense to Noel now. "That's why you were hard on me, huh?" she asked.

"Yes, that woman downstairs is hurting; she isn't a spiteful human being, Noel. She's a woman in pain, and if I had the chance to come face to face with that woman again, I probably would take it. Sometimes, people just have to see that we're human. The woman at home, the wife, the girlfriend, the woman with the kids, we are human, we exist and we hurt," she emphasized.

"How come I didn't know about this?" Noel asked.

"Before this trip, Noey, we hadn't spoken in months. I do take partial responsibility for that too, considering the phone does work two ways. But you were so happy and I couldn't bring myself to be happy for you considering all that was taking place in my own life, so for that I am sorry. I love you and I hope you do truly intend on making things right when you get home," she concluded, making her way out of the room and shutting the door behind her.

Abigail, who was now drenched in sweat wearing only her training bra and tights, rushed into Noel's room and playfully squeezed her, laughing.

"Gross!" Noel shouted. Overhearing their laughter, Frances emerged wearing an oversized robe, her hair uncombed.

"Glad to see everyone so happy," she said as she leaned on the threshold of Noel's door. Alicia and Angelo had awakened once Alicia heard the laughter of the women upstairs. She motioned for him to leave out of the back door and instructed him to wait as long as thirty minutes before knocking and returning to cook. Angelo complied, stepping lightly into his clothes and making his way out of the sliding doors.

After a delightful breakfast, both Alicia and Angelo could not seem to keep their eyes off one another as she volunteered to assist him with clearing the dishes. Africa instructed everyone to get dressed as they prepared for a morning of hiking up a trail that she was sure would have been easy to follow.

Minutes later the women were ready to go. Noel was reluctant but decided to entertain the idea. Stepping outside, it was cold, the wind chills vicious as Frances thought to herself,

"Am I dressed warm enough? What about the baby" She found herself thinking more of her unborn child despite not truly knowing if she was, in fact, with child. The idea of pregnancy was scary for her, but the thought of not being pregnant was now starting to seem scarier. Day by day she was finding herself smitten by the idea of motherhood, all while wondering how she would ever think to afford it. Noel watched as Frances would stare off into space as they now took steps up the hill just outside of their lodge.

Alicia wondered where they would be hiking to and began to grow concerned considering there was no real trail, no guide, and no way of returning home. She wanted to ask but thought it best to simply go along, inquiring would only give the women additional reasons to dislike her it seemed.

As the women treaded along the hills for what now felt like forty-five minutes, the view became apparent overlooking the city. Snow hedges, trees, and the roads all covered in snow. Frances threw her arm around Noel, growing weary. Noel could not help but simply bask in the beauty as Abigail and Africa spoke indistinctly, admiring the world before them. They began snapping photos as Africa decided to stand by the edge of a large foothill where the snow had begun turning to ice, expanding her arms and smiling as her sister snapped a photo of her.

Suddenly, she slipped, falling down the spiral bend, breaking her right ankle on impact once she landed at the bottom. Africa let out a sharp cry. Turning back, the ladies came rushing to her aid, stepping lightly down the mountain, Abigail fighting back tears,

"Africa, I'm coming!" she screamed as she continued to slide. Noel and Frances were now following her, Noel turning to face Frances, advising her not to come down, she feared the slope would be too dangerous for her to travel considering her condition.

"Frances, no!" she motioned. Africa continued to cry as her ankle burned. It was a catastrophe; the simultaneous screams and the tears were turning this brief moment of happiness into what felt like a nefarious plot to awaken every dormant emotion lying within them.

After breaking her ankle, Africa became a lachrymose woman who would not stop sobbing. She thought of many things as she watched her friends meticulously make their way down the slope. She thought of Morris, her recovery time, the amount of money she would lose by not being able to return to work. Africa thought of her life-changing and the thoughts were enough to cause her to feel overwhelmed.

Moments later, Noel, Alicia, and Abigail all stood above Africa, pondering how they would move her, Abigail, now face to face with her sister, removed her jacket and placed it firmly over her. Africa continued to cry.

"Someone needs to head back to the lodge and get help. We can't move her," Alicia said, her hand on her head. The ladies began to pace.

Noel grew annoyed. "Maybe that should have been suggested before we all came sliding down eight feet," she snapped.

"Okay, well, no one was thinking that we were all just worried," said Alicia. Standing still now, the women began to feel the temperature dropping. They were over an hour away from the lodge and the condensation appeared thicker with each breath they took. Alicia now stood with her arms wrapped around herself, Abigail trembling without her jacket on.

"I know you want her to be warm, but we all can't just stand here, someone has to go back down for help," Alicia advised.

"Of course, someone is going to go!" said Noel. Her low-pitched voice making it impossible for her anger to be heard, but Alicia felt it anyway.

"Hey, what the hell is your problem? I am only trying to help," she said.

"So then why don't you go back and get your boyfriend up here?" Noel snapped.

"Boyfriend?" Alicia took a deep breath before continuing. "Something is just wrong with you and now is not the time for this," she said.

Abigail was now growing impatient as she wiped the tears from her sisters' eyes, kneeling before her and attempting to keep her composure.

"Can you two stop it?" she cried. "I will go back, you two just stay here with her!" she instructed. Abigail began making her way back down the mountain—freezing now as she moved with purpose, her arms wrapped around her upper body. Alicia and Noel could not stand to look at one another, Africa now struggling to keep her eyes open as the pain grew unbearable and she felt too cold to speak.

Frances, kneeling at the top of the slope, said, "Hey, are you guys okay?"

Alicia began to feel out of place, far more now than she did a few days ago,

"This isn't your friend, you can go," said Noel.

"I am not leaving her," said Alicia.

"Why? You don't have to be here. It's bad enough you came on this trip to see me, the mistress, you saw me and decided to stay, you should have been gone," Noel scolded.

"Why on earth are you behaving like this?" said Alicia.

"Because your presence is making everyone uncomfortable, especially me. You weren't supposed to be here," Noel continued. Alicia was slowly beginning to lose her patience.

"I have not been a bother to anyone," she replied. After taking a long sigh, she decided it best to simply dismiss herself,

"Okay, you know what, I will go back to the house and just stay in my room," she said calmly as she attempted to climb back up the mountainside.

"No, don't go to the room, go home," Noel demanded as she now kneeled to comfort Africa, running her hands up and down her shoulders to generate warmth. "It's going to be okay, alright? Abby went to get someone," Noel advised her. Inside, Noel feared for her cousin. She wished there was something she could have done to ease her discomfort.

"Um, before I go, I just want to ask that you please stop seeing my husband," said Alicia.

Noel wanted so bad to scream. Instead, she said, "Go home!"

"I will not leave before it is time to do so, until I know you will stop seeing my husband," Alicia quarreled.

"Aren't you busy sleeping with the help now. Your husband must not be that important, so please spare me the theatrics," Noel sniped.

With the air now growing colder Frances decided to head down the slope. She gripped her hands firmly into the walls of the mountainside for balance. After ten minutes she had made it. She watched as Africa was beginning to turn red and despite Noel wrapping her arms around her, she could not stand by and do nothing.

"What can I do?" she said, making her way over. Noel surprised to see her,

"What are you doing down here?" she said. Alicia, now turning a beet red, took a seat on a rock as she used her hands to keep warm. Snowflakes began to fall.

"Where's Abby?" asked Frances.

"She went to get help," advised Alicia.

Noel rolling her eyes. "I asked her to leave," she said. A bewildered Frances did not know how it best to diffuse what was clearly a moment of tension between Noel and Alicia.

"She's been doing nothing but insulting me when her friend needs her the most," said Alicia.

"I would not be able to insult you if you simply weren't here. I mean, why do you insist on staying here?" Noel said. One hour now passed and the ladies now worried for the safety of Abigail, as the snow falling began to pick up—sticking to the ground and impairing their vision.

"Noel, you have to calm down, Africa needs us," said Frances.

"Exactly my point," Alicia agreed.

"Just stop talking," Noel reprimanded her.

"Listen, I am a grown ass woman, you do not get to speak to me that way!" Alicia shouted.

"So then go home to your cheating husband and leave me and my friends alone. You're a forty-something-year-old woman chasing after a younger woman for sympathy," Noel said. Frances was growing impatient as she blew breath into her hands and used her mittens to wipe the snot now dripping from her nose.

"You guys have to stop," Africa mumbled. Alicia was now speechless, but not for long.

"Your haughtiness is unbearable," Alicia said. She couldn't stand the idea of being rejected by both her husband and his mistress, so she now decided it best to leave. "I will pack my things and go." Noel, Frances and Africa remained quiet, much to Alicia's disappointment.

"Great, don't forget to screw the help one last time on your way out," Noel said.

"Noel! Jesus!" Frances cried.

"We don't all have to divide our legs for a man to be loved or respected," said Alicia as she struggled to now climb back to the top of the trail. Fighting back tears, she felt alone, as though she had no one.

Frances turning to face Noel and could not recognize her friend. She had no idea who she was becoming, she was different, now, no longer the timid, kind woman she met two years ago.

Flashback
Kenneth devastated her, he broke her, and she now felt foolish, used, and lied to. She began to question whether or not she was good enough for him. One month later, Noel no longer went looking for work, she was slowly beginning to wonder if she should simply head home, back to Seattle, back to where it was safe. But she began to worry as the money she traveled with was now slowly beginning to dwindle away and she had no luck finding a job in the tough New York City streets. Fifteen interviews in the past two months, none of which had considered her for a callback.

As she pondered this, she noticed Frances preparing for the start of the school year. She was excited, and Noel was excited for her. Frances loved working with children. Teaching had long been a dream of hers since the tender age of twelve when she would line up her Barbie dolls and stuffed animals, teaching them all that she had learned that day in school.

Frances saw teaching as more than a job; it was an opportunity to educate the next generation and was her contribution to society. By 3:15 that Saturday afternoon, Frances made her way inside, stumbling with a large box filled with binders, pencils, markers, and crayons. Noel, seeing her struggle, decided to help as she prepared dinner.

"You're such an inspiration," she said once Frances settled inside.

Frances took deep breaths. "Inspiration? I teach third graders; I think the word you're looking for is suicidal." Frances laughed.

"Well, either way, I think it's commendable," said Noel as she stirred the pot to a recipe she found online and decided to try; pepper steak with garlic mashed potatoes. Although she was failing miserably, she was not hard on herself.

Frances sorting through her supplies bellowed. "Hey, so, I was thinking, I know it's been a bit tough on you finding work and now that school is starting, maybe you can speak to Amber about possibly working at the boutique," she said. Noel was elated,

"Oh, my goodness, that would be fantastic! Do you think she would let me?" asked Noel.

"Of course, I will speak to her tomorrow first thing," Frances said, smiling.

That night the fire escape outside rattled as the neighborhood kids ran up and down, playing what was heard to be a game of tag. Frances decided to retire early, prepping her course notes as the smooth sounds of Jazz tempo bellowed through her *Beats* headphones. Their modern sized millennial home felt cozy inside, the temperature just right, and as Noel lay on her back-playing games on her cellular phone, she realized just how much she missed her mother.

It was the laughter of the children playing just outside that brought along the nostalgia, remembering like it was yesterday the struggles of being the only girl; two boys in the house and one girl proved itself to be nothing short of cuts or bruises. But thank goodness Jennifer knew all the home remedies that had her little girl back up and running with the boys in no time. Noel feared she would not be liked as a child because she was a hoyden back then. Noel would find herself pilfering clothes from her eldest brother to wear to school. The over-sized shirts always two sizes too big, her hair in barrettes, her jeans baggy and her sneakers the off-brand kind. Jennifer never spoiled her children into valuing materialistic things, despite the fact that she had married a man who over time acquired a great deal of wealth.

Both Jin and Jennifer remained humble, as did their children, learning from an early age the importance of hard work, and although Noel did not miss how overbearing her mother was, she missed the life lessons she would every so often bestow upon her. It was the simple things, the things she wished she could go back and experience anew, such as running up to the tree-house and playing alongside her brothers as they all created a mess they knew there would be consequences for. She welcomed the reprimanding. Jennifer did not separate her children when punishing them, they each dealt with their punishments amongst one another, sure, they conversed and they laughed, but she did not mind, although at times she would pretend to. All that mattered was that they bonded.

Lifting her window Noel sat on the heater, staring outside. The Brownstone held many tenants and although the ladies occupied the first floor just above the cemented staircase leading up to their front door, the view of the sun setting just over the Manhattan buildings was absolutely priceless. A home filled with peace, burning incense, smooth jazz on a daily basis and the sweet smell of Pine-sol every Saturday morning after Frances and Noel completed their weekly chores made her feel grateful.

Noel held a bachelor's degree in communications—before she had any idea what exactly she wanted to do with her life. Cradled now in the fetal position, she continued to wonder,

"What are my goals?" she thought as she reached for her journal. Setting the ringed notebook along her lap, flipping the pages to a blank page, she began her journal entry with *Dear Noel*. That evening she wrote over ten pages on what she had now aspired to be. At the tender age of twenty-seven, her life had no direction, she had no real goals, and then it hit her,

"Why on earth did I even come to New York?" she thought. The epiphany causing her to scribble harder, longer, rigid, trying to find new ways in which she could dissect the emotions she was feeling. It was a decision she made out of anger, wanting to get away from her parents and wanting the life she had always seen on television that the celebrities lived, the fast life with the nice clothes—she had no idea she would receive it, despite it coming with a price. As she continued to write, she continued to wonder whether or not she was good enough or made to be anything more than a simple leech.

"Where is my sense of independence?" she thought as she scribbled some more, consumed by her own thoughts, she was drowning out the sound of Frances bellowing her name.

"Noel!" she cried from the bathroom door threshold. Frightened, Noel dropped her writing utensil, climbing over her bedroom mattress she made her way to the adjoining door, swinging it open she watched a partially naked Frances now conditioning her afro, preparing for its evening style.

"Amber called and I asked her about the job, she said yes!" Frances said, smiling past the bathroom shower curtain. Noel leaped for joy, happy that she would now begin to generate some form of income. However, she was also disappointed. After outlining her goals and reasons for being in the big city, she realized she was settling, but she dared not express this.

"Thank you, Franny," she said, hugging her, careful not to slip.

"Yea, so she said to be there tomorrow at nine, bring two forms of identification and she will then discuss pay," Frances continued.

"Should I wear anything in particular?" Noel inquired.

Frances shot her a questionable look. "Why don't you go business casual for the first day, I think that's a safe bet," she advised as she wiped her face profusely with the tucked portion of her towel—the conditioner dripping to her face. Noel could not bring herself to show more excitement, she felt her life was flashing before her eyes, no career, no steady boyfriend, and now a full-time job working for a boutique where she would no doubt be making minimum wage. As Noel decided to settle with her thoughts, she smiled at Frances, closing the door behind her, leaving as she continued the fight against her afro.

Noel, removing her clothes, then began preparing for bed.

She slept like an angel, or what she would consider a sleeping angel. Forgetting to set her alarm the night before, she feared the worst—that she had overslept. Luckily that was not the case as she checked her alarm clock and the time read 7:05 a.m. The boutique only twenty minutes away with no traffic— she hopped out of bed and turned on the shower, careful not to awaken Frances and from the looks of the toilet seat, Maxwell too.

Noel rolled her eyes as she placed the toilet seat back down and began preparing for her first day.

That morning she felt rejuvenated, smiling now from ear to ear as the cab dropped her off curbside amidst the angry mob of drivers behind them. Noel began to think of this opportunity as a new beginning now—a place where she could earn some income and then utilize the income to build her credit and begin looking for an actual career,

"A milestone," she thought feeling optimistic. Once inside, she called for Amber who appeared wearing a pair of bell-footed tan dress pants, an orange blouse, and a gentlemen's tie she had loosely wrapped around her neck in a fashionable manner. Her skin glowing, Noel opted in for a pair of black dickies, a cardigan, and a V-neck t-shirt along with a pair of boat shoes she could afford. In her hand she held a Ziplock bag with her social security card and non-driver's license identification card. Amber had merely caught a glimpse of Noel as she walked over to lock the door from the inside. However, turning to face her, she said,

"What on earth are you wearing? This isn't your first day at McDonald's," Amber said. "Oh my goodness, and we open in fifteen minutes," she panicked. Noel continued to watch in horror as Amber rustled around the boutique tossing together pieces,

"Size!" she yelled from the rear of the store.

"Um, I am a size small in shirts and a size four to six in pants. A size seven shoe," Noel answered nervously. She was concerned she had made a bad impression on her first day, just then Amber emerged.

"Here are some old clothes we didn't sell out at the beginning of spring so head to the bathroom, try them on, and then meet me in the office," Amber instructed. Noel did as she was told as she fumbled to the rear of the boutique where she tried on the satin grey short-sleeved jumpsuit which zipped in the middle. It was accompanied by a necklace, a pastel rose-colored blazer, and a pair of nude stilettos. Noel turned and took a hard look in the mirror, her eyes appeared to be puffy.

She took a piece of tissue and began to dampen them just as Amber called, "Noel, we're opening." Noel wondered if this was a part of her probationary period, quivering as she stepped timidly back to the front desk. With customers now making their way inside, Noel stood greeting them, one lady complimenting her just before making her way to the fragrances. Amber looked her up and down, breathing a sigh of relief.

"Great, you look good. This is the new dress code," she said. Noel stuttered,

"But I don't think I can afford this right now," she said, tugging on the garments.

"There's nothing to afford as long as you work here. Besides, the clothes are to be returned to the warehouse anyway, it's kind of free grab. Now, don't get carried away. Plus, a lot of the designers that we carry typically don't want the merchandise back if it doesn't sell. So, before they head to a department store and start to look very cheap, you can take a stab at them first," Amber advised.

"Is this for real?" she asked, chuckling.

"Yes, one of the perks for working at a high-end store in Manhattan. Once the store clears out, I will take you to the back to go over the training videos. So just sit tight and for now, try to assist as many people as you can," instructed Amber.

Noel took pride in the fact that she was a fast learner and despite never having worked in customer service, she found the experience quite pleasant. The clients were polite, the environment clean, and as long as she made her rounds and offered her assistance to as many men and woman as she possibly could in the boutique, she lessened the amount of work she had for herself once her shift ended. After one week, what she would have expected to be a tedious place of business had proven itself to be far too rewarding.

Noel even began receiving tips from the clients she assisted with fragrances, lingerie, and shoes. One lady had given her seventy-five dollars after shopping for less than thirty minutes, and at twenty-six dollars an hour, she immediately found herself becoming comfortable with the idea of working for the boutique far longer than she had initially intended. Fervid about her work, Noel arrived one hour before her shift every single day and left one hour after her shift ended. She made sure the boutique was immaculate and by week two, clients had begun asking for her by name. With Frances nearing her last day, the girls contemplated how they would celebrate and decided on a big dinner.

With all the tips Noel had begun to earn, she was proud to say she could finally afford a decent meal. After three weeks she earned her first paycheck. It surprised Noel to learn how much New Yorkers were taxed, this bothered her slightly, but she realized what she lost in taxes she made up for in tips. Day by day her outfits changed, one look after the other, and they were all simply mesmerizing. Amber was now on the hunt for a new cashier considering how well Noel was doing with client services. She decided perhaps it best to not distract her with much more than that.

One morning as the sun began to shine, Noel realized she had only a few more weeks of pleasant cardigan wearing weather as she approached the boutique. Entering the alarm code after letting herself inside, she turned her back to place her lunch on the glass countertop. Returning to the entrance to turn on the lights, she felt her legs giving way, and yet she remained standing as Nathan wrapped his arms around her—her eyes widened.

"Why? Just why are you here?" she said. Her long-sleeved fuchsia colored peplum top and matching pencil skirt made it hard for her to maneuver as quickly as her mind had hoped.

"I missed you and I thought we could talk," said Nathan. He was draped in a three-piece suit and tie—his signature.

"No, we cannot talk. I almost died the last time I was with you; I am trying to move on and you should too," she demanded as she attempted to lead him back to the front door.

"No, I've been driving past here for months and yes, I know you've been avoiding me. If I were you, I would avoid me, too. But Noel, I love you. I love you and I want to fix it. What happened in my apartment had nothing to do with me and I had no control over that. I know you believe me. I mean, those guys beat me pretty bad," he said.

Noel believing him to be sincere. Taking notice the scars that were now on his face, none of which took away from his beauty. Noel was now stunned,

"Love? How? You barely spent any time with me, you moved me to your apartment and then left me there with the driver. You weren't around to even get to know me. What's my favorite color, do you even know?" she inquired. "I mean, it's practically unrealistic." Noel knitted her brows as she threw her hands in the air as if to accept defeat—she felt she had lost because she did like Nathan, but not enough. She then turned to proceed to unlock the door,

"Your favorite color is yellow, um, you told me on our first date. We had champagne; your tolerance was pretty low. And again, the night we made loved, as we laid next to each, I asked you some questions. You said yellow because in Seattle where you're from after it rains, the school you went to...their garden only had dandelions, and from a young age you would always admire their bright colors and that helped you forget about how dark and gloomy most of the days were," he said. Her back still to him, Noel now lifted her head.

"You put my life in danger," she whispered. Her heart was torn.

Standing behind her with his hands atop her shoulders, Nathan whispered, "Noel, I promise you it will never happen again. I've moved, there's security everywhere, I will have a new closet of clothes delivered for you by tomorrow morning if you just leave this behind and come home with me," he said.

She was shocked. "Again?" She turned. "You want us to do this again? I don't know if I can. I am definitely not leaving what I have here," she said.

"Okay, I will not force you by any means to give up your independence, I like that about you, too. Whatever makes you happy is what I want for you. Just tell me," he said as he lifted her hands to kiss them softly. Noticing her nails needed to be done, Nathan reached into his back pocket where he removed his wallet and a black AmEx card, handing the card to Noel, he said,

"Nails, clothes, everything is on me," he said, sniffing her perfume. "I like your hair like this, your makeup, I just—Noel, I need you. I promise you I do," he said, caressing her body. Noel trembled.

Noel could not believe the words that left her mouth. "Pick me up at five," she said with her head hung in shame.

After no demur, Nathan accepted. "I will see you at five," he said as he kissed her cheeks softly. Taking two steps back, he waited for Noel to unlock the doors as he slid outside, disappearing now into the large crowd. Nathan was admiring the woman Noel was blossoming into, her hair now combed into a tight bun, her makeup now matching her complexion. She was beginning to take pride in her appearance far more than she did when they first met.

As the day pressed on, Noel felt the pressure of Frances's eyes on her.

"You seem really preoccupied today," said Frances as she cleaned the glass countertop and Noel folded clothes on the display table closest the door. Amber was away steaming; Noel could not hold it back any longer.

"Seattle bae came by this morning," she whispered to Frances as she casually continued folding. Frances, throwing down the cloth and the spritz bottle, made her way around the counter to stare into Noel's eyes,

"Promise me you are not going to re-open that door, Noel. Please, he almost had you killed!" she emphasized. But she had come to know Noel all too well now, and considering the nature of her facial expression, she knew her mind was already made up.

"He did not almost have me killed. He was robbed at gunpoint just as I was," she said defensively.

"I am calling Africa since you clearly won't listen to me," said Frances.

Noel shook her head in annoyance. "What? Africa isn't my mother," she snapped.

"Well, she's the closest thing you have out here to family, and if I can't talk you out of making a terrible decision on my own, then I have to include her," cried Frances. Noel was now irritated. She knew her shift was soon ending and so she decided to retire to the break room where she freshened up and awaited her ride.

Frances, with the phone to her ear, waited patiently for Africa to answer. She stood by the door, staring through the glass when a black stretch limo appeared, pulling over across the street. A now furious Frances wanted to approach him, she wanted to scream, but then she realized Noel was an adult, and although she had come to love her like a little sister, it was simply not her place to interfere.

Noel made her way out of the break room, clocking out on the register on time for the first time in weeks, she sauntered her way through the doors and past Frances who was standing wearing a pair of vintage boots, kimono-inspired cardigan, turquoise necklaces, distressed jeans, and a denim button down. Frances froze, she wanted to grab her, she wanted to do something, instead, she watched Noel climb into the back of what appeared to be hell. Immediately the car took off. Frances stood looking out the door like a sad child watching their parents leave, just then her phone rang. It was Africa returning her call.

CHAPTER FIFTEEN

Once the rescue team arrived, the ladies hitched a ride back to the lodge while Africa was taken down the mountain to get the medical attention she needed. Abigail insisted on staying on with her, promising the remaining ladies that once her sister was well, she would return—she too needed treatment for her moderate hyperthermia. Inside the lodge, the fireplace cracked as Angelo quickly approached them once the door creaked open,

"Abigail could have gotten sick!" he said. "How are the rest of you feeling? I can have another medic up here to check you guys out," he said as he stumbled around to assist the ladies with removing their backpacks, shoes, coats, hats and gloves, but before he concluded, Frances began to sob hysterically. A frightened Noel turned to face her, cradling her on the ground. She sat hugging Frances as they rocked back and forth. Frances could not figure out why she was so emotional, she was upset, she was hurt, but it was unlike her to cry. Noel had never seen Frances sob like this and knew this must have been an unfamiliar feeling for her.

Moments later there was silence. Angelo was not familiar with how to handle such situations, he was not going to leave the women alone, but decided on giving them their much-needed space. He was saddened, for in his short time there he had seen and heard more devastating news than anything worth celebrating. Just then, Frances arose, making her way upstairs into her bedroom. Once inside she closed the door as she dialed a number on her telephone keypad.

After three rings, a husky voice said, "Hey gorgeous, I take it you're having the time of your life!" he emphasized. But Frances could not respond, instead she continued to sniffle, holding the phone tightly to her ear, she cried as she sat on the floor now curled into the fetal position.

"Baby, baby, what's wrong," he said. "Franny, babes, did someone hurt you?" he shouted.

"I—just—want—to come home, I need to come home—please," she cried. Her tears now beginning to create a puddle on the floor. "Africa—hurt her—ankle, baby—she broke it down the mountain and no one is happy, everyone is honestly just so miserable," she continued.

"Baby, I will try my best to come and get you. I promise. I promise, I am so sorry about your friend," he said, trying to console her. But he was at a loss for words.

"And, I think I'm pregnant," she whispered as she sniveled, closing her eyes tightly.

"I will be there first thing in the morning. I love you!" he said. Through her tears, she felt relieved.

Flashback

That evening, Nathan took Noel for a long drive to the Hudson where there was a five-star restaurant just overlooking the river and the sun was beginning to set. The car ride filled with laughter, kisses, champagne, and memories Noel missed dearly. So much so, she vowed to herself to never abandon this lifestyle again.

"Destitution is not for me," she thought, and how could it be? Just when she found herself settling for a lifestyle without financial freedom, here came Nathan to remind her that things did not have to be that way. Once they arrived, Nathan walked over to her door where he opened it, extending his hand. As she placed hers into his, Noel stepped outside, feeling like a princess again.

The Italian restaurant had a red carpet laid out at the entrance and double doors opened by the restaurant staff; the doors heavy, roaring when moved. Nathan placed his hand on Noel's lower back, causing her to clench her clutch tightly, his touch felt foreign. As they made their way inside, Nathan gave his name and they waited patiently to be taken to their table. Standing by the hostess stand, the doors growled behind them once again, Noel continued looking forward when she heard Nathan gasp slightly.

The couple behind them chattered indistinctly.

"But babe, that tie, I told you, you should have worn white," she teased.

"I love it when you try to dress me, you always think you're right, don't you?" he said, tickling her. Her laughter began to resonate by the entrance, just then Noel turned quickly to face Kenneth. There he was, standing there looking down on her with Jade on his arms, laughing and flirting as though she was no one of significance. Noel lost her breath for a moment, a long moment, so long she thought she would pass out, but she caught herself.

"Wow," the woman said, teasing almost. Noel fought the need to faint; she dreaded the embarrassment of it all, but little did she know the embarrassment was going to come either way.

"Hello there, aren't you Jade, from the Hilton on Americas?" said Nathan, playing coy.

"Yes, I am Jade," she said as she pulled Kenneth closer to her, placing one hand on his chest and another behind his back. Nathan turned around as Noel wondered where on the earth the hostess had gone and what could possibly have been taking her so long.

"This is Noel," said Nathan. Noel could not face either of them, with her head held down she watched as her feet in her heels were beginning to shake, in her mind she begged them to please stop. Her palms now getting sweaty as her clutch slipped from her hand, tumbling onto the floor, making a firm landing. As she leaned down to pick it up so did Kenneth, causing them both to bump one another on the head.

"Ow," they said in unison.

"I am so sorry," she bellowed, careful not to touch him as she extended her hand as a reflex but not as quickly as Jade, pulling him back.

Noel was so nervous she caught herself swatting away flyway's that were not there, every inch of her hair strands were tightly pulled into a high-top bun. Jade kept a plastic smile on her face while Kenneth remained unreadable, he simply looked at both Nathan and Noel, his facial expression, however, said nothing. Once the hostess returned a pile of sweat was now brewing on Noel's forehead, leaning over to whisper to Nathan, she asked,

"Can we please leave?"

Nathan turned as he noticed the fearful look on her face, leading him to believe there was something she was nothing telling him,

"Is everything okay?" he asked as he placed his hands on her shoulders, surprised to feel the goosebumps along her arms. Knitting his brows as Jade and Kenneth now made their way past them. Trailing behind the hostess. Noel felt like a fool, a woman in love with an emotionally unavailable man, a feeling she thought she could mask by being with another, but instead, the old wounds had re-opened and now her emotions were heightened. Watching them together again, and realizing now that Kenneth had chosen to forgive Jade despite having to confront her on who Nathan truly was, was just about enough for Noel. Kenneth loved Jade, and there was nothing more to the story, the sad truth was now something for her to face.

"Would you like us to simply do take out, my love?" said Nathan. Noel fought back tears as she remained deep in thought. Her back turned, Noel heard the voice of Kenneth behind her,

"Listen, not sure what is going on with your tables, but we'd love to have you both join us for dinner if you're interested," he said.

Noel turning quickly to beg for Nathan to say no, but instead, he said, "Hell yeah, sounds like a plan to me." Both men shook hands, embracing one another like two frat boys.

Noel scoffed, the hostess now growing impatient. But with wealth comes power, and it doesn't matter how loud and obnoxious you are, your actions will never be called to question as long as you hold some kind of elite status in the hustle and bustle streets of Manhattan. Nathan continued to smile as he took Noel by the hand, never facing her, tugging her along as they paced behind Kenneth, and he behind the host.

The walk was long and Noel was already feeling exhausted from working a long shift earlier that morning, but she kept up the best she could. After all, Nathan did not care. The inside resembled a cathedral, the high ceilings and the glass decorated windows, the theme, volcanic. There was a large fountain filled with red water, the room dimly lit. Once upstairs she saw a large room reserved specifically for Kenneth and Jade. Nathan had not made reservations, but it was safe to assume management was going to accommodate him either way. Just overlooking the Hudson, Noel took a seat closest to the window where her daydreaming would be mistaken for simple admiration. Jade too had her qualms about this arrangement, but she did not allow them to show.

"So Nathan, what do you do for a living?" Jade asked as she unfolded her napkin, placing it meticulously across her lap. The waiter now poured them each a glass of water.

Nathan smiled, he loved opportunities like this where he could gloat about his accolades. "I am the CFO for an intellectual property firm called Benner, Brown and Motley PLLC, been there around twenty years now. It's a tough job, but that's why they have me," he laughed as he took a sip of water.

"That firm sounds familiar. Perhaps we've worked together before," said Kenneth.

"Oh, I doubt it," Nathan quickly interrupted.

Appalled, Kenneth asked, "Well, why is that?"

Nathan shrugged. "I just don't see what kind of business you could offer a place like my firm," he said. Noel now took a large gulp of water as she looked around the empty room, praying for the waitress to make her appearance. She did not.

Kenneth chuckled. "I'm not here to measure dick sizes, perhaps I may be mistaken," he said humbly.

"No, babe, you aren't," Jade interrupted. Noel was unclear; was the mistress upset? She knew her place as the girlfriend and had come to accept Nathan's marriage playing a huge role in their relationship, however, she couldn't figure out why Jade seemed angry. "Cookie, remember your firm put on that Hedge Fund operation for their firm about a year ago? Because of you, they tripled their initial company investments in one night when you created a marketing plan that was golden. You called it the Reign of Assets, and the assets sure did reign. Nathan himself walked away that night with what, a two-million-dollar bonus, all because of you?" She turned to kiss him.

Nathan was speechless. "Is that right?" he asked leaning forward. "Well, please accept my apologies for having been so quick to judge and of course, judge so incorrectly. Speaking of which, Jade, my memory seems to be working as well, that seems to be the night we crossed paths for the first time too, no?" he said with a sinister smirk. Nathan was ready to get to know Kenneth, although he despised him for being with the woman he wanted for himself.

Kenneth, on the other hand, was lost in his thoughts as things began to make sense. The timeline. Knitting his brows, he turned to face Jade,

"Quite honestly, I did forget about that. I am not sure why. But yes, Nathan, you are THE Nathan," he said with extra emphasis. Noel now turning to face him as she realized he was turning red. Just then the waitress appeared.

"Have you all had a chance to look over our drink menu?" she asked politely. Everyone remained quiet until Jade said,

"Yes." She smiled before Kenneth arose.

"No," he said as he began making his way down the stairs. A timid Jade did not know whether to follow him or allow him to go on without her. Noel continued looking around, mad now that she was not home in bed, resting, curled up with Chinese food and Candy Crush. She was soon beginning to feel this fast life was not worth the pain, neither emotionally nor physically. She arose as well, Nathan turning to face her as she struggled to pass him. The waitress continued standing above, awaiting a response,

"I am sorry, my boyfriend seems a bit upset, I think I have to go," Jade said as she shot Nathan a look of worry. He nodded to her in understanding.

Meanwhile, Noel had made her way down the winding staircase and found herself standing outside alongside the valet, waiting patiently for Nathan, who after about twenty minutes had finally shown up with a plastic bag in his hand.

"Is that food?" Noel asked.

"Yea, I got you the scallops," he said as he climbed into the back seat of the stretch limo, not a care in the world. Noel finally removing her shoes, her feet feeling worn down. She desperately wanted to climb into bed. Checking her phone she noticed over seventeen missed calls from the ladies and text messages all begging her to contact them. She decided to create a group chat where she collectively informed everyone that she was fine and simply went for dinner.

In the meatpacking district, Kenneth opted for the stairs rather than the elevator lift. He needed to clear his mind. Jade entered behind him. Once inside the loft, he slammed the door, which Jade later opened with caution.

"Are you going to tell me what your problem is?" she demanded. Their ride home silent.

Kenneth turned as he removed his blazer and began to unbutton his pants. Pouring himself a drink, he took a sip before sitting on the couch.

"How long were you sleeping with that guy?" he was so eerily calm. It was a trait Noel had come to love about him. Jade, however, feared this tone.

"What are you talking about?" she said, standing by the door, her arms folded.

"You know what I hate more than a liar, is a liar who continues to lie even when they're caught, now, how long have you been sleeping with that old guy?" he reiterated.

"We talked about this and we both agreed to move on because we both made mistakes," she said.

"No, no, I didn't ask the tough questions then because I couldn't stand to know the answers, I knew it would kill me. But now, now, I just want to know how long," he said. "Answer me, Jade. Four years, right, and I've never seen the inside of your apartment. Maybe FaceTime your mom and your dad, so it was just about the money and then when you found someone richer you decided to climb under him?" he said as he stood, biting his bottom lip as he threw his glass across the room. Jade covering her head as she began to whimper, the contents flying everywhere, some of which landing on her clothes and hair.

"I am so sorry!" Jade cried. Kenneth remained standing by the large window, staring out into the night. Kenneth, the alpha male, had always been a man of few words. He never allowed his enemies to one-up him because he had come to understand the laws of power and how they truly worked in his favor. Appearing to always be relaxed, Kenneth was constantly smiling, studying, and looking for new innovative ways to prey on the cognitive minds of others. What he did not expect to do was in fall in love so fast and so hard for a woman who had been deceiving him.

Kenneth envisioned a future with Jade, moving out of the big city and relocating somewhere up north to raise the beautiful children they would make. Jade made him a dreamer. Before her, he was stoic because he had come to believe that the only way to make it in the big city was to drown out the background noise and simply focus on your career—and he did—but not for long.

"But what is having all the money worth when there is no one to share it with?" he had begun to think, and then there she was, making her way towards him, serving cocktails at a Gala for a non-profit organization his office had been hired to work for. Jade was simply trying to make ends meet, she told him, advising him of her life with her roommate who she loved dearly but clearly leaving out the details of her relationship. But Kenneth thought he had met the woman of in his dreams, the kind of women in both college and high school he wished he could have dated, and now here she was, choosing another.

It was his ego more than anything that felt destroyed, not his trust for women in the future, but the fact that he thought he had done everything the right way, the way a gentleman was supposed to, he wanted to make an honest woman out of Jade, yet she was never an honest woman to herself. As he took a seat, finally, his bare chest rising and falling with every breath, he parted his legs.

Leaning forward as he placed his elbows on his knees and his hands under his chin, he asked the tough questions,

"What is it about that man that makes him worth losing me?" he asked. His heart was rupturing, the conversation he tried so hard to avoid months ago because he had convinced himself it was a one-night stand and he knew that he and Jade were destined, tonight was the test, the one he thought she would pass. Kenneth spent years practicing the laws of power, one of which: play a sucker, to catch a sucker—seem dumber than your mark, and now he was ready to move on, but not before he learned the truth.

Jade was now on the floor, sobbing, crawling over to him, her hands and feet dragging as the mascara ran down her cheeks and the tears seeped through her lips.

"I just want us to move on from this, and you said you did too," she cried. "Nathan is not for me, I love you, I swear I do," she begged.

However, Kenneth corrected, "No, Nathan likes Noel, you are settling with me. Jade, you had a look in your eyes tonight, there was some jealousy there. You were touching me far more than you normally do, oh and let's not forget that defining moment when you just had to let your ex-paramour know that I am not as broke as he thought I was, for the chance to vaunt because you cared what he thought of me," Kenneth said. "Get out," he continued. But Jade did not budge.

"I don't have anywhere to go and it's very late," she said, wiping her tears and the snot from her nose. Jade knew by exposing Nathan to his wife all of the assets made accessible to her would have been seized, she had a cushion anyway—Kenneth. But now it seemed things were taking an irrevocable turn. Her makeup had completely gone. But Kenneth did not care.

"Go to Nathan's," he said now, making his way up to his master bedroom leaving Jade downstairs in the dark to wallow in her own self-pity.

The Tribeca duplex condo Nathan now occupied was 4,200 square foot with three bedrooms and two bathrooms, accompanied by 24-foot ceilings. It was more than Noel could have stomached. Unfurnished, it was an open space of pure magnificence. The condo was well lit with incandescent light bulbs in the ceilings, standing lamps with beige marble tiling and wood surfaces. Noel glided her hands across the patio doors as she continued making her way around the room. Nathan now standing in the center with the food he purchased removing his coat, placing it delicately on the ground as though it had been a blanket, he then took a seat. Motioning for Noel to join him, she turned and, although difficult, she managed to take a seat in her pencil skirt.

"Do you know why it's still empty in here?" Nathan asked. Noel had not a clue; she was simply just amazed by its beauty,

"No," she said innocently.

"I want to make this feel like home for you. I bought this condo about three weeks ago since it took some time to sell the Park Avenue apartment and the insurance claim is still processing. But, in the meantime, I want you to decorate. If you need to hire someone to assist you, let me know and I'll have my assistant find you, someone," he said, taking a bite into his crab legs.

Noel remained speechless.

"How did you even know I would come back?" she asked.

"Because I know you feel what I feel," he said, staring into her eyes as he wiped his hands. Noel lowered her eyes because she could not decide whether or not that was entirely true. But for the sake of conversation, she went along with it. Noel had not loved Nathan, she lusted after him, it was easy for her to fall into his bed, but it was becoming harder for her to imagine herself staying there. Noel stood, undressing now, slowly, as she removed her skirt and her top, unzipping them from the back. She unwrapped her hair bun, letting her hair fall. Her silky hair now bouncing past her shoulders as Nathan continued to work on his crab legs, sucking the meat out and using his tongue to catch the sauce he used for dip.

Naked now, she went on her knees where she arched her back. Removing his pants, Nathan reclined back as Noel removed his penis and began to perform oral, her head moving up and down as she placed her hands alongside his waist. Nathan had yet to find a woman better than Jade when it came to fellatio, but Noel was now proving herself a strong contender.

CHAPTER SIXTEEN

The clocks read 10:14 a.m. as the doors and windows bang loudly. But there was no one around to answer them. The voices on the other side calling out to no prevail, but could not prematurely depart due to their contractual obligations. Winter was beginning to feel more brutal than ever as the cabin lights were turned down and the fireplace lost its spark. Seemingly almost symbolic. The sun rising barely granting them mercy as the jeep came revving up the mountainside, but as Abigail sat inside, she could think of nothing and no one else but her sister; overridden with guilt that she had returned.

Abigail returned to the lodge still dressed in her clothing from the day before, an oversized coat, a hat, scarf, and boots half-zipped. Thinking of Africa, she found herself checking her cell phone every fifteen minutes as the reception began to fade the further she went up the mountain—the tiny men and snowmobiles now coming into focus as she scooted over to the window for a better look.

They were banging on the windows, their hands in mittens pressed against the windows for a better look inside; she thought they were trespassers and told the driver,

"We don't know those men."

Turning to face her, the driver said, "Oh that's Ned and his crew. They're the snowmobile directors from about two miles south of here."

Abigail reclined in her seat, tossing her waist-length braids into a ponytail after removing her gloves. She was not prepared to face the others because she knew they had questions. As she stepped out of the vehicle and approached the front door, the men locked on their new target, racing over to advise her of the appointment that was made.

"Ma'am, my name is Ned; we had an appointment scheduled for snowmobile training this morning at nine for five women. We've been here knocking and no one has answered. Are you one of those women?" the man said.

Abigail could not make out his features as his face and head were both covered exposing only his eyes, which as far as she could tell were a dark brown. She was confused.

"We had an accident yesterday, is there any way you can come back later, perhaps around one?" she asked politely.

"Unfortunately, no, we have other appointments. But if you're ever in town again give us a call," he said as he motioned for the remainder of his staff to wrap up and get going. Abigail took a long sigh as she used the spare key she had to open the door and let herself inside. The cabin smelled of burned wood, it was dark and melancholy. Removing her shoes at the door, she began making her way upstairs to her bedroom where she let the hot water run, preparing herself to climb inside the shower. Her bones ached, she had no idea just how much pain she had endured until the water touched her body. She groaned, as Noel entered inside the bedroom taking a seat on the edge of the bed waiting patiently for Abigail to emerge. Seventeen minutes later, after the pipes shut off Abigail stepped out of the tub, wrapped a towel around her wet torso, and made her way into the bedroom. Noel's presence startled her,

"How is she doing?" Noel said.

"Jesus!" Abigail trembled, for she was surely frightened. "Oh man, you scared me. There were guys banging outside, why didn't anyone answer the door?" asked Abigail.

"Frances hasn't left her room since yesterday and Alicia and Angelo have been in hiding somewhere downstairs. I sure as hell was not going to answer the door. Now, how is Africa?" she repeated.

"Angelo?" Abigail questioned.

Noel rolled her eyes. "Get over him," she demanded.

"No one is under him, I am simply wondering why the hell he is still here. He had one job, cook and not sleep with his client. Anyways, Africa is not fine. She broke her ankle and it's going to be a while before she's walking again. Noel, she's devastated. I mean, all she can think about are her bills, being out of work and everything. I don't think I'm going to go back to school. I need to stay home and help her," Abigail said as she dressed.

Appalled, Noel blurted, "What! This is your last semester. You can't not go back to school, are you insane? I can help Africa with the bills and things, so don't worry about that," Noel said confidently. "When is she being taken back to Long Island?" Noel continued.

"Well, when I left they were preparing her for transport, the surgery went well and my mom will be there by the time she arrives," Abigail said. Noel breathed a sigh of relief. "What on earth is wrong with Frances?" Abigail continued.

"She might be pregnant," said Noel. Abigail was shocked; she had her suspicions but couldn't bring herself to believe them,

"Pregnant?" she asked, confirming.

"Yep, pregnant, as in with a child," Noel emphasized.

Abigail took a deep breath. "Why is this turning into the trip from hell?" She chuckled.

"This has got to be our karma. I am convinced." Noel laughed.

"Maybe we should do something to cheer up Franny, she seems really down," said Abigail.

"What can we possibly do?" Noel inquired. The ladies began to ponder. Moments later, as Abigail and Noel thought long and hard, it dawned on them,

"Let's cook and play drunk musical chairs," Noel shouted, standing on the bed in excitement. Abigail turning to face her.

"It isn't even noon yet."

"So, we're on vacation, let's live a little. By the way, I can't cook so you can fry up the bacon." Noel smiled.

"I'm a college student, I don't cook, but I guess I can try. Plus, Frances can't drink," Abigail reminded her.

"That's fine, we will give her some sparkling cider, problem solved, let's go!" Noel said, jumping off the mattress and making her way down to the kitchen. Abigail trailing behind her.

Noel searched the ground floor for music before locating an old stereo player accompanied by vinyl's from musicians she knew were before her day. As she struggled to get the record player working, Abigail turned the heat on high and let the bacon sizzle while simultaneously mixing the mimosas. Abigail was feeling ashamed for allowing herself to be happy, but knew her sister would have wanted this considering she was returning to school to endure one of the hardest semesters before graduation, and then it was off to law school. Abigail needed a break, some good fun, and to see her friends all coming together and smiling again.

The music now blaring through the speakers with an upbeat tempo. Bopping her head, Noel snapped her fingers as she fluffed the pillows and began to push the sofa over to a corner. Following this, she moseyed on downstairs, retrieving folding chairs from the basement. Stepping down there, she remembered their first night, Frances scolding her and the tone that was set for the remainder of the trip—things simply hasn't been quite the same since.

Just then, Angelo appeared wearing a pair of pajama pants and a white crew neck t-shirt. "Smelled the bacon," he said. Abigail ignoring him as she continued making her way around the kitchen, stirring the scrambled eggs and preparing the French toast, sizzling the sausages and slicing the strawberries. Angelo felt his presence was not welcomed as he made his way back to Alicia's bedroom, shutting the door behind him. Noel and Abigail exchanged a bewildered look before continuing their bidding. A few hours, fresh breakfast, and glasses of mimosas later, the ladies were ready to add some fun to their day.

Abigail made her way upstairs to visit Frances. She listened as the pipes turned off, indicating her shower was complete. As she rushed inside she could hear Frances on the phone. Her voice just above a whisper,

"Yes, I return home on Monday, I can be there by 8 a.m.," she said. "My boyfriend," she continued. "No, this is my first," she responded now, making her way out of the bathroom. Stepping into the bedroom with the phone to her ear, she was alarmed to find Abigail sitting on the bed, her arms folded. Frances immediately wrapped up her conversation. "Yes, I have insurance and okay, thank you."

The ladies went back and forth discussing the reasons for Frances's decision all while Noel waited patiently downstairs as she refused to collect Alicia and her new lover, who she was still coming to wrap her mind around. She had been trying not to judge, but could not bring herself not to. Thinking, Alicia faulted her husband for his infidelity, and yet she too was proving herself to be no different—whether physical or emotional, it was cheating nonetheless. Just then, Abigail ran downstairs; as their eyes locked, she motioned for Noel to join her upstairs. She needed backup.

Noel was growing impatient as she left her glass on the counter top and began making her way upstairs, dreading the walk. She stopped midway to say a quick prayer. Arriving at Frances's bedroom, she realized she needed help picking an outfit, learning now that Maxwell was coming to visit. Noel was both shocked and annoyed; having thought she had signed up for a girls' trip. But Frances decided to quickly explain,

"I only asked him to come because I need him here, I need a pregnancy test to be sure and I'm way too anxious to wait until we leave. Noel, please don't be mad," she pleaded as she held two dresses against her body for the ladies to choose from.

Despite what her lips said, Noel was irritated. "It is fine," she said as she took her leave. "I'm going down to eat, everyone is taking too long," she said. Just like that, she left the room, Frances and Abigail exchanging a look.

Flashback
Noel opened her eyes to find herself alone, a feeling she had long since forgotten. The sun beaming inside the empty condo was simply breathtaking. As Noel wandered around naked, she walked until she came to the back bedroom where she noticed there was a bed, and inside the closet was a hamper and some of Nathan's personals. Then it dawned on her.

"Where are the rest of his things?" she thought. Searching now, she continued to pace as the birds out on the balcony began to chirp like a harbinger as keys now jingled in the front door. Expecting it to be Nathan, Noel did not budge. She continued searching through the walk-in closet as the voice of a woman was heard in the distance. Running into the foyer, she grabbed her clothing and made her way back into the bedroom into the tiny closet where she threw her clothes and herself into the laundry basket, her knees pressed against her chest and her hands and arms pinned against her body. The sounds of her feet pattering throughout the house had not raised an ounce of suspicion as the two women made their way into the foyer and began examining the space.

"Alicia darling, this place is simply magnificent," a woman said as their heels clapped against the wooden floors. Alicia was smiling from ear to ear,

"Well, Nathan said it was the least he could do for all the trouble he's put me through. Plus, we're downsizing," she chuckled.

"Downsizing?" the woman asked. Noel continued to hide, her neck beginning to hurt. Alicia continuing to pace as the woman now came across a shiny object on the floor. It was a nametag.

"Alicia darling, who is Noel-Lee?" the woman inquired. Alicia turned to face her, as she had no clue.

"I have no idea," she said, inspecting the badge. "Must be the cleaning lady, I mean, with a name like that, right?" she chuckled, praying inside that Nathan had not brought a woman into her home. "But yes, we're selling the house in Rockland," she said. Noel was now beginning to sweat; she could not see Alicia, but heard her every word now as they made their way into the master bedroom, walking past the laundry basket with her in it.

The ladies continued their inspection for what felt like hours. Noel was beginning to lose her balance, and as the door closed she rocked the basket back and forth until it fell and the lid flew open. Noel began crawling out of the laundry when a man approached her, causing her to scream. She had not heard the door re-open.

"Jesus!" she shouted, struggling to gather her clothes to cover her naked body. But he was a gentleman and immediately turned away until she was proper. Standing now, Noel struggled to put on her shoes, praying he would get away from the threshold so she could leave, but he remained statue-still. Noel struggled to push her way past him.

"Oh no you don't. Nathan is a great friend of mine, and I know he isn't perfect, but exactly who are you? You don't seem like the type of woman who would go for this," he said.

Noel grew angry, she had not given this stranger permission to touch her and barricade her in a home she clearly wanted out of. "The questions you're asking are none of your business, now are you going to move so I can leave?" she demanded.

"Wait, I remember you. I haven't been able to get you out of my head since that day I saw you in the elevator," he smiled. "Maybe this is destiny," he continued. Noel was afraid now.

"I have no clue who you are, and I need you to move out of my way!" she said ferociously.

"Listen, I'm no monster and your secret is safe with me. Here is my card. Get home safely, and I look forward to hearing from you," he said reaching into his inside suit pocket to retrieve a business card, handing it to Noel.

Grabbing it as he stepped past her, she scurried her way out the door, down the stairs, and onto the road where she bellowed for a taxi.

Arriving home, Noel prayed Frances had gone for work. Today was her shift and Noel had the day off. She showered quickly, and after washing her hair began searching the internet frantically for Nathan's place of business. Noel dressed in a pair of Seven jeans, an oversized t-shirt she knotted at the bottom, her hair in a ponytail and her shoes of choice a pair of boat shoes. She wanted to be comfortable when she went to confront Nathan; she was now a woman on a mission.

Reaching the tall Manhattan high-rise across from the United Nations building, Noel feared to make a scene, but between the shower and the car ride there she was no less calm than she had hoped to be. Noel moved swiftly inside, catching the elevator door before it closed as she searched for his company's name on the directory. Learning his location was on the fifth floor, she began making her way up.

Outside, the streets were congested, everyone beginning their commute to work and some, from work to home, but Noel had neither on the agenda; she was slowly beginning to feel less timid as she began to understand the importance of being assertive. Stepping past the glass doors and into the high-rise Manhattan building caused her heart to skip a beat, she felt out of place and completely underdressed.

Once inside, she noticed the guard sitting at the front desk asking everyone to sign in and provide their identification cards, and she realized she had forgotten hers. As her turn to approach the desk drew nearer, she knew she would have to resort to other methods in gaining access. She fabricated a lie, advising the guard that she was the sister of Nathan Ramirez, and needed to deliver some chilling news in regard to their parents. She even let some tears flow as she batted her lashes and puckered her lips. The guard hesitated until finally, he allowed her to pass—lackadaisical and disinterested he did not bother to question the issue in resemblance. Noel stepped ferociously past the turnstiles where she entered the elevator lobby. The mundane look of the hall was giving her a headache, the white against brown, mindless paintings, people appearing to look like robots and to complete this catastrophic look were purple ottoman chairs.

The elevator dinged on the fifth floor, stepping out, Noel felt she had entered into a new building—it was warm and organic, yet sleek and modern. The 12,000 square foot office space held an abundance of people, everyone so busy no one noticed Noel walking past reception and staring off into each of the offices to locate Nathan. She continued to go unnoticed, moments later she located him standing in front of his window, staring outside at the construction taking place. Noel pressed firmly against the door as she entered into the opulent room. Slamming it behind her. Surprised, Nathan turned, his hands in his pockets, but he was not astonished to see her, angering Noel further.

"Seems like you were expecting me?" she said.

"Not at all, beautiful, what's going on?" he spoke nonchalantly as he began to rustle through papers.

"Are you seriously that clueless? Your wife, that's what's going on," she said, Nathan now looking up in shock.

"Listen, I told you I will try to get out of that as soon as I can—" Nathan said.

Noel, interrupting him, "No, you fool, she was at the condo this morning!" she said.

"Impossible," Nathan laughed. "She has no clue about that condo, I made sure of it. I went through a broker who is a very good friend of mine. He wouldn't tell her anything," said Nathan, sounding sure of himself.

"Are you calling me a liar?" said Noel as she continued to stand, her arms folded.

"No, but, It's truly just impossible. Would you like me to call her? I can ask her right now," Nathan said confidently as he took a seat now in his brown La-Z-Boy executive chair. Noel was not sure if this was a game or if he should be taken seriously, and so she decided on the latter.

"Fine, call her," she demanded. Nathan reclined once more as he proceeded to dial Alicia's cell, after three rings, a soft voice answered.

"Nathan," she said maliciously.

Nathan now sat upright, Noel watching his decorum closely. "How was your morning?" he asked.

"Nathan why don't we cut to the chase, perhaps you've heard from my realtor by now, the Rockland house is sold and we need to be out by the end of the month. Thank you for the lovely condo, I've begun moving our things there," Alicia said.

"What!" Nathan shouted, Noel gasped; quickly, she covered her mouth so as not to be heard. Nathan continued to take deep breaths.

"Why on earth would you sell the damn house and not consult with me first, and where the fuck are the kids going to go to school?" he screamed—embarrassed now that Noel had to witness their debacle, undoubtedly a blow to his ego as he felt he was losing control.

"You don't get to talk to me like that! We were robbed just a few months ago, all of our most expensive possessions gone, and you go and get an eight-million-dollar condo and not tell me about it! I may not be the breadwinner, but my money is tied up in this marriage as well. It may not be much, but it is something. What were you planning to do with that condo, Nathan, huh? Have a new place for your whores?" she yelled.

Noel heard enough and prepared to leave as Nathan arose from his seat, inadvertently calling to her as she pulled the double doors to make her exit.

"Noel wait—" he said just before realizing Alicia was still on the other line.

"Noel?" she questioned as her brain now registered whom the nametag belonged to. Just then she hung up the phone. Nathan was left standing in his office, feeling a surge of emotions. As Noel made her way down the hall and out of the office doors, she pressed the elevator buttons forcefully. She was feeling lightheaded. Once the elevator light dinged, she stepped inside to find the one person who made her uncomfortable, considering he had seen her naked without permission.

"Are you stalking me?" she said. Benjamin Grayson was a celebrity real estate agent who occupied the tenth floor. Unlike most of the wealthy men Noel had met, Benjamin was not the flashy kind, he was humble. He owned several properties in the tri-state area and the luxury condo building Nathan purchased his new home in. Benjamin had come to know the real estate market so well that he made his first million eleven years prior at the age of nineteen after only seven months of flipping houses in affluent neighborhoods. While Benjamin had some flamboyant tendencies, he was no doubt a lady's man. Twice divorced, no children, and several houses later, he was now ready to settle down, and Noel had become his next target.

Benjamin was 5'8 with broad shoulders, a bald head, and a full beard and was the same complexion as Nathan. However, Nathan was far more attractive. Noel could not stand the idea of being backed into a corner, especially with a man she had since asked politely to leave her be. He was proving himself to be persistent,

"Your phone keeps ringing," she said as the elevator reached the lobby, stepping off she noticed Benjamin remained stationed as others now piled on. Riding his way back to the fifth floor where Nathan was now in an uproar, he opened the doors and took a seat after pouring himself a cup of coffee.

"Alicia was in the condo this morning?" Nathan inquired.

"Sheesh, allow me to take a seat first, please," joked Benjamin. "I did not see Alicia in the condo. I did, however, see a beautiful woman hiding in a laundry basket in your condo," Benjamin said as he cooled his beverage.

"Laundry basket?" Nathan inquired. He was in no mood to solve puzzles, he simply needed answers. "Listen, Alicia knows about the condo, what if she knows about the robbery too?" Nathan said. "Look, if she got to you, you would tell me right?" he asked with discontent.

"No one has gotten to me, the robbery went smoothly, your things are still in storage, and everything is perfectly fine. Maybe you left a note or a receipt or something at the house you perhaps forgot about. I mean, you said yourself she's suspected you of cheating, so maybe she hired a private investigator or bugged your phone. I mean, what did you expect?" he laughed. "Not to mention she did physically catch you with Jade, so I mean that will do it. Spark the elevator of mistrust," he continued. Nathan began to pace.

"We need a plan," he said.

"This was the plan because you have no prenuptial agreement. Rob the place, hide the assets, this was the plan, Nathan," Benjamin said.

"No, no, we need a better plan, I have to speak with Jade," Nathan said—turning his back to Benjamin as he stared out his window.

"What of this sweet young woman? Noel? I'd like to date her," Benjamin said.

"That's fine," Nathan said massaging his temples. Benjamin was now taking small sips of his coffee,

"That woman didn't deserve that, Nathan," he said. "We're better than this," he continued.

"It was never supposed to go this far, nor was this ever really about Noel, Jade just needed to be taught a lesson. She single-handedly fucked me over that night," Nathan said. "But listen, Noel is a good girl, so, treat her right," he continued—looking over his shoulder, his arms crossed.

"Oh, but of course," said Benjamin.

CHAPTER SEVENTEEN

With Angelo now gone, Alicia decided to give Nathan a call. After some much-needed thinking, she was convinced she had found a solution to her problem. Her marriage was not going to end, especially if she could help it. As the day pressed on and Noel and Abigail were heard in the kitchen cooking and playing soft music, Alicia watched as the phone rang on FaceTime.

"Hello," answered a raucous voice. Alicia turned to face him.

"Nathan?" she said.

"Yes," he responded in aggravation.

"Why are you always so short with me? I am trying to make things work and all you want to do is fight," Alicia begged.

"I want a divorce," said Nathan. Alicia's eyes welled as Nathan had yet to be this curt with his tender wife.

"Well I want my marriage, and what that sounds like to me is we both need counseling," she said.

"Counseling is for two people who want to fix things but are unsure how or where to begin fixing what is broken, we do not need counseling, that will prove to be a waste of time for me and the counselor," he said. "Look, I have to get back to work, can we talk about this later?" he said.

"No!" Alicia shouted. "I slept with someone a few days ago. I—I just wanted to see how it felt to step out on someone you love, and for the life of me, Nathan I could not find myself enjoying it, so yes, I know you stopped loving me a long time ago, but how do I change that? How do I make us happy again?" she pleaded.

"You slept with someone?" he asked, intrigued now. Alicia now sobbed uncontrollably.

"I did," she said, taking a deep breath, mad at herself for resorting to such lies.

"Okay, and so what would you like for me to do with this information, Alicia?" he asked.

The conversation between Alicia and Nathan, while unpleasant for her and comical for him, was a revelation unlike any other. Alicia began to realize her self-esteem was no longer intact, that fire in her which Nathan loved when they first met was slowly beginning to burn out, it was the adventure he longed for, the chase, the thrill of not knowing and being with a woman he knew would always take pride in her appearance.

Alicia knew Nathan was shallow but did not expect him to ever turn on her in this manner. He watched as she raised their children, she took care of his mother—much of which she could not help but remind him of—but he continued to remain disinterested. She knew with his mistress there with her there was no way he was spending more time with her, which to Alicia meant he could be swayed. But she was heavily mistaken.

As their conversation pressed on so did Nathan's patience. "Listen, enjoy your trip, the kids are fine, I have to go," and just like that he ended their call. Alicia sat upright, staring at her phone before curling into the fetal position for twenty minutes and looking out the window. She was devastated, her marriage was coming to an end, and this was now the worst time to have this epiphany.

Angelo on the patio knocking to come inside as she sobbed was embarrassing to say the least; she was not physically attracted to Angelo but knew he would make a good friend. She gathered the strength to allow him access, where he stood for a few minutes before realizing there was a loud commotion and the sweet scent of bacon coming from the kitchen.

He would investigate later.

Angelo did not know what was wrong with Alicia, but as she lay in bed sobbing he decided to undress and join her. She needed to be held, although she did not say so, pulling him closer to her, closing her eyes, she drifted off into a deep slumber, dreaming of the days she was once happy.

What was supposed to be a morning filled with happiness and laughter was turning into a day filled with gloom as Noel sat downstairs enjoying her breakfast alone until Abigail and Frances joined her. A faint knock at the door caused Frances to arise in excitement. She thought it was the love of her life, but it was Ned returning to inquire on whether or not the ladies were still interested in going for their snowmobile training. Peeping through the door, Noel and Abigail both jumped up, elated now as they both agreed. They completed their forms once Ned came inside, removing his headgear and exposing his face.

Ned was a Caucasian man with dark brown hair between the ages of thirty-five and forty. The ladies promised to be dressed and ready to go in a matter of minutes. Frances could not bring herself to join them, she was waiting on company, and so she decided it best to stay behind.

Ten minutes later, Noel and Abigail were tucked in on the back seat of the snowmobiles, Noel holding tightly onto the torso of the instructor she had been assigned. Unable to see their faces, Noel was excited and afraid as they began to take off. Frances watched in amazement as the ladies shouted their way down the hill, laughing now, it warmed her heart to see them having fun. Angelo then emerged, standing in the kitchen reaching for a plastic bowl where he placed some pieces of bacon, eggs, and strawberries.

"Well hello to you, too," teased Frances.

Angelo smiled. "Sorry, you looked lost in thought there, didn't want to bother you," he said.

"How is Alicia?" asked Frances, folding her arms. Angelo took a look behind him to ensure they were alone,

"She's not good," he admitted. Frances now took a seat on the stool by the island as she filled her plastic plate with breakfast.

"What do you mean?" she asked with a worried look on her face.

Angelo continued. He did not know much but from what he guessed, it was safe to say that Alicia was heading for divorce, one that she was trying desperately to avoid. But Frances could not wrap her mind around the need to stay with a man who was unfaithful.

"He does nothing but cheats on her, why is she fighting to stay?" she inquired as she bit into her bacon strip.

"Children," said Angelo, putting the lid on the plastic container. "I can understand that aspect. Not to mention, she raised his son like he was her own. How do you separate two children who you've raised together for the bulk of their lives?" he wondered.

"That isn't for her to figure out, it's him, and he seems to be too selfish to care," she said. There was a knock at the door, but Frances was no longer excited, she thought the women had returned. As Frances made her way over, Angelo quickly disappeared to the rear of the room where he retrieved a large gift box he had hidden days before his arrival. The box was fourteen inches thick, ornate, with turquoise wrapping paper and a white bow. Angelo quickly began to unravel it as Frances unlocked the door. Outside she saw no one, she turned to face Angelo, the door still open as she noticed he was now standing behind a beautiful cake, perfectly decorated. She chuckled as she turned to find Maxwell now standing behind her, both Noel and Abigail behind him, they all screamed,

"Surprise!"

Frances was shocked, Maxwell held a large teddy bear in his hands, a necklace around its neck held a pendant and the icing on the cake read,

Will you marry me, Frances Cooper?

Frances began to weep as she held onto the teddy bear, once in her hands it was almost the same size as her. She watched as Maxwell, Noel, and Abigail all made their way inside—Maxwell getting down on one knee. Noel and Abigail behind him, cheering, Alicia was awake now, given the commotion; she stood in the hallway closest the kitchen as the proposal went underway. The balloons now loose in the cabin released by Ned and his crew. Frances felt overwhelmed, she did not know what to say, she was absolutely speechless.

"Frances Cooper, these past two years have been something else. Man oh man, you watched me go from a waiter in a coffee shop to now managing my own accounting firm, and babe you never gave up on me. Even when I had to give up my apartment to pay for classes and I had to stay with you, I felt like a loser and someone who did not deserve you. But you stuck with me, you helped me, stayed up late at night to help me study, and I had to find the best way to repay you. Then I realized I am going to need the rest of my life to do just that," he said. Frances now drenched in tears, Noel crying and Abigail too, as was Africa on FaceTime.

"I know you're not a huge fan of surprises or being fussed over, but I know how much your friends mean to you and so, I wanted this moment to be perfect and have them here while I ask for your hand in marriage. Frances Melinda Cooper, will you make me the happiest man and complete me by marrying me?" he asked humbly.

Squeezing her teddy bear tightly, Frances said, "Yes, of course, I'll marry you," she said as she dropped the teddy bear, Maxell stood now after placing the fancy yellow and white diamond frame engagement ring in 18k white gold on her ring finger. Frances and Maxwell exchanged a kiss as everyone clapped, celebrating their engagement, Angelo searched under the sink for the two bottles of champagne he stashed away.

"Has anyone seen the champagne?" he asked loudly. Noel quickly turned to face Abigail, who whispered,

"Noey, I used them for the mimosas this morning," she chuckled.

Noel placing her face in her palm laughed. "I think it's in the refrigerator," she said. "The bottles are open, though," she said quickly before retreating to hug Frances. Ned and his friends made their way over to Maxwell. Congratulations and cheer spread all throughout the room. Just then, Frances spotted Africa on FaceTime, her eyes opened wide; she quickly forgot how happy she was as she reverted to tears.

"Don't cry, Franny, I am okay!" Africa said. But Frances could not help it. She loved Africa more than life itself. She was her sister, her best friend.

"Africa, I am so sorry this happened to you, so sorry. I love you and I miss you. Once I get back I will be right by your side, I promise!" Frances pleaded.

"Today is your day, Frans, enjoy it. I love you too and I am so happy for you! We have a lot of planning to do," she said, smiling. Maxwell realized the discomfort of his bride-to-be and made his way over to her phone call, placing his hand around her shoulder; he kissed her softly on the cheek as he greeted Africa.

"Africa is fine babe, I went to see her before I came," he said.

"He did," shouted Africa. Frances turning to face him, hugging him as tightly as she could muster. He was perfect.

That day everyone danced and Frances learned the truth of Maxwell's intentions when going to the cabin. Ned and Maxwell shared stories of their time in high school together, and Frances was shocked to learn a lot about her fiancé, but she was heavily impressed. She knew he was a lady's man, she knew he was a man who had a vision for himself, Maxwell made sure that Frances did not have any champagne, whispering to her as the evening was coming to a close,

"I have the test for you in my luggage," he said, smiling. He wanted the news to be positive; Frances had taken a deep breath. She couldn't wait any longer. Carefully she slipped away to locate it as she ran to the upstairs bathroom. No one had missed her, she was gone for all of thirty minutes, and as everyone continued to laugh, listen to music, and enjoy cake and champagne, the questions for Maxwell began.

"How many kids do you want?" Abigail asked.

"Maybe just two," he said, laughing. Upstairs, Frances had finally learned the truth; she was in fact pregnant.

Flashback

Africa made her way inside the brownstone where she and Frances had a long discussion about Noel and how she was holding up. She had not left her room in days. Frances was beginning to worry that Noel was allowing herself to fall into too many toxic relationships, none of which were conducive to her mental health and her growth as a woman.

Noel was beginning to keep her up at night with her crying, at work she was no longer upbeat, Amber was beginning to question whether or not she should take some time off, but feared the thought due to Noel not being herself. Africa could barely get time off from work but knew she had to try and help her cousin and find time to celebrate Frances's upcoming birthday and her last day at the boutique.

"How long has she been in here?" Africa asked. Frances and Africa sat in the living room, it had been four days since Noel confronted Nathan and she did not hear from him, which left her devastated. She hated him but had grown accustomed to his constant pursuit of her. Now, she felt his feelings had perhaps begun to fade, meanwhile, she was finding herself smitten by him, his emotional unavailability and the lack of attention she was receiving made her want to spend time with him now more than she ever did.

The buzzer from the front door caused her to sit up straight; she thought maybe Nathan had found her. Racing out of bed she stood by the window as she watched the postman leave behind a package she was sure had to have been from Nathan. Stomping out of her bedroom, both Africa and Frances watched as she darted to the front door. Stepping outside Noel retrieved the package that was, in fact, addressed to her, the return address unknown. Noel smiled from ear to ear as she made her way back, stepping past her friends and into her room, locking the door behind her.

Frances and Africa exchanged a look. Inside, Noel sat Indian style in the center of her bed as she unraveled the package. Her gift, a black strapless dress from Chloe along with a pair of Jimmy Choo strapped sandals. Noel was ecstatic, a small note inside instructed her to be ready by 7:45 p.m. Frances and Africa were now immersed in *CSI* as Noel rushed to shower, shave, and polish her toes. By 7:45, Noel was putting the finishing touches on her makeup. She loved a night on the town; having been taught there was no better way to say, "I am sorry."

Inside her bedroom, as she strapped on her sandals and let her curly hair bounce effortlessly past her shoulders, she listened as the black town car approached. Grabbing a clutch, she made her way through the front door to notice that Frances and Africa had gone. Stepping outside, she stood at the top of the stairs feeling like Carrie Bradshaw from *Sex and the City* wearing the paper dress. Noel felt beautiful. As she slowly made her way down the stairs, she had now forgiven Nathan and was ready to be treated like a princess again. But Nathan was not inside. It was Benjamin.

Noel scoffed, tripping over her feet out of the limo, Benjamin now calling behind her as he too ran outside.

"Stop stalking me!" she screamed, finally her low-pitched voice made her proud.

"I am not stalking you, I am simply trying to date you," he said. Noel was curious about how he knew where she lived, and this only fueled her anger. "Listen, I am not leaving until you let me take you out," he said. Noel began to wonder if maybe she had been overreacting, Benjamin had not done her any harm. After all, he had been nothing but polite. Turning now, Noel could not stand the idea of wasting such a beautiful dress, plus he had no baggage that she could think of, and so, she decided to go along.

"One date," she said, clapping her heels down into the town car. Benjamin, elated, stepped back inside reaching for a gold box. Inside was a Diamond Mandala Flower fourteen karat pendant necklace. Noel caressed it before allowing him to place it around her neck, she felt like she was being bought. It was as though he could read her mind,

"I am not trying to buy you with nice things; I just feel a woman as beautiful as you should simply always have nice things, plus I am a huge fan of fine jewelry," he said.

But Noel, although grateful for the gift, still did not find him attractive. She figured maybe he would grow on her, but as the car began to move, she was screaming on the inside. Their ride silent as the car ceased in an unfamiliar location. Noel could not stand the fact that she was on a pity date, but Benjamin was not worried, confident she would come around.

The night sky was beautiful once the car came to an abrupt stop at the pier, Noel wondered if he was going to kill her now for wanting nothing to do with him, but that was not the case, Benjamin walked with her, holding her hand as they made their way into a tunnel; on the other side was a 37.60 metered all-white mega yacht. Noel gasped, she had never seen one up close. Benjamin did not wear a suit, he went for the business casual look, a pair of brown pants, boat shoes, a crew neck t-shirt with a cashmere cardigan. Noel wondered why she could not have opted in for a more relaxed look as well. But she decided against complaining. Stepping onto the boat, she was aided by a man wearing a sailor suit and a thick Italian accent.

Downstairs there was a bar, two island stools, a sectional, and a center table. The bar was completely full, there was no space for anything else. Coming from the upstairs down into the well-lit community room, Noel noticed the beige loveseat, the four-piece beige couch closest the wall with four large navy-blue throw pillows, the additional two mahogany center tables, and behind that another beige four-piece sofa, and to the left of that a three-piece beige sofa with one white throw pillow. The painting to the rear, a Picasso.

As she admired the room, Benjamin asked, "Would you like a glass of wine?" He poured himself a glass of bourbon.

"Sure," she said. "So, are we going to be alone?" Noel inquired. "This boat is kind of big for just the two of us," she continued.

"Well no, we have our captain, Dave, we have a chef joining us in a few minutes and some friends of mine for an intimate dinner," he said.

Noel did not know whether to be enticed or afraid. Benjamin took a seat now after handing Noel her glass and crossed his legs. "So tell me a little about yourself," he instructed.

Noel took a seat. "What do you want to know?" she asked timidly.

"Where are you from? You're clearly not a New York girl," he said.

"Seattle," she replied.

Benjamin was inquisitive, he had many questions while every so often reminding Noel of how breathtakingly beautiful she was. After twenty minutes of what felt like an interrogation, Noel could hear the laughter of a man and a woman approaching. She began to feel relieved. Her tensed shoulders now coming down, the couple was a woman named Markie and her boyfriend Carter; everyone stood to introduce themselves because as it appeared only Carter and Benjamin knew one another. In fact, it was later revealed they were brothers.

The chef then made an appearance, and Noel was feeling a tad bit more comfortable as each new face came onboard. Signaling to the captain, Benjamin informed him they were all ready to go. Markie and Noel found a small room where they both conversed for a few minutes as the men headed up to the deck to enjoy a cigar. Markie was very beautiful, a Latina woman with soft green eyes and a voluptuous body. Her skin glowed as she stood to pour herself a glass of wine,

"So how long have you known Benjamin?" she asked. Noel continued to sip slowly, her beverage, she did not want to find herself inebriated amongst strangers amidst the still waters.

"Um, not too long, How about you and Carter?" Noel asked.

"About four months, my life hasn't been the same since," she chuckled. Curious now, Noel asked,

"Why is that?"

"Well, I was working in a small art gallery and he came in and bought some paintings; since then we've been to Paris, Indonesia and Uruguay. It's just been surreal."

"I see," Noel said.

By her third glass of wine, Noel found herself dancing, learning to waltz, the dinner was scrumptious and the conversation insightful. The gentlemen spoke on politics, entertainment, and business. Noel was excited, and she was slowly finding herself attracted to Benjamin, drawn to him due to his intellect and profound kindness. He cleared her dishes, he assisted the chef with providing dessert, and even when her feet began to hurt, he removed her shoes to massage her feet. She was tickled by his extreme generosity.

The chef, later joining in on the conversation, along with the captain once the boat was left on cruise control. There was something in the room Noel had never experienced; it was power, the respectful kind. She was regarded as a woman of high value in his eyes, regardless of the little input she added to the discussion. Hours later, she found herself growing weary. Benjamin knew this as he instructed the captain to the dock. He complied.

The journey home felt like hours, but once she arrived she kissed Benjamin good night and began making her way inside. Unlocking the door to a pitch-black, empty apartment was tranquil. Undressing, Noel found herself now thinking of Kenneth. It was two in the morning and she knew he must have been sleeping. But she wanted so bad to visit him, to see him. She missed his touch. Frances was not home, Noel assumed she was spending the night with Maxwell. She couldn't sleep, and although she had work in the morning and knew she was going to hate herself, she decided to head over to Kenneth's loft.

Noel called for an Uber, using her application after changing into a pair of jeans and a top. Shutting the door behind her, she ran outside and hopped in the car. An all-black Audi R8 with tinted windows parked on the corner began to follow. As she journeyed to the meatpacking district, she noticed the lights in his loft were off. This disappointed Noel, but she figured she would go up and knock anyway. So she did. No one answered. The black Audi now drove to park inside the garage. Noel wondered where all the noise was coming from as she now stood on the outside of Kenneth's loft.

"I guess God has a sense of humor," a voice said from the distance. Noel looking around, confused until she checked downstairs to see Kenneth stepping lightly, making his way up.

"I—I, I just want to talk, I couldn't sleep," she lied. But Kenneth knew the truth.

"Is that so, how was your date?" he asked as he now stood in front of her.

Her eyes directly in front of the lower part of his chest, Noel could not bring herself to face him. "How did you know I went on a date?" she asked, surprised.

"I watched you tonight because I can't stop thinking about you, and I don't know, I just had to see you. Amber gave me your address, she was kind enough," he said, licking his lips. But Noel did not care how he received her address, hell, she was thinking of ways she could thank Amber.

"Are you saying what I think you're saying, Kenneth? Because I can't stop thinking about you either," she said. Grabbing her jawline, Kenneth lifted her face as he began to tenderly kiss her lips. Noel lived for these moments as he lifted her, parting her legs, carrying her inside. Noel removed his track jacket to expose his chest and his biceps. She was in heaven, as she was in love, she had never felt this way before and knew he had to be the one for her.

That night they made love. Kenneth was surprisingly gentle and Noel had come to appreciate every minute of it, any moment they spent together in passion were now moments Noel could not imagine her life without. Three hours and two rounds later, Noel was parched, Kenneth dripping in sweat, and her hair a mess. She kissed him softly as she lay on her back under the covers, the canned lights in his walk-in closet bringing her comfort as the rest of the house remained dark. Kenneth now turned to face the opposite way, and Noel fought her way under his arm, wishing he would cuddle her so they could sleep soundly.

"I almost married her," he said.

Noel propping her head up in annoyance, needing clarification. "Are you going to talk about Jade tonight?" she asked,

"No, I mean—It's just that I know what you want, but I almost married her, so it isn't that easy to simply let her go and move on with someone else," he said.

Noel decided it best to lie. "I don't want you to move on with me, I just, I kind of want to know I'm not wasting my time and you don't just see me as a woman who can scratch your itch from time to time," she said. Kenneth remained silent. He decided to choose his words carefully,

"Kenneth Anderson, if I walk out those doors again, I am not coming back," Noel said, her hand spread across her heart as she sat upright to stare down at him. "Is that what you want?" she continued, praying he'd say no.

"Just lay down, I will take you home to change and bring you to work in the morning if you have to go," he said, kissing her forehead as he turned his head to go to sleep. But Noel could not sleep, she kept replaying his words over and again in her head. The next morning, Kenneth went for a run at approximately 6:15 a.m. Noel wondered where he found the energy, she could not bring herself to get up, let alone run. He made a smoothie and then hopped in the shower, and Noel listened as now she could not go back to sleep. She had to be at the boutique by nine and decided to stay in bed a little while longer. By 7:45 a.m., Kenneth climbed on top of her, Noel was fast asleep again. He knew she was going to be late as he went under the covers and began to suckle between her legs.

Kenneth first went slow, then picked up the pace as she opened her eyes and he felt her body begin to tense up, a master at the art, he aggressively attacked her clitoris, gliding his tongue from the front to the middle and enticingly to her anus. Fifteen minutes later, after heavy breathing and the best orgasmic relief she'd ever had, he arose, wiping his mouth— appearing as though he had just won first place in the Olympics.

"Let's go, before you're late for work," he smiled.

Noel rushed inside of her apartment where she showered and threw on clothes she had placed in the wash. She had no time to search for a proper outfit. Amber would be furious, but the later she was, the more trouble she would be in, so she made an executive decision. Once in front of the boutique, Noel felt like the popular girl in high school. She watched customers make their way in and out of the boutique, sitting in the passengers' seat to Kenneth's coupe had her feeling as though she was on top of the world—kissing Kenneth goodbye, she ran inside to clock in, the time read 10:47 a.m. Just then, Amber appeared,

"Noel, you're late!" she screamed.

"This is my first time being late since I started, I am very sorry," she pleaded.

"Just don't let it happen again. Please fold the clothes on the entrance display," Amber said, walking away. That day Noel worked and could not stop smiling, she was elated, she felt she finally had a chance with Kenneth, a chance to make him happy and a chance at her own happiness. It was surreal.

Amber noticed something about Noel that she loved. She was friendlier, quicker on her feet, and genuinely showing interest in the men and women who entered.

Every day for a week Kenneth began picking up Noel. They would go to dinner in the evenings and then head back to his loft. Noel felt like she was finally in a real, normal relationship. They ate in front of the television, watched movies, drank alcohol, had sex, and even one night played video games. There were no penthouses, diamonds, yachts, it was just her and a simple Kenneth who made hot cocoa in the summer and played GTA before bed. One week turned into one month and nothing had changed, their routine only intensified as Noel found herself now asking for space to leave her things. She felt bad for Kenneth having to bring her home and then to work on the days she was not off. He reluctantly agreed, asking his maid to make space for her. She was given a drawer for her personals under the area where he kept his cufflinks.

Noel was now happier, although she and Frances continued to miss one another at home until one day they had finally crossed paths when Kenneth advised Noel he had to go out of town for a business meeting so she had to go home. Noel did not mind. Once inside, she noticed Frances had completely packed and was ready for the first day of school. It was September seventh. Noel had not realized how much time had flown.

"My last day at the boutique is Friday, Noey," said Frances.

Noel was shocked as she stood in the kitchen making scrambled eggs. "Oh, are we still doing that dinner?" she asked.

"Yea, I'm going to meet you guys at the restaurant though because I close the store that day, and it is also my birthday, Noey, so I definitely expect you to be there," she smiled. "Wow, you and Kenneth, huh?" she teased.

Noel blushed. "Of course, I will! Yep, me and Kenneth, finally. I mean, it's so perfect, it's like we were just meant to be, it's so easy to be with him. He's laid back, he's intelligent, witty, fun, all the things I had no idea he could have been." Noel smiled.

"Well, I'm glad you're happy, that's all that matters," said Frances. "I am going to turn in early, tomorrow is going to be a long day!" she continued.

Noel nodded her head,

"Good night Franny, love you," she said.

"Love you too." Frances closed her bedroom door behind her. Noel sat in the living room where she binge-watched *Grey's Anatomy* until eventually falling asleep.

Friday came quickly as Frances basked in excitement for her first day at school, putting aside the fact that it was also her birthday, she was assigned eleven eight-year-old children and one teacher's assistant. She was having the time of her life. That morning she noticed a woman carrying her young daughter into the building, her daughter crying hysterically. Frances knew she simply had the first day of school blues. As Frances marched over to her, she extended her hand to the little girl, exposing a bag, inside was one Gluten Free chocolate chip cookie. Instantly, the young lady stopped fussing as her mother placed her down to stand on her feet. The little girl was absolutely beautiful, a Latina girl strongly resembling her mother. Frances extended her hand to introduce herself,

"Hello there, beautiful, this chocolate chip cookie is for the well-behaved children in my class. Is today your first day?" Frances smiled at the young lady.

"Yes," she said, hiding behind her mother. "But I want a cookie," she said, her eyes enlarged by her fascination.

"You can have that one, but you have to promise you'll be a big girl now and you won't give mommy and your teachers a hard time. My class is right down there," she said, pointing behind her. "So, you can visit me whenever you want," Frances smiled. "How old are you?" she asked.

"Six," she said, her Dora the Explorer backpack was almost bigger than she was, so Frances knew she was in the younger class.

"Okay, well, you're a big girl. What's your name?" Frances asked,

"Lauren, but my friends call me Moose," she said in excitement.

"Wow, Moose! Okay, well I am Ms. Frances, and so Moose, it is. Nice to meet you," Frances could not stop smiling. Lauren seemed intelligent and kind.

Standing, she now came face to face with her mother.

"Hello, my name is Frances," she smiled.

"Thank you for getting her to calm down," the woman said. "My name is Alicia Ramirez, my husband and I just moved to Tribeca from Rockland, so I was getting her registered today," she informed Frances.

"Well, this is most definitely a change from Rockland, but I will be happy to keep an eye on her for you, my class is not too far down the hall. I teach the third grade. Lauren will be down here with the first graders, so I will check on her periodically," confirmed Frances. This put Alicia's heart at ease.

Maxwell had flowers delivered on her first day back, which made things a bit awkward when the children began to inquire who was sending their teacher flowers and love notes. But Frances did not mind, they were subtle reminders of his love for her, a love she would not have traded for anything else in the world.

That evening the ladies prepared for their dinner at a soul food restaurant in the East Village that Frances had never visited. She spent the day at work wondering what she would wear, but nothing in her closet seemed flattering enough, she was now in a relationship and wanted to look more appealing, her Bohemian chic style did not compliment her curves, which made her wonder how Maxwell was ever able to find her attractive in the first place.

Frances always struggled with having low self-esteem, but it was never low enough to keep her in undesirable situations, rather, it was the opposite; she never felt beautiful enough to be in the relationships she was in and would sometimes question why the men in her life wanted to be there—thinking only light-skinned women were beautiful. But Maxwell was showing her a love she never knew could exist, showering her with gifts, his time, his ongoing affection, it was like something out of a romance novel. As she applied her makeup and took glimpses at her phone, she was surprised to see missed calls and texts from just about everyone, advising her that they were either on their way or running a little late. Everyone except Noel.

As the buzzer dinged, Frances realized she was one year older, which meant she was now twenty-nine, just one-year shy of the big thirty. Frances wore a green Boho dress, designed by Vyshyvanka with custom embroidery in dots long sleeve tunic. The fit and flare silhouette accompanied by a slip-on belt helped to extenuate her curves, the curves she was completely proud of. Her hair was out for the first time in a long time, the bra length kinky curls were moisturized to perfection as her wash-and-go proved itself to be rather appealing. Her mocha caramel complexion, dark roots, and small face all made her look exotic.

Outside, Maxwell awaited her in a checkered taxi. Upon making her appearance he could not keep his eyes off of her. She was classy and beautiful, just the way he liked. Stepping out of the taxi to aid her in stepping down the stairs, he was proud as they stepped inside and Frances had the pleasure of meeting Morris. Frances smiled as she noticed the man occupying the front seat next to their driver.

"So, you must be the infamous Morris Baker," she said.

"That I am, and you must be the Nubian queen that my best friend here can't stop talking about," he replied. Frances turned to face Maxwell, who by now had begun to blush. Grabbing his cheeks and kissing him, Frances could not help but laugh.

"Well I am sure glad you could make it; I have a friend I'd like you to meet," Frances said.

"Playing matchmaker on your birthday, that's different," he teased. They all chuckled.

CHAPTER EIGHTEEN

Announcing the news to her friends, Frances and Maxwell were celebrated—their night festive. As the sun began to rise everyone returned to their quarters, but no one could sleep. Noel had news of her own, and with only a day left she wondered when she would expose this truth she had been keeping for some time. Frances and Maxwell lay awake, Frances cuddled in his arms as they told one another untold stories of their childhood. Frances loved having this conversation, especially now that Maxwell knew of her pregnancy. He was so excited, and she sat up to let him know her thoughts.

"I wasn't going to keep the baby," she admitted.

Maxwell, shocked, turned to face her, his biceps now flexed. "What? Why?"

Frances was afraid. "I just thought maybe we weren't ready for a baby," she said, biting her lips.

But Maxwell understood. "Are you scared?" he asked, placing his hands under her chin to console her. Frances took a deep breath,

"Yes. I am a teacher, I see how these parents in New York struggle with their children, a lot of them, the school systems here are broken, we don't have the means to necessarily just up and leave. I'm afraid for our child, and so I thought it was best to not have one," she admitted as tears began to flow freely from her eyes,

"I will get us out of the city and into a town where the air is clean and the school systems are the absolute best for our children," he smiled. "I will protect us, I promise, as long I'm here you don't have to be scared," he continued.

Frances wept.

Noel sat outside of their room listening keenly, engrossed with jealousy as she marched down the stairs, removing a glass from the cupboard where she began to pour herself a glass of vodka on the rocks.

In a home filled with people, Noel never felt more alone. She was already envious of the fact that Maxwell was going to show his face to disrupt their girls' trip from hell, but she had no idea she had traveled hours across the country to end up lonely, in a freezing cabin, with nothing to show for herself. There she was, turning thirty in a couple of years with no real accomplishments and no direction at all. The more she pondered this, the more depressed she became, taking sip after sip of her vodka. The day beautiful, but she could do nothing but hang onto the negativity, the idea that she was nothing more than a desperate, pathetic woman. Just then, Frances interrupted her thoughts.

"Noey, are you alright?" she asked kindly. Noel took a deep breath; Frances was the last person she hoped to see.

"I am fine," she lied.

"Well you don't look fine," Frances wrapped her robe around her torso as she reached for a bottle of water from the refrigerator. Frances knew something was wrong, Noel had been off all day. "Are you upset because Max is here?" she asked taking a seat on the stool by the island.

"No, we knew he was coming, just had to pretend as though we didn't. I mean it was one thing to know he would be here for the big question, but actually seeing how happy you two make each other, I feel pitiful. I agreed to something, Franny, that if you knew, you would never look at me the same." Noel began to struggle to get the words out, breathing shakily.

Intrigued now, Frances asked, "What is it?"

"You remember when I first came here? The kind of woman I was? Just free-spirited, kind and aloof?" Noel asked. "Well, I feel like I'm changing for the worse. I am deceptive, argumentative, jealous of my best friend." Noel began to sob. "I've lost myself here in New York, and I don't know how to get her back," she continued.

Just then Alicia emerged—the morning sun just on the horizon, as she made her way into the refrigerator carving for herself a piece of the cake from the day before. Noel and Frances remain still as Noel took another gulp of her alcohol. Alicia removed her watch to wash her hands and the utensils before slicing into the cake in silence. Noel took a slight glimpse to her right, noticing the watch she had once been gifted. Lifting it. It was a Tambour black faced 34mm pink alligator strapped LV watch, the same she had been given by Nathan.

"Where did you get this watch?" Noel inquired, breaking her silence. Alicia turning to face her.

"My husband, what kind of question is that?" she said, snatching the watch from her hands.

"Did it ever go missing?" Noel asked. Alicia looked uncomfortable as she entered into deep thought.

"Yes, once, and then I got it back," she said.

"Did you stage that robbery in the apartment?" Noel asked, standing. She was ready to get confrontational.

Alicia, turning to face her, wanted to scream. "How did you know about that robbery?" she asked.

"I was there when the robbers snatched that watch clean off of my wrist," she said. Frances was confused; she was in no condition to part an altercation.

"Ladies, why don't we all calm down," she begged. "It could just be a new watch, maybe it was a present, doesn't mean it was the one that was stolen," Frances continued. But neither woman was listening, Alicia began to wonder as Noel grew agitated. She felt foolish.

"Is Nathan leaving you?" she asked. Both Frances and Alicia knitted their eyebrows, shocked that Noel could bring herself to ask such a question.

"I know you would love that! But my husband and I are going to counseling and we are going to fix our issues and come out stronger than ever! I came here to tell you to stop sleeping with my husband so that he and I can work on our marriage in peace! I don't know what you want to go away, but whatever it is, just name it and it's yours because I am sure sick of this shit!" Alicia said as she ran her hands through her hair.

Noel gathered herself. "I'm sorry you traveled all this way to confront the wrong woman with that speech," Noel said tranquilly as she walked past her, shoving her slightly. But Alicia knew better than to reciprocate her aggression and decided to be the bigger person. Frances did not have anything to say, she too then decided it best to retreat.

Flashback

Noel had decided to accompany Lexington on a car ride to the airport where Kenneth would be returning from his business trip. Emails, phone calls, and even FaceTime between them with Kenneth reminding Noel of the pop-up event set to take place exactly one week from Friday. Noel was excited, she felt like his little secretary, although she was not getting paid, she welcomed any and every opportunity to be around him, whether it was for business or pleasure. Lexington despising her, he thought of her more as a little mouse that simply would not go away. He believed that fateful morning when Elmira had summoned him to dispose of her that that would have been the last he would see of Noel. This was unfortunately not true, as not only did she leave him sitting outside in the vehicle without so much as a word, but she also found herself right back into Kenneth's good graces, a first for any woman who was not Jade.

Gate twenty-three, Kenneth had arrived, and with Frances covering the store Noel had all the time in the world to spend with the man of her dreams. As he stepped through the double doors at the airport, Noel was there to greet him in her overalls and sneakers. Lexington struggled to put away his luggage, tucking the pieces neatly in the truck as he very kindly reminded Kenneth of a meeting he had to attend in forty-five minutes.

"Shall we bring the young lady to her own quarters?" mumbled Lexington. Noel ignoring him, she knew he was simply jealous as she kissed Kenneth profusely. The world around them a black hole, they needed to be snapped back into reality.

"No, Noel, you aren't busy today, right?" Kenneth asked. Noel knew today was Frances' birthday dinner but figured she would not be missed. "No, I'm pretty much all yours," she smiled, kissing him.

"Well, it's settled. Lexington, we can head straight to the meeting. Have you eaten, Noel?" he asked,

"Yes, we stopped for breakfast before heading here," she said. She could not stop smiling, although they had been together for a short amount of time, it was romantic, it was fresh, he was the man she dreamed of and he was finally all hers.

Kenneth loved touching Noel, he liked grabbing her petite waist and running his fingers through her hair. Kissing her forehead and thinking of new ways to pleasure her, Kenneth was in lust. Noel, however, was finding herself falling deeper and deeper in love.

As the day pressed on so did Kenneth and his endless meetings and errands. He had a client meeting with Pepsi Marketing, Tau Iota Mu Psi, Incorporated, CNN, Market Global, and a representative for the Mayor of Washington D.C., Irving Houston. Noel was curious when she heard the name and decided to inquire.

"Who is this Irving guy?" she asked Kenneth as they paced down the long corridor inside of the high-rise on Madison. Noel carrying his iPad, notebooks, pens, and tape recorder for the meetings. She was not always allowed inside but was handed his notes once he left,

"He's going to be our next Black president," said Kenneth confidently. "I've endorsed his campaign, of course, so with myself and a few others, we're going to get him into the oval office," Kenneth continued,

"But that meeting sounded more like damage control," said Noel.

"Wow, you're pretty observant, aren't you?" Kenneth smiled as he ran to catch the open elevator, Noel looking up at him as she remained curious about why he was needed for a political campaign. As they made their way outside, Noel continued her barrage of questions,

"I just don't get it, how are you going to get a man into the oval office? You're just a public relations manager, seems kind of like an aberration," she continued. Kenneth politely changing the subject,

"We're going to head to the boutique now, to meet with Amber to finalize some details. This may take a while, are you hungry?" he asked.

"Please don't do that," Noel said.

"Do what?" Kenneth asked as he held the car door open.

"Dismiss me by changing the subject, I know this isn't my business, but what if on some level I would like to contribute? The man is running for president unless there is something to hide, wouldn't it be prudent to inform more people, curious people such as myself, on his political stance?" she said.

"Ah, see, you weren't asking about his political stance, you were asking why my services would be needed for a man looking to run for president. I believe the phrase *damage control* is what you used. However, I would be more than happy to advise you on his political stance so of course, you can spread the word, but that's as far as we go," he warned, motioning for her to step inside. Noel knew better than to continue to push and so she decided to leave it alone.

Once outside of the boutique, Noel dreaded going inside, she was having a good time running errands and attending meetings with Kenneth, and as foolish as it sounded, she felt like she was slowly finding her calling as his assistant. She loved what he did, the excitement, meeting people of power and finding new clients to poach from competitors. She wondered if this was the position he initially tried offering her months ago when she first arrived.

The boutique was packed and Amber was alone, Frances was not coming in until after class ended, which was around 3 p.m., and Noel had been given the day off. Once inside, Noel decided to assist. Removing her cardigan and throwing her hair into a ponytail, she aided Amber in customer service, steaming, cleaning, and checkout. Amber had never had an incident such as this where she was understaffed on such a busy day. Kenneth smiled as he waited patiently for the crowd to cease.

Turning to face him, Amber asked, "What's so funny?" she snarled.

"Well, when you hire a public relations manager to help increase your business, you might want to consider hiring more help," he said. Amber was shocked,

"This was your doing?" she asked.

"I don't get paid the big bucks for nothing," he gloated. Kenneth was smug, which helped him to do his job very well. Noel turned to face her.

"When on earth did it get this busy?" she asked. But Amber knew better than to complain, she simply waited until the crowd died down to pay Kenneth a visit in her back office, where she poured herself a glass of water.

"So, should I be thanking you?" she scoffed.

"Not at all, this is what I get paid to do, our staff put out an advertisement blast for your event, everything is all booked up and we are ready to go. We have over two hundred RSVP's and counting, remember this advertisement went up two days ago, so this kind of turnaround is very good for a boutique this size," Kenneth said. "We have nine vendors also attending, trade show set-up as we discussed, a press kit is scheduled to go out Tuesday at 9:09 a.m. and again on Thursday at 10:36 a.m. We want this event to be the most talked about event of the year, especially with the year coming to an end, people are looking for things to do," he said.

Amber struggled to keep up. "I don't know what to say," she said.

"Say nothing, on the 16th, next Friday, just allow our office to do all the work for you and I promise you this will be one of the best nights of your life," Kenneth said as he began to take his leave. Wondering if Noel would be staying back, he prepared himself to carry out the remainder of his meetings alone. Amber walked him outside having noticed the influx of customers had gone. Noel did a wonderful job assisting them. Walking inside, Jade fanned her weave as she stepped mindlessly into a table, speaking out loud as directed to no one in particular. Noel, Kenneth, and Amber stood watching her. Noel gulping loudly, immediately she felt her position threatened as she turned to face Kenneth, who was now frozen in his tracks. He could not help himself, he missed Jade terribly, and she knew it.

"Kenneth," Noel whispered, dropping her cloth as she came around the counter to grab Kenneth by the arm, indicating their relationship status. Jade and Noel exchanged a look that could kill. Kenneth removed his arm from Noel's clutches and decided it best to take his leave. Noel followed.

"Hey, I think I'm going to just finish the rest of the day on my own, plus it looks like Amber can use a hand," he said walking away, Jade leaving behind him. Amber then called to Noel as she noticed her wanting to trail along as well.

"Have some self-respect, what are you wearing to Frances's dinner party tonight?" Amber asked, scolding her almost. But Noel could not bring herself to respond as Jade and Kenneth went out of view. Noel held her breath as she could only imagine their conversation as she fought her inner demons, the ones telling her to go outside, but Amber would not let her, hugging her now for she knew Noel's worst nightmare had come true.

"Kenneth, wait," Jade bellowed, tilting her head to say hello to Lexington, who smiling back, greeted her. "I gave you so much space because I thought that's what you needed, but you don't get to ignore me and throw away years all over a mistake I made when you made one too. We love each other and it doesn't matter how much you try to rebound with Noel, she isn't us, she is not Jade and Kenneth. I made terrible choices and I want the chance to fix them," Jade begged.

Kenneth remained stoic, he decided to hear her out. "Tonight, you can meet me at my place around eleven. Lexington, we need to go to Birkin," he instructed climbing into the back seat, and just like that he was gone. Jade did a happy dance right there on the corner of Lexington. She was going to get her man back by any means necessary.

Just then the phone rang; she was reluctant to answer as she realized it was Nathan calling, but she could not bring herself to go down that road and so, she decided against it. Returning to the boutique, she wandered as Noel gave her a chilling look.

"Listen, we don't have to like each other, I just came by Amber to ask if you could bring me along as a plus one to Frances's get together tonight? I know she hates me, but I got her this really nice gift that I think she's going to love and I decided to wait until today so I would have an excuse to give it to her," Jade said. Amber remained apprehensive as Noel listened in silence.

"Sure," Amber said as Noel shot her a baleful look.

"If she goes, I will not be there," Noel cried.

Amber knitted her eyebrows. "Are you crazy, this isn't about Jade, this is about your best friend, you better be there," said Amber.

"So, it's settled, see you all tonight. What time should I be here?" asked Jade.

"Frances will come in to close around seven, so you can meet me here around eight and we'll head on from there," said Amber. Jade was elated.

"Perfect," she confirmed, turning to leave. Noel stood with her arms folded.

At 2:30 p.m., Noel left the boutique. She knew Frances would soon be making her appearance and she could not bring herself to face her. Noel felt defeated, her calls to Kenneth ignored. Feeling lonely, she dialed another number after calling for a taxi, once inside she instructed the driver on where to go. Standing outside the loft, she waited for the door to open, listening as the clicks came undone and the door widened, she let herself in, kissing him on the cheek for making himself available to her, she decided to remain there for the rest of the evening.

Their table was filled with laughter, champagne flowing freely between them and the sweet sound of a live Jazz orchestra playing adjacent them. Frances, Africa, Morris, Abigail, and Maxwell all sat at the large dinner table draped in a white satin tablecloth. Frances dialed Noel as she wondered where she could have been. Soon, Jade and Amber made their appearance. Frances could not bring herself to be mad at Jade, instead, she hugged her, thanking her profusely for her willingness to show up. Africa and Morris found their way to one another, their attraction instant once they were inside and Africa exposed her petite shoulders wearing a strapless silver maxi dress accompanied by a pair of strapped sandals, her nails and toes painted a snow white, her braids sitting on the top of her head in a tight bun accompanied by a golden head chain.

Abigail wore an ivory pantsuit, her hair cut into a nice bob, her shirt a crop top. The ladies were dressed to impress. Africa began to notice that Noel had not arrived yet, and she forwarded a text as everyone prepared themselves to order their appetizers. Maxwell and Morris, who was 6'2 wearing a navy-blue blazer buttoned once in the middle, began to reminisce on their college days. Morris was Caucasian, insanely handsome, and knew how to make everyone smile.

The dinner lasted for hours as the soul restaurant allowed the party of what was to be eight their own quarters to enjoy a live show. Buried in Maxwell's arms, Frances could think of no better way to have spent her birthday, there were gifts, cake, balloons, and of course Jazz. But this did not take away from how hurt she felt considering that Noel did not show up. She continued to check her phone, praying she would simply say something, but nothing. Africa excused herself to the ladies' room and soon found herself on Noel's voicemail, screaming, demanding answers and in the same breath praying she was in fact safe. Just as she was making her way back downstairs, Morris came to approach her.

"I don't think I had the chance to properly introduce myself," he said, extending his hand, Africa felt uncomfortable, for the corridor was small.

"The pleasure is mine; my name is Africa," she said.

"Beautiful name for a beautiful woman. If you're not busy, I would love to take you out some time for dinner maybe," he said.

"I would love to, I can give you my number," she said as he removed his cellular phone,

"Sure, what is it?" he asked.

"631-555-1488," she said

"Oh, Long Island," he laughed,

"Yep, born and raised," she said.

"Fantastic, well, I will be in touch," he said, lifting the back of her hand and kissing it gently. Africa blushed as she watched him take his leave, and Morris returned to the table where he amicably bid everyone a farewell. Maxwell walked him downstairs to the car. Before they knew it, it was midnight, and with Noel nowhere in sight, Frances gathered her gifts, the ones received from her friends, as Maxwell settled their bill downstairs.

Once home, Maxwell assisted Frances with bringing her things inside and decided to take his leave as they stood outside of the brownstone kissing on one another, Frances thanking him copiously for a wonderful evening. Maxwell knew Frances was unhappy as he watched her walk inside, but could not bring himself to do more than he had already done.

"I love you," he shouted, climbing in the back seat of the taxi cab.

"I love you more," said Frances as she waved him goodbye. That night, Frances hoped that Noel would return home, but she did not.

Across town, Noel found herself entering the home of one of the richest men she knew, Benjamin Grayson. The only loft in the building to have a balcony, she remembered the day they met, she was bringing Kenneth flowers and ran into him on the lift. She had not known until now that he was that same man, he'd smelled differently then, putrid, as she then realized he too was one for going for long runs in the mornings.

Benjamin's loft was stylish with an elegant white-look interior design. Finely furnished and composed of three floors: entering at ground level there is a bright living room with two wide windows, furnished with a comfortable large revive unholstered fabric sofa, a table, and a fully operational kitchen with a stainless-steel stove, oven, and microwave. Moreover, a washing machine and dryer and a fully operating dishwasher as well as comfy bathrooms with large showers and appliances. Past the stairs extended the first floor, where a delightful bedroom, complete with large wardrobes, overlooked the living room and the private access to the roof garden. At the push of a button, the retractable glass ceiling opened to reveal the large terrace where he enjoyed living in the open air. The hi-tech amenities included a flat-screen TV, Wi-Fi internet access, and an electrical curtain for the roof window. His favorite colors were white, beige and forest green and his home was by far the best she had seen.

Noel stepped lightly through his home as she wondered why a man with such wealth had any trouble finding women his own age to date, and then she asked,

"Why is a man like you single?"

"What exactly is a man like me?" he replied, being inquisitive. Noel hated this, as she wondered to herself why she had truly contacted him. Placing her glass on the kitchen countertop, she decided to waste no more time, she was craving attention and wanted it from anyone who was willing to provide it. As she removed her clothes, her conscience eating at her, she wondered how Frances must have felt considering she was not there. Benjamin took a seat and watched in amazement as she undressed, one garment at a time, but little did she know Benjamin was not the type to make love.

Noel was demanded to satiate his desire for submission as he tether her wrists, thrusting her against the mattress, Noel did not know whether to cry or scream and so she did neither, she endured the pain as much as she could, praying she would not feel this weak in the morning. Benjamin did not kiss her, he did not perform oral sex, and he did not caress her body, rather he entered her with force, throwing his body against hers, creating a puddle of sweat; she had no choice but to allow him to drench her naked face and body. Benjamin propelled her body against the walls where he parted her legs and began to enter her from behind, slapping her backside with brute strength as Noel let out a shrieking cry what felt like hours later. She had never been handled with such brutality, her medium skin tone now a beating red.

But Benjamin did not care. His breathing increased, he grabbed her hair, twisting her stands around as he created a ball in his hand for a better grip to pound his body against hers. This went on for hours, her legs pried open as he entered her, exiting and switching positions she had not been familiar with, Noel begged him to slow down, but he would not hear of any such thing as he turned her face to the wall, pressing it against the concrete—Noel began to flutter her hands in the air for she was now free, but not quite—begging for him to stop, but Benjamin continued, smacking her torso and her buttocks as hard as he could muster. Noel now screamed when a loud bang came to the front door, Benjamin, releasing her, turned around. Noel fell to the floor lifeless. She curled into the fetal position, weeping silently. The voices were indistinct, she could not make out who was at the front door, and as Benjamin reentered the room she continued to cry, pushing her body into the corner using the soles of her bare feet. Benjamin had now put on a pair of boxers as Noel sniffled. Pulling her close to him gently, he laid her head on his chest, embracing her.

"I am so sorry!" he exclaimed as Noel continued to cry. He was truly sorry. That night, Noel examined her bruises as Benjamin became a whole new man once they were not intimate. He explained to her why he was into submission and this was the reason that led to his divorces. He was not proud of this, but as a rich man, he found that many women were willing to comply whether he disclosed this information to them or not, but he felt truly embarrassed because he had come to value Noel, she was a treasure in his eyes. Noel wished she had known these things before finding herself inside his home, she knew she was in his domain and anything that he wanted to go, was going to go. She continued to listen to him, asking him a series of questions, she wanted to learn more as she contemplated the idea of exploring this dark, twisted side of him.

Benjamin was elated to know she was somewhat interested, he was more than willing to give her exactly what she wanted in exchange for her cooperation,

"I can have a lease drafted in your name as early as tomorrow morning for a beautiful apartment in the Belmont, Upper East Side, just say the word." Noel could not believe her ears.

"And I just have to have sex with you, like that?" she asked.

"That's it," he nodded. Noel took a deep breath before she unenthusiastically agreed.

The next morning the contracts were signed, Noel had no furniture and although she hated having sex with Benjamin, she did it, forcing herself to find solace in the fact that she was living in a beautiful home for which she did not have to surrender a dime. Arriving at the brownstone to apologize to Frances two days after her birthday was proving itself to be a daunting task, and as she made her way up the stairs, unlocked the front door, Noel found that her things had been folded neatly and placed in the hallway. She demanded answers as she contacted everyone in her phone book: Africa, Abigail, Frances, and even Maxwell, who was the only one to answer,

"Hello," he said.

"Max! Why on earth did Frances put my things outside?" she questioned. Max was absolutely stunned as she looked through her belongings,

"I have no idea, she knows she shouldn't have done that," he said.

"Well, she did and now I'm calling her and she won't answer," Noel shouted.

"Today is Monday, Noel, she has class, I can call her once I leave work. Did you try using your key?" he asked. Noel felt foolish because she hadn't tried using her key and for good reason, she knew once her things were outside then most likely the locks had been changed, and they were.

"Locks are changed," she scoffed. Maxwell grew silent as he took a deep breath,

"I can just give her a call when I leave," he said, trying to diffuse the situation.

"Thanks," Noel said, hanging up the phone as she stepped outside to call for a taxi. Once inside she thought long and hard whether or not a battle with Frances was one she wanted to enter into, but her emotions got the best of her as she instructed her driver to take her to the school. Pushing her way through the crowd of parents, teachers, and administrators, she spotted Frances by her hair. As Frances lined up her students, preparing them to walk inside, she spotted an irate Noel stomping viciously towards her.

Frances tapped the woman next to her, asking her to lead the children inside as she stepped towards Noel.

"You can't be at my job!" she said, walking away from the students.

"Right, and you can't throw my things out all because I missed a damn dinner!" shouted Noel.

"What on earth is going on with you? A damn dinner?" she mocked. "We cannot be friends if you're here just to attack me with vituperative words," Frances said.

"Friends? What kind of friend puts their friend's things on the outside of an apartment? What if my things got stolen, Frances? Huh, then what?" Noel shouted.

"I was angry, a part of me still is, I haven't heard from you in two days and you missed my dinner because you wanted to be laid up with yet another man!" Frances screamed. Noel's low-pitched voice was no match for her.

"Who told you that?" she asked.

"Jade, she was at Kenneth's the night you were with some old man named Benjamin, how many men are there?" Frances said. Noel ran her fingers through her hair as she wondered who was at the door that night. It was Jade.

"So, I guess Jade is now the token best friend and girlfriend, huh?" said Noel. Frances felt terrible, she was watching her friend diminish right before her eyes—Noel fidgeted.

"Listen, maybe you need some counseling, but you can't stay hung up on that man. He loves Jade, Noel, he does, and I am so sorry to say this, but maybe it's time you move on and grow up," Frances bashed. "Oh, and they're going to be at the pop-up event this weekend, maybe it's best if you don't come," she continued.

Noel couldn't believe her ears, Frances had completely turned against her, in addition, she had the man of her dreams and lost him to the one woman she thought she stood a chance against. She pondered this as she returned back to the brownstone where she gathered her things and began stuffing them inside the back of the taxi cab, pleading that she be taken to her new apartment.

"1775 York Avenue, please," she sobbed. The two-story, two-bedroom apartment containing a washer and dryer was surrounded by a lavish environment; sauna, 7,000 square foot fitness club, swimming pool, and enough space to fit her family. Noel was miserable. As she made her way up the stairs, she couldn't help but feel as though she had sold her soul. Mild furnishings slowly arriving with large windows overlooking the Harlem River and in full view of the Triborough Bridge; the 9ft ceilings were truly a luxurious way to live. Landscaped gardens, framed entrance, and a sparkling fountain with a rooftop sun deck. As she made her way around the apartment, she realized she needed a hot shower and so she took one, in the opulent bathtub large enough to fit three, maybe four persons at a time.

Noel ran herself a bubble bath, pressing along the bruises found on her inner thigh, a small price to pay for luxury, she thought. That evening, Noel dreaded watching the sunset, a first for her, as the keys to the front door jingled.

She stood by the window, contemplating throwing herself from it as Benjamin made his way towards her, dropping a leather flogger, leather handcuffs, a blindfold, and restraints. Noel gagged. Walking over, Benjamin grabbed her chin, rotating her neck in a circle before taking her hand and using it to caress his penis as he sniffed her neck,

"You smell delicious," he said. A motionless Noel remained standing. Benjamin now walked away as he unbuttoned his shirt, removed his pants, and made his way over to the elaborate bar where he poured himself a glass of D'Usse cognac, his favorite. That night, Noel had an experience; she was handcuffed, beaten, blindfolded, and sexed until the sun came up. She had no safe word and found herself exhausted by morning. She was growing to despise him, the fire that once burned in her was slowly being put out as she found herself now contemplating suicide day in and day out as she waited patiently for her owner to return home. By Tuesday they were doing it spread-eagle, her wrists and ankles secured to the four corners of the bed, faced down, allowing Benjamin complete access to the back of her body where he whipped her unremorsefully until she cried.

By Wednesday it was chair bondage, an entry-level position for Noel to perform oral sex on Benjamin as he did not return the favor. Ultimately it resulted in the leapfrog position where Noel came to the sad realization that she was not as flexible as Benjamin would have thought. With her wrists tied on the inside of her ankles and her back firmly arched downward, Benjamin had the time of his life. Thursday morning Benjamin came by early, hog-tying Noel in a position where she could not move until he returned in the evening. He had finally broken her. That night, Benjamin took notice of the light going out in her eyes as he untied her and decided to spend the evening conversing over food. But Noel had no appetite, she wondered why he was being kind and saw no desire to break bread with a man she had come to loathe.

"I had no idea you would have hated this so much," he admitted. "I don't want you to feel like I'm some horrible man who is just here to bring you harm, Noel, I truly do value you as a woman, and if this is not something that you are into or can see yourself being into, then we can stop," he said as Noel sat upright, her arms folded and tears falling from her eyes. She was silenced by her depression.

"Noel, please speak to me," he pleaded. "What can I do to fix it?" he begged.

Later that evening, Noel had awoken to find Benjamin putting away his toys in a garbage bag and setting it by the front door. She walked down into the kitchen where she took a seat on the couch, the sheets wrapped firmly around her. Benjamin noticed the bruises along her arm and went into the freezer where he removed ice, wrapping the cubes in a table cloth placing it gently on her body. For the first time, he kissed her cheek. Smiling now, Noel reciprocated this act as she laid down in his lap, Benjamin continuing to ice her hand until he too had fallen asleep.

It was a big day for the boutique; ladies from all areas around town were spending their evenings getting ready for what was advertised as the most important event to attend amidst the fall season. Kenneth and Jade had spent the previous day shopping for outfits which would complement one another, and Kenneth realized how smitten he was by Jade when she came by a week before and did that thing he liked so much. Jade was talented in the bedroom, but outside of that she was kind and he was ready to do what he had waited months to do.

Frances and Maxwell had not spoken because Frances was disappointed in Maxwell for scolding her about changing the locks and having Noel's things thrown out of her apartment, to which she was clueless on where she had gone, or with whom she was now staying.

Africa and Morris had been dating heavily for a week now; Africa was looking forward to their first event appearance together as she quickly saw a future there, as he was proving himself to be attentive, communicative and a hard worker.

Nathan contemplated attending the event alone, but Alicia would not hear of it. She wanted the town to know exactly who she was and that she was in fact married to one of the wealthiest men on the island. Abigail had not yet found love and took pride in the fact that she would attend alone, as Amber and her husband prepared for their big night.

With stunning views of downtown NYC, the rooftop location was the ideal venue as Amber's vision was captured perfectly. Inside, their eleven trade show sponsors would begin their booth set up, other boutiques, manufacturers, business owners, company programmers, and hotels were all present with their marketing materials. Amber decided to leave home five hours early, accompanied by her wardrobe stylist and makeup artists as she worked with the event coordinator Jelani Hardwell to bring to life the event she only dreamed of.

The renovated 3,000 square foot glass enclosed multi-purpose space came equipped with hardwood floors, large enough to fit over 300 people, a wraparound, one of a kind outdoor terrace with phenomenal downtown Manhattan skyline views. The room came fully equipped with AV sound, systems, Bluetooth connection, microphones, and a projector system. Amber could not wait as she and her husband began to bring in their more desirable pieces to showcase at their sponsor table. The room was nicely decorated, with a fall theme, centerpieces that were remarkably done with apples infused into the décor. The apple trees, the floating balloon lights were all simply perfect. Scheduled to begin at six, Amber requested that the lights be dimmed and the music begin to play, contemporary music as the mannequins were set into place, the spotlights to shine directly on the material and the racks of clothes Amber herself had begun to wheel inside.

Disappearing downstairs into the stage room, Amber began to ready herself as Frances and Maxwell first made their appearance, their looks not complementing one another considering they had not been speaking up until the day of the event. But Frances did not mind, she was happy he was there and that alone mattered. Frances was in no mood to be dressed up and so she found herself wearing a light cardigan, jeans with the ankles rolled up, a pair of boat shoes and a v-cut blouse. Making their way inside were the sponsors and guests as they began to pile on in, Frances was kind enough to greet everyone while Amber continued to get ready in an effort to make an appearance, her husband now making his way over to greet

Frances and Maxwell. Christopher was 5'6, fetching and mild-mannered, perfect for Amber.

As the room began to fill, Frances spotted Abigail, who was dressed in a pair of overalls and an ankle length cardigan with a barrel hat. She greeted Frances and Maxwell with air kisses to their cheeks. Maxwell decided to pass as he wandered the room for anything that may catch his eye. Moments later Jade and Kenneth made their fashionable appearance. Jade, wore a mid-calf length lavender colored pencil skirt, tight enough to accentuate her curves and a bralette attached to the skirt, a pair of silver strapped sandals, her hair slicked to the back with a weave ponytail reaching just below her buttocks, and a pair of diamond hoop earrings and matching bracelet. Frances and Abigail exchanged a look of confusion,

"Did we get the same invitation?" joked Frances.

Nathan and Alicia arriving shortly thereafter. Alicia standing a few steps behind Nathan as he made it apparent they had not come together. Alicia wore a vintage Tom Ford dress, her hair straightened and extending to the middle of her back. Nathan wore a pair of jeans and a button up shirt accompanied by a blazer. As he laid his eyes on Jade, he followed her all around the room like a lost puppy. Noel and Benjamin had arrived in a stretch limo, Frances laid her eyes on her and immediately made her way across the packed room to greet her.

"Hey," Frances said. Noel was dressed in a long sleeve sequin shirt, much to Frances's surprise considering how warm it was outside, and a pair of ivory pants with heels. Noel looked as though she had been crying. Frances leaned in to hug her and Noel let out a sharp cry, a cry she immediately wished she could take back. Her bruises were aching; both Frances and Benjamin shot her a look of discomfort.

"I don't believe we've met," said Frances, extending her hand to Benjamin.

"No, we haven't. Benjamin Grayson, and your name?" he said, trying to speak over the loud music,

"Frances Cooper. Noel, do you mind if I speak to you alone?" she asked, looking down at the bruises found on her friend's hand. Noel quickly covered them.

Africa and Morris made their entrance, and by now the room was completely packed with sponsors, a DJ, photographers, and the event coordinator making his rounds as he and Kenneth exchanged words every so often. Africa made her way to Frances, leaving the men to mingle, and Noel agreed to spend time with her friends who she knew were all still quite angry with her. Jade made her way over. As she took a long look at Noel, she felt pity.

As the event went underway and Amber made her appearance bringing everyone to their feet with a round of applause, she felt accomplished. By the time she had come out to take center stage, she noticed all of her designs had sold, and Amber decided it best to show her gratitude.

"I just want to thank each and every one of you who came out this evening and thank you all so much for your expressed interest in my designs. I started *Crystals* about eleven years ago, the store is named after our beautiful daughter, my husband Christopher and I," she continued, as she spoke the ladies retreated to the terrace, where the conversation began.

"I am really sorry about missing your birthday dinner, I have this thing where I begin to self-loathe and I shut down, but it's no excuse. I should have been there front and center, and Franny, from the bottom of my heart I am so very sorry," Noel sobbed, careful not to ruin her makeup. She and Frances exchanged a hug as Amber continued her thank-you speech inside.

"You have to tell me what's been going on with you," said Frances. Africa and Abigail looked on; Jade stood inside, holding a cup of fruit punch as Kenneth stood by the stage next to Amber, who thanked him profusely,

"Next, please help me in welcoming Mr. Kenneth Anderson to the stage, who was responsible for tonight being a huge success," Amber said as the room filled with applause. Jade was shouting in the back as Nathan and Benjamin turned to face her. Grabbing the microphone, Kenneth spoke swiftly, searching the room with his eyes he noticed Noel on the terrace speaking with her friends, and Jade now stood next to him, looking up to him. She wondered why he had not begun speaking and when she turned to find what his eyes were locked on, it was Noel. Immediately she kicked the foot of his pants, and clearing his throat, he began.

Jade was not happy as she had expected Kenneth to propose. The thought crossed his mind, but he could not bring himself to follow through as he stared at Noel, with Benjamin now catching him.

"Hey, can she help you?" Benjamin asked angrily—speaking loudly above the chatter around the room. Frances was now making her way back inside after learning that Noel had bruises on her body, she marched and marched until she found Maxwell.

"Max, Noel is bruised up, I mean all over her body," she said, trembling. Noel wished Frances had not gotten so worked up, she did not get to finish telling her that Benjamin vowed to stop. Frances broke down crying as Morris, standing next to Maxwell, overheard,

"Who did she come here with?" he asked. Frances was now panicking as the crowd grew thicker and the women were making their way inside, Noel searching frantically for Frances before she could spread the wrong information. After expressing a few words of kindness, Kenneth stepped off the stage—irritating Jade further. However, Kenneth and Jade continued to work the room as Alicia now stood in a corner, completely oblivious to what was taking place until moments later when she decided it best to spare herself any further embarrassment by leaving. Nathan had not introduced her to anyone, the moment they stepped inside he went his separate ways.

Maxwell and Morris now searched the room for Benjamin; they had questions, and as Noel now made her way over, Kenneth and Jade stood with their backs turned as the DJ resumed the music. Jade was livid as she questioned Kenneth, wondering why he was staring at Noel, but Kenneth was speechless overhearing the commotion making its way to him.

"She's all bruised up," he heard a voice say, walking past him. Benjamin and Nathan laughing over a glass of bourbon, neat, as Maxwell made his way over. Noel, begging them to stop, accidentally bumped into Kenneth, who turned to grab her. She screamed as her arm began to hurt, and he immediately let her go.

Jade grabbed him by the arm now as he asked, "Are you okay?" Kenneth was confused, and with everything happening so quickly, he followed her. "Noel," he screamed, Jade continuing behind him. Jade called to Kenneth as Kenneth called to Noel, infuriating Jade further.

In the corner by the stage, standing face to face, Maxwell turned to Benjamin, Kenneth now standing behind him, as he asked, "So you think it's okay to hit women!" Maxwell shouted, and without a second thought, Kenneth questioned, "Hit who?"

He was enraged as Frances shouted to him, "Noel!"

Without thinking further, Kenneth and Noel made eye contact, her eyes filled with sorrow, and just as she looked away Kenneth made his way past Maxwell, balling his fists, punching Benjamin in the face. This caused an uproar as they both fell to the floor. Everyone began kicking, knocking over the equipment, as Kenneth yelled, "You put your hands on her? Did you put your hands on her?" he shouted with every punch aggressively tugging on his shirt collar—breaking Benjamin's nose.

Nathan now intervened in pulling him back, and Maxwell punched Nathan. It was a catastrophe as the guests began racing out of the room, Frances grabbing Noel as she pulled her away from the crowd, Jade stood watching Kenneth and Benjamin tussling and all she kept wondering to herself was, *'why is my boyfriend fighting to defend another woman?'* Jade and Noel locked eyes. As security came piling in, removing Kenneth and a gushing Benjamin, Benjamin screamed, "You're finished in this town, my guy, done. You have no idea who you just put your hands on," Benjamin shouted as Kenneth was soon escorted from the building, everyone now in complete anarchy.

CHAPTER NINETEEN

Their trip coming to a grisly end, with no more activities planned, the morning dragged. Five days came and went, just like that, and Alicia wondering to herself what exactly did she accomplish. The night before she did not sleep, she stayed up wondering what Noel was talking about, the words replaying in her mind like a broken tape recorder as she politely asked Angelo to allow her room to grieve. She decided it was may be time to mourn the death of her marriage as she took a long walk down the mountain where she made it to the edge of a cliff. Thinking of nothing and no one but her daughter Lauren, she wondered how Nathan was not able to think of her as well.

The cold breeze caused her ears to change color as she stayed outside, waiting patiently for an answer from someone, anyone, on what she was supposed to do next. Convinced that Noel was the problem, Alicia simply did not know anymore. Was Noel truly her issue, or was her issue simply with the man she was fighting to continue to love, a marriage dead long ago that she was trying so hard to resuscitate. Watching Frances and Maxwell happy reminded Alicia of the days when she and Nathan first decided to get married. It was almost so sudden.

Alicia met Nathan at a county club she frequented when her ex-husband would take her there. Warren was his name, and at the time Alicia desperately wanted children.

Unfortunately for her, Warren was infertile. Alicia begged Warren to adopt but he would not hear of it because he never felt you could love an adopted child as much as your own. This Alicia begged to differ as she found herself doing extensive research on adoption on her own considering Warren had no desire to start a family the non-traditional way, before she knew it she was venting to an unlikely source, a man who wanted more children but had just lost his wife and was beginning to give up on love. Their paths crossed at such an odd time in both of their lives Alicia considered it to be destiny. But she decided to stay true to herself, asking Warren for a divorce so as not to commit adultery, and Nathan waited patiently for the ink to dry. Before she knew it, she was pregnant with Lauren, her miracle baby.

Alicia prayed long and hard for a man like Nathan, prayed that God would design him specifically for her, especially when she knew she could not have children with Warren, she begged for a man she would spend the remainder of her life with, and then he came. As Alicia continued to pray, she found herself receiving all the answers. Stepping back into the lodge, the girls were beginning to bring their luggage downstairs.

Alicia decided to take a seat as Noel struggled to bring her things down. She watched her as she began her monologue, the story went on and on, Alicia outlined in detail how she had to come to learn about Noel from the nametag on the floor to the pop-up shop to the abrupt visit to their condo. She knew everything. But she needed the courage to confront her. Noel stood, confused, as she had thought this was all now behind them.

Everyone gathered around, bewildered on whether they were to console Alicia, scold her, or rid themselves of her toxic company.

The room felt dark and with little to no resolution, the ladies decided it was time, time to intervene the only way they knew how; turning to face her, Frances said, "I think it best you leave; what time is your driver going to be here?"

Unfamiliar to her now, the joy had been taken out of the room, the air was now brisk as she prepared to take her leave, Alicia stared at Noel with malice, something she had never felt nor seen. The thumping in her heart meant her anxiety was beginning to flare, and without so much as a second thought, as Alicia began to gather her belongings and roll her suitcase through the front door to await her driver, she heard Noel say the words she knew was going to be enough to change her life forever.

Peacefully, Noel said, "Alicia, please tell Nathan that I am pregnant."

Frances turned to face her, "Pregnant?" she questioned. The women were aware of the affair, but no one could have seen this coming. Maxwell moved quickly now to pack the truck, Abigail remained standing in shock,

"How many of you are having babies?" she questioned.

Alicia could not move, as the next question left her lips, she knew she had reached a new level of desperation. "How much do you want?" she asked, removing her checkbook from her handbag. Everyone gasped.

"What? You can't pay my friend to go away," Frances shouted. "Jesus, what is happening?" she said, placing her hand on her head,

"Five million," replied Noel.

"Over my dead body are you getting that kind of money from me and my husband!" Alicia scolded.

"Noel, this is madness, what the hell are you doing?" Frances demanded answers, but Noel was paying her no mind,

"Five million and I go away for good, you never have to hear from me or even about me and my baby ever again," Noel repeated. "You and I both know how Nathan feels about me, he will be back, and you know he will love my child," Noel bluffed.

Alicia took a deep breath before answering, "Fine, I will have the money wired to you," she said as she gathered her suitcase and took her leave, listening as her driver made his way to the front door, Maxwell politely advising her of same. Quickly, as Alicia climbed into the back seat, she rang Nathan, sobbing hysterically, but her service would not allow the call to connect.

Flashback
Arriving home, Jade threw her clutch down as Kenneth walked across the loft holding a bag of ice to his head. He was in no mood to quarrel.

"You have to explain to me, what am I doing here? Huh? I thought we were going to fix things, I found a Cartier box in your closet two nights ago and I even thought you were going to propose, and then you fight someone for Noel!" she screamed.

"It wasn't even like that, my uncle used to beat the crap out of my aunt, I don't like the thought of any man hitting a woman, ever!" he replied.

"That's bull and you know it, I am no fool, you heard her name, you heard it was her who was the so-called injured party, and you couldn't wait to become a superhero," she shouted. But Kenneth refused to pay her any mind as he continued to ice his head, closing his eyes and reclining on the sofa.

"Do you love me?" asked Jade, her arms folded.

"Of course, I love you," Kenneth mumbled. His eyes remained closed,

"You can't even look at me and say that," she cried.

"Jade, I love you," he said, turning to face her, but Jade did not believe him, and for good reason. Kenneth remained disconnected and Jade felt him drifting further away from her, but he was a comfort to a fool as she knew there could be no future, their hearts were in different places and their minds in separate times. But for the sake of not wanting to feel like a failure, Jade continued to fight, holding onto what she thought would never come to such a bitter end. Realizing now their union had been no more than a filibuster; Jade spoke her peace before deciding to make amends with the internal conflict growing inside her.

"I watched you leap across a room to fight a stranger because you thought he had hurt your precious Noel," she sobbed. Kenneth was now standing as he tossed the ice pack onto the center table, unsure of why he had been so dramatic, he wanted peace, he wanted to be left alone, but he knew the best thing he could offer was an apology, not in an attempt to make her stay, but to allow her the peace he knew she was seeking to simply let him go. Kenneth had a warm touch; he provided a safe and comfortable environment for Jade—one she would not soon forget.

"I am so sorry," he said, cuddling her. But Jade would not hear another word, pushing him away; she marched out the front door, slamming it behind her—her eyes welling. She waited a few minutes for him to chase her, but inside Kenneth was relieved. Glad to be alone with his thoughts.

Jade cried as she made her way down the stairs, Noel, outside in the taxi cab she had taken to the loft, waited before going up and thanked God she did, considering she had no idea Jade would have been there and Benjamin was not home, either, his car not outside.

As Jade left, Noel made her way inside the lift where she allowed it to take her upstairs. Knocking on Kenneth's door she waited patiently for him to answer. Taking his time, he thought Jade returned and Kenneth had enough fighting for one night. Unlocking the door and seeing Noel on the other side made his heart skip a beat as he wondered if Jade had seen her.

"Did Jade see you?" he asked, concerned now for both of their safety as he pulled her inside.

Noel said, "No, I watched her leave, crying."

Kenneth now turning to face her, his suit ripped and his head hurting, he made his way back to the couch where he took a seat.

"I just wanted to say thank you for what you did tonight. I, um, I didn't know you would do that," she said.

Kenneth continued to recline. "Come here, Noel," he said, his eyes closed once again. As she hesitated to make her way towards him, he pulled her closer as he felt her body heat. Noel opening her legs to sit atop his lap. Kenneth opened his eyes to look at her now, unraveling her hair as he played in it, unbuttoning her shirt and kissing her passionately between her breasts, he whispered, "I would kill for you." As he exposed her wounds, kissing them lightly, Kenneth and Noel made love. She missed his touch, although it had not been long. Kenneth finally realized, she still meant everything to him.

The following morning Noel had awoken to find Kenneth in the kitchen making them breakfast when the phone rang. She stepped lightly onto the winding stairs, wearing his t-shirt, overhearing the conversation, it did not sound good.

"Wait—What? That's not even true, you have witnesses, they're lying, everyone is lying, you know that. Doug, that's not how it went. Jesus, Doug!" he shouted. Kenneth banged the phone on the countertop, smashing the receiver—breaking it. Noel made her appearance as Kenneth stood in the kitchen, afraid to approach him as he rubbed his head in disbelief.

"Are you okay?" she whispered, Kenneth staring past her.

"No, no, I'm not alright, I just got fired," he said. Just then a loud thud came to the front door; Noel raced downstairs now as Kenneth ran to open it, affixed to his door was an eviction letter dangling from the peephole. Kenneth made his way down the ironclad staircase, catching up to the man who had put it there, a frail man.

"What the fuck is this?" he shouted.

Timidly, he said, "It's Mr. Grayson—wants you out in thirty days," the strange man shouted, climbing in the back of a town car as if he feared for his life. Everything was happening too fast as Noel stood inside, Kenneth's oversized shirt hanging from her as her hair bounced along her shoulders. Kenneth could not help but notice how beautiful she looked, pissed as he looked down at her arm to find the bruises still there.

"I'm so sorry," Noel cried as Kenneth placed his hand gently behind her neck, pulling her closer to him, kissing her forehead. She had an innocent look on her face.

"I'm not, it's going to be okay," he assured her.

Weeks passed since Noel and Benjamin had spoken, she screened his calls and after multiple text messages, she realized he was responsible for having Kenneth fired and having him evicted. Noel had no desire to continue to have him in her life, but the longer Kenneth went unemployed the more difficult it became to deal with him. As Noel found herself boxing up his belongings, she noticed all the things he held onto that belonged to Jade. Without his permission, Noel began keeping a separate box for her things, after a few weeks, she showed up to the hotel where she returned the box to Jade. Jade was infuriated.

"How dare you come to my job and return a box filled with my things? Obviously, if he still has these that's because he wants to hold onto his memories of me," Jade sniped.

"He has me now, he doesn't need your memories," said Noel.

"Well, perhaps you can tell him to stop calling me," said Jade. Noel turning to face her.

"He doesn't call you," she said with confidence.

"Every single day," Jade bragged.

"Stay away from my boyfriend," Noel warned her. As Noel made her exit, Nathan made his way inside, marching aggressively; he did not notice Noel stepping past him. Jade rolled her eyes as he approached the counter.

"I have nothing to say to you," she said as she walked away.

"Take a break, come and sit with me," Nathan demanded. Jade did not like being told what to do, but Nathan had a hold on her. She followed him to the bar located in the hotel restaurant, where he ordered them both, vodka over ice, Jade politely chose to decline. Nathan shot her a questionable look.

"No alcohol?" he asked. "That's a first."

"What is it, Nathan?" she asked, growing impatient.

"I have a proposition for you," he said, taking a sip. "You know I love you and will do anything for you, you've been asking me for this divorce and believe me, I am trying everything in my power to get it for you, but there's an issue," Nathan said.

"I've been asking for two years, if you truly wanted the divorce, Nathan, you would make it happen!" she sniped.

"Do you love me? You're parading all around town with this Kenneth guy and trying to make me jealous," he said.

"Really, I wanted that ring, it would have been worth so much, but no, your friend had him fired, Noel ends up sleeping with him, it turned into one big mess, and now I'm pregnant, Nathan," she said, lowering her voice. Nathan was speechless; he could not bring himself to question the child's paternity, knowing the truth would simply crush him.

"I have a plan, but it will involve Noel. I don't have a prenup, and if I'm going to get out of this, we, if we are going to do this, we have to both do this the right way," he said to Jade, smiling.

As the conversation continued, Nathan could think of nothing but the child growing inside her, bringing him to finally ask, "Is the baby his?" Inside he was crying, emotionally devastated considering he already knew the answer.

"I do not know, you and I were together the night of the fight, so I truly don't know, but I won't keep it if you don't want me to," she said as she let a tear fall from her eyes. Nathan took the time to outline the details to Jade, believing if the child was to be his, they could in fact be very happy together. Surprisingly, Jade was happy to take part.

Jade knew it was time to now play nice, she was ready to get exactly what she came for as she left work and made her way to the boutique where Noel had just begun her shift. Stepping inside, Jade removed her sunglasses. With the holidays nearing, the streets were congested and now the boutique filled with customers; she patiently waited for her turn to have Noel to herself.

"Noel, we need to talk," Jade demanded as she made her way to the counter. Noel ignored her.

"This is about Kenneth," she continued. Noel took a deep breath.

"Jesus, you just don't quit, do you?" Noel said, making her way into the back of the store.

Jade, taking a seat, began. "So, I'm pregnant," she said.

Noel turned to face her. "What! With what?" she sniped.

"A baby, you idiot, and yes, it is Kenneth's baby, but him and I weren't supposed to make it this far, I mean, Nathan took too long for his divorce, which led me to stay with Kenneth longer than I had anticipated, so, now I'm pregnant, but Nathan wants the divorce. But his overly clingy wife won't grant him one and they don't have a prenup, so this is where you come in," Jade continued. Noel listened on.

"You have to get his wife to pay you somehow to go away. We will give you some of the money, I will go away with my baby, and Nathan can divorce his wife," she said.

"Something in that plan is illegal," Noel snapped.

"Listen, you and I both know if I tell Kenneth about this baby, he will want to be in this baby's life and mine, but quite frankly, I don't love Kenneth as much as I thought I did, and now that Nathan is ready to move on, I am too. We just can't allow this woman to take everything he's worked so hard for," she continued.

"Get out," Noel snapped.

"Noel, think about this, if I leave, I will keep this baby and there is a good chance that Kenneth will leave you and I have no problem continuing to pretend my love for him is real, he doesn't want to leave me and we both know he is going to land on his feet," said Jade.

"Get the hell out," Noel repeated. "You don't love anyone but yourself, wherever the money goes, that's where you go, huh? Jesus, Jade, people have feelings, Kenneth has feelings, and the only reason I'm not mad at him for loving you the way he does is because underneath all of that macho demeanor and that smooth talk, walk, and large bank account is still the boy I went to high school with, the boy who can't believe he moved from a small town and landed a good job and got with a woman as beautiful as you—but you are so ugly on the inside, it hurts me that he can't see it. But I will change that for him, I swear, so women like you can't hurt him anymore," she said.

Jade remained disinterested. "All of that sounds sweet, but give it some thought, otherwise this can get very messy for everyone involved," she warned as she made her way back outside, pushing her way through the crowd.

Alicia and Nathan settled into their condo in Tribeca, Alicia warming up to the idea of living in the city, but being a stay at home mom proved itself to be far less rewarding than she had hoped. After hearing of the fight at the pop-up, she begged Nathan to spend more time with her and the children. Over breakfast, their conversation was anything short of pleasant,

The next day inside the Ramirez household, Alicia was feeling slighted as Nathan had begun giving her the cold shoulder after their brief exchange. "Why don't we start planning a mini-vacation?" She suggested as their kids ate and Nathan responded to emails. She stood over the table, slicing her cantaloupes before suggesting the kids begin to get ready for school,

"Nathan?" she questioned as she waited patiently for his reply, but he did not reply, instead, he joined the children in their upstairs bedroom where he assisted their youngest in finding something nice to wear for school,

"Sweetheart, this dress is nice," he said, holding up a white dress she had worn to church once before.

Lauren giggled. "Daddy, that dress is for church." Nathan smiled as he listened to her giggle, Alicia listening on from the foot of the stairs as his son came racing down with his backpack on and ready to go,

"Hey, hey, Junior quit running," Alicia warned him as he ran into the kitchen, pouring himself another glass of orange juice. Nathan and Lauren made their way downstairs once they agreed on a pair of overalls, a sweater, and a light jacket for school,

"We're going to go apple picking next weekend," he said to Alicia as he retrieved his coat from the hanger in the closet closest the exit. Alicia tried to pretend to be happy as she assisted him, but realized he was pulling away. She smiled at Lauren, who had her eyes fixed on them both,

"Nathan, after you bring the kids to school can you come home so we can talk?" she begged.

"No, I have meetings," Nathan said as he turned and made his way out the door holding his daughter's hand. "Junior, stop running," he shouted, shutting the door behind him. Alicia sobbed as she watched from the upstairs window as Nathan took their children to school. She felt excluded in a family she had worked so hard to bring together. Moments later, after watching the Cadillac SUV take off, a knock came to the door.

"Who is it?" she bellowed as she ceased clearing the breakfast from the table. Making her way over to the door, she took a look through the peephole where she noticed the back of a woman's head. Again, she said, "Who is it?"

The woman on the other side quickly took her leave once she heard that Alicia was inside. Noel ran down the stairs and out of the door where she remained hidden for a total of twenty seconds, giving Alicia just enough time to look out the window and see that no one was there. Noel wanted to have a talk with Nathan but completely forgot that Alicia now resided with him in the condo. She slapped herself for almost having been caught.

Noel could not focus as she wandered the streets of New York's Upper East Side. When she realized she was still in possession of her apartment keys, she made her way into the building, letting herself in, she had expected to find the locks changed, or even a new woman occupying the unit by now, but it was empty. It was the exact way she had left it. Her makeup, her hair bows, racks of clothing Benjamin had delivered for the pop-up, shoes, and the unfinished champagne. She thought about how free she would be if she truly had the money to support herself. Jade did not disclose how much she would get for fooling Alicia, but she imagined it would be sufficient enough to afford the luxury she stood in. Plus, with Kenneth out of work, she wondered how they were now going to make ends meets once his savings depleted. Although she did not believe Kenneth would be out of work for long, Noel did not want him to be the only breadwinner in their relationship.

As she paced the sky-rise, she left a note for Benjamin on stationary she found just beneath the bar. She thanked him for his generosity and apologized for the misunderstanding which led to the altercation between Kenneth and himself. She could not get the visual out of her head as the events replayed, snickering as she recalled the first blow that Kenneth made as he leaped into the air, landing a punch right in Benjamin's face. As she scribbled away on the notepad, she felt her hands beginning to hurt. Filling an entire piece of paper with her thoughts, thoughts she knew Benjamin was not going to be pleased reading.

But she had to be honest with herself, and of course, with him as well. She concluded by thanking him once again for his willingness to change who he was in an effort to make her happy, she thought, had it not been for Kenneth, she could have possibly been happy with Benjamin, he was kind after all. She was rambling now as she decided it best to stop writing, placing the key along with the note next to the D'Usse, she took another look around. It was time to say goodbye to the dating scene and hello to responsibility and a life with the man she had come to love.

Noel made her way to the loft with a bag of groceries she purchased from Whole Foods, her duffle bag, and some other belongings she gathered from the apartment. Arriving in the taxicab, she watched Lexington outside of the loft throwing a suitcase into the back seat. She hurried inside as she wondered what was happening, the bags breaking as she ran into the lift making her way to the third floor. Kenneth's door wide open as strangers entered and exited. She searched the room in a panic, looking for Kenneth, calling to him now as the food dropped everywhere, angering the men who were trying to wrap the furniture and move it down into the center of the loft.

"Watch it, lady," one man grumbled. Noel now made her way up the winding stairs after placing what was left of the groceries on the countertop. Entering the bedroom, she saw Kenneth sitting on the edge of his bed in a pair of jeans and a Hanes t-shirt, a baseball cap on his head, his walk-in closet had been completely emptied.

"Hey Noel," he said, standing to face her. But Noel was not feeling amicable,

"What's happening, you don't have to be out for another week," she said, standing by the staircase.

"I know, but, um, I decided to head to Seattle and, uh, visit my family for a while and enjoy the house I have there until I decide to rent it again," he said nonchalantly. Noel did not understand.

"You're going back to Seattle, for how long? Did you want me to come? I needed some more notice, I mean, what do I tell Amber?" she spoke quickly and in such a panic she caught herself losing breath. Kenneth rushed over to her, placing his hands along her shoulders.

"No, no, I mean, I am going alone and I just need some time," he said. Noel slapped his hands away, growing angry,

"When were you going to tell me about this?" she questioned. Kenneth placing his hand on his head grew tiresome of the constant bickering between women.

"I mean, I didn't really think about it, I just figured you would find out eventually. I mean, no one would be here," he said. Noel smacked him. She had enough of the games. Looking up at him as he tilted his head and now straightened his neck to face her once again, his hands placed in his pockets,

"Well, I'm glad you got that out of your system. My flight leaves in a few hours," he said.

"Listen to me, if you leave right now, we are over. I am not a masochist; I do not enjoy being hurt. If you don't love me, or want to spend your life with me, then…" Noel snapped and yet her voice just above a whisper,

"Whoa, whoa, you know I just came out of a serious relationship, surely you didn't think I was going to dive right back in. You see, Noel, you have these expectations, and then when you don't get your way, everyone else is at fault. I'm not taking the blame here," Kenneth said. "I am not saying that I don't have feelings for you, but Goddamn, I just lost the love of my life, my job, my home, all that I worked for. Jesus, stop being selfish, I need time!" he shouted. Noel flinched, she did not want him to yell at her, she did not care to understand,

"I don't want you to go," she sobbed.

Kenneth took her hands as the man downstairs shouted, "All set!" He banged on the staircase railing. Noel looked around frantically. "Don't go, please, don't go!" she cried. Kenneth was not used to a woman begging him for anything, unfamiliar to him, he had no reaction towards her, he simply thought it best to walk away.

"I'll be in touch, alright?" he said, and just like that, he was gone.

Noel, falling to her knees, felt completely foolish as she wondered how many more times was she going to have to be a fool for him before finally realizing it was time to let him go. The doors slammed downstairs, and then the car door. Noel knew now Kenneth was gone for good. Did she truly mean nothing to him? Where had the time gone and what if he knew about the baby, what if that was the real reason he had chosen to depart? As the questions flooded her mind, she could do nothing but allow herself the time to grieve. He was gone, gone for good, and there was nothing she could do about it.

The rain came down so hard that night she realized it was time to go. The loft was pitch black and Noel was finally peeling herself from the floor. As she took one final look around, she threw her duffle over her shoulders, her nail chipping as she struggled to open the door and make her way outside. She stood quivering when she spotted Lexington across the street sitting in the town car with the light on inside, completing what appeared to be a crossword puzzle. Lexington was an African American man who appeared to be in his late sixties. He wore an all-black suit with a black hat. Spotting her, he proceeded now to remove an umbrella from the passenger's seat, making his way towards her.

"Young lady, allow me," he said, removing her duffle from her shoulder. "Kenneth asked that I take you where you need to go." Noel did not want his pity, but she needed it.

"Houston Avenue, please," she muttered as she continued to shiver. The night grew cold as she stepped lightly to the car.

Once they had arrived at Frances's house, she listened as the laughter resonated from inside, the bright lights blinding her as she thanked Lexington, removing herself and her bags from the town car, turning to face her he asked,

"Will you need the umbrella?"

Noel politely declined as she climbed out, her hair now soaking wet as the water beating against the door frame continued to splash on her. She rang the buzzer, standing out in the cold, listening as Frances and Africa shouted, "Who is it?" in a joyful manner. But she could not bring herself to respond, Frances now grew worried as she unlocked the door to find Noel standing drenched in the rain, her mascara running as she sobbed, falling into Frances's arms. Her heart was beating faster than she had ever felt it, she thought it was the beginning of a heart attack, the hairs on her arms rising, the sweat on her forehead building; it was the symptoms of a broken heart, she thought, physically taking its toll on her once again.

Frances and Africa were determined to help Noel find peace in the situation after she disclosed to them the events that took place that afternoon. Africa and Morris were now in a serious relationship, spending more time now with Frances and Maxwell. Noel was wondering if she would be left to feel like the pariah of the group, but Frances assured her that would never be the case.

In an attempt to lighten the mood, Maxwell said, "Hopefully in a few years I will be able to afford a nice vacation for you ladies. Noel, you sure seem like you need it," he chuckled.

As the months passed, Noel decided to occupy her room and embark on a quest to finally find the peace and the direction her life so desperately needed.

CHAPTER TWENTY

Present Day... January 2018

Once the vehicle took off with Alicia sitting in the back seat, Maxwell toggled in his mind an idea, whether or not he should let the remaining ladies in on one last surprise. Angelo beside him, nodding his head in excitement. If there was one thing Maxwell always knew to avoid, it was an angry woman.

His hesitation caused Angelo to grow antsy, and so he shouted, "Maxwell is now the primary accountant for the Brimson Family Estate!"

Maxwell turned to face him. "Man!" he said, extending his arms in disbelief. The news abrupt, her eyes widened, Frances ran to hug him.

"I am so proud of you," she said, kissing his lips abundantly. Abigail and Noel were confused, but they were happy nonetheless,

"So, you're going to be managing Michael Brimson's billion-dollar accounts?" Noel asked.

Smiling as Frances hung off of his arm, Maxwell said, "Yes, every single one, the commission is ridiculously large, and this is truly the start of a brand-new life for us," he said, kissing Frances.

"Why don't we all head home and go out to dinner to celebrate?" said Frances.

"That sounds like a good way to end the trip on a good note, so finish getting packed up and make your way to the cars outside!" he said with excitement. Angelo assisted Noel and Abigail with their luggage, tossing it in the back seat of one of the Cadillac trucks. Frances and Maxwell occupied their own car as they now made their way down the hill away from the lodge. Noel was excited!

"This is so exhilarating," Frances said as they cuddled in the backseat of the Jeep. "It is, you can even quit your job and start planning for your dream wedding," Maxwell said. Frances turned to face him.

"Are you serious? I can't leave my students, and of course, I was going to begin planning the wedding, I don't want to be a fat bride." She smiled, Maxwell tickling her; the pair horse playing around in the back seat, laughing.

"I will never tell you to leave your job, just know the option is there, and you are going to be a beautiful bride," he said, kissing her forehead. Frances could not have been happier,

"I will think about it," she confirmed.

It had been one week since the ladies returned home. With Frances no longer working at the boutique part-time, Noel had taken over full-time as a manager. She was promoted prior to their girls' trip, and although she felt it was bad timing, she figured given the circumstances she should, in fact, go. Now she was one million dollars richer and looking forward to meeting with Jade before the day's end.

"You can fold the clothes, but please be mindful of where you're placing them," she said. It had been eighteen months, and Noel had finally begun feeling like she'd found her calling. As the manager of *Crystals*, she was making it in a world of competitors as she also sought work as a full-time paralegal to a Mr. Corey Williams, Esquire. Things were beginning to calm down at home as Frances found her wedding dress, however, their apartment now began to resemble a bridal warehouse and a pregnant Frances was anything but fun.

Jade made her way inside the boutique as Noel stood waiting for her store clerk to clock out so she could leave.

"See you tomorrow," she told the young lady who by now had only been working a full two days and was beginning to feel overwhelmed. Jade and Noel found themselves forming an unlikely friendship once Kenneth departed and Maxwell had given up his apartment to reside with Frances while he finished school. This made their living situation anything but comfortable. The two-bedroom apartment now housing three adults, two of whom were in a relationship. Noel found herself renting hotel rooms the majority of the time, and when she came to realize how quickly the cost was adding up, she called on Jade for a generous discount at the Hilton.

After almost two years, and Noel felt different now, in control, she was not the same woman she was when she arrived in New York, and with a new style, new attitude, new job position, she felt empowered and was determined to begin making her own way.

As the ladies took a seat on the outside of the terrace of a rooftop restaurant only blocks away from the boutique, Jade began by saying, "Thanks for finally coming around."

Jade gained about twenty-five pounds during her pregnancy and was now the mother of a young man by the name of Elijah Ramirez. She was ecstatic to announce that Nathan was finally filing for divorce. Noel did not feel good about this; the money she wired her was later divided amongst them, leaving Alicia with absolutely nothing during their settlement.

"Where are you guys going to go?" asked Noel placing her hair behind her ear. Arriving home from the lodge, the first thing she did was get a new hair-cut, a bob to be exact. Her hair no longer doing as it pleased, and once she began making good money, she started having facials on the regular, along with manicures and pedicures.

"Not sure yet, but as a new mother, I feel bad for her. Nathan is fighting for full custody of the kids and leaving her high and dry," Jade continued.

"Do you honestly think she deserved that?" Noel questioned. "Also, what about Kenneth, that's still his son," she continued.

"Listen, Nathan and I are far from perfect, but we wanted each other and we didn't want the financial baggage. Aren't you even the least bit appalled that this woman was even willing to offer you money to rid herself of you and your unborn child?" Jade asked. "She isn't as innocent as she appears," she continued.

"No, but she's still a human being with feelings, Jade, and now Kenneth won't even know his child. All of this hurt to two people who didn't deserve it," Noel pleaded. The waitress now making her way over to them as Jade continued to evade a conversation involving Kenneth.

"Hello ladies, can I start you both off with something to drink, perhaps water?" she asked politely.

"Sure, a glass of water for us both, please," Noel said.

"Look, you can act innocent all you want to, but something made you pick up the phone and call me that day, something clicked in your mind that made you want in on this plan to get the money you needed to be the woman you always wanted to be, and now you have it. My number is going to change tonight. Nathan still has some details to iron out since Alicia sold the condo and pretty much everything they owned to pay you and she's now living with her mom, poor thing didn't see this coming. Well, I wish her all the best," Jade said. But Noel was not through,

"Just answer me one thing, the robbery. Were you there?" Noel asked.

"No, I was not there, but I did have a request that you be roughed up a bit," she said, walking away, and that was the last time Noel would ever speak to Jade again.

Arriving home, Noel dreaded turning her key. Inside resided a pregnant bridezilla, her husband-to-be, and a house filled with wedding favors, dresses, gifts, vision boards, placement cards, and all the wonderful girly things she had come to despise.

On January 19, 2018, when Noel left the lodge, she vowed never to think of those moments again. Surprised that Alicia had shown up, she wondered how Jade managed to pull that off, but knew better than to ask; Jade, after all, was a determined woman and Nathan was her priority then. Noel was different now, refined and mysterious, and after learning a lot about herself and her standards, she decided to re-evaluate the people she allowed into her life.

After months of wedding planning, cake tasting, and multiple trips to venues, Noel was tired and grateful that the wedding was now only a few days away, although this saddened her because she knew with Frances now becoming a wife and mother there was no longer any room for her here. Day in and day out she thought of no one but Kenneth. She wondered how he was doing, envying her best friend at times, thinking to herself that this life Frances is living should have been hers, but then she wondered, is this a life she truly would have wanted? Or was the fear of turning thirty soon and ending up alone causing her to resent the life she was currently living? She should have been happy, but she wasn't. There was something missing, a void she wondered how she was going to fill.

Once inside, she noticed she was alone. Noel decided to order food and delve into this YouTube channel she had begun hearing so much about, entitled, *Even My Hair is Mad* from a woman named Nova Higgins. Nova, like most other African-American women, were fed up with the Black man and the self-hate they've been projecting on women of color as it pertains to dating and their refusal to court them. However, if her best friend were not getting married to a Black man, she too would have no doubt believed the words coming from dear Nova. But Black Love exists, she told herself. She had seen it with her own two eyes. It was seldom, but it was there.

That night, Noel lay awake in the dark. One year and six months later, she pondered just how far she had come, planning her next move as she now had over a million dollars in an account to call her own after stepping off of the Amtrak two years prior with only seven hundred dollars and a credit card with a meager spending limit. She then decided to call on someone she had come to know all too well. As he answered on the second ring, his voice as always put both her mind and body at ease.

Noel was not some boring Korean and Black woman to him, she too was exotic, a fascination of some kind. She was the woman who he saw himself sneaking kisses and oral sex in the back of the taxi cabs and Ubers with. He was exciting and exciting is what she craved.

"Good night beautiful," he said; her stomach filled with butterflies, as always, as his tone was so deep and rich. Noel was not afraid to speak her mind and be as graphic and detailed as she wanted to be, she was free whenever they spoke, she was the woman behind the phone and he was the man who at night unleashed the part of her she otherwise had no idea existed. The two spoke for hours, and once the night seemed to begin phasing itself out, she decided to end their call.

"I am feeling sleepy," she said.

Teasing, he said, "Will you think of me tonight?" Noel now blushed with her fingers buried between her legs, sweating, her cheeks pressing heavily against the cellular phone speakers.

"Of course!" she said. But she was not sure who she was going to think of, she just knew that it was going to happen, and she was going to welcome it. Noel was in such a rush to get off of the phone she could hear herself beginning to grow impatient.

"Good night, I have to go." Immediately she ended the call.

However, she could not go to sleep; instead, she turned to lie on her back. Eyes closed as she turned her head to the right, removing her hands from the insides of her pajama pants, throwing the covers over her as she began to fall into a deep slumber and then it happened like it always did.

Noel began to imagine him, someone, a prince, a sexual knight, climbing on top of her, stroking her, but not just any stroke. He was pounding the fuck out of her, relentlessly, harder each time she moaned. It was as though he enjoyed the feeling of power and the control she had given him over her body, over her soul! He was demanding and rightfully so, never letting up. As Noel placed her manicured nails atop his imaginary chest, as she lie facing upward, his abs and muscles protruding, his face still a mystery to her. But Noel did not mind it. She gasped and gasped, gripping her pillows tighter, she let out a faint cry.

Noel's imaginary lover was slowing down, winding his waist, picking up speed, he continued to penetrate her, shouting now, she felt him, and she felt it! Her thighs began to tremble as she began caressing my hair with her right hand and gripping her breasts with her left. She was in heaven. Placing her head back as she widened her legs, allowing him, this being, undeniable access to insert himself fully into her. She imagined that his penis felt like love, with each stroke she felt her heart skip a beat, twitching once, she moaned and moaned as he stroked deeper and deeper, pounding with anger, but she loved it! She moaned until finally she was released. Noel felt her juices trickling down her thighs, and before she knew it, she felt the pleasure from a prince.

The light in her bedroom switched on as Noel slept. The ladies returned and everyone energetic, the time now 2:14 a.m. Noel squinted, as she had no clue what was happening. Abigail threw herself atop the mattress and onto Noel, causing her to shriek in pain,

"Jesus Abby!" Noel shouted,

"Wake up sleepy head, our best friend is getting married in just two days!" shouted Abigail. Africa and Frances had driven to the airport to fetch her that night. Noel could not think straight, she did not know whether to be angry or annoyed, her emotions completely in disarray.

"Auntie Jenn is flying in tomorrow," said Africa who was now in the kitchen fixing herself a sandwich. Frances now sat in the living room caressing her stomach. Everyone gathered in the living room as they turned on all the lights exposing the pigsty she had been forced to live in for months. Noel continued to groan changing her clothes into something lighter, a nightgown. Taking a seat next to Frances, she planted a big kiss on her cheek.

"We're losing you to a guy," she pretended to sob.

"Oh please, how many times did I lose you to a guy?" Frances teased,

"Hey, but I always knew where home was," Noel laughed. Frances was right, each time she met one of her affluent lovers, she abandoned her friends only to call on them once things went downhill. But she vowed no more. "You know I'm trying to change," Noel said, intertwining her fingers into Frances's.

"I know, so, I have good news," Frances said.

Noel now sat Indian style as Africa flipped through the television channels.

"Max and I discussed it, and since he bought us a house in Long Island, I'm going to sublet you this apartment. Of course, that's if you want it," Frances said. Noel was elated, she could have cried,

"Wait, seriously? I wondered where I was going to go, but oh my God Franny, thank you!" she said, hugging her, Africa turning to face them,

"Aww, Franny is a nice baby momma," she joked.

"Only forty-eight more hours until he makes an honest woman out of me!" she confirmed. Turning to face Noel, she continued, "I can't imagine you not being here," she said as her eyes began to well. Noel took a deep breath as she leaned in to give her a hug.

"Are you going to need a roommate," cried Abigail. Everyone chuckled.

"Surely, I mean this rent is ridiculous and now with everything that's happened to Shawn, who knows what the new owners will look to charge," Noel said sadly, placing her hand atop Frances's lap,

"And you will be in Long Island, closer to me," Africa smiled as she pointed to Frances hoping to restore the joy in the room.

"We have to leave the bachelorettes to enjoy this city life, we're boring housewives now," she continued.

"Oh, did you tell them the good news?" Frances asked Africa, Africa was reluctant to say.

"Well no, I mean, we're still working out the kinks and going to therapy, we have Max to thank most definitely for talking some sense into him, but Morris and I have a ways to go before we're back together," she scoffed,

"Hey, but at least it's progress," Frances said as she was feeling optimistic. "Plus, he's been more than apologetic, just hurry up and forgive him so we can have these babies and start planning play dates," Frances demanded. Everyone laughed.

"One uterus at a time," Africa shouted.

"Speaking of which, Noel, are you bringing Corey to the wedding?" Abigail asked.

"Yes," Noel said, bringing her knees to her chest as she sat upright.

"Who on earth is Corey?" Africa asked.

"You will all meet him at the wedding, he's an attorney and a super sweet guy," she continued.

"So you're over the public relations guy?" joked Abigail. The room grew silent, immediately Noel wanted to throw herself back into her room locking herself inside, but determined that would have been a tad bit too dramatic.

"Well, I'm not over him, but I have to start getting back out there. It's been long enough and, he's gone, I guess," she said, her voice breaking up. Frances could not help but feel bad, she knew how much Noel loved Kenneth and it saddened her to have heard about his abrupt leave.

"Yea, your prince charming will come too, Noey," Abigail continued. Africa was growing tired now; as such she knew Frances must have been exhausted,

"Well, as the appointed maid of honor, it is my duty to ask that the bride now retire in her quarters for some rest. Frances, you have a long day tomorrow and Sunday," Africa said. Frances nodded in agreeance.

"You're absolutely right, plus, I am feeling sleepy," Frances arose from her seat, walking over to Abigail and Noel giving them both a kiss on the cheek and a hug to Africa, she closed her bedroom door and went to bed. Once the girls were sure she had been tucked away, the conversation began,

"So, what are we doing tomorrow?' Noel asked,

"We are having a spa party for her tomorrow, it's all day so we have to be at the spa on Madison at ten in the morning and then once we leave, Frances has an appointment to get her hair and makeup done and then we are doing dinner," Africa said. "No bachelorette party for the pregnant bride, I figured that would have been too tacky," she continued, both Noel and Abigail agreeing.

"Well, I am going to turn in as well, Abby, are you sleeping with me?" asked Noel.

"Yea, I'm going to brush my teeth and I'll be there in a minute," she said.

"Good night," Africa bellowed, turning to face Abigail she continued, "We are losing one of us, it's so bittersweet," she laughed.

"You were technically the first to go when you and Morris decided to live together, but here comes extravagant wedding and the baby to match," Abigail said. "Good night sis, see you in the morning," she continued.

The next morning was proving itself to be completely catastrophic as the woman struggled to get dressed, showered and prepared for the day ahead. Stumbling over one another Noel wished greatly that she was able to stay somewhere else, at least until the wedding was over.

"Okay, ladies! Up and alert, we have spa at 10 a.m., rehearsal dinner and church from 3 p.m. to 5 p.m., makeup and hair for Frances at 6:30 p.m. and dinner with the relatives at 8 p.m., then its bed by 11 p.m. no playing around because we have to be up bright and early tomorrow," Africa shouted from the front door where she knew everyone could hear her as she read the itinerary from her cellular phone.

"I am tired already and we haven't even left the house," Frances mumbled, Noel laughing.

"Careful, you don't want the drill sergeant to hear you," she joked about Africa, Frances tilting her head back as Noel slipped her a Kit Kat bar, her face lit up with glee.

"Oh my God, thank you Noey, can you slip me these all day?" Frances begged as she whispered to Noel.

Noel chuckled. "Of course, preggers," she said smiling, kissing Frances atop the forehead.

"So, who is heading in the shower first?" Noel beckoned,

"Me!" shouted Abigail as she hopped across the luggage as though she were on an obstacle course. The morning went smooth and with Frances now four months pregnant her clothes were beginning to feel less comfortable. She dreaded having to wear her wedding dress as she was not looking forward to the zippers, ribbons and all the struggling it was going to take to get her inside.

"Franny, our parents are on the plane and will call once they've arrived. Noel your mom and dad are coming too okay!" she said to Noel who was now in the bathroom brushing her teeth as Abigail showered.

Noel was shocked, thrusting her head out of the door, she asked, "My parents? As in Jennifer and Jin? Why on earth are they coming? None of us are getting married," she said with toothpaste foaming in her mouth. "Franny? Please explain?" Noel begged, her eyes lowered,

"Well, I've only met Africa's parents one time and she's my maid of honor, so I figured it only right to invite them, and then once they heard we were all friends, her mom invited your mom and then your mom invited your dad. I guess they just want to see you, Noel, it's really not a big deal," Frances said. Noel's jaw dropped, Africa was now making her way into the bathroom,

"Abby, hey, come on, in and out, there're three other asses that need to be cleaned out here!" Africa shouted. Abigail growling in annoyance as she turned off the pipes. One by one the woman all utilized the latrine, showering and getting themselves organized for the day ahead. Frances looked forward to seeing Maxwell, since their engagement she had never spent the night without him, this was feeling foreign to her. Texting her mother until she arrived at the airport Frances could tell just how elated she was, she and her brother Freddie to which Noel had yet to meet him.

"You haven't met Freddie yet, have you, Noel?" said Frances with a sly grin on her face, this worried Noel.

"No, I haven't and perhaps I shouldn't want to," Noel laughed, Africa, interrupting.

"Believe me, you don't want to, he is so smug," Africa confirmed.

"Not true, you've met him once," Frances laughed. She knew her brother was a lot to handle, but she was secretly hoping he and the girls would come to get along considering they had put aside their own differences.

"Where are your family flying in from?" Noel asked as she prepared for her shower,

"San Francisco," said Frances.

"Wow! And so, tell me about this Freddie guy?" Abigail interrupted,

"Well here's the most important part, he is engaged," said Frances. "So, ladies please be on your best behaviors, his wife to be is such a sweetheart, I think she's working so she won't be able to make it. Noel, I know how you like married men," Frances joked, everyone laughing hysterically.

"Oh, so we can joke about it now? A few months ago you all wanted to murder me," she said.

"Listen, we all learned and grew from that experience in the woods, I think it was just what we needed, although my ankle will never be the same, it was a revelation for us all," Africa said.

"Cheers to that!" said Abigail as she blended a batch of tequila and orange juice.

"Why are you such a lush?" Africa asked.

"I am a college student, that's all we do is drink and study, give me a break, will you?" she said.

"Noel, time's up in the bathroom!" Africa shouted. Noel tilting her head back said a quick prayer while the shower beat against her naked body. By 9:35 a.m., the women were dressed and waiting on their Uber, the spring weather feeling amazing. Now April, Noel, and Frances were the last to enter the back of the taxi cab. Once at the spa the woman enjoyed their full body massages, manicures, pedicures, facials, and vaginal rejuvenation—a special gift from Africa to Frances. Their morning filled with laughter and inexplicable joy, Frances describing her brother to the women once her mother confirmed they had arrived at the hotel and would be heading to the church within the hour. Nothing felt more perfect and now Noel was beginning to realize just how real this way, Franny was tying the knot and they were all getting along so well and all present for it.

Frances hated the fact that she could not enjoy a glass of wine or even champagne and it annoyed her that everywhere they walked strangers were congratulating her on her pregnancy. Petite, weighing only 135 pounds, and so her belly was round and palpable under her shirt and cardigan. Arriving at the church, Frances could not wait to see Maxwell, she missed him dearly, and upon entering she noticed the empty seats, her parents sitting to the far front by the altar along with her brother, who after one look had become smitten with Abigail who was paying him no never mind.

"Who is that?" he whispered to Frances as she made her way past him to hug her mother and father,

"Mom, dad, these are my friends, Africa who you've met, her younger sister and my bestie, Abigail, and this is Noel, the newest addition to the fabulous three," everyone said hello, Africa leaning in to give her mother a hug.

"Hello Ms. Elle, she smiled." Eleanor was a tiny woman, her hair cut short, she was of stocky build, dark-skinned with a heavy southern accent. Her husband, Frances's stepfather, was Mr. Myles Carter, Cherokee and Jamaican, he had a ponytail and stood about 5'11, caramel complexion. Frances would joke when she called him coolie. Freddie bared a striking resemblance to his father. After everyone made their acquaintances, Frances and her mother had much to discuss, her mother thrilled to see that her baby girl was pregnant and wearing her pregnancy well—after all, Frances was glowing. A few minutes later in walked Maxwell, Morris, his friends Dwayne and Karym, and his parents Gloria and Joseph Miller. Everyone exchanging brief introductions as Frances and Maxwell made their way to the altar to visit the pastor.

Frances and Maxwell previously introduced one another to their parents, so they were simply making conversation as Mr. Carter told the joke of when Maxwell contacted him asking for permission to marry his daughter.

"That boy was so afraid," he chuckled, everyone laughing along, the day was going smoothly as the rehearsal got underway. What was supposed to be two hours quickly turned into four as no one would stop speaking long enough to follow the directions provided by the pastor. Both Frances and Maxwell were asked to write their vows apart from one another, and after more than forty-five minutes the couple emerged. Frances handing her vows to Africa for safe keeping and Maxwell doing the same to Morris. She was feeling drained as she turned to face Noel, who reached into her cardigan pocket removing a Kit Kat, Frances grabbing it with excitement found her second wind.

"Thank you," she mouthed.

As the day pressed on, Mr. Carter took countless bathroom breaks, and when he was present did nothing but complain about his placement and the seating arrangements. Freddie was embarrassed.

"Dad, you have to just stand there," he whispered, Noel overhearing them.

"I am an old man, I can't be standing so long to light no candles," he grumbled. When given a break, Noel checked her phone to find thirteen missed calls from her mother. Dialing her back, she wondered why she had been sent straight to voicemail. Africa was now drifting off to sleep, Abigail growing anxious, and Noel just praying the day would end, they were all finding themselves bored and growing impatient. As 8:30

p.m. made its way upon them, their pastor finally concluded, closing everyone out in prayer. Noel and Africa were the first to exit, taking in the fresh air. Frances laughed hysterically,

"You two are such children," she teased. "Well, we have to go to dinner now," Frances said. However, Africa would hear of no such thing,

"What! We need to get you home so you can change, you completely missed hair and makeup—" she panicked, but Frances did not care, she was more concerned with simply spending time with her friends and family, not the glamorous look Africa wanted so badly for her. Leaning in, she gave Africa a long hug, grateful for all she had done as the sun now began to go down, her brother calling to her from the foot of the church as they all piled into the taxi cab,

"Are you guys coming along?" Frances asked, Abigail quickly agreed, marching happily down the staircase, Noel, and Africa exchanging a look before Noel shouted,

"I will be here bright and early, I love you," she said. Africa said the same as they watched Frances and Abigail depart. Noel stood watching Africa pace back and forth, she was exhausted, it was showing in her eyes,

"I need a bed so badly," she cried. Just then, Noel took pleasure in amicably reminding her that their parents were also in town and they should consider finding them. Africa had completely forgotten, shouting obscenities now as she was mentally prepared to head to sleep. Stepping past her, Noel chuckled to herself. She liked seeing Africa come mildly unhinged in an effort to coordinate this wedding.

"Noel, you are such a bitch," Africa said jokingly, walking behind her as they waited on their Uber. A cynical grin wiped across Noel's face.

CHAPTER TWENTY-ONE

A Day to Remember...
April 17, 2018

The big day arrived and everyone looked absolutely stunning. By 9 a.m., the church was completely packed on both sides. Frances underestimated how many guests she had and the marvelous turnout considering they had only four months to plan and prepare. The 1100 square foot church with 29-foot ceilings was heavily decorated by the wedding planner Frances hired. Jelani was a recommendation from Amber, and she could not have been more pleased with the turnout.

Frances stood in the bridal suite wearing her maternity wedding dress. This beautiful white wedding gown featured a one-shoulder design with organza flowers and a long and flowing Ganza skirt. The high waist concealing her belly while lengthening her torso, a stunning silhouette. The built-in bra and petticoat underneath helped the dress to maintain its structure and shape. A long train Frances needed help with bustling extending seven feet from her waist. Noel marveled in how beautiful she looks, her makeup simply flawless. Frances was pleased with her overall appearance, disappointed slightly that her dress had to bear the look of a belly bump, but as she favored the impeccable Anika Nani Rose with her bright smile and her hair curled and pinned back exposing her blemish-free skin. She had little to no complaints.

The romantic greenery theme is what Frances had longed for, the colors of elegant, vintage romance. Her bridesmaids draped in a veiled rose elegant V-neck sleeveless zip-up Ruching dress and silver sandals. Frances insisted on everyone having their hair pulled back into a tight, sleek, low ponytail. Applying her veil, Africa began to sob, which angered Frances as she was beginning to ruin her makeup.

"Let's just enjoy the day," said Frances as she smiled and held onto her bouquet, making her way to the main hall, stepping past the roses and the décor. Frances could feel her heart thumping through her chest as Dwayne and Noel walked first, his white tuxedo accompanied by the rose-colored handkerchief found in his jetted pocket as with all of the groomsmen. Karym and Abigail walked next to the sounds of the organ player, followed by Africa and Morris, who smiled at one another. Frances took a deep breath once the doors opened, revealing her to her guests and her husband-to-be. However, once she looked into his eyes, everyone now standing, as her stepfather, in his black tuxedo, and her brother in his white tuxedo, made their appearance, one to the right and the other to the left of her, she was no longer afraid.

Maxwell could not take his eyes off her, and while everyone stared at her, she looked at him, Noel watching him closely, his reaction and admiration for Frances causing her to weep. This was slowly beginning to feel like the happiest day of her life as she replayed all the wonderful moments she and Frances shared, she was no doubt losing her sister, the only sister she had come to know. Noel thought back to that moment on the train, she had no idea the people she would meet or how they would change her life forever, this moment was one for the books as Frances, her brother, and her father all made their way down the aisle.

Arriving to the altar, her father and brother both kissing her cheeks as they took their seats, the ladies moved swiftly to straighten her train, Noel noticed that Frances was drenched in tears. She blew her a kiss. At that moment, Noel realized they were all late bloomers, with Frances now thirty-one,

Abigail twenty-seven and finishing her bachelor's degree to enter onto law school, Africa thirty-four with no husband and no children and she, herself, Noel, now twenty-nine. She wondered, why had society put a time clock on women to ascertain the things that they should have no problem acquiring if and when the time is right?

As their vows were exchanged, Noel took a glimpse at her parents, who despite it all, she knew deep down were happy for her and proud. Everyone gratified and as humble as Frances was there was no reason to feel anything less than, she had fallen in love with a man who would move the ends of the earth for her. Maxwell could not take his eyes off of her, and as they exchanged their beautifully written vow everyone was now in tears, the ladies had all heard and seen a side of Frances they would have never known existed. Noel learned so much from her, she learned the importance of submission, the wonders it can do for and with the right man, and of course showing appreciation, before the pastor could instruct them to kiss, Frances removed her veil to kiss her husband-to-be for, she had come to appreciate all that he had done and was willing to do for her and their unborn child and she wasted no time letting him know.

"...by the powers vested in me by God and the State of New York, Mr. Miller, you may now kiss your bride," said the pastor. Hearing those words sent Maxwell into a frenzy as he reveled in her beauty, having no idea years ago he would find himself standing before her on this very day. From the moment they exchanged their vows and their rings Maxwell made a promise to himself, *this is forever*, he thought, no matter how long forever would take.

Frances and Maxwell danced their way out of the chapel and down into the limousine that awaited them outside. Noel greeted her parents and her auntie and uncle as everyone now made their way to the reception in the vehicles following behind them. Frances and Maxwell played around in their limo like two children, laughing, telling jokes, and preparing themselves for eternity. The car ride was one they wished could have gone on forever once they arrived at the venue thirty minutes later.

Jelani escorted the bridal party, the bride and groom, to the rear of the building just under the greenhouse-inspired reception tables for photographs. The ladies smiled, frolicked and tossed around jokes as they all happily enjoyed the day. Frances and Maxwell posed for their photos, Frances could not have been happier as her parents now made their way across the lawn, snapping photos of them on their cellular phones, a proud moment.

Everyone was then redirected to the upstairs ballroom where they waited and had a quiet snack for themselves as their guests were settled in downstairs and served appetizers. Noel, along with the other groomsmen and bridesmaids, all sat along the rectangular table, later on, Frances to the left of the groom and the bridesmaids seated alongside her. The Carters and the Millers seated at the round table closest to them both. The romantic greenery featured themes such as woody, green, nature, and romance. The flower details were the most indispensable part of the wedding, paired with an elegant white that literally transformed the outdoors.

Frances was so impressed with Jelani that she could not wait to thank him, stepping outside the floral greenery wedding table decorations done on top of the neutral colored table linen helped her décor to simply stand out. As the ladies prepared for their photos, Noel smiling from ear to ear until her eye caught a glimpse of a shadow, she had to convince herself was not really standing just by the threshold congratulating Maxwell. She shook it off as she continued to converse with the ladies over salmon. Corey had chosen to accompany Noel.

Corey and Noel danced the day away! Noel felt like Baby from *Dirty Dancing* in her rose dress, and after a few shots of vodka, the party was divine. Corey was smitten by her, but the attraction on her side was purely physical, she could not have the man she wanted, subconsciously comparing every guy to him, not that she wanted to do this, but although Corey was great, he was no Kenneth. As she danced and minded the dance floor, Africa and Morris retreated to more quiet quarters. Noel asked Corey to be patient while she used to little girls' room. Stepping into the bathroom—Jelani also had the sink counters decorated—she overheard Amber in the stall.

Noel waited patiently for her to emerge, inebriated now, she could not help but listen to the conversation Amber was having,

"I had no idea he would be here; I can't even bring myself to look at him," she said into her phone. Noel could no longer hold her pee as she rushed inside one of the stalls to release herself, stepping back out, she and Amber made eye contact,

"I am drunk, but I am not on your clock," Noel slurred.

"It's fine," Amber said with her arms folded. She appeared to have something important to say, Noel barely being able to stand, wondered what was going on.

"What is it?" she asked.

"That public relations guy is here," Amber whispered. "I was speaking to my husband because I had no idea he was going to be here," she continued. As she spoke, Noel stood still, her eyes widened. Amber thought it was something she had said.

"Are you alright?" she asked Noel. But Noel was not alright, her heart was skipping beats, her pulse was racing, she was feeling lightheaded and words began leaving her mouth that she was no longer aware of.

"Public relations?" she slurred, concentrating hard on standing straight.

"Yes, that belligerent man I had to have fired from the night he ruined my event," said Amber. Noel turned away and began splashing water on her face. She did not care about ruining her makeup as Amber continued speaking, Noel fighting hard to sober up so she could focus, as she splashed more water on her face.

"Fired?" she questioned, knitting her brows.

"Well of course, Christopher and I were so angry we called his firm and demanded he be let go for his decorum. I mean we were so embarrassed, Noel," she chuckled.

Noel took a deep breath before turning to face her.

"Kenneth was my boyfriend, Amber. You made my boyfriend lose his job and then he left me," she sobbed. "It was you."

"Oh, wait a minute, you have clearly had too much of the juice, that man cost us our reputation and surely you weren't dating him," she scoffed. "Noel, you're so much better than that," Amber continued.

"No, he was protecting me. I had bruises all over me from that guy, and Kenneth just wanted to defend me." She hated herself for going back down that road, she stood crying as she found herself falling in love with him all over again. She took several deep breaths trying to catch a grip on what was happening, but Amber remained unfazed.

"Noel, I'm sorry, but he cost me a lot of money!" she pleaded. But Noel was growing angry by the second,

"How much?" she asked as she fought the nausea,

"Almost eleven thousand dollars; his fees plus the fees for the venue damage," she said.

Noel resisted the urge to act inappropriately. "Amber, I handled his paperwork for weeks leading up to that event. He only charged you five thousand dollars, his fee, because he was doing a favor for you and included an event coordinator, then he got you eleven freaking sponsors at three-thousand dollars a pop! Which more than covered his costs and the cost of the venue, but because of your white-privileged ass you had a Black man fired because he struck a piece of shit who takes pleasure in bringing physical pain to women in exchange for luxury," Noel said. "I fucking quit," she continued walking out of the latrine, Amber trailing behind her.

"Noel wait, I can fix it!" she shouted. "I will fix it!" she begged. "I had no idea, I swear to God, and I will fix it," she continued. Noel could hear the excitement continuing on in the grand ballroom as she stepped ferociously out of the bathroom, ignoring Amber, she moved hastily until she bumped into the chest of a man wearing a grey pantsuit, a pink handkerchief hanging from his jetted pocket.

She thought it was one of the groomsmen, dashing past him, her back turned until he said,

"Noel, may I kiss you?"

THE END

LIMITED EDITION

Hello Cabineers:

I hope you enjoy this extended version and I thank you from the bottom of my heart for your continued support and dedication to my craft.

Until we meet again...

Lisa K. Stephenson

Noel remained frozen, she could not bring herself to move, turning slowly she saw no one behind her, only Amber, who continued to scream as everyone was heard shouting joyfully. Corey, now standing behind her with his hands in his pocket, she thought she heard Kenneth, but it was simply Corey checking to make sure she was alright. The 6'4 lawyer had small dreads, an athletic build, and a medium to dark skin tone. He dressed casually, at times his inscrutability turned her off. But Noel felt it best to tolerate him; he was someone to date until Mr. Right came along. However, it saddened her that as she turned it was not Kenneth there to greet her. Eight months of dating Corey and she was still hallucinating about another man, what did that mean, she wondered.

"*Dear Noel,*" as she walked and thought to herself, holding hands with her date now who had no idea just how disconnected she was. "*Will I never get over that man?*" her thoughts consumed her. Noel was now needed in the ballroom as she overheard Mr. Carter stand to recite a limerick; Noel was not going to miss this as she tugged on Corey, the two of them racing inside like school children leaving the playground after recess. Amber, now giving up her chase, realized there was simply nothing she could do. It was now time to accept defeat. Corey was playful and willing to do whatever it took to see a smile on Noel's face, even if it meant acting foolish around her friends and family. When the time came for toasts, Africa had everyone brought to tears with her moving speech for Frances, who was seated at the center of the rectangular table alongside her groom.

Inside, the greenery flowed freely from the table, across the china and down the long rows leading into the hallways. The microphone now passed to Abigail, who also delivered a heartfelt speech. Once Noel held the microphone in her hand she felt her heart skip a beat as Kenneth slid inside, taking a seat at table number twenty-two along with Freddie and a few other gentlemen she had not been introduced to.

All eyes were now on her; as she stared at him, Noel thought she had seen a ghost, the awkward moment causing Frances to giggle as Maxwell leaned in to whisper, "I told you this was a bad idea," he said, tapping her thigh gently. But

Frances would not hear of it, she smiled from ear to ear as she stood and made her way gracefully over to Noel, prying the microphone from her hands, kissing her gently on the cheek as Noel mindlessly took a seat. Corey now turning to face Kenneth as his eyes darted back and forth between them.

"Ladies and gentlemen, thank you all so much for the kind words, my beautiful poem..." as Frances continued her speech Noel began to fidget as her view of Kenneth was now obscured by a teenager.

Africa turning to face her, whispering, "If you don't stay still," she warned.

Noel turned. "I have to find Kenneth," she said as she stood to make her way out of the ballroom.

"You cannot leave in the middle of her speech," Africa reprimanded. "Sit down and stay still, please, this is unacceptable, Noel," she continued. By now, Noel was in the hallway as Corey too made his way outside.

Grabbing her by the hand, he asked, "Baby, is everything okay? You're acting strange, do you want to go home?" he asked kindly. Noel felt horrible, there was a compassionate man standing right in front of her, one who she knew for sure would never break her heart, and yet she was struggling to find the one who had proven time and time again that he is willing to do so. She was confused, regressing back to that muddled young woman who stepped off the Amtrak a few years prior. She was once more finding herself making imprudent and selfish decisions.

Kenneth now made an appearance, standing behind Corey with his hands in his pocket like a GQ model. Noel caught a glimpse of him out on the terrace now, just under the floral arch. The outdoors reserved for the elaborate dinner set up under a draped arrangement of green leaves, flowers, candles, lamps and additional rectangular tables. Frances was so busy she had not noticed Noel had slipped away and was now in the hall, standing in front of two men who no doubt were expecting her to choose one of them.

Although her choice was simple, it had become complicated; she just had to hear him out.

"Corey, I am so very sorry," she cried. Corey was heartbroken, he had fallen in love, staring into her eyes, he realized there was someone before him, someone who no matter how hard he tried, he would never be able to replace. A heartbroken Corey decided it best to take his leave, retaining whatever dignity he had left as he took Noel by her hands, kissing the back of them gently, admiring her soft skin and manicured nails. She was perfect. Noel let a tear fall before watching Corey disappear. *Did I make a mistake?* She pondered, resisting the urge to go after him as she stood face to face with Kenneth, who she wanted so desperately to run to. She wanted the fairytale ending, his arms around her. She scoffed as she continued watching him, his suit gray and the handkerchief in his jetted pocket the same color as her dress, was this fate or a simple coincidence?

"You have some really nice friends," he said.

Noel quivering as his voice began to resonate through her body; she missed his honeyed tone and gentle mannerisms, his touch, his sense of humor. Noel remained silent in fear of saying the wrong thing and losing him once again, and so, she listened as he made his way towards her.

"I like the hair, you lost some weight, and you smell wonderful," he said, now looking down at her, playing with her hair. "I missed you and I owe you so many apologies, I honestly don't even know where to begin," he continued. Noel suffered from moral gaucherie, her eyes twitching, and her hands lifeless, she was hanging onto his every word, but thought to herself she was remaining stoic without the ease of temptation written across her face. Kenneth caressed her lips as the wedding party and guests cleared the dance floor for Maxwell and Frances to have their first dance as Mr. and Mrs. Miller. Once their dance concluded, the real fun began as Maxwell was tasked with removing the garter from Frances's thigh, everyone gallantly cheering him on.

Noel did not want to miss the bouquet toss, but found herself in a trance, as Kenneth continued to sweep her off her feet with his words, but Noel could not allow him to continue, she wanted to tell him the truth, she wanted to tell him about the baby. There he was, standing adjacent to her, pouring his heart out and speaking as though he was finally ready to take make a commitment, to fall in love and to have the beautiful children she only dreamed of for the past two years. She was stuck, stuck between losing him again and holding onto a secret that had been eating her alive for months.

Africa and Abigail now made their way outside, watching as Noel and Kenneth stared lovingly into one another's eyes. Africa was growing weary, her ankle no longer the same, she could not stand for long periods of time nor dance, opting in briefly for the electric slide and a slow dance between her and Morris. Morris also delivered a heartfelt speech, pleading for his love once again, but this time in front of her friends and family. Africa was moved to tears.

Frances hoped her love would influence her friends and their relationships in a positive way, and it did. As the festivities were coming to an end, Noel and Kenneth decided to leave before the bridal bouquet and garter toss, the warm sun beating on her face as she ran across the lawn hand-in-hand with Kenneth, her dress blowing in the breeze.

Just then Frances spotted her, shouting across the lawn. "I love you, Noey!", placing her hands around her lips to assist in projecting her voice, her dress blowing graciously behind her as Noel turned and smiled.

The sun began to set as Noel and Kenneth walked along the park, where they found a fountain, admiring the view only few blocks from the reception hall. Noel was feeling anxious, she had no idea what to expect because Kenneth was always full of evil surprises, but this time was different.

"I live in Seattle," he said as he walked along the sidewalk, enjoying the views and the desolate walkway. "I am not asking you to move, but kind of asking you to consider the idea." Noel shot him a bewildered look. "New York is beautiful, but it is simply no longer for me; the fast life, the women. I know your friends are here, and I would never ask you to leave them without promising you some type of security," he continued, laughing now. "I had no idea what I was coming home to, no idea if you would be married, or had a baby, or pregnant. I had no clue, but I wanted to return anyway, I had to see for myself, and when Frances called to tell me she was getting married..." he continued.

"Wait—Frances called you? How?" she stuttered,

"I think she got my number from your dad, he and my father are still very good friends and I was spending a lot of time with my father, so, word got back to me that she wanted to speak with me and so we got in contact," he confirmed. Noel was surprised, she had no idea Frances had done that,

"I just need time to think about it," she said, for once she felt in control with Kenneth and vowed to never be at his beck and call again, she had learned her lesson." Although he did not like her answer, he had no choice but to be understanding. Nodding his head as he kissed her forehead, he said,

"I leave next Thursday," informing her, "so, I'll wait for your call," handing Noel a business card, and just like that Kenneth stepped towards the sunset, his right hand now tucked away in his pocket as he made his way south, the sun behind her as Noel stood by the fountain all alone, contemplating her next move. The love of her life walking away.

Noel arrived home to the brownstone where she saw that all of Frances's things had been neatly packed and labeled. Movers were hired to gather her belongings as the wedding was underway; Noel could not bring herself to check the boxes, as her mind was now completely occupied. Kicking off her shoes and grabbing for a box of Häagen-Dazs ice cream from the freezer, she slammed the door shut, sending her bob to the rear of her neck.

She was getting used to the idea of living alone, the peace, until the front door clicked open; it was Africa making her way inside with a large box wrapped in red gift paper with a white bow annexed. Noel stood, holding the door to assist her,

"Why on earth do you look so sad?" Africa asked her cousin.

"Kenneth was at the reception, he asked me to move to Seattle with him," she said, kicking boxes aside so as to make room for the new box. Africa, with a shocked look on her face, thought to take a seat.

"Okay, so what have you decided?" she asked.

"He doesn't know what I did, if he found out it would devastate him, and the last thing I want to do is build a relationship on lies," she continued. Noel could think of many reasons why she was reluctant to relocate to Seattle to be with Kenneth, but she needed advice on this one particular area, which is why she decided to mention it to Africa.

"Well, something tells me he may already know," she said as she slid Noel her cellular phone, an article came up with a headline that read: *Wife to Millionaire Snubbed in Divorce Settlement.* As Noel read through the article, she was confused.

"I don't understand," she said to Africa, handing her the phone.

"Well, apparently Nathan is a tycoon and Alicia isn't going down without a fight. She got the media involved, who then involved Kenneth in a paternity battle because of Jade, also known as the mistress with the baby. Alicia's attorney was trying to build a case against Nathan, saying he was hiding assets and set up a fake pregnancy to have the money paid out. But the baby is his and Jade didn't receive a dime, allegedly, so that money is lost and she's fighting a losing battle. It's been in the papers for weeks, but Frances and I did our best to keep it from you. We weren't sure if you were ready to hear the news. Your name wasn't even mentioned," Africa continued.

Noel took a deep breath before asking, "So what should I do?"

"If he's here, Noel, it's because he knows and he's forgiven you. I say go to Seattle and be happy for once. We all deserve it, don't we?" she asked. Over the next few days, Noel thought long and hard. She stumbled through the boxes, and when the movers came to gather Frances's things, she assisted. Arriving at their house in Long Island, Noel was blown away, the 4200 square foot house, colonial built took up 0.84 acres of land, had five bedrooms and three and a half bathrooms. Though still empty, Frances hobbled around, showing her friends the entire house. She was radiant. Seeing this helped Noel to make up her mind as she had one final conversation with her best friend.

"Franny," she called to her making her way to the master bedroom where Frances was unfolding baby clothes.

"Hey Noey, are you okay?" Frances asked, her shirt hanging over her protruded belly, her hair in a ponytail. Maxwell and the movers could be heard downstairs.

"How do you feel about me moving back to Seattle?" Noel asked taking a seat on the floor, crossing her legs. Frances smiled.

"Noey, I think that's a great idea. This is for Kenneth, right?" she asked.

"Did Africa tell you?" she asked.

"Well, of course she did," chuckled Frances. "I think you should go. But, the brownstone will always be there, and if you want, Abigail can sublet so we always have a place to go when we simply need to get away from our men." She laughed. "Seriously though, I want you to be happy and so, of course, I think you should go with him. He has stability, structure and you both love each other," encouraged Frances; Noel began to cry.

"But what about you and the baby?" she sobbed. Frances hugged her.

"Awe don't cry Noey, Africa is here and we're all going to Georgia for Abigail's graduation in just a few months, so, we are always going to be together," she said. Noel sobbed, she was finding that letting go was proving itself to be the hardest thing for her to do, but Frances was right and it was time to grow up and move on.

"Franny, I love you so much!" she said, squeezing her. The ladies exchanged a moment of solidarity.

"Noey, go get your man and call me when you get there!" Frances said, pushing her away, Noel struggled to stand as she raced down the stairs and out the front door, retracting her steps she located Maxwell in the kitchen where she gave him a long, hard hug.

"Take care of my friend, Max, or I will kill you," she said, flying out the door; Maxwell and his friends exchanging a look of confusion.

Inside John F. Kennedy airport, Noel checked her messages, she contacted Africa, who informed her of the next flight to Seattle, the earliest leaving that day.

As she scurried through the airport, making her way past the crowd, purchasing her one-way ticket and checking her luggage, she thought to herself, "*Deal Noel, you get to be happy, too. It is finally time to grow up, time to be a wife and one day a mother. You are a woman with so much passion and love to give and finally there is someone for you to give that love to. Dearest Noel, thirty is your next chapter to begin expressing yourself and finding joy in those around you, create a long-lasting life with a person who is deserving of your smile, your compassion for others, and your ability to love beyond yourself. New York has taught you that there may be many luxuries, but nothing compares to finding your soulmate,"* she thought.

There he was, sitting with a pair of headphones in his ears reading through a magazine, periodically taking a glimpse out of the airport window. Noel stepped lightly towards him, removing the hood from her head on her hooded sweater allowing her hair to fall, she stood watching him for what felt like five minutes before he noticed her. Kenneth turned in annoyance wondering who had been hovering over him; but once their eyes connected, he arose from his seat, grabbing her face as he tossed his book aside, the strangers there to witness their union. Kenneth was elated to have her in his arms as he leaned down to kiss her passionately,

"I love you so much," he smiled.

It had been two years, three months and two weeks since the ladies all gathered at the brownstone where Abigail was now residing while prepping to go to trial for a hate crime case. Noel was married to Kenneth and now the mother of two, Frances the mother of three, and Africa still trying to figure out why she had not yet met Mr. Right, decided to go the IVF route and was now six months pregnant with a healthy and feisty baby boy.

As the ladies laughed over margaritas and mocktails, they reminisced on their time there. Frances was now ready for the longest vacation of her life as she and Maxwell recently welcomed their son. As the evening pressed on and the ladies laughed, danced, and celebrated their unions, a black stretch limo pulled up outside. Noel noticed her phone dinging and discreetly went to answer it.

"I'm stepping out for some fresh air," she told everyone as she skipped down into the limousine. Once inside, she was greeted by a handsome stranger who held a white rose adjacent to his face.

"Well hello there," he said, lowering it, Noel chuckled. "This is for you, my beautiful lady," he said, causing her to blush.

"It's been a while," she smiled, as she leaned in to kiss him.

"Only a few months, I did miss your smile though," he said.

Noel, lowering her head in shame, said, "Nathan, we probably shouldn't keep doing this."

Nathan, taking her hands, sliding his fingers gently through hers, replied, "In the circle of love, wrapped with loyal bonds, clever demons play their songs," he said, kissing her hands as he continued, seductively, just above a whisper, "*In mortals' weakest moments the tunes of love and lust creeps within their core silencing all their morals rendering these mortals to their emotions clever demons laugh whiles their legs split apart and a sinner rushes in to eat the forbidden fruit*," he concluded with his hands buried deep between her legs, kissing her softly, her eyes now closed,

"A poem about us was written by Eyan Desir, just let it happen, flower," and just like that, she was playing a devil's game.

Coming soon....

58804539R00163

Made in the USA
Middletown, DE
08 August 2019